Everything e...

When the rakehell Lord Jack Tremont kissed Miranda Mabberly, mistaking her for his mistress, neither realized his reckless act would cost Miranda her reputation, her fiancé, and her future. But for Jack, it was a kiss unlike any other.

Years later, hiding incognito far from London—as a teacher at Miss Emery's Establishment for the Education of Genteel Young Ladies—Miranda has made a respectable life for herself, away from the *ton* and the dangerous men who inhabit it. When a penniless, much humbled, though still damnably attractive Jack arrives at the school to escort a rebellious young niece home, Miranda does her best to avoid the rogue, only to end up tumbling into his arms—and reawakening a desire that is anything but proper.

She might want to deny her heart, but Miranda's resolve is no challenge for three schoolgirl matchmakers who know true passion when they spy it. Now they won't rest until their all-too-proper teacher and the reprobate lord discover the love that is their destiny.

"Ms. Boyle . . . is sure to leave you smiling."
Stephanie Laurens

ELIZABETH BOYLE

THIS RAKE OF MINE

An Avon Romantic Treasure

AVON BOOKS
An Imprint of HarperCollinsPublishers

AVON BOOKS
An Imprint of HarperCollins*Publishers*
10 East 53rd Street
New York, New York 10022-5299

Copyright © 2005 by Elizabeth Boyle
ISBN-13: 978-0-06-078399-0
ISBN-10: 0-06-078399-0
www.avonromance.com

First Avon Books paperback printing: November 2005

Avon Trademark Reg. U.S. Pat. Off. and in Other Countries, Marca Registrada, Hecho en U.S.A.
HarperCollins® is a registered trademark of HarperCollins Publishers Inc.

Printed in the U.S.A.

10 9 8 7 6 5 4 3 2 1

To Maureen,
for being a good friend
and an even better sister-in-law.
You are always there to listen,
and your kindness, generosity
and beautiful spirit have brightened my life,
as well as all the lives you touch.
Bless you always.

Prologue

London, England
1801

"**W**ell," Lady Oxley huffed, "I suppose there are worse things than having some *cit*'s daughter marry into your family, but for the life of me, I can't think of it. Our bloodlines will be tainted by this forever."

The Duchess of Cheverton, seated next to Lady Oxley, couldn't agree more. "I fear for your standing, my dear. I do, indeed."

"If there is some consolation, she did go to Miss Emery's," Lady Oxley conceded, though grudgingly.

"Miss Emery's, you say?" The duchess twisted in her seat and looked at the girl in question, eyeing her from top to bottom, as if she were gauging the quality of a length of silk. "A mite young, wouldn't you say? I daresay she's fresh and innocent."

"Oh, she looks innocent enough," Lady Oxley de-

1

clared, ignoring the hot glances from the people in the other boxes, who were actually watching the opera. "So there is some hope there. Gads, the trollops these merchants pass off as daughters is just appalling. My greatest fear is that Oxley will marry the chit and discover she's been ruined. Oh, the shame of it."

Ruined.

The word rang through the Oxley box and to everyone around them.

Miss Miranda Mabberly, the object of this scorn and speculation, wished herself a thousand miles away. Her cheeks burned with shame and embarrassment, not so much from her future mother-in-law's loud denouncement but from the fact that her mother and father were willing to sit here and listen to their good name being tossed about in such a ragtag fashion.

She wished right there and then that she was ruined.

Miranda took a deep breath and tried to concentrate on the performance on the boards, not the one Lady Oxley was staging here in her private box. This wasn't the first time the lady had lamented her son's betrothal in public, and it most likely wouldn't be the last.

Still that one word rang in her ears. *Ruined.*

Not completely ruined, Miranda reasoned, for that was hardly proper, and despite Lady Oxley's opinions, she was a proper young lady. Besides, being completely ruined went far beyond her knowledge on such matters.

Her mother nudged her and whispered in her ear, "Gracious, child, smile! You are going to be a countess in a sennight."

Miranda did her best to turn her lips upward, but it

was hard to bear, despite the way her mother beamed over the wonderful news.

Why, such a match had exceeded even Mrs. Mabberly's designs for her daughter. But Mr. Mabberly, a *cit* with the fortune of Midas behind him, had thought nothing of procuring for his only child the most lofty of husbands.

Yet no one in all this brokering and maneuvering and social engineering had ever thought to consult Miranda on the subject of marriage.

Her marriage, she would like to point out to her title-mad parents, Lord Oxley, and the various solicitors, bankers, and the earl's numerous creditors, all of whom were arranging this blessed (and financial) union.

Didn't anyone realize that in all this deal making, *she* was the one who was going to have to marry Oxley? Take his name. Live in his house. And she shuddered to think of the next logical step in this progression—share his bed.

Not that marrying an earl was objectionable, for Miranda had gone to Miss Emery's Establishment for the Education of Genteel Young Ladies and knew her duty to her family and country. But it was marrying *this* earl that Miranda found so objectionable.

Earls were supposed to be elegant and sophisticated. Charming company in any situation. A gentleman at all times, and, well, frankly, more often than not, they should be a little bit heroic.

Was that too much to ask for?

Unfortunately, the Earl of Oxley was none of these things.

Even while his mother bemoaned his lowering

match, the earl sat beside his future bride and boasted to anyone who would listen about the pair of "goers" at Tattersall's he'd picked up now that he had a rich little "goer" of his own. Miranda had closed her eyes and snapped her mouth shut to refrain from telling the obtuse man that she thought he was putting the cart before the horse, since they weren't married. *Yet.*

Oh, if only she was a little bit ruined, Miranda thought. Just enough so Oxley would cry off. So she could have a chance to find the man of her dreams. A knight in shining armor, who would love her for more than her fortune. A proper gentleman, who would kiss her gently and lovingly. Make her toes curl inside her slippers and her heart beat fast.

But such a fate seemed well beyond her grasp as the houselights came up and there was her "hero" beside her, leering at her as if she were a combination between a ripe peach and a bucket of gold. He sent her stomach lurching.

She would even have been content to marry a dull sort like Lord Sedgwick, if the man hadn't already been wed to his delightful Emmaline.

If only Lady Sedgwick had been part of their party here at the opera . . . she would have put Lady Oxley in her place and buoyed Miranda's sagging spirits in that sparkling way of hers.

Instead, she had only Lord Sedgwick's company, and he was quite preoccupied by some problem, given the deep crease in his brow. Even if he hadn't seemed so worried, Miranda knew it was hardly proper to pour her heart out to the staid baron, no matter how exceptional Lady Sedgwick claimed him to be.

So instead, Miranda made a hasty excuse to her mother as the intermission began, ignoring the good woman's protests that she shouldn't leave "poor Oxley" alone and fled the box, looking for someplace to escape to, if only until they darkened the lights again.

What she found was an alcove in the back of the hall, far from the rest of the *ton*, who were parading about the opera, showing off new gowns or gossiping about the latest news.

There in the privacy of that darkened corner, Miranda gave herself over to a very improper spate of tears. She cried until the bell rang for everyone to return to their seats. The humiliation of it all! She was no better than one of the horses down at Tattersall's.

Bloodlines, indeed! Miranda's mother came from a good and noble family—one with a far greater history than anything Lady Oxley could claim. So calling up that proud tradition, Miranda wiped away the evidence of her despair and straightened her shoulders, girding herself for the rest of the evening.

For the rest of her life. But suddenly her life took a very different turn.

"Giselle, my dearest goddess, how glad I am to see you," a man whispered into her ear, taking her by the hand and spinning her around. She flew into his chest, and before she could utter a word, he caught her lips in a searing kiss.

Miranda struggled against the rogue, twisting in his grasp, her hands balling up and pounding at his shoulders. Oh, dear heavens!

Her eyes sprang open. Lord John Tremont? Kissing her? Dear heavens, didn't he know this wasn't proper?

Obviously not, for his lips teased and taunted hers, and when she opened her mouth to protest, his tongue swiped across hers, sending the most frightening thrill through her limbs—the kind she could never have imagined.

Why, it made her toes curl up inside her slippers. No wonder most of the *ton* called him Mad Jack Tremont.

For this—this spell he was casting over her—was utter madness!

She continued to struggle (only because she knew she was supposed to), and Mad Jack responded by pressing her up against the wall, pinning her in place with his hips, making his point that there was no escape.

Miranda gasped as his entire body covered hers, left her with an intimate knowledge of this man's intent, for there it was, hard and insistent, riding against her.

And worst of all, she wanted to feel it. His kiss, his touch, the feel of his body, it made her ache in response to having him up against her.

Oh, this wasn't proper.

She was betrothed. To another man. Whose name she couldn't for the life of her remember at the moment.

A man, she dared venture, who would never kiss her like this.

Not teasing her tongue to come play with him, tugging at her bottom lip with his teeth, nor deepening his kiss until a soft moan whispered and trembled up from within her.

For one wondrous moment, she clung to him, let him

kiss her, let his hand travel up the length of her hip, rising along her waist. His touch brought with it this tantalizing glimpse of the very temptation that made innocence seem a poor commodity.

Ruin me, she thought. *Ruin me, thoroughly.*

That is, until his fingers roamed higher, until they came to cup her breast, rolling over her nipple. His touch sent shock waves through her body, made her thighs clench together, made her ache *down there.*

She sucked in a deep breath and rose up on her toes. Oh, dear heavens, this was too much. She struggled to issue a protest, to flee all the way back to her betrothed, even as Lord John's expert and talented fingers teased her bodice open, leaving her breast exposed—and if that wasn't bad enough—he was taking advantage of her nakedness by letting his mouth roam over her soft, silken flesh, leaving her nipple hardened and puckered, her knees buckling beneath her.

"So my sweetling, show me where we can be alone," he whispered into her ear, the scent of brandy assailing her senses, "and I'll make good my promise to see you well completed before the curtain arises."

There was more?

Oh, dear heavens, how could that be? How could she stand more of this torment?

That, as it turned out, was the least of her worries, for just then she spied her mother and future mother-in-law standing a few feet away. Lady Oxley gaped in shock, and her mother looked positively ill.

"Leave me be!" she sputtered, trying to get free of him, but to her horror, the lace on her sleeve caught on one of his buttons and held her tangled in his arms all that much longer.

Long enough for Lady Oxley to find her voice, the lady's deafening shrieks bringing an end to Miranda's betrothal, and leaving her utterly ruined. . . .

Chapter 1

*Miss Emery's Establishment for the Education
of Genteel Young Ladies*
Bath, England
1810

"**I** don't see why *he* has to be allowed in," Lady Philippa Knolles complained to her cousin, Miss Felicity Langley, as they crept down the back stairs of their school.

"Pippin, when the Duke of Parkerton sends his brother to perform an errand of such a delicate nature," Felicity explained, "one cannot simply bar the door to the man. Even if he is a disreputable . . . a horrible . . ."

"Rake," supplied Felicity's twin sister, Thalia, who brought up the rear of this illicit party. Tally, as she was known, was not one for delicacy of words, and besides, she was rather excited at the prospect of getting a look at such a man.

To Tally the word *rake* conjured all sorts of dreamy possibilities, like *pirate* or *highwayman* or *smuggler.* And the very notion that Miss Emery had banished the entire school to their rooms for the afternoon until their "visitor" had departed was just too much to bear.

A rake at Miss Emery's? Why, it was like history in the making, a moment not to be missed.

"Really," Tally had declared, "how does Miss Emery expect us to recognize this sort of man if we have never seen an example of one?"

Felicity had readily agreed. Pippin had been a bit more hesitant than her daring cousins, but in the end, she'd relented and joined the party, if only because she too held a secret curiosity about the infamous rake, Lord John Tremont.

"Who was it that Lord John ruined?" Pippin asked.

"Miss Miranda Mabberly," Felicity supplied without hesitation. "He kissed her rather inappropriately at the opera."

Felicity's knowledge of the *ton* never ceased to amaze Pippin, especially given that up until two years ago, the Langley sisters had never even set foot in England, having spent their entire lives traveling the world with their father, Lord Langley, a distinguished member of the Foreign Office.

"Oh, dear," Pippin said. "If that is so, why didn't he just marry Miss Mabberly?"

Tally finished the story, for at the moment Felicity was timing their descent to ensure that they didn't run into the headmistress or one of their other teachers, especially their decorum teacher, Miss Porter.

"Miss Mabberly was betrothed to the Earl of Oxley at the time," Tally whispered. "Oxley cried off when he learned what happened."

"And Miss Mabberly?" Pippin asked. "What of her?"

Tally shrugged. "I don't particularly know. Probably the usual in those circumstances. A fatal decline, banishment from good society, not that it really matters, she was ruined after all."

"How dreadful!" Pippin whispered.

Not to let the story pass without her own stamp upon it, Felicity added, "I daresay Miss Mabberly ended up in some Eastern harem or married off to some Colonial merchant." To Felicity, either fate was of equal degradation, considering her own matrimonial aspirations were nothing less than to marry a duke, thus having earned herself the nickname of "Duchess" at a very early age.

Taking another look down the stairwell, and seeing that the coast was clear, she waved her accomplices to follow her.

Down the steps they crept and then dashed across the hall and into a nearby closet. Having feigned a megrim earlier, Felicity had been excused from Miss Porter's class and had used the time to remove the buckets, mops and brooms that usually filled the tiny space.

After they wedged themselves in, Tally looked about their quarters and sighed. "I suppose this is the best we can do," she said, setting down the fourth member of their party, Brutus, her ever-present companion. Though the small black dog had been a gift to Felicity and Thalia during their father's tenure in Austria, Brutus had taken to Tally from the first moment she'd gathered him up into her arms.

And Tally never minded (well, maybe a little) that her dog appeared to most like a little clown, with his big round eyes and funny tufted mane of hair. She took great pleasure in pointing out that Brutus possessed the heart of a lion, fearless and loyal, despite his demure stature.

Brutus immediately went to work inspecting their hiding place, sniffing at the pungent smells in the closet and finally giving his opinion by shaking his monkey-like head in protest. "Ruff!"

"Tally," Felicity whispered sharply. "Do make him be still! He'll ruin everything with his sniffing and yapping. I still say we should have left him with Nanny Gerta. It's a wonder Miss Emery allows him."

Tally gathered Brutus up and hugged him close, shooting her sister a dark glare, which the Duchess ignored with the imperial grace that only a future wife of a duke could possess.

Dogs at Miss Emery's were as much against the rules as rakes, however Lord Langley's infamous charm had gone a long way in convincing the usually impervious lady to allow Tally to keep her dear dog at school.

After all, Brutus could trace his bloodlines to Marie Antoinette's own beloved affenpinscher. Such lofty connections had a way of bending even Miss Emery's rigid rules.

"Are you sure Miss Emery is going to make Lord John use the back stairs?" Tally asked. She wasn't overly fond of dark enclosed spaces and had a growing look of panic about her.

"Yes," Felicity said with her usual certainty. "She can't let him go up the main stairs—why, everyone would be peeping out their doors at him." She opened the closet door a bare crack to afford Tally some light.

"Besides, with Bella's room in the back of the house, it is the most expedient route for him to take."

And expediency was the order of the day.

Lady Arabella Tremont, the Duke of Parkerton's daughter and Lord John's niece, was being sent home in disgrace. She was the first student in the history of Miss Emery's to have caused such a scandal, having been caught kissing one of the stable lads, and her removal was being conducted with as much discretion and secrecy as one could hope to find in a house full of young ladies prone to gossip.

Tally hugged Brutus close and looked around their hiding spot like it was turning into a prison cell. "Duchess, I don't know how much longer—"

Her words came to an abrupt halt as the bell over the front door jangled with a solid tug. Almost immediately the click of Miss Emery's sturdy boots echoed forth.

The girls held their breath as they listened intently, peering through the cracked door, praying they would spy their quarry.

"This way, my lord," Miss Emery said.

Now if only Felicity's prediction would come true—and Miss Emery would escort Lord John in their direction.

And sure enough, she did.

"Make certain you get a good look at him," Felicity whispered in Tally's ear. "I want you to draw his likeness for the *Chronicles.*" In the unlikely case that the Duchess wasn't able to find her duke, she kept a very detailed journal of all the eligible bachelors in England. And while Lord John was a rakish devil, hardly deserving mention, he was still unmarried and therefore qualified for a place in her *Chronicles*. She turned to her cousin. "Pippin, you as well. You have an excellent eye for detail and will ensure that Tally gets his likeness correct."

And then the moment came, and all four pairs of eyes peered through the crack at the rare sight of a rake.

In a flash he strode past their hiding spot, and then all they saw was his back as he climbed the stairs to his niece's chamber.

"I never," Tally whispered.

"Nor I," Pippin added.

Felicity, for once, was silent. Dumbfounded at what they had seen.

Lord John was nothing like they'd been led to believe.

"I thought he'd be—"

"No, I was convinced he'd be—"

Felicity put it most concisely. "Why, he's dreadful!"

Dreadful was the word that Lord John Tremont would have found most fitting for the situation—though not quite in the same way as Felicity.

At the moment, any place, even Newgate, would have been more welcome than having to endure another moment in Miss Emery's politely strained company. The narrow, pinch-faced woman's unforgiving arched glances and barely concealed glare were yet another reminder of the lowly regard Society held for him.

He, who had once been the *ton's* favorite, the most invited Corinthian about town, was now reduced to being his brother's errand boy, fetching home his disgraced niece in quiet obscurity, rather than have

Parkerton lower himself to such a task. Certainly, there was no love lost between the duke and his disgraced sibling, no familial sense of obligation that could have enticed Jack to come to Bath on his brother's behalf. There was, however, the matter of Jack's outstanding debts, and his brother's willingness to pay some of them in exchange for this favor. And since his brother hadn't allotted him a single penny from the family coffers since the Mabberly incident, having cut him off completely, it was an offer Jack could ill afford to pass up.

So here he was, walking on eggshells through this all-too female domain, when he should be home minding his own affairs instead of carting his niece's various hatboxes and trunks and portmanteaus down the back stairs like a common footman.

It didn't escape his notice that he had been led to the rear of the house, or that there wasn't anyone else about, the students having most likely been banished for fear the very sight of him would infect their sensibilities (as if young English ladies possessed any measure of sense), but he ignored the insult and turned his thoughts to matters far more pressing than his errant niece's behavior.

Gads, perhaps if his brother had spent less on clothes and shoes for the girl and more on decorum lessons, she wouldn't be leaving school early and he wouldn't have been summoned up from Sussex to perform this ignoble chore.

Lost as he was in these thoughts on this, his fourth trip down the stairs with Arabella's belongings, he didn't pay any heed to where he was going as he bounded off the last step and found himself colliding with someone.

And not just anyone, he soon discovered as his arm-load of luggage went flying into the air with what looked like a sewing basket—threads and yarns, knitting needles and poor bits of ribbon mixing with Arabella's ludicrously rich collection of belongings.

Even as the yarn tangled, the threads unraveled, and a feminine cry of "Gracious heavens!" rose in the air, Jack realized his adversary was about to fall as well, so he quickly wrapped his arms around the warm and curved lines of only one such creature.

A lady.

And not some young, soon-to-be debutante, but a woman grown.

Such curves he knew all too well. Had spent years seducing and exploring. Despite the fact that it had been some time since he'd been in such close proximity to any woman, like most inherent talents, his memory and his blood surged with bold clarity, and he pulled her close.

To keep her from falling.

"Oooh," she gasped as she slammed into him, her breasts pressing against his chest, her fingers splayed across his shoulders. Fingers that quickly turned into balled fists and began to pound against him, undermining his already tenuous stance.

"Careful, miss," he told her. Certainly he wasn't to be blamed for keeping her from hurting herself? Why, he'd done her a favor.

Perhaps it didn't help matters that his hand had landed right on the curves of her sweetly rounded bottom and his arm had wound around her slender form until his palm had come to rest beneath a perfectly formed breast.

He looked down at her, feeling a bit bemused; surely,

if there was to be some reward in this errand, it was a short lapse back into his rakish past.

A gratuity of sorts, found in the sight of pink lips, the rosy hue of fair skin. And considering her other endowments, could a former rake be held responsible for the temptation she had hidden beneath her ugly black bombazine gown?

Besides, it had been a long time since he'd done anything to retain his title of Mad Jack Tremont.

So could he really be faulted if he nearly forgot himself and lowered his lips to hers, to taste a bit of their pert promise, to see if the rest of her charms could be matched by her kiss . . .

That is, until he spied her hair.

The devil take her, the chit was a redhead! How he had missed it before, he knew not, but there was no denying the color now.

Even tied up and contained as it was in a spinster's knot, he knew without a doubt what was bound beneath that prison of pins and ribbons.

Red, tempting flames of passion.

He nearly tossed her into the heap of luggage as he released her, his rediscovered ardor fleeing like the hordes before the Huns.

She stumbled out of his grasp and, like any good woman, shot him a most aggrieved look.

Whether it was for the state of her tangled sewing basket or ruffled senses, he wasn't too sure. To be honest, he didn't care.

For while the Tremont family motto was *Justus esto et non metue* (Be just and fear not), he had added his own addendum to that brave credo.

And no redheads.

Demmed beguiling, mysterious creatures. Sent like the ruddy hounds of hell to be his undoing.

Thankfully, the lady didn't look all that pleased to make his acquaintance. Her fair brow furrowed, and she backed away from him like he was showing signs of plague.

"You!" she sputtered, her greeting coming out like an accusation or the warning cry of "Bar the door."

The flashing look of horror in her green eyes pricked at his sense of honor. Despite what his brother, or obviously Miss Emery and her cohorts thought of him, he was a gentleman these days . . . well, most of the time.

"Lord John Tremont, at your service," he said, mustering his out-of-practice manners and managing a decent bow.

"Harrumph," she stammered, still looking at him expectantly, fists planted on her hips, her elbows jutting out.

Now he was getting annoyed. She needn't look so put out. It wasn't like he'd actually kissed her. But that was a spinster for you. Only a lady who had avoided matrimony as long as she obviously had could hold such a look of outrage.

"I know who you are," she was saying as she bent to the task of retrieving her fallen belongings. "You should be well and gone by now."

So much for a polite welcome and an offer of tea and biscuits.

Still, it wounded him that this lady, whom he'd never met, regarded him with such open disdain.

Maybe it was the fact that he had always been partial

to redheads, but maybe it was the fact that she also had a look of sharp-eyed intelligence about her.

As he went to work picking up Arabella's belongings, her strained silence drove him to distraction. It was as if he could hear the crackle in her straight spine and ramrod shoulders.

He decided to try again.

"Hard to believe one chit requires so many hats and gowns," he said, hoping to ease the tension. "Perhaps a few less trips to the dressmakers and more lessons in decorum might have been in order." As he stacked up his niece's hatboxes, he thought he saw a slight flash in her eyes, as if she shared his unspoken opinion that Lady Arabella Tremont possessed more gowns than sense.

"By the way," he said, taking her hint of a smile as a crack in her spinster's armor, "I didn't catch your name."

She glanced over at him, her arched brow in perfect imitation of Miss Emery's glare. Even as she stared at him, he thought there was a sense of a brewing tempest between them, as if she were on pins and needles over such a simple thing as an introduction.

Finally, she took a deep breath and offered the barest of introductions. "Miss Porter."

By Jove, it was as if even that much were a great imposition.

"Are you a teacher here?" he asked, hoping to engage the lady in even the merest hint of conversation. It had been a long time since a lady had even spoken to him.

He received a curt nod in reply. So much for a polite exchange, he mused. Bending over to retrieve an upside-down valise, he asked, "And what do you teach?"

"Decorum," came the clipped reply.

Jack cringed. So much for his earlier remark about Arabella's need for additional lessons.

Oh, yes, he'd made a muddle of all of this. He'd rather intimately tangled with (and if he was honest, contemplated kissing) a spinster who specialized in training young ladies to avoid such situations. And he'd insulted her capacity as a teacher.

He could hear his brother now, casting it down upon him that he wasn't capable of venturing into any society without allowing his sinful nature to overtake the good sense he'd been given.

Of course, Jack's more wicked senses would have said that the real sin was having a lady with Miss Porter's curves and tempting red hair trapped in this spinster's museum, especially now that she was bent over to catch up a ball of yarn and he had an excellent view of her rounded behind and a hint of her curved ankles . . .

Oh, yes, it had been too long since he'd been in a lady's company, for even the mere sight of her ankles sent his imagination running wild.

In the height of his rakish days, he might have been tempted to pull her into his arms and tell her that he found her hair divine, her breasts tempting, and her lips perfect for kissing. Then rather than let the lady protest, he'd prove his point by devouring those lips, stroking her breasts, and holding her so close he'd leave her with an intimate knowledge of the power a beautiful woman could wield over a man as imperfect as he.

Stealing another glance at the prim and proper teacher, he had to imagine that if he undertook such a declaration, she'd go into a state of apoplexy that would be her undoing.

And his.

Demmit, it would take another ten, nay, fifteen years, to live down such a ruinous scene.

She was in the midst of picking up the last of her belongings, tucking them into the sewing basket with all due haste, clucking with disdain over the state of her yarns, and muttering something about "dropped stitches."

Try as he might to go back to his own task, Jack couldn't help but watch her.

Dear Lord, if ever there was a woman who needed something really important to worry about, it was this Miss Porter. Properly folded napkins, perfect curtsies, and posture pointers were her life. She probably spent her days lecturing young girls on how to return calls, the correct seating of guests at dinner, and, most of all, how to avoid the likes of libertines.

A rather dull existence, he surmised, for a woman with hair that hinted at a passionate nature and a sharp tongue that could skewer a man as easily as it could tease him to distraction.

Jack heaved a sigh. As much as it grieved him to see a life wasted—for he knew a thing or two on the subject—there was nothing he could do about it. If he were to liberate Miss Porter with a kiss, there'd be hell to pay.

And Parkerton would most likely use it as an excuse not to pay the debts he'd promised to redeem.

So instead of giving Miss Porter a taste of the wicked temptation that could be found in a misspent kiss, he bent over to pick up Arabella's remaining valise. There beneath it lay one last treasure from Miss Porter's sewing basket that she'd missed.

A silver button.

He turned it over in his fingers and realized it wasn't just an ordinary button but an expensive one. Most likely from a gentleman's jacket or waistcoat.

Glancing up at Miss Porter, he wondered if he'd underestimated her. She kept a man's button as a keepsake? Perhaps from the coat of a beloved brother, or the vestment of her sainted father, the vicar?

Or even that of a lover?

"Is this yours?" he asked as innocently as he could muster.

She glanced over at him, then her gaze fell to his outstretched hand. Instantly her cheeks colored. Her hand moved so quickly that he barely realized it when her fingers swept over his palm, snatching back her treasure as if it were gold.

"Thank you," she said curtly.

A chill ran across his still open hand, while a disconcerting niggle whispered in his ear.

Remember.

Remember what? he thought, closing his fingers and stuffing his hand in the pocket of his coat, letting the warmth of the wool chase away the lingering echoes that urged him toward something disagreeably familiar.

The only lesson he had learned in the past was that the days long gone were best forgotten.

And what about this Miss Porter? What did her past hold? Her hasty reaction spoke of a scandal she'd rather forget as well. Still, she'd held onto her token for some reason, held onto this reminder, and he couldn't help but wonder what had driven Miss Porter and its former owner apart? Forced her to spend her life teaching manners to spoiled young chits while the villain (for who else would have been idiot enough to let this redheaded handful get away) left her in this feline prison of sorts.

"A man's button, Miss Porter?" he said softly. She glanced up at him, her shoulders returning to the taut, wary lines she'd worn earlier. Whatever he thought of her tart opinions, her sharp manners, they all fled in the face of the fear he saw in the most beautiful pair of green eyes he'd ever beheld. They pinned him with a grief he couldn't fathom, filled him with guilt for his earlier notions.

For there was only one reason a woman looked like that, and it was because a man had wreaked havoc on her heart. Left her to twist alone in a scandalous breeze.

"I'm . . . I'm . . ." he stammered. *I'm sorry*, he tried to say, but the words faltered in the face of her private anguish.

He straightened his shoulders and stood like a nobleman, instead of his brother's lackey. "Oh, demmit. My apologies, Miss Porter. For whoever he was, he was a fool to leave you here."

With that, Lord John Tremont bent to the lowly task of fetching the last of his niece's belongings and left Miss Porter standing in the hall gaping after him.

Miss Porter stood rooted in the hallway, biting back a thousand retorts before she found the right one.

But by then it was too late. Mad Jack Tremont was gone.

Departed yet again from her life.

"Dreadful man!" she muttered anyway, unwittingly echoing her students' earlier assessment.

Why, he'd barreled into her like a stevedore, barely managed a decent apology, and then had possessed the audacity to hold her . . . not just hold her but *claim* her, as rakes were wont to do.

Well, some things never changed. Or rather, she corrected herself, some men. He'd been a degenerate sort without a care in the world back then, and he was still a bounder.

She took a deep breath and smoothed her hands over her skirts, hoping it would be enough to still her trembling limbs, her beating heart.

It wasn't that the man affected her, not in the least. It was just that it was so . . . so . . . unsettling to see him again.

And despite her best intentions to turn heel and march away, she slowly and reluctantly made her way to the window at the front of the house and peered through the opening in the curtains at him, as half the girls in the school were most likely doing at this very moment despite her earlier admonitions to the contrary.

Gazing down at the man who had ruined her with just one kiss.

For having neither been sold to a harem nor married off to some Colonial merchant, nor even succumbed to some dramatic decline, Miss Miranda Mabberly had done what any lady of good sense would have done in such circumstances—she'd picked up the ruined pieces of her life and gone on living with what was left to her.

By society. By her unforgiving parents.

And when it had become obvious that Lord John

would not marry her, she'd been packed off with due haste to live with distant relations, the Hibberts, in a remote corner of the north of England.

Mr. Mabberly, livid at the irreparable loss of her reputation, and, as such, the end of any noble marital prospects that could improve his business standing, cut off his only daughter with the same cold business acumen that had made him one of the wealthiest *cits* in London.

A clean sweep of the ledger book, as it were, written off like a lost ship or a hold full of wet powder kegs.

Having grown up in the hustle and bustle of London, the north country held few delights for Miranda. Especially when the Hibberts decided it was their moral duty to see her wed before her unnatural tendencies reared their ugly head again and brought shame on their upright home.

Besides, there was always the hope, Miranda suspected, that having seen her respectably married, her wealthy father might reward the poor couple.

So they'd brought forth vicar after widower after yeoman farmer for her choosing.

But Miranda had clung to her girlhood hope that she could marry someone who fit her original list of attributes. Someone noble and honorable, charming and heroic. And one other thing, a trait that her encounter with Lord John had etched into her heart.

He must be passionate.

Mad Jack's kiss had given her a tantalizing glimpse into the very improper world of passion and temptation, one she couldn't shake from her memory, her imagination.

Yet as the years passed, and the line of eligible men slowed to a trickle, she still couldn't let go of her dream. Not that time hadn't compelled her to realize that making some concessions would be necessary.

The lonely English countryside had a way of forcing one to forsake some of one's more lofty requirements. Yet, if she must marry, what was sophistication if the man couldn't inspire her heart to beat fast? And weren't heroism and nobility slightly overrated if the man's lips held all the appeal of week old mutton?

So Miranda had continued to wait.

And wait. And wait.

Appeals to her parents went unanswered, though she knew that the Hibberts received intermittent correspondence from her father's solicitor, along with funds for her keep.

But nothing came for her.

And then one winter, she read in a months-old copy of *The Ladies Magazine* the following note:

DEATHS.
August 15. At her house in Mayfair, Mrs. Jane Mabberly, wife of Mathias Mabberly.

Miranda dropped the journal and gasped.

She furiously sent off an urgent missive to her father demanding to know how this had transpired, why she hadn't been told. When that went unanswered, she sent another, a more contrite page, begging him to allow her to come home. She could keep house for him, they could share their grief.

Please, could she return home?

And still she waited.

Then the hand of time intervened. Mr. Hibbert passed away early that summer, and Mrs. Hibbert followed him to her reward before the leaves had turned to autumn gold. While these were sad events, for the Hibberts had been well-meaning, Miranda saw it as an opportunity to finally go home. But shortly after Mrs. Hibbert was laid to rest came a letter addressed to Miranda.

She'd opened it with trembling fingers, certain this was going to be her summons home. But to her dismay it was a terse note from her father's solicitor instructing her to travel further north to take up residency with a cousin of her father's. Enclosed were the funds for her travel expenses.

Nothing more, nothing less.

The letter and notes fell from her hands and she stood for some time in a state of shock.

And then something happened, something inside her snapped. Anger at Lord John, anger at her father's stubborn refusal to acknowledge her, anger at herself for being bullied and pushed into this wasted life. She'd spent the last five years waiting for her life to begin anew.

She wasn't going to wait another day.

Packing up her valise, she'd bought a ticket on the mail coach going south, but not to London   rather to Bath.

Over the years she had corresponded with her former teacher, Miss Emery, for the dear lady seemed to be the only person who still held any regard for her. In her most recent letter, Miss Emery had lamented that her decorum teacher had eloped with a naval officer. Such a scandalous situation and now there was no one to be found to take the position.

Miranda smiled to herself, the irony of such a proposal almost too funny. Who better to teach young ladies to preserve their reputation than someone who knew firsthand the experience of ruin?

However, she found Miss Emery hesitant to accept her proposal, for she had the sterling reputation of her school to consider. So Miranda came up with a solution: she would change her name, thus to keep Miss Emery's polished standing in tact.

So, Miss Miranda Mabberly ceased to exist, and Miss Jane Porter became the new decorum teacher at Miss Emery's Establishment. And on that day, Miranda made one other change in her life; she vowed never to give the rake who had ruined her life another thought.

And until today, Miss Emery's had provided her a perfect haven for such a course.

Until *he* had come barging back into her life.

Now, unhindered by the shock of seeing Lord John so close, Miranda, aka Miss Jane Porter, took the time to study the man and see what nine years had wrought upon him.

Well, perhaps she'd been hasty in her estimation that he hadn't changed, for in fact, he had.

The Corinthian who had been beloved by the *ton* for his expensive taste was all but gone.

How had she not noticed the shabby jacket and boots that looked like they hadn't seen a decent polish in years? And his hair, which had always been styled *à la*

Brutus, or some other noted cut, looked like it had been trimmed with a kitchen knife. Long and ragged, he wore it brushed back in a poor attempt at civilization.

Not only that, it was gray at the temples. Gray hair on Lord John?

Her hand went to her own head and touched the strands tucked into her very proper chignon. Heavens, if he looked so ancient, what must she look like? Did she look so different as well?

She must.

For he'd held her ever so close, looked deeply into her eyes, and—if she wasn't mistaken—been about to steal a kiss, detestable beast, yet he hadn't even blinked in recognition. Hadn't known her from any other lady.

She took a deep breath and tried to still her hammering heart.

He didn't recognize her.

The astonishment of such a notion nearly bowled her over as she tried to fathom how he couldn't know who she was.

For even after all these years, when she had all but forgotten the dark hue of his hair, the blue of his eyes, the breadth of his chest, and his commanding height, (well, perhaps she hadn't forgotten *those* things) there were other bits and pieces of Lord John she had forgotten, but that didn't mean she wouldn't have recognized him anywhere.

Even as ragtag and tattered as he looked now.

So how could he not know her? She took another breath as a second, more damning notion thudded into her thoughts.

Lord John had recognized her and had neither the desire nor the honor to acknowledge her.

What did she expect? He'd ruined her and hadn't possessed the wherewithal to offer for her. Why she thought time would have afforded him a sense of honor or responsibility, she knew not.

Pushing the curtain shut, she turned from the window, having realized that in some foolish, dark corner of her dreams, she had always thought that one day he would seek her out, proclaim that he had never forgotten her kiss, and redeem her ruined reputation with a proposal of marriage.

"Harrumph!" she sputtered. Lord John had held her and tossed her aside once again like a week-old mackerel.

Worse yet, he pitied her!

My apologies. Miss Porter. For whoever he was, he was a fool to leave you here.

"Yes, you were a fool," she muttered. No more than she had been to carry such ridiculous romantic notions around all these years. She was five and twenty now, a woman of means and certainly no longer susceptible to the bird-witted memories of a man's kiss.

Shoving her hand into the pocket of her apron, her fingers closed over the solid silver reminder of that fateful night.

The button that had fallen from his coat. A keepsake from a rake who had kissed her until she'd been senseless, breathless.

And very ruined.

She didn't know why she had kept it. Then again, perhaps she did.

Miranda shivered, her body still tingling where his hands had touched her, her lips parting, as if waiting for the kiss she had thought for one blissful moment to be hers yet again.

So when she turned and glanced once more out the window at Lord John, she knew he still did. Somehow. Some way. Even after all these years.

Leave her breathless, that is.

"Dreadful, wretched man."

The front door opened and Miss Emery bustled inside, closing it behind her with a decided thud.

"There you are, Miss Porter," her employer said, coming to stand beside her at the window. "Sorry business all this, but don't think for a second I feel that Lady Arabella's indiscretion reflects on you in the least. She is a Tremont, after all."

Miranda nodded her appreciation but said nothing.

Miss Emery, who never liked silence, continued on unabashed. "My dear, I wish you would think again of staying on. Are you sure you want to leave at the end of the term?"

Nodding, Miranda smiled at the lady. "Yes. I think it is best that I go." She had gained her inheritance recently and with it, a measure of independence that she'd never thought she'd possess. So she'd taken a house in Kent and invited an elderly cousin to come live with her. It was all very respectable and proper.

Miss Emery wasn't so convinced. "My dear, I worry about you."

"I am quite capable of managing for myself," Miranda told her. "Look what I've done for your accounts and the school's budgets. You of all people should know that I will not squander my father's money."

Miss Emery waved her off. "Yes, I'm not disputing your business acumen." She lowered her voice to a whisper before continuing, "But Miranda, my dear girl, the world isn't made up of account ledgers, and life can't simply be tallied up in a column. I fear you've been far too sheltered—"

"Sheltered?" she protested, shaking her head. "I think you know as well as I that I've—"

"Yes, yes, I know all about that. But it was years ago," Miss Emery said. "And only a kiss. It is high time you stop hiding—"

"I am not hiding, I'm—" Miranda protested.

"Retaining your respectability," the lady said. "Yes, I know. But, my dear, you have nothing to be ashamed of and nothing to hide. Quite the contrary. Besides, your newfound fortune will most likely smooth your way back into Society's embrace. I would guess it will even help you find a man who—"

"You mean marry?" Miranda shook her head. "No. I think not. I am well past such folly."

Miss Emery persisted. "But a husband would give you the protection you need. Would keep you safe from harm. It isn't right for a woman of your age to be on her own. To be *alone*."

"I'll be well enough," Miranda told her, patting the lady on the hand and smiling at her. "Miss Emery, I want only to live a quiet and exemplary life. My solicitor tells me Rose Cottage is a fine house, the housekeeper of excellent repute. I'll be quite content to spend the rest of my days working on the charities my mother loved and tending my rose gardens."

The lady put forth one last plea. "When you leave here, you will be on your own. I wish you would reconsider. The world is full of—"

Miranda straightened her shoulders and looked out toward the now empty street before them. "I am well aware of the sort of people one finds in the world, and having taught decorum for you for the past four years has given me a fair regard for propriety. It is highly unlikely I will ever do anything improper or untoward."

Gathering up her basket, she nodded to the lady and went up the stairs to her room.

"That's what I'm afraid of, my dear," Miss Emery whispered as she watched Miranda ascend the stairs in modest and perfect precision. "That is exactly what I fear most."

Chapter 2

Three months later

Miranda Mabberly might have thought her perfectly ordered future well in hand, but Lord John's visit had changed all that.

The button, which had fallen from his coat that night and had sat all but forgotten in her sewing basket for so many years, had suddenly become a beacon.

She found herself digging it out and putting it in her pocket. Fingering the smooth shank, tracing the engraved design on the front.

Remember his kiss . . . remember that night . . . it seemed to call to her.

Every time she found herself reaching for it, hunting through her ribbons and threads and needles and pins to spy its shiny temptation, she swore it was going to be the last time she picked it up.

By heavens, she was going to take the blasted thing

and give it to the first beggar she spied on the street. But when it came to actually marching out the door and giving away the token, something stopped her.

Pride, perhaps. She didn't need to get rid of the button to forget about Lord John, she told herself. She could do that on her own. And so she'd tuck the button back into the bottom of her sewing basket where it was safe.

Out of sight. But hardly out of mind.

She soon realized that seeing Lord John had opened a Pandora's box inside her, far more dangerous than a single button. It was a tangled, niggling whisper of desires that wheedled and wound through her limbs, her thoughts. For years she'd banished such feelings as hardly proper, but now they'd become intrusive.

Barging into her thoughts when she was planning lessons or knitting, or worse, intruding upon her sleep, bringing dreams that no proper spinster should ever have . . .

Dreams of a dark-haired man who lured her to a shadowy corner. Once there, she'd find herself trapped in his arms, unable to escape (perhaps slightly unwilling to leave) while this devilish fellow whispered offers and enticements into her ears, upon her lips, that left her bolting up in bed and shivering for all the wrong reasons.

And much to her chagrin, filled with a sense of disappointment and longing that the dreams didn't continue until he made good his enticements . . .

So finally, when the time came to leave Miss Emery's Establishment, Miranda heaved a sigh of relief and packed up her belongings, ready to make a new life for herself. She'd even gone as far as to leave the button behind, but at the last minute, she tucked it into the bottom of her valise, determined that somewhere in the next fortnight, she'd find a new home for that pestering little piece of silver.

As it was, three of the students—the Misses Felicity and Thalia Langley and their cousin Lady Philippa Knolles—were going to spend the summer with a Lady Caldecott in Kent, and had offered a space in their carriage to Miranda for her journey, in exchange for chaperoning them during their travels.

Miss Emery provided the party a letter of introduction and suggestions for proper places for them to spend the night, as well as a list of historic and educational sites along the way that would give some substance to their days.

"I expect a full accounting, ladies," she told the girls. "Sketches, historical vignettes, and a well-written expense account. Do not waste your summer lolling about and daydreaming." And then she turned to Miranda and, with tears in her eyes, said, "And I wish you find the answer to whatever has been on your mind these past few months. If anything, don't be afraid to do more than tend roses, my dear Miss Porter."

Now, a sennight later, Miranda looked out into the dismal night and wished that tending roses was the least of her problems. Unrelenting rain beat against the carriage, and a fierce wind rocked the elegant conveyance nearly off its well-hung springs. Their trip, which until today had been entirely uneventful, had now turned harrowing. As they had dipped toward the sea, traveling along the edge of Sussex, a horrible storm had blown in from the Channel, leaving the road a mire of mud and slowing their progress down to a crawl.

"Do you think we will ever find Thistleton Park, Miss Porter?" Pippin asked, her voice edged with a bit of panic. "I don't see how Mr. Billingsworth could have led us so far afield."

In addition to Miss Emery's list of proper sites to visit, the girls had also taken to using Mr. Billingsworth's travelogue to find other interesting venues. The Langley sisters, Miranda quickly discovered, were intrepid travelers, having spent most of their lives gadding about the globe with their father. For most of the day, they'd taken this delay and the storm in stride, Felicity with her nose buried in a newspaper they'd procured in the morning, and Tally reading a French novel that Miranda had to imagine Miss Emery would hardly approve of.

But even those diversions were no longer working, for it had grown too dark to read and now Miranda had three unhappy young ladies in her care, and no idea of where they were going to spend the night.

"I just hope we can find an inn out here," Miranda said under her breath, even as she began to feel the same bit of panic as Pippin.

They had intended to spend the night in Hastings, but early in the day Philippa had pointed out an entry in *Mr. Billingsworth's Accounts of Sussex for the Accomplished Traveller, with Details on Sights for the Artistic and Historical Aficionado* that sounded worthy of a slight detour from their prescribed route.

It read:

> *Thistleton Park is an ancient manse, the original portion of the house having been built not long after William the Conqueror arrived in England.*

Entirely walled, it is a relic of another time, the gates guarded by an ancient oak whose mammoth size is worthy of note and is said to have been planted by Eleanor of Aquitaine before she was banished. Beyond these historical delights, Thistleton Park also offers a quaint and pictur-esque setting, just right for a seaside nuncheon al fresco, which the delightful and generous owner of the house can be counted on to provide. Those with an artistic bent should bring along their tools for they will find great delight in sketching the craggy and romantic tower, referred to as Al-bin's Folly. . . .

That had been enough for Thalia—the words "roman-tic" and "sketching" lure enough for her. And "nun-cheon" was probably what had piqued Pippin's attention.

By now, whatever romance Thalia had thought she'd find was long forgotten. She cast herself back into the deep, comfortable confines of the rich leather seats and complained dramatically, "We're done for. We'll perish out here, for certain." To add to her performance, she threw her hand over her brow. "Lost, never to be found, that is what is to become of us."

In her lap, Brutus let out a pitiful howl to match his mistress's mood, though Miranda suspected the little dog more likely shared Pippin's despair over their long overdue nuncheon. And tea. And supper.

"I don't see how we could be so lost," Pippin said, tossing aside her guidebook. "Mr. Billingsworth's di-rections were quite specific. We should have reached Thistleton Park hours ago."

Miranda suppressed a smile. She knew the girl's chagrin wasn't so much that they hadn't succeeded in seeing the infamous folly but that they hadn't found an inn or common house at which to dine. That her beloved Billingsworth had let her down in that respect was probably the most disheartening experience of her young life.

But dear heavens, Miranda wondered as she looked out into the growing darkness, what would they do if shelter couldn't be found? She'd given up all hope of making it to Hastings. That left them with few options, the most likely of which appeared to be spending the night in the carriage.

She shuddered to think what Miss Emery would make of such an arrangement.

Just then they came to a quick stop. Miranda parted the curtains and, with the aid of a massive crack of lightning, spied a heavy iron gate before them—the kind that was usually a portend to a great house.

"Miss Porter," the driver called down, "it appears we may have found this Thistleton Park of Miss Thalia's. Should we seek shelter there?"

"Oh heavens, please, Miss Porter!" Philippa begged. "'Tis well past supper as it is. They may be eating late!"

Miranda wasn't so sure. "We don't know the family." She glanced once again at the heavy gate. Goodness, spending the night by the side of the road was one thing, but in the house of someone who was beyond the pale . . . why, it could be ruinous for the girls. All their stops and nights had been spent with respectable families, handpicked by Miss Emery to ensure that they didn't come into the company of "certain" people. "I rather think we should continue on."

Immediately, Felicity reached over and caught up her cousin's book, paging through it with all speed. "According to Mr. Billingsworth, Thistleton Park is the home of an elderly spinster. The sister of a duke. Surely, an old lady in her dotage would provide an acceptable haven for us."

Taking another glance toward the house, which was now once again obscured by the storm, Miranda reconsidered. Certainly if anyone knew what the gates of Thistleton Park held, it would be Felicity. The girl was title mad and could probably cite the location of every lord, heir, heir apparent and second son in England, as well as those in the nether parts of Scotland. The relations to a duke were probably just as important in her quest for the right spouse, and therefore if she said the mistress of this mansion was the sister of a duke, there was no need to doubt it.

Taking one more glance back at the muddy road behind them and the gloomy, shadowy house before them, Miranda knew she had no choice but to apply to the owner for shelter.

"Go on in, Stillings," Miranda told the man, and the carriage lurched forward, the horses probably as anxious to be out of the rain as their driver.

As they drew through the huge gates, the house came into view almost immediately, a dark, shadowy manse, without a single light within.

"I don't know if your spinster is in residence," Miranda remarked.

"Someone will let us in," Pippin said. "There must be

a servant about, a footman, or the housekeeper, maybe even the cook."

Everyone in the carriage knew what Pippin truly meant. There must be someone inside who could prepare a decent meal.

When the carriage came to a stop in front of the house, Stillings went up to the door and pounded on the great oak panels.

After what seemed like an eternity the door opened a mere crack, a tiny shaft of light from a single taper offering a meager and mean welcome. A discussion ensued, then Stillings came down to the carriage.

"It's the secretary, Miss Porter," the man told her. "He's not the most obliging fellow. Says we can seek shelter at the inn in Hastings."

"How far is that?" Miranda asked.

"A good twenty or so miles," Stillings said.

At this, Pippin groaned.

"Twenty miles! Why, that is ridiculous." Miranda pulled her cloak up over her head. "I'll apply to the mistress of the house directly. Twenty miles, indeed!" She got down and marched up the steps. She pulled her hood off and patted her hair into place.

It never hurt to make a proper impression.

Thus prepared, she took the door knocker in hand and gave it a polite rap.

Then waited. And waited.

When she took it up again, she gave it a little more insistent thud. By the third time, she had lost patience with standing in the cold and wind, so she hammered at the door, hoping it roused the entire house.

Really, how could a place be so ill-run? Most likely,

the lady was elderly and the servants took a terrible advantage of her dotage. Finally, after another volley of knocking, Miranda spied the light of the candle returning.

When the door opened, a great looming figure stood before her. His face was scarred, and his long hooked nose crooked to one side. A more fearsome man she had never seen. Without even realizing it, she stepped back off the shelter of the porch and into the rain.

This was the family secretary? Really, what sort of lady kept such a servant?

"I said afore, go away with ye," he bellowed. "Or I'll set the dogs on the lot of you."

So much for Mr. Billingsworth's assurances of generous hospitality.

Even as the fellow made his rude greeting, a torrent of icy water from the ill-kept gutters ran down the back of her neck. It was enough of a hint as to what a night spent in the carriage would be like to screw up her courage.

Besides, Miranda would put her money on Brutus against any mongrel this ill-mannered fellow could produce. She squared her shoulders and stepped forward. "I would speak to your mistress," she said in her most authoritative voice.

"She's gone," he said, starting to close the door in her face, paying no heed to her confident and commanding request.

Not about to spend the night listening to the girls complain and Brutus snore, she wedged herself into the doorway. "To London?" she inquired.

"To London, that's a fine one." The man made a loud

snort, as if her question was foolish. "She ain't in London. She's gone aloft, if it's any of yer business."

Dead? This news sent a chill down Miranda's spine that had nothing to do with the leaky gutters and their persistence in draining their contents on her head. This entire house and night were like something out of one of Tally's gothic novels.

Oh bother, Miranda chided herself, now she was being foolish.

Gothic, indeed!

"We need shelter for the night," she told him. "You obviously don't understand that I am escorting three young ladies from Miss Emery's—"

The man didn't let her finish. Once he heard the word "ladies" his eyes widened in horror. "We'll not have a lot of doxies in this house, even if they are from some fancy brothel like Miss Emery's," he said, starting once again to shove the door shut.

Miranda bristled. Brothel? Doxies? How dare he! If anything, she was determined to stay now, if only to see this vulgar, impertinent man sacked from his position.

"My charges are young ladies of character," she told him. "Their fathers are highly respected noblemen of the realm. Any family would be honored to give them shelter for the night."

He snorted once again. "Ye look like a lot of doxies to me, and we won't have none of that here, so just be gone." His words were punctuated with a loud clap of thunder and another deluge of rain.

Miranda glanced back at the carriage where four noses were pressed to the window.

"Sir, I promise—" she began, even as from the dark

recesses of the house came a voice that sounded like a soothing calm amidst a fury.

"Mr. Jones, what is going on here?" came the question, the inquirer's voice cultured and refined, holding all the comforts of a London town house.

Then it struck Miranda who this could be. The butler! It had to be.

"Mr. Jones, who is at the door?" came another inquiry.

"Now see what you've done," came the secretary's disgruntled snort as he struggled to close it before this newcomer spied her.

Miranda heaved a sigh of relief. It *was* the butler. No one else (save the mistress or lord of the manner) could elicit such a disgruntled response from another servant.

"Vagabonds, Mr. Birdwell. Seeking shelter."

"We are not vagabonds, sir," Miranda called out, pushing on the door against this Mr. Jones without any thought of decorum, shoving her head into the opening so she could look the butler in the eye.

Let him see her poor bedraggled state.

She hadn't been raised in London not to know how the majordomo of any house hated to see a lady in dire circumstances. "My name is Miss Porter, and I have in my charge the daughters of Lord Langley and the daughter of the Earl of Stanbrook. We seek but the barest of shelter for the night. If you could allow us to come in and let me explain—"

Her plea worked before she could even come to the end.

"Yes, of course, miss," this Mr. Birdwell said, hurrying forward with a welcoming brace of candles in his capable hand. "Mr. Jones, open the door immediately."

The secretary clung to his position with the same resolve as Brutus after a squirrel. "But Mr. Birdwell," the man said in a low voice. "We can't have strangers about. And certainly not a gaggle of misses, if you know what I mean. They'll be nothing but trouble. I for one won't be responsible if one of 'em starts wandering about. Sides, they'll be wanting warm milk and trays of chicken and cakes, and hot water and all sorts of 'necessities' that we ain't—"

While a lady—especially not a former teacher of decorum—wouldn't dream of eavesdropping on such a conversation, Miranda was not about to lose the inroads she'd gained with the butler.

"We will be of little notice," she rushed to promise. "And will keep to our rooms. We are simply too fatigued to continue, and our horses need rest."

"There you have it," Birdwell said to a glowering Mr. Jones, prying the secretary away from the door and throwing it wide open. "Welcome to Thistleton Park, Miss Porter."

That was enough of a signal to the girls, who tumbled out of the carriage in a rush and came bounding up the steps to get out of the weather. Miranda was pleased to note that Thalia had possessed the good sense to hide Brutus under her cloak. Hopefully the little dog would stay quiet long enough for them to gain their rooms before he made his reliably unpleasant presence known.

Their mud-splattered arrival led to another aggrieved huff from Mr. Jones, who stood to one side, a frown creasing his ugly face, his big meaty arms folded across his massive chest.

Meanwhile, Mr. Birdwell was surveying his guests

with that knowing air that only a London butler could possess. After a moment of consideration, he nodded to the secretary. "Mr. Jones, if you will, please take their trunks up to the east wing. The Blue Room for the young ladies, and the adjoining chamber for Miss Porter."

"I won't, Mr. Birdwell," Mr. Jones said, making one more protest. "When the master finds out—"

"The master?" Miranda inquired. "Is the owner in residence?"

"Yes, miss," Birdwell said. "But he is currently not at home. Allow me to speak for him and say that he would not mind your necessary intrusion. He is a fine gentleman and wouldn't think of denying the hospitality of his home to ladies in need."

Mr. Jones let out an inelegant snort that seemed to contradict the butler's claims, and for a moment Miranda paused and glanced around. The house was in shadows, so she couldn't see much beyond the foyer or the stairs that rose into the darkness above.

There was no telling what lay in the murky environs beyond, and for a moment she felt truly transported into one of Tally's wretchedly overwrought novels. Each and every one of the unwitting heroines in those books fell prey to the sinister master of a shadowy mansion not unlike this strange house.

She shivered, as if suddenly filled with a premonition of disasters untold awaiting them. It was almost on the tip of her tongue to tell Mr. Jones not to bother with their trunks and hasten the girls back into the carriage, when a gust of wind came blustering in through the still open door, sending a raft of cold air to banish her fears.

Premonitions! Whatever was the matter with her? She was just being foolish.

All it took was one look back out the open door to know what a night spent out there would hold, and the thought of a suite of rooms, no matter how dusty (or gloomy) seemed a fine sight more welcome than a night in the carriage with three complaining girls and that rapscallion Brutus.

"Is the master at home?" Felicity was asking, as if such an innocent question were nothing more than a polite query.

At this, Miranda's wandering thoughts fled, and she turned her gaze on the girl. While Felicity did her best to keep the contents of her *Bachelor Chronicles* a secret, Miranda had heard enough gossip about the girl's infamous encyclopedia of eligible men to know exactly what the young lady was about with her inquiry.

A folly of another sort, Miranda guessed. And more fodder for her *Chronicles*.

"Not at the present, miss," Mr. Birdwell told her. This gave Miranda a moment of relief before he finished it by saying, "But I expect him home later this evening. He has probably been detained by the storm."

"Then we shall see him in the morning?" Tally asked, a little too expectantly

Birdwell shook his head. "The master never arises before two. But I am sure he would be delighted to meet all of you then."

There was another derisive snort from Mr. Jones.

Miranda could well imagine what sort of "gentleman" kept this run-down house or such a scurvy servant and, further, felt the need to maintain city hours while out in the confines of the country.

For truly, what sort of gentleman was out on a night like this?

A rake, no doubt. And a down-on-his-luck one at best.

"Sadly, we shall be long gone before your master arises," Miranda said. "And will not have the opportunity to make his acquaintance."

"But Miss Porter," Felicity protested. "We must not leave before we thank our host. It is only polite."

The girl said it so sweetly that it was hard to imagine that she had the tactical mind of Wellington and the ruthlessness of Napoleon running through her veins when it came to collecting "bachelors" for her *Chronicles*.

"A well-penned note will suffice," Miranda replied. "Our rooms are in which direction, Mr. Birdwell?" Better to get the girls in their beds and well out of sight before the master arrived home in some unholy state.

"This way, Miss Porter," Birdwell said, before turning to Mr. Jones. "See that their trunks are brought up, Bruno." As they started for the staircase, he added, "Once you are settled, I'll see if a tray of refreshments can be found. If you have been traveling all day, you must be famished."

"Oh, bless you, sir," Pippin enthused.

Then in proper fashion, they were shown their rooms, the trunks arrived, and a tray brought up by Mr. Birdwell. If anything, the butler's fine manners eased Miranda's misgivings.

It was only after she'd gotten the girls settled in their beds and sought the sanctuary of her own adjoining room that she realized one very important thing.

She'd forgotten to ask *who* the master of the house was. Unfortunately, the gloomy portrait of an unhappy woman glowering over the mantel gave little hint to a family name.

"Oh, heavens, this is a tangle," she muttered up at the dour-faced woman.

But instead of giving over to worries, she turned to more practical matters. The room was cold, and there was no wood for the hearth, so she pulled on her night-rail, threw her favorite blue shawl around her shoulders, and climbed into the chilly, narrow bed.

Wind rattled the windows, while torrents of rain beat against the panes, only adding to her bleak plight. She thought she'd never fall asleep, but it had been a long day and before she knew it, she drifted into an uneasy spate of dreams, only to be jolted awake some time later by the sound of voices from deep within the house.

From the tenor and pitch, she could tell that an argument was ensuing, and before she could discern anything that was being said, a door slammed shut, and heavy footsteps echoed down a walkway somewhere beneath their rooms.

She rose from her bed and went to the window, cautiously parting the thin curtains. It was hard to see anything at first, but aided by a flash of lightning, she thought she saw a man go striding into the night, as if the storm were but a tiny tempest in a teacup, his great cloak swirling about him.

There was something about his stance, his fortitude in the face of nature's onslaught that made her tremble . . . made her back away from the window as her breath quickened. And when she looked again, there was no sign of him, and the entire episode left her wondering if he hadn't been but a lingering figment from her dreams.

That is, until the chill of the floorboards started to nip at her toes and she shivered.

"Miranda, you are chasing shadows," she muttered under her breath as she tugged her shawl tighter around her shoulders.

This, she told herself, was what came from letting Tally read to them in the afternoons from her collection of forbidden novels.

Turning to get back into bed, determined to dream of something wholesome and sensible, Miranda instead found herself drawn once again to the window, if only to convince herself that her mysterious phantom was just that—a figment of her imagination.

Yet all she could see was the storm raging outside, the rain pelting against the panes, the wind howling and buffeting the old house.

Not unlike the turmoil within her that had started when Mad Jack Tremont had held her once again, leaving Miranda, the most proper of spinsters, wondering how long she would continue to have to weather the storm left in the wake of a rake's kiss.

Jack Tremont had yet to go to bed for the night, but that wasn't unusual for him. Luckily for him, his years in Town had left him fit for the haphazard schedule of Thistleton Park, a legacy inherited from his great-aunt, Lady Josephine Tremont.

It made him wonder sometimes whether he would

ever have left London if he had known what this inheritance would have in store for him.

Not that he'd had much of a choice at the time. It was flee to the south of England or off to debtor's prison. Thistleton Park had seemed the lesser of two evils.

Little had he known.

He came to a side door and shrugged off his greatcoat, which was soaked all the way through. It had been a wretched night out in the rain, and all for naught. He glanced back at the path that led to the cliffs and the sea.

Where the hell was Dash? Why hadn't he arrived last night? Even a storm like that would hardly cause his contact concern. The foolhardy American would probably take the challenge of landing ashore in such conditions as nothing more than a jolly good time.

The fact that Dash hadn't arrived spoke of more ominous tidings.

No, there was something wrong, He could feel it in his veins.

He stopped himself right there. Now he was even starting to think like his crazy old aunt. It was this house, this place, this life. He wasn't cut from the right cloth to do the task he'd been left, but no one believed him. He'd inherited Thistleton Park, lock, stock and secrets, and now he was the master of it all.

Whether he liked it or not.

"Harrumph," he snorted, in perfect imitation of Josephine. At this rate, the only thing he'd master was an early demise from chilblains.

No, he needed something hot to eat and a few hours

of sleep—that is, if he could manage it—and then he'd have to determine how to proceed.

He walked through the long hallway toward the dining room, when a noise from the east wing stopped him. A noise so unusual he wondered if he wasn't already taken with fever, for it was something he hadn't heard in years.

Why, it sounded like giggling.

Giggling?

He shook his wet head. The torrential rains must have not only soaked him to the skin but filled his ears as well. The only other explanation was that Park was haunted, as his secretary, Bruno Jones, averred.

Haunted! Now that's a lark, Jack thought. Right up there with his premonitions of disaster.

But then, oddly enough, the scent of freshly cooking sausages tickled at his nose.

Sausages? Birdwell was cooking him sausages for breakfast? He was lucky to get cold toast most mornings from his disapproving butler.

Sausages were as likely as the giggling.

Jack heaved a sigh, convinced he was going as mad as the rest of the Tremonts who had ever lived at (or rather, been banished to) Thistleton Park, and continued toward the dining room.

He pushed through the doors, his thoughts focused on what he would need to do once he arose.

First and foremost, he'd need to compose a report to London on the events of the night, or rather the lack of events, and then there was always the estate business.

While the place looked ready to tumble down, and the grounds were in a state of *déshabillé*, it actually took some work to make Thistleton Park so inhospitable.

So very unrespectable.

He was about to continue through the dining room to the kitchen, being led by the rich scent of not only sausages but also bacon and . . . he sniffed yet again . . . if his senses were to be believed, the warm, enticing scent of fresh scones.

Scones?

Lord, he was more tired than he thought, for he had to be hallucinating. Yet, lo and behold, there was a bounty laid out on the sideboard before him, enough so that it stopped him in his tracks.

Though not for long.

Not one to look a gift horse in the mouth—not on his meager income—he filled his plate and turned toward the table.

What he spied before him nearly made him drop his breakfast. Nearly, that is, for Jack Tremont was many things, but negligent with a good plate of food was not one of them.

But still, he could be forgiven this lapse, for seated before him was a sight he couldn't fathom.

A woman? Seated at his table? It was as likely as the sausages and bacon on his plate.

"What the devil—" he managed to say as she clambered to her feet.

"Yo o u!" she sputtered back.

Jack set his plate down on the table before he took a good look at this unexpected, and all too unwanted, guest.

There was something rather familiar about the plain dress and startling eyes.

"What are you doing here?" she demanded.

"This is my house, madame," he said, trying to place the chit.

Then it struck him. The red hair. The outraged moue. "You're that handful of a teacher from Miss Emery's," he said aloud before he had a chance to stop himself.

Demmit, he'd been out of Society too long.

But then again, like his aunt before him, he'd come to see the benefit of being plainspoken and getting straight to the point. "What are you doing in my house? Did my brother send you? I'll tell you right now, Miss . . . Miss . . ."

"Porter," she reminded him pertly.

Oh, yes, he had the right of it. As outspoken and to the point as ever.

"Miss Porter," he said. "I'll not be party to yet another of my brother's schemes to see me—"

Before he had the chance to finish his statement, he heard that odd sound from above stairs yet again.

Giggling.

His earlier premonition of impending catastrophe enveloped him like the sheets of rain that had been driven off the Channel the night before.

"There are more of you?" He wasn't a man given to panic, but more women? In his house? "This is inexcusable. If Parkerton thinks he can foist—"

"Lord John, it is nothing like that. If you would just let me explain—"

Jack didn't care to hear anything more from her. "Birdwell!" he bellowed at the kitchen. "Birdwell! What is the meaning of this?"

"Lord John, there is no need for such a display," Miss

Porter chastened, as only a spinster schoolteacher could.

He shot a hot glance at her. She was, in his practiced assessment, in her late twenties, a spinster by Society's reckoning, but that didn't mean (in his humble and experienced opinion) that she deserved a place on the shelf. Of course, his estimation, gained in their tumbled introduction at Miss Emery's, had given him a rather intimate understanding as to the rather tempting curves the lady possessed beneath her dark muslin.

Yes, just get her out of that ugly gown and pull the pins from that severe chignon, and the lady had all the makings of a beauty.

Jack shook his head like a wet dog. Egads, he was in dire straits when he found himself fantasizing about tumbling a spinster who taught decorum!

"Mr. Birdwell!" he barked again, panic truly setting in.

Finally, and thankfully, his butler arrived. "Yes, my lord?"

"What is the meaning of this?" he said, pointing at the lady as if she were a blight upon his house.

"Ah, my lord, I see you've met Miss Porter and her young charges."

Young charges? Jack didn't like the sound of that in the least.

Then, much to his horror, the door swung open and into the dining room bounded three young girls. Like a trio of kittens in muslin, giggling and wide-eyed.

Three of them! Now he was convinced of it. The only disaster missing from the Old Testament was now being visited upon him—a plague of females.

Certainly, his years in Town had been filled with

vice, but Lord, how many ways did a man have to atone for his sins?

"Grrrr."

He looked down to find attached to his one decent pair of boots a small black dog of some misplaced origins.

"Get off," he said, shaking his boot to no avail.

"Brutus," one of the girls called out, snapping her fingers. "Enough! That is our host!"

The little beast promptly let go, sitting back on his little haunches and eyeing Jack like a stray piece of bacon. The dog's fierce expression and lionlike fur made him look much more furious than his small stature warranted.

The girl came forward and scooped up her wretched, snarling little companion. "My apologies, my lord. I fear Brutus is a bit overprotective." The girl covered her dog's ears and said in a soft aside, "He has the heart of a wolfhound but hasn't the vaguest notion that he's just the size of a sewing basket."

"Are you sure it is a dog?" Jack asked.

The coltish miss with her wide blue eyes looked askance. "Of course he is!" She held the animal up, pushing it forward to afford him a better view—as if Jack needed another close-up meeting with the growling, snapping mongrel. "He has the most royal of bloodlines. His grandsire belonged to Marie Antoinette."

He was being visited by a descendant of Marie Antoinette's dog? He must be fevered. It was the only explanation.

The girl continued with her recitation of her dog's merit, in tones that suggested he warranted a place in

Debrett's. "Brutus was a gift for my eleventh birthday from the Austrian ambassador."

Jack wasn't so convinced of the dog's worth or his vaunted bloodlines. "Are you sure it was a gift, or was the poor man just trying to rid his country of some very ugly vermin?"

Before the young girl could say another word, Miss Porter rushed forward. "My lord, I am sorry that you weren't made aware of our arrival last night, but your butler assured us—"

Birdwell! Jack's gaze swiveled in the man's direction, but the cagey fellow was busy tidying up the already perfectly set sideboard. Oh, yes, this certainly smacked of his meddling. If his brother wasn't pestering him to marry, Birdwell was always making it a point to mention the need for a mistress in the house.

A legitimate and properly married one.

Meanwhile Miss Porter was still nattering on. "—for you see we were caught in the storm and your secretary was reluctant—"

To have anyone about, Jack would guess. By nature Bruno Jones wasn't the trusting type, least of all of women; the man had an unholy fear of the feminine sex, ladies especially.

"—but then your kind butler assured us—"

Leave it to Birdwell to ride to the rescue.

And risk so much. Jack's panic returned tenfold. If one of them took a wrong turn or overheard anything . . . Or worse, if Dash arrived . . .

"—I assure you, we had no intention of being—"

"Madame," he said, interrupting her before she could get any further in her polite explanation. "You and your charges are not welcome here. I want you to leave at once."

One of the girls, a tall, blonde creature, gasped at such outright rudeness, while the other pair—twins by looks of them—shared a determined glance that only spelled trouble.

And made him even more resolute to be rid of this pack of females and their toplofty dog.

"Our apologies, my lord," Miss Porter said, gathering her composure together with the dignity of a queen, all the while shooing her charges toward the door—most likely before he said something truly untoward. "We will be gone within the hour and intrude upon your . . . your . . . *hospitality* no longer."

The ice in her words would have chilled every bottle in White's cavernous and renowned cellars.

"Without breakfast?" the tall one whispered to Miss Porter.

"Yes, Pippin," her teacher replied in a tight voice. "Without breakfast. One doesn't remain were she is unwanted. We will be gone before his lordship decides to call the magistrate on us for pinching the sausages and rolls Mr. Birdwell went to so much trouble to provide."

Oh, he'd forgotten how peevish a woman could get. Not to mention the twinge of guilt he felt upon spying what appeared to be tears in this Pippin's big blue eyes over the loss of her breakfast.

Tears! Oh, gads, not tears from some soon-to-be debutante. A woman's tears he could guard against (well, at least he told himself he could), but a young girl's watering eyes were enough to melt his resolve.

No, he was made of sterner stuff. He was disreputable. A ruined man, living a lonely, bitter exile. Jack wasn't about to be turned by the sight of a girl's tears.

And over sausages, of all things!

"Yes, well, see that you are gone by then," he told Miss Porter, pointing at the clock on the mantel as if to mark their agreement. "Or I will send for the magistrate."

"Really, milord. Without their breakfast?" Birdwell interjected, echoing Pippin's lament and stepping into their guests' paths. "It seems a dreadful waste—"

Jack's jaw worked back and forth. Then he made the mistake of looking over at Pippin, with her great big dewy blue eyes.

"Fine," he ground out. "Breakfast for our guests. But then please see that Miss Porter and these young ladies are well on their way to—"

"To your folly," one of the twins said brightly.

"My what?"

"Your folly." The girl had the cheek to sidestep her teacher and bound forward.

Jack suspected he was standing before one of the future patronesses of Almack's or some other denizen of Society. Give this chit a few years and she'd have the *ton* following in her determined wake.

"We are quite keen on sketching your tower," she said. Really, it was more of a command than a request.

And he wasn't about to be ordered about by some schoolgirl. "My folly is not a tourist vista."

"Actually it is," she had the nerve to say. Turning to Pippin, she said, "Cousin, do you have the guidebook?"

Pippin nodded and handed over a thick leather-bound tome. "The description is on page seventy-four."

His all-too-determined and unwanted guest thumbed

through the book until she came to the page, then she handed the entire thing over to him. "If you please, my lord, read what Mr. Billingsworth says."

She pointed at a passage and looked at him with such a sweet, compelling look that he found himself, against his better nature, reading the text.

Albin's Folly is a spectacular example of classical architecture and should not be missed by any traveler intrepid enough to venture into such a lonely reach of the Sussex coastline. Lady Josephine Tremont, the owner of Thistleton Park, is a fine hostess and all too willing to entertain guests. Though some view her as eccentric, this author knows from firsthand experience, she is a rare and charming lady who loves nothing more than to regale visitors with local histories and . . .

The passage continued on at great length, but he had neither the time nor the patience to read such nonsense.

Lady Josephine's charms, indeed! What was it about his aunt that had left every man between the ages of fifty and one hundred blathering on about her as if she were some octogenarian Venus?

"Miss? . . ." he said to the girl before him.

"Miss Felicity Langley, my lord," she replied very properly. Then she nodded over her shoulder, "My sister, Miss Thalia Langley, and my cousin, Lady Philippa Knolles."

"Yes, nice to make your acquaintance, but I have only two things to say about your"—he flipped the book over and read the name of the author—"Mr. Billingsworth. Thistleton Park is under new ownership."

"Yes, but—" the girl began.

"And unlike my aunt, I have no time for entertaining or 'recounting local histories.' Furthermore, my folly is not open to visitors. So I will say it again, you and your teacher are not welcome."

"There goes breakfast," he heard Pippin mutter, her great blue eyes turned in covetous longing toward the sideboard.

The Misses Langley cast him glances that all but branded him the worst curmudgeon this side of the House of Lords, while their beast of a dog was once again eyeing his boots with a renewed interest.

Even Birdwell had the nerve to make a disloyal *"tsk-tsk"* behind his back.

But it was the scathing look from Miss Porter that sliced into his gut. It said only too clearly that she had expected nothing less of him.

And that cut Jack to the quick.

Wasn't that what he wanted? To be left alone to the tasks at hand? Not to have a bunch of curious cats nosing about his estate?

The ruder he was, the more likely these ladies would flee Thistleton Park and spread the word of his inhospitable and ungentlemanly ways from one end of England to the other, or wherever it was their travels took them.

Which was exactly what he wanted. Not some spinster's regard—even if she was a redhead with an enchanting form hidden beneath her dour and proper gown.

Jack ground his teeth together, trying to remember he was now a disreputable boor, not a gentleman, and in no way the rake who had once charmed the *ton*.

It was a battle he won only partly.

"Very well. Give them their breakfast, Birdwell. But no tours, no folly. After you've picked my poor larder clean, ladies, I want you gone so I can have some peace in *my* house."

From the shocked looks on all their faces, that had probably done the trick, but to shore up his case, and before he took another glance at that one stray red tendril that was threatening to spill from Miss Porter's otherwise tight chignon, he stormed out of the room.

There were times when even a rake knew to flee.

With the impossible Lord John well and gone, it was much easier for Miranda to take charge of the situation.

As long as she could also take charge of herself— still her beating heart, calm her ruffled sensibilities.

What was it about this rakish man that put her at sixes and sevens?

His kiss, perhaps, a tiny voice teased from some dark, unbidden place in her heart.

His kiss, indeed!

No, she'd been right back at Miss Emery's. He truly was a dreadful man. How she had ever thought him capable of possessing a thread of honor, she knew not. Why, his state of *déshabillé* suggested a night spent . . . well, it was best not speculated how Mad Jack Tremont had spent the night.

However, now that she was over the shock of seeing him yet again, she couldn't help but think his rude display would serve well to dispel any more of her ridiculous notions about him.

And with his departure it was easier to think straight. First and foremost, she knew she must let Pippin eat or they would have to endure her complaints until another hot meal could be procured.

Who knew, in this remote and obviously inhospitable section of England, when they would find another willing host with a decent kitchen?

So they ate quickly, Miranda prodding the girls along so they could meet their deadline to be gone from the house in less than an hour.

"I don't think he'd call the magistrate, Miss Porter," Pippin said, glancing over her shoulder at the still laden sideboard.

Felicity looked up from her notebook, probably amending her notes regarding Lord John's eligibility. "I wouldn't be so sure," she said, taking a quick bite of a roll from her sister's plate and washing it down with a hasty drink of tea. "I have it on good authority that men of his age tend to be given to bouts of melancholy."

Men of his age? Miranda bit her lips together to keep from laughing. But then to these girls, Lord John probably did look ancient.

To Miranda, he looked . . . oh, bother, she didn't care how he looked. He certainly wasn't the same handsome gadabout he'd been years ago, but time had only added a fine patina to his carved features, giving them a craggy, hewn look, the gray at his temples, an air of mystery . . . leaving her wondering how he'd spent the last nine years.

Really, Miranda, she told herself, *that is no mystery.*

As if a rake like Mad Jack Tremont could ever change his stripes. Not even a storm as horrendous as the one last night had been able to keep him caged up and away from his sinful pursuits.

Tally, it seemed, didn't share her sister's aversion to Lord John's thirty some years. "I still think he looks like a pirate," she said as she folded her napkin and set it on the table beside her.

Miranda was about to chide her for such a remark, but the girl's words echoed like a church bell, tolling a warning that sent a chill down her spine.

I still think . . .

Still?

Miranda turned a slow, inquiring look at Tally. Suddenly their arrival at Thistleton Park took on a less innocent and accidental quality. "Still think, Miss Langley? What other time did you meet Lord John?"

Tally's hand paused as it reached for the teapot. The telltale blush rising on her cheeks answered the question better than if the girl had tried to come up with a handy fib to cover her misstep or even a believable fiction to conceal it entirely.

Felicity continued scribbling in her *Chronicles* as if nothing were amiss, but then again, Miranda suspected the girl could brazen her way out of a charge of high treason.

Still, there was Pippin as the final side to this devious triangle, and being the weakest link, she proved Miranda's suspicions quite handily. The girl looked ready to toss up her precious and hard-won breakfast.

Confirmation enough for Miranda.

They'd tricked her. They'd plotted to come to Thistleton Park—all along, she dared imagine—and it hadn't been for the reasons they'd professed.

Oh, Miss Porter, may we go to Thistleton Park to sketch the folly. It sounds terribly romantic. Oh, please may we go?

How innocent their pleas had sounded yestermorn. And how foolish she'd been to believe them!

But why? Why Thistleton Park? She glanced once more at Felicity and her meticulously kept *Chronicles,* and the answer bore down on her like a runaway mail coach.

Gads, they hadn't come down here thinking one of them would make a match with this infamous rake? Miranda's stomach rolled.

Lord John and one of these girls? Why, it was preposterous!

Not that she wouldn't put it past their scandalous host to take advantage of an innocent young lady, despite his assertions about wanting to be left alone, especially if he discovered the fortunes these young girls would bring to a marriage.

Thistleton Park obviously wasn't prosperous enough to keep him in his usual extravagant Town style, so the lure of a rich dowry to finance a return to London in the lavish and misspent fashion he preferred might be enough to tempt him from whatever dark region of the house he'd retreated to.

That thought sent a broadside of panic through her.

Miranda shot to her feet and into action. "We've imposed on Lord John's hospitality long enough," she announced. "Ladies, let us get our things packed." Ignoring Philippa's protest over her unfinished breakfast, she added a definitive, *"Now."*

The girls knew better than to lodge any further protests, but still, they rose reluctantly from the feast before them and their obviously unfinished task—whatever that was.

Pippin, not one to waste a meal, pocketed a roll or two and looked to be considering whether a couple of sausages would fit as well.

While Miranda knew she should rebuke her, at this point she didn't want to risk a mutiny.

She was in enemy territory with three rake-mad girls. The only course was to hie them out of Thistleton Park as quickly as she could.

Get them well away from Lord John Tremont. A pirate of hearts in ways that these three ladies should never discover.

As she had only too late.

Chapter 3

Jack stormed into his bedchamber and threw off his sodden clothes. He had every intention of getting what he considered his due: some well-needed rest. Climbing into the large bed, he pulled the coverlet over his head and willed himself to go to sleep.

But in spite of the fact that he had been up all night, sleep eluded him, and he knew exactly what the cause of his unrest was.

Miss Porter and her charges. How the devil could a man get any peace knowing there was a pack of females in his house?

Truly he'd been quite magnanimous in giving them an hour to depart, but even that seemed foolhardy as he lay in his bed and conjured up a thousand and one ways his unwanted guests could ruin his life.

Especially that tart-tongued Miss Porter.

He rolled over and closed his eyes. He didn't like admitting it, but ever since he'd bumped into her at Miss Emery's, the redheaded minx and her mysterious button had haunted his thoughts.

Jack wanted to imagine that it was her red hair that had captivated his lonely imagination, for he'd always had a weakness for auburn-haired beauties, but there was something else about her . . . the way she seemed so tightly wound . . . the wary light in her eyes . . . that made him want to unravel her that much more. . . .

Perhaps he did need to get up to Town, as Temple was always urging him to do. Get this restless need out of his blood in some fancy brothel. But not even that enticed him, for to go to Town . . .

Jack shook his head. He'd burned far too many bridges in London to find respite there. No, for better or worse, his life was here at Thistleton Park.

His Aunt Josephine had seen to that.

London
Four years earlier

Rap! Rap! Rap!

The hideous pounding in Jack's head was, he knew, the harbinger of a hangover that threatened to equal the three days of drinking and gambling that had come before. Having been on one of his infamous benders, Lord Jack Tremont had passed out only hours earlier and was certainly in no mood to be disturbed.

Besides, for all he could remember, he had won the night before, so there shouldn't be anyone at the door to collect on vowels or issue a challenge for some remark or comment or insult he'd made during the course of the last few days.

Rap! Rap! Rap! continued the insistent caller, pounding on the door as if they were trying to escape the gates of hell.

Gads, at this rate they'd break the demmed thing in, and he could no more afford the door than he could the rent on this rat-infested disgrace of a flat.

"What do you want?" he growled, still lying atop his bed and unwilling to test his legs while the room spun at such an unholy rate.

"Get up, you no-account rascal, or I shall give this address to your brother."

The voice belonged to only one person, but it was enough to rouse Jack so abruptly that he nearly emptied his accounts into the bucket beside the bed.

Dear Lord, not Aunt Josephine!

Struggling up from his bed, he made his way to the door. Since he hadn't bothered to remove his clothes when he'd toppled into bed, he was, for all intents and purposes, still decent.

If you could use that word to describe Jack.

Ruinous Jack. Drunken nit. That wastrel Tremont.

He opened the door and, without even waiting for an invitation, she barged in.

He must have gone pale, for the indomitable old girl nudged the bucket over toward him and turned her back on him while he threw up.

When he'd finished, she tossed a towel at him. "Some greeting this," she said, taking the one good chair in the room and sitting.

"Aunt Josephine, what are you—"

"Silence, you fool," she said, cutting him off.

Jack clamped his lips shut. From anyone else, he might have ignored such an order, dared to defy them, but this was Lady Josephine Tremont, and he doubted even the king would naysay her.

"You are a disgrace," she declared.

Leave it to his great-aunt to get right to the point.

"Yes, but a happy one," he muttered.

She snorted and looked about the room with a measure of disgust. "Seems I've arrived in time. You appear to be alive."

"Much to Parkerton's dismay."

This time she laughed. Though it was more of a cackle. "Your brother is a stiff-rumped fool. 'T'would give him apoplexy to see you thusly."

"Not such a bad idea," he conceded, shoving aside the bucket and propping himself up against the edge of his bed.

To be honest, he didn't think he could stand, for the room was still spinning like the very devil. "Aunt Josephine, what do you want?"

"It is about time you took your place in the family."

"Parkerton will never stand for it," he told her.

"Still holding that Mabberly chit's ruination over you, is he?"

Jack shrugged. All Society held him responsible for Miss Miranda Mabberly's disgrace and the calamity that had followed. They hadn't cared much for the *cit*'s daughter beforehand, even when she'd become engaged to the Earl of Oxley. But all it had taken had been one mistaken kiss on Jack's part to propel Miss Mabberly into a state of disgrace and make himself a pariah.

"Yes, well, all that nonsense is in the past," his aunt was saying. "Time you take your rightful place."

"I don't think the *ton* will be all that welcoming." After the debacle with Miss Mabberly, Jack's brother, the Duke of Parkerton, had cut him off without a farthing. He'd then managed to insult and offend every single one of his friends, until even his best friend, Alexander Denford, Baron Sedgwick, had given him the cut direct. Not that Jack hadn't deserved it. He'd made a complete cake of everything, and now here was Aunt Josephine droning on and on about duty and "being a Tremont."

"You've got the wrong man," he muttered, wondering if this bad dream was ever going to end.

"Wrong man? Rubbish. I'll make a man of you, a Tremont of you, if it is the last thing I do."

Those words echoed in his head as he once again passed back into a dark, dreamless sleep. One that offered no happy dreams and little respite.

Until some hours later, when he was roused again.

Once again, insistent pounding interrupted his sleep.

"Demmit," he muttered, as he struggled up off the floor. What did his aunt want now? Yet it wasn't Aunt Josephine on the other side of the door, but a small, bespectacled man, who blinked owlishly in the dim light of Jack's Seven Dials flat.

"Lord John?" he inquired, adjusting his glasses. His tone implied that he hoped he was in the wrong place.

"Yes," Jack replied. No use denying the fact. If the

man was here to dun him, let him. There was nothing more to take. "So who sent you? Caldwell? Rodney? I haven't the funds to pay either of them."

"Um, no. I'm from Mr. Elliott's office."

"Mr. Elliott?" Jack heaved a sigh. "I don't recall owing him a thing." He tried to close the door, but the man persisted, pushing his way in, much as his aunt had earlier.

"I'm here about your aunt. Your great-aunt. Lady Josephine Tremont. I work for her solicitor, Mr. Elliott."

Jack rubbed his eyes. "You just missed her. Try for her at—"

"Excuse me?" the fellow said.

"I said, you missed her. She left some time ago."

The fellow's mouth fell open. "You say your aunt was here?"

"Yes," Jack said, growing impatient. "A few hours ago, I suppose."

"I don't see how—" The man's nose twitched at the rank odors coming from the apartment; spilled brandy and worse—the bucket having yet to be emptied. "Yes, well, that is interesting. But as it is, my lord, Mr. Elliott sent me to—"

"Listen, if you've come to find my aunt, she isn't here. So go around to my brother's house in Mayfair, where she's probably bedeviling some other poor sot to straighten up." He opened the door a little wider. "Good luck to you and good riddance."

But the man was, if anything, persistent. "My lord, I haven't come to find your aunt. I've come for you. I've come about your aunt's estate. I need you to sign the necessary documents. There are procedures to be followed if the estate is to be properly passed along."

Jack shook his head. Gads, where had Caldwell gotten that brandy last night? From the Thames? Because he was having a devil of a time following what this fellow was talking about. "What estate?"

"Why, your aunt's, of course. Thistleton Park."

"And why would my aunt want to give me her house? Where is she going to live?"

"Live, my lord?" The fellow got that owlish blinking sort of look going again. "I don't think that is at issue. Now if you could be so kind to come with me down to Mr. Elliott's office, he can go over the terms of your aunt's will and—"

"My aunt's will?" Jack repeated, gooseflesh rising on his arms, a sense of foreboding, of destiny hurtling toward him with the same rude insistence as Aunt Josephine's walking stick pounding against the floor. "Are you saying my aunt is dead?"

"Yes, my lord. A fortnight past. I would have been here sooner, but we had some difficulty locating you."

"But she was—" Jack stammered. "I mean to say she was . . ." He glanced at the door and around the room and tried to reconcile his memory.

I'll make a Tremont of you yet . . .

"My lord?" the man asked.

Jack shook his head. Shook away the cobwebs from the night before and listened to what the man had to say.

"Demmit," Jack muttered, as he glanced over at the clock. There were still a good thirty minutes before his unwanted guests would be gone.

And Birdwell's excellent breakfast was sitting down there on the sideboard growing colder by the minute.

Considering his conduct this morning, he doubted his butler could be induced to warm any of it up.

So with that semblance of an excuse in hand, he climbed out of bed, rummaged around his disorderly room to find some relatively clean clothes, and tugged them on.

If anything, he told himself, he needed to go downstairs and ensure that his *guests* were well and gone.

Bounding down the steps, he spotted, to his relief, the back of Miss Porter's skirt as she shooed her charges out the front door.

Excellent! Out of his house and out of his life.

Even while he congratulated himself on scaring them enough with his boorish manners to make them leave well ahead of his deadline, he found his gaze straying back toward Miss Porter for one more glance at her soft, curving hips and the luscious red curls peeking out from beneath her bonnet.

Remember, that aggravating voice whispered up from inside him.

What was it about this woman that made him feel he had met her before?

Perhaps they'd met in London. . . . He winced. He hoped not. He'd rather forget his life back then . . . he'd been the worst sort of sponger, and after the Mabberly debacle . . . well, it was better no one recalled those days.

Much to his chagrin, before he could take one more guilty glance at the lady Bruno closed the doors on their guests with a decided thud.

One that said, *Don't even think of coming back.*

Hardly dignified, but Thistleton Park had never really been a proper house, despite Billingsworth's effusive praise.

Jack spared another glance at the door. Perhaps it wouldn't hurt to send them off with a good set of directions. Obviously their travel guide couldn't be counted on to steer them on the correct course.

That was it, he told himself, just a bit of help getting them on their way, if only to make some amends.

He continued down the stairs, willing to help in this small fashion—or, at the very least, catch one last glance at Miss Porter. Perhaps if he could see past her starched manners and distracting auburn tresses, he might be able to remember why this vexing lady teased his senses so.

Yet as he came through the door, he nearly ran into the party, for instead of having already climbed into their coach and, hence, out of his life, they were gathered on his front steps like a gaggle of geese.

"Come to call the magistrate?" the one called Thalia asked, sounding only too hopeful for such an adventure.

Christ, that chit was going to give her good parents, and then some poor man, a devil of a time when she came of age.

"No," he said, trying to look a little contrite over his earlier words. "I came to wish you well, and offer some directions that may be of more use than those of your illustrious Mr. Billingsworth."

"That would be well and good," Miss Porter said. "*If* we were leaving."

Not leaving? Jack felt that flare of panic rising anew in his chest, but he did his best to hold it in check. "Is there a problem with your carriage, your horses?" he asked, willing to offer them the best of his stables to see these meddlesome girls and their redheaded chaperone gone.

"Not quite," she said as she stepped aside and pointed at the main gate.

To his horror, the storm the night before had lent more damage to his life than these unwanted houseguests and the missing Dash.

The mighty oak that had stood sentinel at the gates of Thistleton Park for centuries lay across the drive.

Billingsworth had been right; the carved wall around the manor house was a unique sight, a defensive curtain from a time long past. But who would have thought that the wall designed to keep out invaders was now going to prevent the invaders in his house from making their retreat?

Miss Porter apparently shared his horror at the sight. "Lord John, your man says that this"—she pointed at the blocked gate—"is the only way out of the yard. Surely this can't be so?"

There was an edge of panic to her voice. What the devil was she panicked about? She wasn't the one with the weight of the world on her shoulders.

"This can't be," Jack muttered, sparing the ladies the curse he would have liked to use. Taking the steps two at a time, he bounded across the yard.

There was a gathering of men from the estate, as well as some of the villagers from the nearby hamlet, who'd obviously heard that the infamous oak had fallen.

They parted at his arrival.

"A sorry sight, milord," Jonas, his stable master, said. " 'T' was a fine tree."

"Yes, a fine tree and now a fine hindrance." Jack paced up and down the breadth of the gate, trying to determine how they were going to get the mammoth trunk out of the way.

And his guests and their carriage out. As quickly as possible.

He turned to Jonas and said, "Hire as many men as you need. Get axes, saws, rope, block and tackle, whatever you need to cut it up and get it out of the way."

"Oh, you mustn't do that, my lord," came a feminine protest.

He turned around and stared at the proponent of this unlikely objection—Miss Porter.

She stood behind him, her hands knotted into fists at her sides. "That tree doesn't belong to you. It isn't yours to cut up willy-nilly."

"I beg to differ," he told her. Not his tree? Why, that was ridiculous. "In case you've forgotten, Miss Porter, this is my house, my land, and *my tree.*" He turned to Jonas. "Offer double wages to any man willing to help."

The lady was not so easily deterred. She caught him by the elbow and steered him closer. "Do you see that plaque?" She pointed at a small metal plate nailed to the trunk.

"Yes," he said, having never paid the medallion much heed. He assumed it had been placed there by one of his previous errant relations. Hadn't Thistleton Park always been the last bastion for the wayward and outlandish members of the all-too-proper Tremont clan? Marking a tree wouldn't be that far a stretch for one of his ramshackle forebears.

"That's the King's crest," Miss Porter was saying. "That means this tree belongs to the crown."

"The wha-a-at?" he stammered. Now she was starting to sound as dicked in the nob as Aunt Josephine. Yet, even as he drew closer to study the plaque, if only to humor the woman, he realized it was indeed the King's seal upon the tree.

What the devil did the king of England want with the Thistleton oak?

"Ships," Miss Porter told him, as if she had read his mind. "The tree was most likely consigned"—she glanced around the weed-filled garden and ill-kept grounds—"or sold to the crown for the construction of naval ships. It is a common practice, since oak, good oak of this size, is in high demand."

"She's got the right of it, milord," Bruno said, coming up alongside them. "I came across the papers some time back."

"And you didn't think to mention it?" Jack asked him.

"Didn't think it was important. It wasn't like this tree was about to go anywhere. At least not 'til last night," Bruno said. "Now that it's gone and toppled over, it is subject to the bill of sale, which says the oak can't be moved or cut until the king's man or some bloke from the navy yard approves it."

Not cut? Not moved? *Impossible.* He needed it gone. Now.

He turned from the tree and shook his head, well considering the treasonous act of chopping the damned thing up into kindling and pleading innocence if anyone ever came to claim it.

Then Jack glanced back at the sea behind them—the

channel that separated England from her enemies—and knew that it was ships that guarded them well. Ships made sturdy because of the solid English oak that kept them afloat.

His tree could make the difference between England and tyranny. A lofty, impressive notion, but hardly one of comfort given the circumstances.

He had enemies of his own, right in his very camp. Though one might be hard-pressed to put a school-teacher and three slips of girls on the same pedestal as a hostile nation, Jack knew only too well what curious, inquisitive creatures ladies could be, especially young misses. Nosing about, peering into his life, asking questions . . .

"Demmit," he cursed.

Miss Porter didn't look as shocked as he thought she should be. In fact, he suspected she shared his sentiment.

She wanted no more of his company than he desired her . . . her company, that is. Yes, that was it. Her company.

"There must be some way out of here?" she asked, an edge of panic underlining her words.

So she wanted to be gone as much as he wanted the same. That was good news indeed.

"If we cannot remove our carriage," she was saying, "then can you loan us yours?"

Bruno snorted at such a request.

"I haven't a carriage," Jack told her. "And if I did, it would be like our wagons, trapped inside the yard as well."

"Then we'll hire one," she told him. She turned to Jonas. "Perhaps there is someone in the village willing to lend their carriage . . ." Looking around at the poor company gathered, she amended her request. "Or a wagon we could use for a few days until we can find a more suitable conveyance."

The stableman rubbed his chin. "Not likely to find something like that, miss. Everyone is out clearing the roads. Ain't a wagon to be had between here and Hastings. What the lads from the Henry say is that the entire shire is a bloody mess. Pardon me, for saying, ma'am." He shrugged. "I don't see that anyone is going to get very far for the next few days. Trees down blocking the roads, why, even the bridge at the crossroads is washed out. Terrible storm, that."

"You could ride," Jack suggested to her. "I'll be more than happy to send along the earl's carriage once the tree is removed."

"Oh, no," the driver protested, "the earl wouldn't like that in the least. Doesn't like his carriage horses rode."

"Oh, yes," Pippin chimed in. "That would never do. Papa is quite particular about his cattle. Besides, Miss Porter doesn't ride." The girl shook her head woefully, as if this was a terrible shortcoming, but it just couldn't be helped.

"You don't ride, Miss Porter?" Jack asked.

"No, I don't," she said, straightening her shawl again. "But that won't keep us at your doorstep, let me assure you. There must be an inn nearby we could remove ourselves to, so as not to impose upon your hospitality any longer."

An inn? He had to admire her determination. "An excellent idea," he told her. "There is a small public house down in the village, the Good Henry. They have a couple of rooms that I've been told are quite—"

"My lord!" came the shocked explosion from Birdwell.

Jack cringed. That had been the only problem with having Birdwell follow him into this remote exile. The man had retained all of his proper London sensibilities. And of course felt the need to impose them at the most inopportune moments.

Birdwell drew himself up into a regal state. "You cannot mean to suggest that Miss Porter and the young ladies stay at the Henry?" He lowered his voice. "You know very well that the company there is highly improper and that those rooms are used for—"

Miss Porter glanced from the butler back to Jack, her brow arched, apparently awaiting his confirmation of this bit of news.

"Yes, yes, Birdwell," Jack said. "You are right—the Henry probably isn't the best place."

Birdwell sniffed. *Probably?* his look reproached.

"If the inn is unavailable," Miss Porter said diplomatically, "then perhaps a neighbor or the vicar can take us in?"

Her true point was that she wanted to find someplace, any place that was a respectable distance from Thistleton Park.

There was a part of Jack that admired her tenacity, but he also felt a slight prick of conscience. Certainly he'd been a mite rude, and perhaps a little overbearing, but that really didn't require quite so much haste on her part.

It wasn't like he'd made good on his reputation and

tried to ravish anyone . . . lately. And their encounter at Miss Emery's had been but a brief lapse on his part.

Too brief, by his way of thinking, but he wasn't going to tell Miss Porter that.

Still, if she wanted to leave, he could hardly stand in her way. And she'd sprung on an excellent notion.

"Yes, yes, Miss Porter. The manse is quite roomy, and Mr. Waters is—"

"My lord!" Birdwell interjected with the same vehemence that the Good Henry suggestion had elicited.

Jack glanced over his shoulder at the man. "What is wrong now?"

"Mr. Waters?" Birdwell shook his head with a woeful wag.

"Is there a problem with the vicar?" Miss Porter asked.

"The vicar is . . . well, shall we say," Birdwell stammered.

"What my very observant and only-too-helpful butler is trying to say is that the vicar is a drunk. He's fine enough on Sunday mornings, but the rest of the time, well, I don't think you'd find him the best of influences."

Miss Porter shook her head. "A neighbor?"

"Miss Porter, there is no need for you to think about leaving Thistleton Park," Birdwell asserted. "Lord John is honored with your presence, despite his earlier greeting. You and your young ladies will lend the house a feminine touch that it has been sorely lacking. You must stay." Birdwell shot Jack a pointed glance.

"Stay??!" Miss Porter and Jack both protested.

"Oh, say we can, Miss Porter," Felicity pleaded.

"Oh, yes, please may we stay?" Thalia enthused like a happy chorus.

"Impossible," Miss Porter said, tugging her blue shawl around her shoulders. "We may be delayed, but we are not deterred." She turned and took a few steps over to where their driver was standing. "Mr. Stillings, I am afraid we cannot remove the earl's carriage at present. Would you please find the means to continue on to Hastings and hire a carriage and proper horses and return for us with all due haste. We are going to keep to our schedule as planned. We will not impose on his lordship's hospitality for another night."

"Yes, miss," the man said, slanting a disapproving glance at Jack. "But from what these lads have been saying, miss, I might not be back afore sundown. Possibly not until tomorrow, with the roads the way they are." He leaned forward and lowered his voice, though it carried for all to hear like a warning. "Something not proper about this place. Doesn't seem right, leaving you and the young ladies here—let alone leaving his lordship's horses and carriage unattended. The earl is right particular about his horses."

"Be assured," Jack offered, "the earl's horses and carriage will be ready and waiting for you."

Miss Porter nodded. "Mr. Stillings, I don't see that we have any other choice. Just make haste and I'll see to the girls . . . and the earl's horses . . . until you return." Then she turned to Jack. "Since Mr. Stillings is going to Hastings, I would suggest having him take your documents to the shipyard there. If I recall correctly, it is a small one, but they have had navy consignments in the past and should be able to fulfill His Majesty's contract quite ably."

Jack stared openmouthed at her, as did Bruno and Birdwell. Much to his chagrin, she took this as a form of acquiescence. So she turned to Stillings and finished giving her orders. With Jack's business.

"Ask for Mr. Norman," she told her driver. "Explain that this is an emergency of sorts. Tell him the oak is"—she turned and eyed the tree—"about thirty feet in circumference, give or take. That ought to ensure that he sends adequate workmen for the job."

Stillings nodded, as if it were perfectly normal to take such instructions from, of all people, a decorum teacher.

Jack recovered enough to ask, "And how is it that you know all this, Miss Porter?"

She shrugged. "My father was in the trade. Naval matters and such. I suppose I learned a bit of it over supper."

Over supper? She sounded more like a master ship-wright.

"Lord John, do stop gaping. A woman can possess a mind. If men gave more countenance to what ladies thought, the world would be a much more prosperous place." She glanced over at the workmen and villagers lolling about and frowned. "With that in mind, I would suggest putting your men to work removing the small limbs and leaves. It will make the cutting of the trunk that much quicker when the shipwright gets here." Her hands were on her hips. "Better than having the lot of them standing about gaping like jackanapes when there is work to be done."

Jack did his best to ignore the way Birdwell was smirking. "Thank you, Miss Porter," he said. "Your suggestions are quite helpful." *Rather like plague.* "In the meantime, feel free to remain at Thistleton Park as long as necessary." *Or until I throttle you.* He tried to smile, but the words had been forced from his lips to begin with, and a real look of delight was more than even he could muster.

"I wonder then," Pippin said to a delighted Birdwell, "if breakfast has been put away yet?"

From the nearby hill, shadowed by another great oak, a tall, angular man held a looking glass to his eye. He wasn't so much interested in the Thistleton oak as he was in the party in front of the fallen tree. "Who is that with Tremont?"

He handed the glass to the man beside him. The fellow looked, then shook his head. "Never seen 'em before. And they can't be from Dashwell's ship, for he hasn't crossed yet."

"And we should both pray that Captain Dashwell is right now at the bottom of the Channel. Along with his precious cargo. There will be hell to pay if his passengers ever set foot in England again."

"Oui, monsieur," the smaller man agreed. "They'd ruin everything you've done."

"We've done, my good friend," he said, patting his partner on the back. "But all is not lost yet, and we have much work to do."

Retrieving his spyglass, he took another look at the ladies retreating back to the house. Ladies could be harmless enough, but then again, he knew from experience they could also be as lethal as a nest of asps. "Find out who those women are and what they are doing with Tremont."

His partner nodded and both of them slipped into the countryside, on separate paths, but with the same determination to see England fall to her enemies.

Just as the storm had toppled the mighty oak.

Chapter 4

As Miss Porter and her charges returned to the house, Jack muttered a curse.

"Me thoughts exactly, milord," Bruno said, spitting at the ground. "Women! They're nothing but trouble, mark me words."

At the steps, Miss Porter glanced over her shoulder. Her brow furrowed—not so much in annoyance but in intelligent assessment, as if she were measuring the oak and calculating what the board feet would fetch.

And how Jack had yet to take any of her good advice.

Organizing, meddlesome spinster. Obviously, there was more to Miss Porter than what met the eye—for while she had the hair and curves of a siren, she also possessed the managing mind of a London *cit*.

A dangerous combination, indeed.

"What is it that bit o'muslin teaches?" Bruno was asking.

"Decorum," Jack replied, wondering how it was that a lady of good form and manners could possess such a knowledge of naval business. Oh, she'd explained it quite readily that her father had been in the trade, but her understanding went far beyond that of the typical daughter sitting through mealtime complaints of business strategies and government policies.

Then again, it seemed that Miss Porter was anything but typical.

A thought echoed by Birdwell. "Miss Porter is quite an exceptional lady."

"That's one way to describe her," Jack muttered.

"She may well bring a civilizing influence about here," the butler continued, his tone suggesting it was well overdue.

Bruno wasn't convinced in the least. "They'll bring ruin, Mr. Birdwell, that's what they'll bring."

"I hardly see how three young girls and their chaperone can bring ruin upon our heads, Mr. Jones," the butler replied.

"I'll tell you how," the larger man said. "They'll be nosing about, peeking into closets, listening at the doors and asking questions. And when they leave, they'll be like magpies, carrying their stories all about the countryside."

"Miss Porter strikes me as most discreet," Birdwell told him.

Bruno snorted at the notion. "I don't see no choice," he said, rubbing his meaty paws together, "but to sell them to Cap'n Dash and be done with the lot of 'em. He could probably take 'em East and get a tidy price for 'em from one of those foreign fellows, those sultans."

"Mr. Jones!" Birdwell exclaimed, his face going purple. "You are talking about kidnapping the daughters of respected noblemen. Not to mention Miss Porter, who is a good Englishwoman. Why, the very idea—"

Jack held up his hands between his two loyal servants. "Enough. No one is selling anyone. Besides, I don't think even our immoral friend Dash would take them. We just need to make demmed sure that Miss Porter and her young companions haven't the opportunity to discover some of the . . . the . . . incongruities of our household."

Like the former highwayman who served as his butler and the forger and sometime pugilist who stood in stead as secretary to the manor.

"Good luck there," Bruno muttered.

"Ignore him, milord," Birdwell offered, shooting Bruno a scathing look. "Elton's mother had a saying that may serve well in this situation."

Jack was almost afraid to ask. Elton had been Birdwell's partner when he'd been a highwayman, and Elton's mother, a disreputable hag if ever there was, was in Birdwell's mind the pinnacle of nefarious wisdom. Though most often enough, her advice had to do with giving Bow Street the slip or how to make a misplaced knife in the back look like an accident.

"And Old Mam would want us to do what?" he finally queried.

"Keep your friends close, your enemies closer still."

Bruno eyed the butler. "Keep 'em closer, you say?

Bah! I still think we could convince Cap'n Dash to sell them for us. He's a greedy enough fellow. You could talk him into it, milord. Throw in some of those gold coins me cousin got for us. The fancy lead ones."

"I'm not selling the ladies," Jack said, hoping his tone sounded final enough for Bruno, because if there was a chance that Miss Porter and company discovered the truth about Thistleton Park, that may well be their only choice.

But his butler wasn't far off the mark either, he realized.

"If we are to keep our guests sufficiently diverted, Mr. Birdwell, I am putting you in charge of the arrangements."

"Me, milord?" Birdwell looked askance.

Bruno, on the other hand, grinned from ear to ear at this proposal.

"Yes, *you.* I haven't got the time," he said, waving a hand at the oak. "What with this mess, and . . ." he lowered his voice. "Dash's pending arrival with our cargo."

"But my lord," Birdwell insisted. "It isn't proper for me to entertain the ladies. It is your duty as master of the house."

"Decorum and all," Bruno said, nudging Jack, obviously enjoying this further turn of events, especially since no one was likely to put him in charge of their guests.

Jack shook his head. "What do I know of entertaining ladies?"

Birdwell and Bruno glanced at each other, then laughed uproariously.

"Milord," his butler said once he recovered, "you

know more about entertaining ladies than either of us."

"Oh, aye," Bruno added. "I remember yer aunt saying you could charm any bird out of her feathers . . . or her corset or stockings, for that matter. Why, I heard tell that once you kept three mistresses and that you could visit each of them in a single—"

"Enough, Bruno," Jack said, holding up his hands. "Besides, that was years ago, and the ladies I kept company with back then weren't exactly . . ."

"Innocents?" Birdwell suggested.

"Yes, those," Jack agreed. "I never really fit in with the crowd at Almack's and the doe-eyed belles of the *ton*."

"Surely it isn't that much different," Birdwell said. "Entertain them as you did your lady loves, albeit without the more compromising aspects of those relationships. A picnic, dinner, a tour of the estate, perhaps an excursion to the shore or the folly."

Entertain them? Jack groaned. Birdwell didn't realize what he was asking. That would mean keeping company with *her* . . . her and her red hair.

Her and that demmed button.

Jack raked his fingers through his hair and groaned.

He didn't know why that button bothered him so much, but it did.

It made him wonder what sort of man evoked a passion within a woman that had her still holding onto the memories.

Not that there were any ladies out there holding onto a fond remembrance of him. He'd been the worst sort of rakish cad, stealing kisses and breaking hearts and with no more thought than his next meal, next willing lightskirt . . .

No, the sort of man who held a woman's unwavering affections was usually a gentleman, loyal and elegant, and always considerate. Like his old friend Sedgwick, or even his boorish brother Parkerton.

So what had happened that had separated Miss Porter from her heart's desire?

The war? The fellow—an officer, no doubt—had likely fallen at Corunna.

Or maybe the man had been too toplofty, and she too poor, without the connections to traverse such a divide.

Oh, hell's fire, what was he thinking? He closed his eyes and rubbed his pounding head. This is what came of spending too many years trying to devise the most outlandish wagers for the hallowed pages of White's betting book . . . or what came from having been alone for far too long.

He was getting as odd as Aunt Josephine.

The front door opened anew and out marched Miss Porter with her trail of ducklings behind her. Each of them carried a workbag, making them look like an industrious lot.

Bruno nudged Jack forward. "Here's your chance to show Birdie and me how it's done, milord."

Before Jack could come up with an affable and credible-sounding hail, Miss Porter beat him to the punch. "Lord John," she said in a tight greeting. "The girls and I are going sketching. If we must impose upon you, we might as well make the best of the situation and use this extra time to our advantage through some much-needed lessons." She shot a quick, pointed glance over her shoulder at her charges. "If you could direct us toward this tower of yours, we will put the rest of the morning to good use."

"I'd be more than happy to show you," Jack offered, bowing slightly and forcing his best Town smile on his face—the one that had conquered some of the stoniest of hearts. "To spend the morning with you fair ladies would be my greatest joy."

His gallant offer failed to melt Miss Porter's frosty demeanor. She took a step back and stared at him, her brows furrowed with suspicion.

Either he was very out of practice or Miss Porter's icy exterior extended deeper than he'd suspected.

"Oh, would you take us, Lord John?" Thalia asked. Her hopeful words gained an arched glance from her teacher.

"It is kind of you to offer, my lord," Miss Porter replied. "But we wouldn't think of separating you from your duties here. I am sure that your obligations to your estate take precedence."

"Oh, of course, but I believe things are well in hand—"

Her gaze swept over at the still lounging workmen. After a brief moment, she heaved a sigh.

He ignored her unspoken chastisement and went forth with all gallantry. "Besides, the path along the cliff can be dangerous. I would be remiss to have you venture forth without a guide."

"We have Brutus," she said, nodding toward the little gruff dog. "He is quite sure-footed, I assure you."

Forsaken for a mutt. The sting of it did not pass unnoticed. Bruno was having a hard time muffling his guffaws.

Jack held up a finger. "Ah, but your Brutus will not be able to regale you with some of the interesting facts about Thistleton Park and the history of our esteemed folly. History lessons that could prove quite edifying for the young ladies."

Miss Porter shook her head. "I would never think to impose upon you, my lord, nor take advantage of your newfound hospitality. Why, you told us not an hour or more ago, 'I have no time for entertaining or recounting local histories.'" She folded her arms across her chest, as if she dared him to contradict her. When he couldn't think of something to say, she let out another disgruntled sigh and started shooing the girls past him and his servants. "The folly, my lord?"

That did it. With his masculine pride completely trampled beneath her sturdy and practical heel, Jack made a vow. *The moment this ends, I am going straight up to London to cut a swath through Society that will ensure my place in history alongside Casanova and every other great rake. There won't be a woman's heart safe from my charms.*

Including Miss Porter's? That wretched voice teased.

He pointed toward the narrow door in the wall. "Through there and follow the path." He couldn't help but add in a happy voice, "Be careful along the cliff, 'tis a long drop to the rocks below. 'T'would be a terrible shame if you fell."

Behind him, Birdwell gave him a not-so-gentle nudge. "Dinner, milord. Ask them to dinner."

Hadn't his butler just witnessed the dressing down the lady had given him? Well, if anything, he might as well get every last bit of this humiliation over with in one lump.

"Miss Porter," he called after her.

She paused, then slowly turned back around.

Girding himself, he said, "I would be honored if you and the ladies would join me for dinner this evening."

She looked about to naysay him, but then he realized he had her on the ropes. To outright refuse his offer would be rude, hardly the act of a decorum teacher, and a glance over at his grinning butler said Birdwell had guessed this point all along.

"If we are still here, Lord John, that would be most kind," she replied through what looked to be gritted teeth. Then the ladies departed, the girls chattering merrily while their teacher marched ahead as if she were being led to an execution.

"Excellent," Birdwell said. "A dinner party. I've got my work cut out for me." The man began ticking off his list of preparations, then came up short. "Oh, dear."

"What is it?" Jack asked.

"We can hardly feed them mutton."

Bruno snorted. "I told you last night not to let them in. Ladies are all alike. It's chicken and warm milk. That's all they'll be wanting. Might as well have let in the French!"

For once, Jack had to agree.

When they were well out of sight and earshot from the house, Miranda pulled to a stop. The girls, busy debating which would be better to marry, an impoverished duke or a wealthy baron, didn't notice and tumbled into the back of her skirt.

She let them compose themselves for about two seconds, then launched into her investigation.

"You will tell me immediately why it is we are here," she demanded, ready to go to any length to ferret out their plans.

"To sketch?" Pippin offered.

"Oh, yes, to sketch," Tally added.

Even Brutus gave his mangy head a shake, as if he too had thought that such a plan was their intent.

She ignored them and held out her hand toward Felicity. "Your notebook, Miss Langley."

The girl paled and looked about to protest, but the set of Miranda's jaw was enough to send Felicity digging into her workbag. She tried at first to hand over her sketchbook, but Miranda just shook her head and nodded at the workbag yet again. With a great sigh, Felicity dug out her precious *Bachelor Chronicles*. Clutching it to her chest, she made one last plea, "Miss Porter, this isn't meant to be read. 'Tis private."

Miranda felt a tinge of guilt, for the girl maintained an air of secrecy about her writings that would put the Foreign Office to shame. But if one of these harebrained, title-mad girls thought to make a match with Lord John, Miranda didn't care if she had to commit treason—she was going to stop them. "Then I won't pry any further then the pages pertaining to Lord John."

Pippin and Thalia exchanged mirrored looks of horror.

Oh, yes, Miranda was on to something.

"But, Miss—" Felicity protested.

Miranda held out her hand. "Now!"

Slowly and reluctantly, Felicity opened the journal and carefully thumbed through the pages until she reached the entry for Lord John. She looked away as she handed over the book, as if she couldn't bear to watch this sacrilege.

One side of the notebook had a sketch of Lord John. Miranda guessed this was Tally's work, because she was the most skilled of the three of them and possessed a talent for capturing her subjects with a realism that was uncanny.

And there he was, much as he had been on that day at Miss Emery's in his ragged coat and brushed-back hair.

So they had been spying that day.

But from where and how? And why had they gone to such great lengths to arrive on his doorstep?

Taking a deep breath, Miranda read the entry, looking for her answers:

Tremont, Lord John
   B. 1772. Third son of the 8th Duke of Parkerton. (See also, James Tremont, 9th Duke of Parkerton, Tremont Lord Michael.) Current residence: Thistleton Park.

Miranda glanced up at the girls. So they'd known all along that Lord John was in residence here. Instead of remarking on this happy coincidence, she continued to read:

Having disgraced Miss Miranda Mabberly, a former student of Miss Emery's, Lord John has been given the cut direct by all Society. His income, if rumor is to be trusted, is nonexistent and is supplemented by gambling and other reckless pursuits. He is a rake in all the worst ways.

And this was the man they had diverted their journey out of the way to meet? Miranda could only guess why they thought him worthy of a closer inspection.

Lord John, while ancient by the exacting standards of these Chronicles . . .

Miranda suppressed a smile and wondered what the man would think of being described as "ancient." Then she read the words that wiped even the lingering beginnings of a grin from her face.

. . . has left behind the fashions of Town and now maintains a pirate look about him that some ladies claim is intriguing.

The pirate comment, Miranda guessed, had probably come from Tally, given all her gothic fancies.

While his age and lack of a title relinquish him to the lower rungs of eligibility, it has been noted that he admits to a fondness for red hair and appeared quite taken with Miss Porter this afternoon in the downstairs foyer.

They'd been in the foyer? Watching him arrive . . . come down the stairs . . . catch her in his arms.

Miranda's gut twisted as she started to see the threads of their outlandish plan weave together, and she read on only with the hope that her supposition was entirely wrong.

However, the sentences that followed pushed Miranda right past surprised and into stunned.

As a respectable lady with excellent manners and now a good inheritance (if Sarah Browne's maid is to be believed), Miss Porter would be the perfect bride for a former rake of limited means like Lord John.

"Me-e-e?" she managed to stammer. The perfect bride for Lord John? "You thought to match me with . . . with . . . with that—" She couldn't even say the word.

"Rapscallion?" Thalia suggested.

"Ruffian?" Pippin offered.

"Rake," Felicity said unrepentantly. Now that her plan had been unmasked, she wasn't above getting to the point. "It is undeniable, Miss Porter. You are a perfect match for Lord John."

"Me?" Miranda shook her head at them. "I think not."

Tally rushed forward, taking her by the hand and settling her down on a large stone. "I know it seems a little bit hard to believe, but he already has a *tendre* for you."

Miranda snorted. Of all the ridiculous, irresponsible . . .

"It's true," Pippin said. "At least with your hair, he does. And if he likes your hair, it is only a matter of time before he likes the rest of you."

"Think of it, Miss Porter," Felicity rushed to add, "you could be Lady John Tremont, the mistress of all of this." She glanced over her shoulder at the leaning wall and tumbledown manse beyond and bit her bottom lip. "Such as it is," she conceded. "But you have a way with such things, Miss Porter. You would be a considerable asset to Lord John. And you of all people can't forget Miss Emery's credo: It is the duty of every lady to seek a respectable union."

A respectable union with Lord John? Now that was absurd. The man knew nothing of respectability, let alone responsibility—hadn't he refused to marry her when Oxley had cried off? Not that she had wanted to marry such a faithless rogue, but it was telling as to his character.

Why, she'd never even had the chance to refuse him. For certainly she would have. She had wanted to marry a gentleman, an honorable man. Not a rake.

Liar, a small voice whispered. *Would your gentle hero have kissed you like Lord John?*

"Did you ever consider that I might like being a respectable spinster better?" Miranda asked, folding her hands in her lap.

Felicity shot her a look that suggested such a notion was nothing short of foolishness.

Be that as it may, Miranda thought, there were other attributes on her long-held list that could hardly be lain on Lord John's doorstep. For a moment she was hard-pressed to remember a single one, but then one by one they came back to her.

Elegant . . . now there was a lark, given Lord John's ramshackle appearance and dilapidated home.

Or well-read. Only if she included the faces of playing cards.

Good company? He'd demonstrated his capacity for that trait when he'd ordered them from his property.

But what about passion?

Miranda bounded to her feet, frightened by the familiar ache of desire that spread quickly through her limbs when she put those two together.

Passion and Lord John . . . it was a dangerous combination, and she didn't trust these tangled feelings he brought forth inside her.

They listened to reason and common sense about as well as the Langley sisters.

And the girls had gotten her this far—she didn't dare discover what they could do with their remaining time at Thistleton Park if they continued unchecked. Or worse, what her rebellious thoughts would have her considering.

No, it was time to make it very clear that their matchmaking was to cease and desist.

"While it is commendable that you would like to see me suitably settled"—they all grinned at her compliment, but their joy was short-lived—"it is hardly proper to start matching people without their consent."

Pippin shot an "I-told-you-so" sort of glance at her cousins and took a step away from Felicity, as if to distance herself from the forthcoming censure.

Miranda warmed to her subject and continued, "I do not desire a match with Lord John, and you will end your efforts immediately." She shot a hard look at each one until all three nodded in agreement.

But there was a glint in Felicity's eyes that suggested

the girl wasn't ready to completely relent, so Miranda added, "I suggest we spend a good part of today revisiting your accounting, and then if all three of you get your columns tallied correctly, we can sketch this infamous folly."

They groaned, for not one of them liked lessons in ledgers, but none of them offered any complaints; they knew they could find themselves adding and subtracting for the rest of their lives if they weren't careful.

"Come along," Miranda said, starting back down the path.

Pippin ambled alongside her. "I can see why you wouldn't want to marry Lord John. His house is dreadful."

Tally concurred. "Such a dreary place."

"Yes, but with the right hand and management, it could be quite respectable," Felicity said.

Miranda's gaze rolled skyward. The girl was utterly incorrigible.

"In his favor, his stables are fine enough," Pippin said. "He's got a couple of real goers in there. Funny that a man with such limited means would have such expensive cattle."

"Such is the way with men like Lord John," Miranda pointed out. "They put their money into fancy horses and harebrained ventures and not into the foundation of their estate. It is why Miss Emery cautions all of you to be on your guard against rakes and wastrels."

Tally bent over and picked up Brutus, carrying him along in her arms. "Can you even call Lord John a rake?" she asked. "Isn't he rather old for such things?"

Not really, Miranda wanted to tell them. And while he certainly wasn't the same Corinthian he'd been all those years ago, when he'd held her at Miss Emery's, even for those few moments, he'd left her shaken and tempted by his charm and the masculine power that seemed to surround him.

No, Lord John was still a dangerous rake. And worst of all, as a woman grown she was only too aware as to what that meant, and how any good sense she held seemed to flee in his presence.

Her heart beat faster, her breathing became more shallow, her limbs were unresponsive.

Perhaps that was the inherent danger of a rake, she concluded; he left a lady so flustered, so diverted, that she wasn't able to fend off his lascivious attentions . . . would be drawn to the temptation he offered as to a light in the window on a stormy night.

The light, she mused, like the ones wreckers used to lure hapless ships onto the rocks.

However, as much as Mad Jack Tremont might have been a devilish foe once, she was no longer six and ten, and he wasn't the showy, glittering Corinthian he'd once been.

Perhaps his tarnish was to her advantage . . .

They walked for another few minutes and then rounded a bend along the cliff until a magnificent structure came into view. The stone tower stood on the edge of the cliff, as craggy and rough-hewn as the landscape around them. A solitary sentinel standing above the Channel.

Below, the hiss and crash of the waves lulled at the senses, while overhead gulls rose and fell with the sturdy breezes or their own fickle whims.

There was something solid and commanding about it, and at the same time wild and ancient, as if it held the very secrets of the capricious wind, could reach up into the stars.

Enchanted by the sight of it, they quickened their pace until they came to stand beneath it.

Felicity walked around the base, then eyed the distant horizon. "I would wager you could see the shores of France from up there."

"Let's find out," Tally said and went to the door before Miss Porter could stop her. The last thing she needed was one of them tumbling from one of the open windows above.

But it was of no matter, for the door was locked.

"Whoever locks a folly?" Tally complained. "Why it is . . . it's . . . inhospitable."

Miranda suppressed a grin. Surely they should have gathered that much from Lord John's ill-mannered reception this morning.

"Come along, ladies," she said to them. "Shall we get to work?"

With a minimum of grumbling, the three girls found a resting place that suited them best, and they began to add and subtract the costs of their journey to date. From her own carrying bag, Miranda plucked out the pair of socks she was making and took out her frustrations in the soothing rhythm of knitting.

The morning passed quickly, and eventually each girl was released from her dreaded accounts. Felicity reached for her *Chronicles* and busily scribbled new notations—most likely about Lord John, Miranda suspected. Tally pulled out her sketchbook and began a drawing of the tower, while Pippin pulled out her beloved copy of Billingsworth and began to read aloud the rest of the entries on Thistleton Park. It turned out the house had held a lively place in history, from its origins after the Battle of Hastings to Elizabethan times to Cromwell, ending with the historian's lavish praise of the previous mistress, Lady Josephine Tremont.

"I wonder what happened to her?" Pippin said.

"You want to know what happened to Lady Josephine?" came a reply. "Well, I'll tell you. The old gal was murdered."

All four of them sprang up and turned around. There on the path along the cliff stood a short, portly gentlemen of an indeterminate years. He wore an unfashionable jacket, brilliant red waistcoat and scuffed-up boots. In his hand he carried a walking stick.

"Pardon, sir?" Miranda asked, rising and nodding at the girls to do the same.

"The gel asked what happened to Lady Josephine, and I told her. She was murdered." He stomped along until he got to the bench where Miss Porter had been sitting, then sat down. "Lady Josephine was murdered in cold blood right over there," he said, waving his stick at some low bushes clinging to the edge of the cliff.

Tally gasped. At the sound of his mistress in distress, Brutus, who had been snoring happily since they arrived, awoke. Upon sniffing the air, he must not have liked what he smelled, because he immediately bounded to his feet. Spying the stranger in their midst, the dog let out a low growl and rushed toward the man.

The gentleman let out a bellow of a laugh, even as Brutus circled him, barking and growling.

"What the devil is that?" he managed to sputter, waving his stout stick at Brutus.

Tally rushed forward. "My dog," she told the man as she scooped her beloved pet up and out of range.

"So says you," he said, taking another smirking glance at the animal. "Now where was I?"

"Lady Josephine's murder," the always practical and to-the-point Felicity reminded him.

"Ah, yes, Lady Josephine."

"Sir, I implore you," Miranda said, "perhaps this isn't a tale for young ears."

"Ain't much of a story, Miss—"

"Porter," she said. "And you are?"

"Sir Norris Nesbitt. Live just over that hill." He pointed the way with his walking stick.

Miranda finished the introductions, giving the girls an opportunity to practice their deportment lessons, but they were hardly done when Felicity persisted with her questions.

"But if Lady Josephine was murdered, Sir Norris, how could that not make a good tale?"

"Miss Langley!" Miranda reprimanded.

Sir Norris snorted, then spat at the ground. "You'd think that it would, gel, but as I said, it ain't much to tell. She went out walking on this here path and never came back." He shook his head, a worrisome little movement that suggested he had his own theories on how the lady had perished and that with a little urging he'd be more than happy to oblige them.

"Never?" Pippin prodded, giving him just the opening he wanted.

He shook his head. "Never. 'T'was on a stormy eve

much like last night. Wind and rain like you hope to never see again."

"But what was she doing out on a night like that?" The practical question came from, of course, Felicity.

"No telling," the man conceded. "But Lady Josephine was her own gel. Not one to listen to sense." He prodded the ground with his stick again. "Magnificent woman. Had the eyes of an angel and the voice of a lark. Offered for her myself countless times, but she always turned me down." He sighed, then spat again.

"Then her death was an accident," Felicity corrected.

"Oh, no, miss, it was murder. For the next morning, they found evidence of a struggle. Her glasses were smashed into the ground, and the brush just over there was all torn up."

"Hardly evidence of foul play," Felicity insisted.

"Yes, well, that may be, but tell me how convenient it was when that jackanape nephew of hers inherited the place, lock, stock and barrel. Mighty convenient timing, with him being ruined and up to his neck in debt."

Now it was Miranda's turn to take a deep breath, words rising up inside her like a sudden squall in the face of Sir Norris's implications.

It wasn't true.

She didn't know why she found herself feeling this overwhelming need to defend Lord John, because goodness knows, there were plenty of acts he'd committed in his life worthy of condemnation. But murder? Preposterous.

"My lord," she said, "I hardly think Lord John is capable of such a crime." Behind her, she could sense the girls nodding their heads just as vehemently.

"Know the bounder, do you?" Sir Norris asked, his bushy brows rising, his mouth tipped in a smile that suggested something rather unseemly.

Miranda backed away—from both her convictions and the man's sordid notions. "Not really," she lied. "We just met this morning."

"We're staying with Lord John," Tally added with imprudent glee.

"Staying with him?" The man spat again. "Now, miss, you can't be serious?" This he directed at Miranda.

"I fear it is a situation not of our choosing," she informed him. "An oak has fallen across the gate and we are unable to leave without our carriage and horses. It will be remedied quickly enough. Our driver has gone to Hastings to secure a new conveyance."

He rose and walked toward her, taking her aside and putting his back to their young audience. "You had best hope so. I don't think you realize the sort of man you are dealing with."

Miranda wasn't about to enlighten Sir Norris that she knew exactly what "sort" his neighbor was.

Not that this puffy little baronet seemed worried about her sensibilities. "He was a wild buck in London, miss. These young ladies might not know the type, but I don't suppose you haven't got to your age without learning a thing or two about 'em."

Miranda bristled at his jab. *Your age.* How old did the man think she was? While having the girls opine as to Jack's ancient status might be amusing, she didn't like it in the least when her years were being given the same scrutiny.

Sir Norris continued unabated. "Why, it would turn your hair white to hear the sort of tawdry and unnatural acts he partook in." He winked at her, his bushy brows coming together. "Let me just say, no one in the neighborhood was pleased to see him inherit, let alone move in." His hand, which had before been cradling her elbow, slid and landed on her hip. "There now, miss, I think you could find better accommodations for yourself and yer gels."

Already piqued about the comment on her age, she took his invitation and his familiar touch with even less aplomb. And this odious man thought Lord John was low company? She plucked herself free from him and took a steadying breath.

"Your invitation is kind, but unnecessary. Our man will return forthwith, and we will be gone as quickly as possible."

"Suit yourself," he said with a shrug. "But when that devilish Tremont starts tipping those girls, remember I'm the magistrate around these parts, and I'd love an excuse to hang the bastard."

"I hardly think a few hours more in Lord John's company will prove our ruin," Miranda told him.

"You'd think," the man snorted. "But I'll tell you again, the man is as crazy as his aunt was. Riding about the countryside at night, keeping company down at the Henry. But who wouldn't stay away from that house at night, for everyone knows it's cursed."

"Cursed?" Tally asked. Obviously she'd been eavesdropping, and had heard enough to leave her wide-eyed and clutching Brutus to her chest.

"Oh, aye, has been since it was built," Sir Norris told

her. "Wonder why it has such a secure wall around it? Well, it ain't to keep anyone out, I tell you. It was built to keep those crazy Tremonts in."

"Oh, I never," Miranda sputtered.

"You would if you had them for neighbors. They've been locking up every crackbrained, halfwit relation down here for centuries. And those Tremonts are fair full of odd ones. Cursed they are. Cursed. And that Lord John, he's the worst of the lot. Ruin you all without a second thought, he would."

"Sir," Miranda said, squaring her shoulders, "I'll have you know Lord John has given me his word as a gentleman that we are welcome in his house." He'd done no such thing, but perhaps it would be enough to keep this gossipy old goat from telling the world of their imprudent house party at Thistleton Park.

"His word!" the man scoffed. "His word, she says." He spat again. "Miss Porter, is it?"

She nodded.

"You obviously have no thought for your reputation or that of your charges, for if you did, you'd move heaven and earth to get them out of that house. Mark my words, Mad Jack Tremont is no gentleman."

Chapter 5

No gentleman. Those words rang in Miranda's ears the rest of the day. Especially when Stillings returned from Hastings too late for them to continue on their way. However, he had procured a suitable carriage, and nothing would prevent them from traveling directly to Lady Caldecott's at first light.

One dinner and one more night at Thistleton Park, and then Miranda would be able to draw a deep breath and get back to the life she'd planned for herself.

Well and away from the rake who had ruined it to begin with.

"Miss Porter, that isn't what you are wearing, is it?"

This question came from Felicity, who stood in the doorway that connected their suite to Miranda's chamber. Her comment was followed by a *"tsk, tsk"* before the girl disappeared back into her room.

Miranda glanced heavenward. Still matchmaking, even after her earlier lecture. There was no denying it, the Duchess was impossibly determined.

Thankfully, the girl hadn't much more time to maneuver her matrimonial plans.

But to her chagrin, Felicity returned, a small valise in one hand, her sister and cousin in tow.

Tally took one look at her and shook her head. "Oh, no, Miss Porter, that will never do." Even Brutus shook his bushy head in dismay.

Miranda stood her ground. "And whatever is wrong with what I'm wearing?"

The girls shared a glance, as if they were trying to decide how best to break the bad news.

Meanwhile, Miranda stole a quick glance at herself in the mirror and saw nothing wrong. Her chignon was properly tucked at the nape of her neck, her dress, a somber gray gown, was entirely respectable, and her favorite blue shawl lay modestly over her shoulders.

A decent and proper ensemble for a country dinner—with a very improper and highly questionable gentleman.

"Don't you have anything, well . . ." Tally bit her lip as she tipped her head and studied her teacher this way, then that. "A little less severe? Nanny Lucia always said a lady should have a bit of color to her dress."

Miranda had heard enough. "If this is more of your matchmaking nonsense—"

"Oh, no, Miss Porter," Pippin told her. "Not in the least. What my cousins are saying is that it just seems a shame that you must look so old, when you can't be more than nine and twenty."

"I am not nine and twenty," she shot back a little hastily, taking another glance at the mirror. *Nearly thirty?* First Sir Norris, now the girls. Did she really look so old?

Felicity was in the process of unpacking her valise on the bed. "Then let us make sure no one else makes that mistake," she said, pulling out ribbons and laces, a set of fancy hair combs and a few cosmetic pots. "Nanny Tasha always said a lady's age should be a mystery."

Miranda closed her eyes. Truly, she was starting to wonder about Lord Langley's choice of nannies for his daughters. Most of what the girls repeated from their dear caretakers sounded more like the advice of an experienced Cyprian, not that of a doting governess for small, impressionable children.

Felicity approached her with a brush in hand, a paint pot in the other.

Miranda shook her head. "Oh, no, you don't."

Tally moved to stand at her sister's side. "Nanny Rana said it was a lady's duty to see that she was the brightest light at the table." She smiled at Felicity, and together they recited, "Never hide your light, for how else is a man to notice you? Your spark, your fire, is your most cherished possession." They both sighed, as if they had just shared the cure for all that ailed the world. Then Tally slanted an assessing glance at Miranda. "I fear, Miss Porter, your light is positively dull."

Having heard enough of their nanny nonsense, Miranda shooed them from her room. "I will be as dull as I like."

"But Miss Porter, it is only for one night," Felicity protested.

One night too many, in Miranda's estimation.

"Now off with you," she told them, trying to sound as severe as if she were indeed nine and twenty. "Pippin, find your shoes. Felicity, wash your cheeks. You know Miss Emery strictly forbids cosmetics of any kind. Tally, your shawl does not belong in a heap on the floor."

Having dispatched them, she closed the door between their rooms and took a deep breath. *Tenacious little minxes.*

Well, she was having none of their plans.

Before they went down to dinner she was going to line them up and lay down the rules for the evening. Any infraction, any deviation from her guidelines would see the three of them doing ledger lessons for the rest of their travels. . . . Why, she'd—

There was another burst of giggles from the next room, and Miranda turned toward the noise. Such high spirits and antics were . . . were . . .

Almost at the door, she caught a glance of herself in the mirror and came to an abrupt halt.

The woman staring back at her was like a stranger.

Ancient, she admitted, moving closer to her reflection. *When did I get so old?*

What other explanation was there for why Lord John didn't recognize her?

Turning her head one way, then the other, she tried to determine what about her had changed so much in the last nine years.

Perhaps it was the chignon. Mayhap the girls were

right, it was a bit dull. Her gaze fell on a bit of ribbon that had fallen from Felicity's collection. She retrieved it and for a moment considered just how one did put something like that in her hair.

In truth, she'd never really been one for baubles and ornaments. Why, the last time she'd been all dressed up had been that night at the opera. Her mother had taken great pains to see her turned out as befitting a future countess, albeit a modest one, and what had it gained her—Lord John mistaking her for his mistress.

She took another discerning glance at the mirror. There'd be no mistaking her for someone's mistress now.

And that's the way it should be, she told herself, setting the ribbon down and patting her respectable chignon to ensure that every hair was in place. Then, for some reason, her gaze fell on the reflection of a candle in the mirror. Its flickering, glittering light caught her attention, held her gaze with a magical quality.

Like the light Nanny Rana espoused.

A light, indeed, she scoffed. What sort of woman was this Nanny Rana who encouraged young girls to make spectacles of themselves?

And for someone like Mad Jack Tremont! She shook her head.

Besides, he was far too passionate to make a decent husband. Why, a lady would spend all her time having to endure his overtures, his insatiable demands.

Miranda thought about how unsettled he'd left her back at Miss Emery's, and all he'd done had been to hold her in his arms.

And she knew only too well what his kisses were capable of doing—making her knees buckle, her breasts ache with longing to feel his touch.

No, it wasn't this house that she feared, as Pippin had suggested earlier—a bit of managing and accounting could bring it up to snuff. And it wasn't the idea of marriage that had her at sixes and sevens. It was what Lord John's kiss could do to her senses, to her grasp on propriety, that made her tremble.

His kiss had her hiding her light. And had been for all these years.

If Miranda thought she could rein in Felicity, Tally, and Pippin, she was very wrong. Despite the fact that she had told the girls, *in no uncertain terms*, that dinner was to be conducted with nothing but the finest example of their best manners, Lord John had undermined her ruling from the moment he entered the dining room.

He'd settled down in his chair, and then insisted they dispense with all the usual formalities.

"Call me Jack," he'd told the girls, and the threesome, so delighted at this change of events, introduced themselves by their nicknames. Within moments it was Jack, Tally, Pippin, and the Duchess chatting like old friends.

"Is it true, like Sir Norris claims," Tally asked, "that this house is cursed?"

"So you met Sir Norris, did you? Lurking about as usual," he said. "I'm sure he was quite eloquent on the subject."

Tally nodded her head. "Sir Norris warned us that if we stayed here too long we'd be as crazy as the rest of the—"

"Thalia! That is enough!" Miranda told her, using the sharp tones of a schoolteacher. "How many times do I have to remind you not to repeat gossip."

"Ah, but it is usually far more interesting than the truth," Jack said, winking at Tally. "Besides, this house is cursed."

"Really?" Pippin asked, while Felicity scoffed at such a notion.

Jack nodded. "As cursed as any house could be, but how can you expect otherwise when nearly every occupant has been tainted with the Tremont stain."

"The Tremont stain?" Felicity's eyes narrowed to a dubious squint. "I've never heard of it."

He leaned forward and lowered his voice. "In every generation of Tremonts there is always one of us who ends up here, hidden away, and for good reason."

While Jack took a moment to refill his wineglass, Miranda thought of several points that qualified Lord John for his residency within these walls.

"You might say," he told them, "Thistleton Park was built as a means of hiding the family sins."

"Lord John," Miranda said. "Please do not fill the girls' heads with such scandalous nonsense."

"It isn't nonsense," he told her. "And I can prove it."

"How?" Felicity asked, still retaining her air of skepticism.

"With a tour of the house," he told her. "Thistleton Park is filled with some very dark secrets, and it is best to know where not to go traipsing about in the middle of the night lest you run into one of my forebears."

"Of all the ridiculous notions," Miranda said. She had to imagine the worst of the shades haunting this house was currently seated at the head of the table.

"You may come along as well, Miss Porter, and I daresay you'll not be so apt to scoff by the end." He waggled his brows at them and said, "But I will exact a payment for my services as guide."

Payment? She could just imagine what that would be.

"Do tell?" Tally was asking.

"Yes, anything," Pippin echoed.

He leaned back in his chair, his hands crossed over his chest, looking every bit the pirate described in Felicity's *Chronicles*. "To know what it is that the Duchess keeps in that precious journal of hers."

Felicity immediately slid her notebook into her lap and folded her hands over it.

"'T'isn't a journal, my lord," Tally told him, "but a list of—"

"Tally!" Felicity chastened. "Don't you dare!"

Miranda found it a relief that apparently some things were out of bounds. Egads, she didn't even want to think of what he would say if he read the entry Felicity had written.

. . . Miss Porter would be the perfect bride for a former rake of limited means like Lord John.

She didn't even want to think of what he'd make of that little *on dit*. But to her amazement, it seemed that Jack possessed some scrap of scruples.

"Never mind, Duchess," he was telling the girl. "If

the contents of your notebook are confidential, how can I do anything but respect your privacy?" Then the roguish devil winked at them. "That doesn't mean I can't speculate as to the topic of such devoted scribblings."

The girls giggled, and Miranda knew there was no taming the rake inside this momentary gentleman.

And so the meal continued, with Tally relating stories and quotes from their beloved nannies. Felicity shared her matrimonial strategies for securing the affections of a duke. Pippin spoke of books and horses, and all the while, Miranda listened and watched Jack.

She couldn't help but feel the pull of his natural charm. It was more than just the captivating twinkle in his blue eyes as he recounted one amusing story after another. Jack had a way of involving his audience in his stories that left one feeling as if they had been to Lady Dilling's soiree or the Pritchards' infamous costume ball along with him.

No wonder he'd been considered such good company during his years in Town. The kind of guest who was guaranteed to liven up even the dullest gathering.

But there was more to a gentleman, Miranda reminded herself, than just charm.

Besides, she couldn't shake the notion that there was something more at work behind Lord John's jovial company. He was being too charming—even for his legendary reputation.

Why, just look at how he had the girls laughing uproariously with tales of his own beleaguered nanny.

"I can't believe you locked the poor woman in the cellar!" Felicity giggled. "You would never have managed such a trick with Nanny Gerta."

"That's because she wouldn't have fit," Tally pointed out.

They all laughed, and Miranda found herself smiling, despite her resolve to remain aloof and unaffected by Lord John.

Really, what did it hurt to enjoy an evening of laughter? For such company would be rare indeed in her new home, her new life. For all she'd professed to Miss Emery about wanting to spend her days in quiet toil, suddenly the solitary days before her appeared rather dull.

But that is exactly what you wanted, she reminded herself. Wasn't it?

"I think I would have fared much better with one of your Tashas or Lucias or Martas," he was saying to the twins.

The girls laughed, while Miranda glanced heavenward. Given her suspicions about these so-called nannies of theirs, she could just imagine what lessons they would have had for a man as striking as Lord John.

She slanted a glance over at him and found the devilish fellow looking over at her with a sultry, inquiring gander that sent shivers down her limbs.

How improper, she told herself, focusing on her plate and willing herself not to look at him.

For the rest of the meal.

But when she took another peek, just to assure herself that he wasn't looking at her, the man had the nerve to wink at her.

Why, of all the cheek!

Did he really think she could be seduced so easily?

Her heart fluttered slightly, and she faltered with her

napkin to bring it to her now dry lips. Perhaps she had best not test his tempting charm.

'T'was of no matter anyway, she decided, as Birdwell came in to see the plates cleared away and all that was left to do was thank their host for the excellent meal and then shoo the girls upstairs to their rooms.

Yes, everything was going almost according to her carefully wrought plans.

She wiped her lips with her napkin and placed it beside her plate, nodding at the girls to do the same. They were doing their best to dawdle, but Miranda could see through their intentions.

Then, to her horror, Tally piped up. "Jack, is it true you murdered your aunt to gain possession of Thistleton Park?"

Miranda choked, as did their host, who sputtered over the last sip of his wine.

But he recovered first, wiping his chin with his napkin, saying, "Ah, I see Sir Norris was in rare form today."

"He made some very ugly comments about your aunt's untimely end," Felicity said diplomatically. "But really, they weren't worth repeating." She shot her sister a hot glare.

For his part, Jack laughed. "I'm sure Sir Norris gave you an earful as to how I hastened my aunt onto her eternal reward in an unscrupulous effort to gain this house."

"Something like that," Pippin told him. "We told him that it couldn't be."

Miranda had recovered enough to rise to her feet. "Ladies! That is enough on this subject, which, dare I point out, is hardly proper conversation." She turned to their host, who had also risen from his chair. "Lord

John, my apologies for their impertinent remarks. Now if you will excuse us—"

"Miss Porter, there is no need to apologize," he told her. "I have been accused of far worse. And Pippin," he said, turning to the girl. "I thank you for rising to my defense."

Pippin blushed. "It wasn't me. It was all Miss Porter's doing. She gave Sir Norris a regular wigging for saying you were a—"

"Pippin!" Miranda cringed, then dared a glance over at Jack, who was staring at her, a quizzical tip to his brow. "It isn't worth repeating," she told him, sitting back down, Jack and the girls following suit.

"A regular wigging, did you now, Miss Porter?" he said.

"I would hardly call it that," she told him. "Now if you will excuse us—"

Jack grinned and turned to Tally. "What did your illustrious Miss Porter tell that old fusspot?"

"She said—" Tally started to say.

"Nothing of consequence," Miranda interjected. "Suffice it to say that I didn't think it appropriate to stand by and allow one's host to be maligned."

"You thought I was being maligned?" Jack asked. "You have your work cut out for you, Miss Porter. Most of the *ton* shares Sir Norris's opinion of me." He studied her a little more closely, more so than she felt comfortable with, before he asked, "How is it that you don't share their sentiments, especially considering my boorish behavior this morning?"

"I . . . I . . ." She closed her mouth and drew a deep breath, trying to think of something to say. She *did* think him a wretched bounder, but giving voice to such a condemnation was another matter.

Having spent the evening with him, looking now into his dark eyes and remembering the man who had kissed her with so much passion, left her at odds with her convictions.

"Miss Porter doesn't give much credence to gossip and idle speculations," Felicity told him in an aside. "She says one must use common sense and good judgment when determining a person's character."

"She does?" Jack leaned back in his chair again. "And what does your common sense and good judgment tell you about my character, Miss Porter?"

The room fell silent, and Miranda cursed herself for letting the evening get out of hand. She should have kept the girls in their room and dined from a tray . . . she should have . . .

What she should never have done at that instant was look up at Jack and into his mesmerizing blue gaze.

What she saw there defied good judgment, made common sense flee in the face of such perplexing mystery.

"You are a man not easily understood," she said with all honesty.

Jack studied her for a moment longer than was proper, as if he too was trying to use common sense and good judgment to gauge the woman before him. "Nicely put, Miss Porter. But don't we all have our mysteries? I would venture you have a few of your own." That handsome brow cocked again, while his fingers plucked at the top button of his jacket. She could all but hear him silently finishing his insinuation.

Like your silver button.

"Me?" She managed a short, unconvincing laugh. "I think not."

Oh, bother! She should have thrown out that button years ago. For that matter, she should have married the Hibberts' diminutive vicar or the bushy-browed widower with fourteen children.

Really, what should Lord John care if she kept a man's button? It was none of his business. None of his concern.

If he were a gentleman . . .

Then again, if he'd been a gentleman, he wouldn't have kissed her all those years ago, lifted the veil on her innocence, shown her the delirious power of a kiss, and left her with a button that had become nothing but a millstone around her common sense. A little token that weighed her down with ridiculous dreams of a heroic, dark-haired knight riding up to the Hibberts' lonely cottage and carrying her off with a breathless kiss and his ardent pleas for a Gretna wedding.

But instead, the Fates had left her to her lonely dreams and then mocked her by dropping that wretched button back into his hand.

Well, the Fates may be getting a good chuckle at her expense, but she still had the last laugh.

Lord John recognized neither his button nor her.

She rose anew. "And now, Lord John, it is time for us to excuse ourselves."

There was a general round of protests.

"Miss Porter, Jack promised us a tour of the house," Felicity complained.

"That I did," he agreed, getting to his feet. "And I would be remiss as a host not to keep my word." He slanted a glance at Miranda. "It is only good manners, is it not, Miss Porter?"

"I think dinner was more than adequate," she told him, despite the rising chorus of objections from the girls. She shot the trio her most quelling glance.

Had they completely forgotten her plan?

Dinner. Then they would excuse themselves. And nothing more.

Looking at the sparkling light in their eyes, she realized forgotten rules were not the problem. Ignored was probably a better word.

"Lord John, we've imposed on you long enough," she said. "I think our time would be more properly employed packing for our departure tomorrow morning and—"

"Packing? If that is all that awaits you upstairs, I daresay we have time for a tour," he said, cutting her off and directing his next statement to the girls. "A tour it is."

"No," Miranda said, "I don't think—"

"Come now, Miss Porter," he said, sounding more like the teacher than she. "A tour of the house is expected, isn't it? And I would hate to be anything other than the perfect host. But if you would like to go pack, I'll take the girls around myself and send them up later."

Miranda nearly swallowed her tongue. Then to her horror, he started from the dining room, the girls following in his wake without so much as a "by-your-leave."

And by the time she recovered, they were well down the hall and almost out of earshot. Marching after the tour party with a determined step, she could just imagine what sort of alcoves and deserted corners this house sported.

No gentleman. This time Sir Norris's proclamation rang in her ears like a battle cry. Over her dead body would she let Mad Jack Tremont lead one of these girls astray.

"Have you met the Duke of Lynton's heir?" Felicity was asking.

"Oh, no, no, no!" Jack was saying. "Not Sedborough! He will never do for you, Duchess."

This stopped Miranda dead in her tracks. Marital advice from Mad Jack Tremont? She glanced at the ceiling. Was there no end to the man's nerve?

"Felicity," he continued, "my money is on the Duke of Hollindrake's heir. Set your cap for him. I think you would make him an admirable duchess."

"The Duke of Hollindrake," Felicity repeated, as if she was making a mental note of this recommendation.

"How is that you never married?" Pippin asked him.

Jack flinched, and Miranda paused to enjoy seeing him being skewered with the subject he seemed so willing to offer advice upon but so very unwilling to partake in.

"I don't think I need to repeat that old gossip," he demurred.

And why not, Jack? Miranda wanted to ask. *Because you don't want to tell these girls the truth—that you were a bounder and wretch? That you ruined an innocent young girl and refused to do the honorable thing?*

"Gossip is hardly the best source," Felicity pointed out.

"Oh, yes, do tell, Jack," Tally urged him.

If he didn't, Miranda was of half a mind to give them a good accounting of their hero's conduct.

Why, to look at him, one might think *he'd* been the victim in all this. He stood leaning against the post at the end of the stairwell, looking unabashedly woeful—a pose that might have worked if it hadn't been for the twinkle in his eyes. "It all started when I kissed the wrong lady."

"How does one kiss the wrong lady?" Felicity asked, her suspicious tone a credit to Miss Emery's.

Jack scratched his chin. "Earlier in the evening I'd partaken in a little too much brandy."

You were utterly foxed. Miranda silently clarified.

"And I was late meeting a friend at the opera."

Given your state of intoxication, I'm surprised you could even find the Opera House.

"There I was in crowded hallways, and down the way I thought I spied a lady of my acquaintance."

You thought you saw your mistress loitering in an empty alcove and wanted to take advantage of this momentary boon.

"So I went over and kissed her," he told them.

"You kissed a lady who was merely an acquaintance?" Pippin asked. "That sounds rather forward."

Good for you, Pippin. Once again, Miss Emery's fine standards of education shone through.

Though not for long.

"Cousin," Felicity whispered over at her, "Father was forever kissing our nannies. A man can kiss a good friend of the family or a dear employee and it is of no consequence."

Miranda closed her eyes. That confirmed her suspicions about Lord Langley and his bevy of inappropriate governesses. She made a note to add a much-needed lesson on whom one kisses, or rather does not, on the way to Lady Caldecott's.

"So you kissed this lady you thought you knew," Tally said, steering the story back on course. "And then what?"

"It wasn't the lady I thought it was, but another man's betrothed."

"Miss Mabberly," Felicity whispered.

"Yes, Miss Mabberly," Jack admitted.

Well, finally a bit of truth in this ridiculous fiction. Miranda mused.

"Then what happened?" Tally persisted.

"Well, once I realized my mistake, I apologized immediately and profusely."

Miranda didn't even dignify this bouncer with another thought.

"Then I went to the Earl of Oxley, the lady's fiancé, and tried to make amends."

Buy him off so you didn't have to offer for me, or end your days with grass for breakfast.

"When the earl proved hard-hearted to the situation—"

Most likely because you didn't offer enough money.

"—I went and made an honorable request for Miss Mabberly's hand in marriage."

Miranda shook her head, for in truth she couldn't believe her ears. *An honorable request?* Why the lying, *dis*honorable . . .

"So why didn't you marry her?" Pippin asked.

Possibly because he never proposed, she thought indignantly.

"Tragically, by the time I came around—"

Sobered up—

"—Miss Mabberly had taken ill," he was saying.

"From the scandal, no doubt," Felicity said with all the sage wisdom of an eighty-year-old.

"I don't know how she contracted her illness," Jack said, "but by the end of the week, Miss Mabberly had . . . had . . ." He took a deep breath and shook his head, as if he was unable to finish.

Left Town! Miranda wanted to shout. *Been packed into a carriage by her irate parents and sent to Northumberland to live with distant relations.*

"She'd what?" Tally pleaded, her eyes wide and looking misty.

They all held their breath as Jack composed himself. Even Miranda was leaning forward to see how he'd finish this corker of a story.

He put his hand on Tally's shoulder, bracing her for the truth. "Miss Mabberly perished from her fever before I could declare myself."

"Perished?" Miranda blurted out, without realizing it. Almost immediately, she clapped her hand over her open mouth.

"Yes, Miss Porter," he replied, his quiet words carrying down the hall and washing over her. "She passed away."

"She died?" whispered a wide-eyed Pippin.

He nodded, as if saying it thrice in one night was too much to bear.

"A decline," Tally whispered. "Just as I always said."

She'd died? What utter nonsense! Miranda marched down the hall, insensible to what her words could do.

She stopped before him, tapping her finger to her chin, and said, "Let me get this straight, Lord John."

The four of them looked up at her in shock, as if they couldn't understand why she too wasn't taking a moment of silence for the soul of the dear and departed Miss Mabberly. Only Brutus seemed to understand what she was about, and he very uncharacteristically left Tally's side to sit beside her, as if adding his considerable opinion to hers.

He glanced up at her with his little monkey face and let out a small "woof."

And with his encouragement, Miranda continued. "You kissed another man's betrothed at the opera—"

"By accident," he clarified.

"Yes, by accident," she said, offering him that much. "And then once you reached an impasse with the Earl of Oxley over repairing this mistake, it was your intention to marry Miss Mabberly yourself to save the lady's tarnished reputation?"

"Of course," he said, straightening and looking her in the eye. Suddenly, he was no longer Mad Jack Tremont, willing to lie and jest his way out of any bit of trouble. The man before her was eight and thirty, his face lined with lessons hard learned—but it was his eyes that shook her right down to her proper and upright boots. Eyes as steady as the marble beneath her feet.

The steady, honorable gaze of a gentleman.

"Miss Porter, whatever you may think of me," he said in a voice cut with steel, "consider this: while I regret kissing the young lady and causing so much scandal, what I am ashamed of more is that she went to her death without having her good name restored. I paid my respects at her funeral—"

Funeral? How could that be?

"—and though her parents were insensible to my condolences, my old friend Lord Sedgwick stood with me, for his wife, Emmaline, was quite fond of Miss Mabberly . . ."

Lord and Lady Sedgwick? Her parents?

Then from some long-closed memory, her mother and father's voices echoed forth. . . . They'd been arguing the night she'd been sent from London, their heated words ricocheting through the house, impossible to avoid.

I would rather see her dead than have a penny of my money go to that no-account wastrel.

But Cyrus, if she doesn't marry him, she'll never marry.

Good! Then I won't have to see the fruits of my labors cast into the Thames. Because that is what I'll do before I'll give one farthing to Mad Jack Tremont.

Dead? The truth of it crashed down on her. *Father, Mother, what did you do?*

They'd told one and all that she'd died!

And everyone had believed them. Including Jack.

This was why her father had never allowed her to return to London. Why her inheritance from him had come to "Miss Jane Porter" and not her given name.

Because everyone else thought her dead.

Miranda tried to draw a calming breath, but instead the foyer spun around her.

Jack stepped back from her and folded his arms

across his chest. "After that, everyone blamed me for her demise, and rightly so. If I hadn't kissed her, she would be the Countess of Oxley now, and I . . . well, let's hope I wouldn't have blundered elsewhere and have had to endure the cold shoulder of Society for so many years."

"Why, it is as if you both died," Tally said in a dramatic, mournful voice.

Miranda felt a chill ripple through her veins, as if she really had perished that day. Her knees wavered beneath her as she tried to focus on something steady, something solid.

And her gaze fled of its own volition to Jack.

All these years, all this time, she'd thought no one had sought her out because of him, and now she realized it was because everyone had thought her dead. Because of her father's lie, his insensible anger at her ruination.

"Was she pretty, Jack?" Pippin asked.

"Miss Mabberly?" He laughed a little. "I think so."

"You think so?" Felicity made a *"tsk-tsk"* sound under her breath. "Either she was or she wasn't."

His jaw worked back and forth. "I don't really remember her face . . . the hallway wasn't very well lit, and I must confess, I was a bit in my cups, but I do remember her hair. 'T'was a red like one would never forget, full of fire and passion."

"Like Miss Porter's?" Tally asked.

He glanced over at Miranda. "Yes, very similar."

His confession pulled her out of her trance. What had he said? *Full of fire and passion.*

Her?

"And you don't remember anything else about her?" Pippin asked, sounding all too disappointed.

He laughed. "Yes, Pippin, I do remember one other thing about her. I remember her kiss." And there was a wistful note to his confession that brought a sigh from the girls.

Miranda thought her knees were going to buckle. *Her kiss?*

"Come now," Jack said. "That is enough melancholy talk for one night. I promised you a tour, and a tour we shall have." And then he led them down the hall.

Miranda stood rooted to the floor. She was still trying to comprehend all that had been said. Little, steadfast Brutus sat at her feet, a sentinel in the battle of emotions going on within her.

"Miss Porter, are you coming with us?" Felicity called to her.

"Um, uh, yes," Miranda told her. "In a moment."

Jack cocked his head and eyed her. "Are you well, Miss Porter?"

She straightened and did her best to breathe. "Yes. I'll be right there."

He frowned and looked ready to say more, but the girls pushed him along, their excitement to see his cursed house a tide he couldn't turn.

Even as they rounded the corner and left her sight, she collapsed to the steps, her hand clinging to the post. Brutus lay down at her feet, looking up into her eyes and offering whatever solace he could.

She'd never done it before, but she reached out now

and scratched his little head. "What if what Lord John said was true?" she whispered to the dog. "That he intended to marry me?"

Brutus made no reply but tipped his head so she could continue to scratch him, this time on the side she'd missed.

"Oh, Papa, why would you do such a thing?" she said softly, the breadth of her father's deception fanning out before her.

It was as if the ledger of her life had been turned upside down, the orderly columns and tightly held opinions that had been her foundation, now merely a jumbled, indecipherable mess at her feet.

She closed her eyes and recalled what he'd said.

What I am ashamed of more is that she went to her death without having her good name restored.

And more so, he'd said he remembered her kiss.

Her fingers went to her lips, and she regretted every time she'd tried so very hard to forget his.

Miranda slowly rose to her feet. Down the hall she could hear Jack's deep-timbred voice.

Whatever should she do now? Tell him the truth?

No, never! cried that very ingrained spinster inside her. *Don't say a word to the man.*

Really, what was there to be gained from telling him that she lived?

Then even as she asked herself the question, her gaze met the mirror across the hall, and this time when she looked at herself she saw what everyone else saw—the woman she'd become.

With her too-tight chignon, her dull gray dress, and her brows forever pinched together.

Gads, she *was* as ancient as the girls politely refrained from telling her. And they were right, there wasn't a hint of light, not a spark of fire anywhere to be seen about her.

Even worse, she hadn't the vaguest notion how one went about igniting such a light.

She looked again at her chignon, and, biting her lip, reached back and pulled a pin free. Then another. Then another. Until her hair came loose.

Well, it's a start, she thought, looking at herself. And if she needed some more help, a wild notion came whispering in her ear, offering just the answer.

Mad Jack Tremont knows how . . .

Chapter 6

Jack had spent the entire evening watching Miss Porter. He couldn't help himself. It was like driving past a mail coach accident: While manners and good taste dictated that one not look, you couldn't help but steal a glance.

And as his gaze had stolen over her time and time again, he'd come to the conclusion that he had never seen a woman whose corset was tied so tight. She looked positively trussed up by her convictions—proper this, respectable that.

No wonder she never smiled.

Yet all the while, that red hair of hers defied reason—why, it was wasted on her. Such a glorious titian hue belonged on a lady willing to admit to the passion it proclaimed. A woman unafraid of the temptation she represented.

His fingers had itched to pull those sturdy pins out of her tightly wound chignon and set those ruby tresses free. To run his fingers through their fiery silk and whisper into her ear—

Remember . . .

"The tour, Lord John?" Felicity prompted.

Jack glanced over to find the girls staring at him.

"Uh, ah, yes!" he managed to say, taking another glance down the hall and wondering what was taking Miss Porter so long. "Let's start in the library."

"A library?" Pippin enthused. "How wonderful."

He picked up a candelabra on the sideboard and led the way down the shadowy hall. "A regular library might be: our library is quite different."

"Is it haunted?" Tally asked.

He paused, looking into their wide eyes and serious expressions and realized he might have gone too far. Well, Birdwell had told him to keep the girls occupied, and he supposed a good curse and a few ghost stories would keep them tucked in their beds for the night, not venturing about the house when he had business to conduct.

The irony of it was that while he was supposed to be diverting these girls, the bulk of the evening had passed and he'd all but forgotten what awaited him later. He hadn't even been aware of how much he'd missed company until this evening. Why, the entertaining and engaging little chits had got him confessing his darkest secrets like a schoolgirl!

He was out of practice.

For one, he'd never told anyone that he'd gone to offer for Miss Mabberly. Most everyone thought he'd disavowed doing the respectable thing, and he'd let them think the worst of him.

He hadn't cared. When his head had finally cleared, his only thought had been of a kiss that couldn't be forgotten. Jack had gone straight to the Mabberlys and pleaded with the old *cit* to let him make amends for the girl's ruination.

The cagey man of business had refused, convinced Jack was only after her fortune . . . and while, to be honest, that had held some appeal, there had been another reason he had wanted to see Miranda again.

He'd wanted to kiss her once more.

It didn't matter that he couldn't recall her face; he could recall her kiss. Her lips, the way she'd smelled, the sound of her first sigh of longing as he'd teased it from her.

Somehow, through the brandy and the hubbub, her innocent kiss, her passionate response had marked him.

Haunted him. Still did.

In the years since, months might pass when she never entered his thoughts, but then he'd spy some chit with auburn tresses at a posting inn or in the village, and for a fortnight his dreams would be haunted by a red-haired vixen whose lips did more than kiss him, whose hands roamed over his body, who begged the rake he'd once been to take her . . .

And just as he'd roll this tempting lover over, cover her body with his, give her the pleasure she demanded, he'd wake up in a cold sweat, hard as a rock, and longing for a lady all but forgotten, a fiery miss long passed from this world.

It had been even worse since he'd bumped into Miss Porter at his niece's school. Tangled with her, held her, gazed into her eyes and seen a hint of long-forgotten passion.

Now the dreams had taken a new turn, and the woman in his bed was older, more mature, a living testament of innocence lost, and his desire for her all that much more demanding.

How ridiculous, he thought, that someone like stiff and proper Miss Porter would remind him of Miranda Mabberly.

Why, she'd even scoffed at Miss Mabberly's death! How heartless could a woman be?

Kiss her and find out, a wicked voice whispered in his ear.

Kiss Miss Porter? Now he was going as mad as Sir Norris alleged.

"My apologies for the state of the house," he told the girls when he planted the candelabra on his desk and a cloud of dust rose up. "I'm not the best at managing these things."

"You should ask Miss Porter for some suggestions," Felicity said, while Pippin wandered over to the bookshelves.

Jack saw no need to do that. He already had a pretty good understanding of Miss Porter's opinions on how Thistleton Park was run.

"Besides decorum," the girl continued, "she also teaches classes in household management. Why, give her a month and she'd have your estate so you would hardly recognize it."

Yes, he could well imagine what Miss Porter would say once she delved beneath the dust and carefully constructed eccentricity and ruin of his household.

Tally joined in the chorus of praise for Miss Porter. "She is also very good at managing investments and such, especially now that she has gained her inheritance and will be overseeing her own accounts."

Her own accounts? An inheritance? This took Jack aback. Why, she hadn't said a word of it all evening.

Well, for that matter, she'd been hard-pressed to say anything.

Before he could delve into this any further, Miss Porter arrived in their midst, tumbling into the room in a rush.

"So sorry," she said. "I dropped one of my hairpins."

The girls gaped at her, and he did as well.

Her tight little knot of a chignon was gone, and her hair fell in a long curl to her shoulder. Without her hair pulled back, her face appeared softer, the severe tip of her brows gone.

"Have I missed anything?" she asked brightly, looking about the library as if she had never seen one.

"Not in the least, Miss Porter," he managed to say, trying not to stare but at the same time captivated by the sight of her freed tresses.

If he weren't a gentleman, he would have sworn she'd lost more than her hairpins back in the foyer.

"You said something earlier about proving your family curse, my lord," she said. "Shall you proceed in convincing us of your claim?" Her lips were turned upward. As if she meant to smile.

Jack looked at her and then at the doorway. Was this the same woman they'd left at the stairs? What the devil had happened to her?

Any other lady, and he might have thought she'd discovered his brandy stash—not that she'd had the time—but he was still of half a mind to march down to the cellar and start counting the bottles.

"Um, yes, the curse," he muttered, trying to get his thoughts back on entertaining and diverting his guests. Especially since he was supposed to be diverting *them*, not the other way around. He pointed at a great wooden chair in the corner. "That is, if Tremont legend is to be believed, the rightful throne of England."

The Langley sisters gaped at the massive piece of furniture. Even Pippin took her nose out of the bookshelves long enough to give the chair a good inspection.

Miss Porter gave his pronouncement a snort of disbelief, then covered her mouth as if ashamed of her hasty judgment.

"My apologies, my lord. Please do go on," she said, smiling at him.

The sparkling light in her eyes was like a Cyprian's invitation. Was it him, or had the room suddenly gotten terribly warm?

"The throne of England? How is that?" Felicity asked, barging into his reverie.

He coughed and struggled to stay focused. *Family history. Diverting their attention.* Yes, that was it.

"The original part of the house was built in 1111," he told them, "as a residence for Lord Harold Tremont. He ran afoul of Henry the First by insisting he was the legitimate heir to the throne of England. Rather than have the entire family disgraced, poor Lord Harold was banished here to continue his single-minded reign. He commissioned the throne and installed it himself, with great pomp. Even bullied the local priest into blessing it."

Felicity gave a disapproving shake of her head.

"How sad for Lord Harold, to think himself the king and no one to believe him," Pippin offered, eyeing the chair with a newfound curiosity.

"Don't pity him too much, fair Pippin," Jack told her, winking at the girl. "Hal had a fine time establishing his own court—which included a court jester, a poor fellow he hired from a traveling troupe." He glanced up and spied Miss Porter running her hand over the wide arm of Hal's throne.

As her fingers trailed over the wood, he felt himself take a deep breath, a delicious chill running down his limbs.

All of them.

Whatever was this woman doing to him? He was going mad, cursed not by this house but by this mercurial woman.

"One poor fool doesn't sound like much of a court," Tally was saying.

At this Jack decided to test Miss Porter's newfound boundaries. "Oh, no, Tally, he also had an entire bevy of ladies-in-waiting he hired from a London bro—"

"Lord John!" Miss Porter interrupted, turning from the chair, her hand clenched on the wide, thick arm.

So she hadn't completely lost her sense of propriety—and for some reason he was glad of that. Yet even as he looked at her, there was that mischievous sparkle in her eyes again despite her protest.

A sparkle? An odd light as incongruous as her red hair.

No, he was imagining things. But where was the expected admonishment on propriety, the lecture on proper restraint? Just when he thought he understood the lady, knew how to knot up her corset strings and keep her at sixes and sevens, she'd turned the tide on him.

What had she said? *You are not a man easily understood.*

Perhaps she understood him better than he'd given her credit for.

"Miss Porter," Pippin was whispering, "why did Lord Hal need ladies-in-waiting if there was no queen?"

Jack waited expectantly to see how Miss Porter was going to answer this, and he smiled as she blushed a bit before she made her tart reply.

"I assure you, if there had been a queen about the house," she said, "Lord Hal's rule would have come to a quick and decisive end."

He had to imagine that Miss Porter wouldn't let a man get away with such indiscretions. She'd hold him to the highest of standards—the kind no man could ever achieve.

Even with a lifetime to perfect . . .

A lifetime? Jack didn't have a lifetime to give. Not to any woman. No matter the temptation.

The clock struck the hour, one toll shy of midnight. He half expected Miss Porter to begin shooing her chicks up the stairs before the witching hour struck, but instead, she turned to him. "Where to next on your tour, my lord?"

Where next? She wanted to see more of his tumble-down house? He glanced again at the clock and wondered what it would take for the old Miss Porter to return and put an end to this tour.

An offer to see your bedroom, came an errant thought.

"What would you like to see?" he said instead, making sure he didn't look at Miss Porter. This madcap reincarnation might be able to see right down into his dark soul.

"Something tragic!" Tally enthused. "Romantically tragic."

"That," he told the girl, "this house has in spades."

He led them back down the hall to the foyer and stopped right before the steps. No, what he needed was a good Tremont tragedy, a story that would have them in their beds with their sheets pulled all the way up to their chins for the rest of the night. And perhaps it would put a chill in his blood as well.

"This," he said, pointing at a spot in the marble, and using his darkest, most menacing voice, "is where Isolda Tremont, the wife of Lord Douglas Tremont, died when she tumbled down this very staircase."

The girls stepped back, as if the lady's broken body lay there still.

That was a good sign, he thought, and so he continued in the same vein, to put a shiver of fear in their hearts. "Douglas swore it was an accident, but others claimed he pushed her, for they had heard the lord and his lady arguing violently a few minutes before she met her demise. Apparently Douglas thought Isolda was paying too much attention to a neighbor, and he was wild with jealousy."

"So he killed her?" whispered a wide-eyed Tally.

"Who's to say?" Jack demurred. "But over the centuries there are those who have claimed to see Isolda late at night rising from this very place and making her way through the gardens to seek her lover."

The girls sucked in a collective breath, their eyes riveted to the spot on the floor.

Instead of frightening the girls and their chaperone into hiding, his dark story only seemed to incite their interest further.

"Are there more such stories?" Tally asked with all the enthusiasm of a girl who'd just received her vouchers to Almack's. She turned to her cousin. "Pippin, think of the play we could write from all this: *The Tremont Tragedies.*"

Pippin nodded, as enthralled with the idea as Jack was stunned. "Yes, oh yes," she said. "And the subtitle would be: *A Cautionary Tale of Remorse and Regrets.*"

Felicity, practical to a fault and without a bit of drama to her soul, just glanced up at the ceiling and heaved a sigh, as if to say, *How can I be related to the two silliest girls in all the world?* "I doubt Lord Douglas regretted a single moment of his wife's demise," she told them.

Jack turned to her. "In poor Douglas's defense, he never remarried and spent the rest of his years tending the roses around Isolda's grave."

"The ones near the gate?" Pippin asked.

"The very same," Jack said, noting the girl had an observant eye and good memory.

"The poor man," she said softly. "Oh, Tally, we can have a scene where Lord Douglas waters his dear wife's grave with his tears."

"Bah!" Felicity interjected, probably before her sister started rehearsing for the role of Isolda. "He watered them with his guilt."

"Ah, Duchess, I think you are being too hard on Lord Douglas, for part of our family curse is that we love only once in a lifetime. Once a Tremont man falls in love, he shall never have an eye for another."

Tally sighed. "Just like you and Miss Mabberly. Is that why you never married?"

Now during his wild days in London, he'd gotten into more than one scrape when he thought he'd end up sticking his fork in the wall for certain, but nothing had prepared him for having four pairs of feminine eyes gazing at him intently, awaiting his reply.

Even Brutus sat at his feet, paying his boots no heed and looking up for his answer.

His gaze flew to Miss Porter, looking for some help, some admonishment about proper conversation. But there was none forthcoming. The vexing woman just stood there, her head tipped to one side and a look that challenged him to deny it.

And as he looked at her, really looked at the woman before him, he found himself forgetting the girl who'd stolen his heart so long ago. Suddenly all those things about Miranda that had left him filled with regrets and longing—her innocence, her quicksilver passion— seemed a quaint dream in the face of this managing, proper spinster with her tempting tresses and tart opinions.

A woman that challenged him in ways he didn't yet understand, didn't know if he wanted to.

What the devil was he thinking? He might not understand what was happening to him, but he knew how to put a stop to it.

"Yes," he told them quickly. "That's exactly the reason. My affection for Miss Mabberly has become my curse." He shrugged his shoulders, if only to cast off any last lingering notions about Miss Porter, and said, "Now we have one last stop on this tour. The Great Hall. If you'll come this way—" He turned to lead them down the hall when Brutus gave a short woof and darted between his legs, then under and through Miss Porter's skirts.

The little dog's mischief was enough to topple the lady, sending her feet skidding out from beneath her.

Jack was having his own problems remaining upright, and they collided somewhere in the middle, falling into each other's arms.

They slammed together with a mighty *whoosh*, and Jack caught her and steadied them both—though the same couldn't be said for the bolt of desire that ricocheted through his veins.

"Bad, Brutus!" Tally shouted and went dashing off after her dog, her sister and cousin in her wake— leaving Jack and Miranda alone.

Alone. And in each other's arms. What had Birdwell said? Keep his enemies closer still?

Ah, but Jack discovered an enemy of another kind, a devilish temptation that could steal a man's heart. He glanced down at her, a tightening thread of passion pulling her closer to him.

Even worse, she was supple and pliant in his arms. Perhaps it was the shock of being upended, but there she was, as fluid as a willing lover, her breasts pressed against his chest, their legs tangled, his arms wound around her ever so tightly.

Through the muslin of her gown, he could feel her corset, the stiff linen, the rigid stays, the tightly pulled strings, but the living, breathing woman all but defied her prim prison.

Around him, he could swear he heard the roar of a mighty wind, feel the cold chill of time wind around them, marking them, marking him. He looked at this woman in his arms and wanted her with a depth that swept all the way down to his soul.

He forgot everything around him. All the problems that haunted his days, made up his nights, turned to ash. With her in his arms a calm settled into his soul, lending him a peace he hadn't felt . . . well, ever.

It was this house, he averred. This woman . . .

Enchanting him. Whispering impossible notions into his ear.

Kiss her. Kiss her.

And her lips parted in answer, as if begging him to cover them, to explore her, to conquer her desire. She looked as if she had something to say, something she wanted so desperately to tell him, and yet the words—

"I am so sorry, Miss Porter," Tally was saying as she and the other girls returned. "I don't know what got into—" The girl came to an abrupt halt.

Jack knew right then and there he was indeed cursed.

"Oh, my—" Pippin gasped as she stumbled into Tally.

Felicity for once took a romantic turn. "Lord John, how heroic you are to save Miss Porter. I just knew you were what Nanny Lucia would call a *'preux chevalier'*."

Whatever spell had been cast over Miss Porter in the last half hour—demmit, in the last magical minute—evaporated in the blink of an eye as Tally translated her sister's words in a breathless whisper of acknowledgement.

"A knight in shining armor."

"I think I'm well enough to stand now, my lord," she said, clambering out of his arms. "Thank you for catching me." Her hasty tone and the way she swiped her hands over her skirt made it seem as if she were brushing away the last vestiges of the web that had entangled them. "There, now," she said, tucking her hair up and deftly pinning it back into place. She turned to the girls. "Do you have that beast in hand, Miss Thalia?"

Tally nodded. Their prim chaperone was back, and there wasn't a single soul in the room who felt like cheering her return.

Least of all Jack.

"Very well," Miss Porter told them. "Girls, let us thank Lord John for the tour and—"

"Oh, Miss Porter!"

"No!"

"We've hardly begun," came the protests.

From the pinched expression on her face, the disapproval knit across her brow, he knew their protests were falling on deaf ears.

"Really, Miss Porter, what is your hurry?" he asked.

She didn't look up at him this time but instead went

to work settling her shawl around her shoulders like a mantle of chain mail. "If we are to be gone at first light, we need to finish our packing."

"Delay your departure until after breakfast," he found himself suggesting.

Oh, the devil take his tongue! What was he saying?

"That isn't possible." She looked up at him then, her face once again composed and set. "We have other stops to make before we reach Lady Caldecott's. Educational diversions. Houses of architectural interest, ones that offer lessons in history."

Jack grinned. Lessons? She wanted lessons? "There are some excellent architectural points to Thistleton Park that are quite educational, if you would give the house a chance."

Give me a chance.

Her eyes widened, and she stepped back. Oh, she understood exactly what he meant.

"Come now, Miss Porter, you hardly strike me as a spoilsport. In truth, I can see it in your eyes, you are as immensely curious about my Tremont ancestors and Thistleton Park as your charges are."

She shot him a wry look, one that most would believe was filled with disdain. But not Jack. He'd seen that spark in her eyes when he'd held her, and for some unfathomable reason, he wanted to see it again.

"At least come and see the Great Hall," he cajoled. "My Aunt Josephine had the original medieval portion of the house turned into a portrait gallery, and I know that Birdwell asked the girls from the village to clean it up before they left this afternoon." He turned a wide-eyed expression on the hopelessly romantic trio behind

him to gain their help. "'Tis said that Eleanor of
Aquitaine dined there before she was exiled by her husband. Much to Lord Harold's delight."

Pippin, the obvious bluestocking of the bunch,
nearly swooned. "Oh, please, Miss Porter. Such a room
would be worthy of recounting to Miss Emery. You
know how keen she is on medieval history."

If there was one thing Jack did remember about
women, it was how to spot the moment when they begin
to capitulate. In a flirtation—or even an improper
invitation—there is that split second when a woman
goes from being downright unwilling to cautiously entertaining.

"Well, I don't know—" Miss Porter began.

Jack didn't wait for her to finish. "Excellent!" he declared, catching her by the arm and spinning her toward the hall. "I think you will find it a most
illuminating experience."

"I can only imagine," came what might have sounded
like a tart reply but to Jack's ears was a tempting challenge to see if he could rediscover the lady he'd
found . . . and lost.

Pushing the double doors wide open, Jack announced, "While to most this would be your typical
portrait gallery, it is what we Tremonts refer to privately as our own version of Bedlam. When a family
member is banished to Thistleton Park, any and all portraits usually follow—we Tremonts don't like to keep
reminders about that there are branches on the family
tree that have failed to exhibit our requisite noble and
lofty traits."

"Ooooh," came their excited sighs as the girls gazed into the dazzling room.

Birdwell and his helpers had done their part—all the Holland covers were pulled and every sconce filled with candles. The gallery was ablaze in light.

For the first time since Jack had taken possession of Thistleton Park, he felt a sense of pride for his disreputable residence.

The girls followed him eagerly, spellbound by the sight, as well as by the scandalous taint that the room seemed to hold in its depths.

"Who's this?" Felicity asked at the first portrait they came to.

He stopped before the great oil canvas and set the candelabra he was carrying on a nearby curio cabinet. "May I introduce you to my great-aunt, Lady Josephine Tremont."

"The one who was murdered?" Tally breathed.

"So avers Sir Norris," Jack told them. "But there has never been any proof of foul play. Nor was her body ever found. I think the old girl went out for a walk and got too close to the edge."

"On a dark and stormy night?" Miss Porter asked.

Well, there was that bit of untidy business, Jack mused. Leave it to Miss Porter to point it out. "My aunt was here at Thistleton Park for a reason. She wasn't always counted on to do the right thing."

"Harrumph," Miss Porter said and continued further into the hall.

"She looks rather formidable," Pippin added.

"She was," Jack told her.

"Why was she here?" Tally asked.

"She made a very inopportune marriage as a young girl. Then her blighter of a husband abandoned her, and she was left with nothing. Rather than see her become an even greater scandal, she was given Thistleton Park, as the previous inhabitant had died a few months earlier. Of course it came with the proviso that she not go out in Society but remain here."

"How terrible," Felicity opined.

"Not really," Jack told her. "Aunt Josephine had her admirers, far and wide, and they were more than willing to come here to see her, much to the family's horror."

"Mr. Billingsworth was quite taken with her," Pippin said.

"And how lucky for us," Jack told her. "Or we wouldn't have met."

There was another "harrumph" from Miss Porter.

It only served to pique his rakish heart all that much more.

"Jack," Tally called out, "who is this?"

"That," he said in a conspiratorial whisper, "is my great-great-uncle. They called him Mad Jack Tremont because he had a propensity for gaming and drink."

Miss Porter came to stand just behind the girls. "So you were named after him?" Her question held that sharp-witted irony, which the woman used so well.

"Yes," Jack said. "Much to my mother's dismay. She said it was sure to mark me with Mad Jack's tendencies. Instead, she had hoped to name me after her great-uncle, who was a respected vicar."

"What was his name?" Pippin asked.

He shuddered. "No, you'll only laugh."

The three of them shook their heads. "Surely we won't, Lord John."

"Orson," he told them.

They promptly fell into a spate of giggles. "Never!"

He grinned at them. "What? Don't you think I would have made a good Orson, or is it a good vicar?"

Their giggles were now turning into a gale of laughter. "Neither!" they told him.

"Really, girls," Miss Porter admonished. "I don't see anything funny about Lord John being a vicar."

"Nor do I," he teased. "However perhaps Miss Porter thinks I might have made a good clergyman. What say you, Miss Porter?"

"It might have been a better employment of your talents," she said, staring at him with a straight face, but there it was, in her eyes (if he wasn't mistaken)—that spark of passion that defied her words.

A hint of what they had shared in the hallway.

Jack couldn't help himself. "And those talents would be?"

Her eyes widened, and for just a moment that bit of magic wove them back together. She looked like she was about to say something, as she had in the hall, but she was interrupted by Tally, who had wandered away and now stood before another portrait.

"Jack, who is this?"

"Don't think you'll get off so easily, Miss Porter," he whispered at her as he passed her by to join the girl. Taking a quick glance back at the lady, he saw the slight hint of a blush on her cheeks.

Oh, no, he wasn't mistaken. Her corset was loosening, whether she liked it or not.

Pulling his attention away from the redhead who perplexed him, he glanced up at the portrait Tally was looking at.

"That is Lord Albin Tremont," he told her. "He lived here just before my Aunt Josephine. He built the tower, thus the name, Albin's Folly."

"Why did he build it?" Pippin asked.

"So he could see France more readily, so the story goes," Jack said.

"He looks very sad," Pippin said.

"Spent every penny he could get his hands on building his tower."

"Was he a student of the classics?" Miss Porter asked.

"No," Jack told them. "Nothing more than a man with a broken heart." He glanced over his shoulder at her. She was gazing up at Lord Albin's sad expression with a light of understanding in her own eyes. Was she thinking of the man whose button she still kept? Jack tossed the notion out of his thoughts and told them Albin's heartrending tale.

"The story goes that Albin fell in love with a young girl from a noble French family. They were to be wed, but when it was discovered that he suffered from spells—fits, I suppose they were—the girl's father called off the engagement. She wrote to him and promised him that somehow she would escape her family and come to him. Shortly thereafter, word came that she had been married to another, and the news left Albin bereft. He removed himself here and built his tower so he could watch for her. So he could see France, and in a sense, see her every day that the sky was clear. He died up there, waiting for her. When they found him, that was in his hand," he said, pointing to a miniature of a lady hung beside the grand portrait.

Tally and Pippin gazed up at the man who'd spent his life waiting for the bride who would never come, and then at the lady herself, sighing in unison. Even the ever-practical Felicity turned away, wiping her eyes with her sleeve.

But it was Miss Porter whose reaction surprised him. She backed away from them and stared up at the portrait with shock in her eyes. "What a terrible waste of a life."

Jack felt only the condemnation in her words, as if they'd come from his brother or some other illustrious and opinionated Tremont. "You think he should have given up on his true love?"

Her brow furrowed as she gazed up at Lord Albin. "He gave up when he built that folly, climbed up inside it and turned his eyes away from the possibility of love."

There was an unmistakable bitterness and anger in her words, which tugged at Jack all the way down to the bottom of his boots. Is that what she thought of *him*? That he'd retreated to Thistleton Park in defeat and despair and was hiding here from life?

And he'd thought her disdain for him had been born out of his disreputable past, but there it was; her true scorn lay in the fact that he had seemingly wasted his life since leaving London.

Perhaps that had been true at first, but he'd found a purpose here at Thistleton Park that few people could ever imagine—even him. One, he supposed as he glanced over at the tall clock that stood in the corner, he needed to get back to as soon as he could. No matter how the consequences weighed on him, no matter that the fear of failure tore at his soul. But he could hardly tell Miss Porter any of that. That he was in no way like his distant cousin on the wall.

But she was right about one thing—he had turned his heart against love. He'd seen firsthand the power of it, how it changed a man, leaving him helpless to the whims and charms of a woman.

Look at how it had changed his old friend Alexander Denford, with his beloved Emmaline, who'd re-arranged the stodgy baron's life quite literally. And how about Templeton, his old partner in revelry and charm? He'd gone agog for Lady Diana and chased her all the way to Scotland, against every rhyme and reason.

And then Jack looked at Miss Porter, really looked at her, and felt another kind of tug. One that perhaps made him understand his old friends a little better. The kind that made him want to show her what kind of man he was, give her a glimpse into the character and traits she thought him so lacking.

But why her? Why Miss Porter? he asked himself. *And why now?*

"What a sad, terrible waste," she was saying.

Then he spied something different in her grief-stricken gaze. A sense of regret that he understood only too well.

She wasn't talking about him or Albin. How he knew

it, he didn't know, but he knew it with a certainty that she was talking about herself.

About that demmed button.

So why was it that his veins coursed with jealousy suddenly? That a single ornament could taunt him so thoroughly? That the very notion of another man holding her heart hostage infuriated him?

"I believe, Miss Porter," Jack said before he could stop himself, with the same foolish, headlong passion that had driven Albin to build his tower, "that we all have our follies in which we hide. Albin just built his for all to see." He paused and glanced once more at his lovelorn relation before he looked back at Miss Porter, at those devilish red tresses of hers, at her eyes that spoke of a life of regrets. "However, if there was ever a woman who could have tempted my poor besotted relation out of his prison, you might have been the one to do it." He nodded at the miniature beside Albin's portrait. "You see, he had a fondness for redheads, as well."

And with that, Jack bowed to the ladies and marched from the hall.

Fled was more like it.

Chapter 7

Miranda continued to stare after Jack long after he'd gone striding out of the Great Hall, her heart hammering in her chest. The windows in the long hall rattled as the wind outside picked up again, heralding a new storm.

Not unlike the tempest of emotions raging inside her.

"Whatever was that about?" Felicity asked.

"I don't know," Miranda lied, cursing herself for taking such a chance. For listening to Nanny Rana's advice. Lights, indeed! It had nearly upended her life.

Somehow, in the course of her grand experiment, something, so very subtle and dangerous, had happened between them. In just a moment in his arms, they'd made that strange, tangible connection once again.

She shivered and wondered what would have happened if he had kissed her. Would he have truly remembered her kiss, as he claimed?

As she remembered his?

"I think it is time to go upstairs and finish our packing," she told them, taking one last glance at the portrait of Lord Albin.

What if she and Jack were indeed cursed? Marked together for the rest of their lives?

Albin's sad, haunting eyes seemed to follow her out of the room, as if mocking her from his prison of wood and oil.

We all have our follies in which we hide.

Miranda hurried out of the room. Really, she wasn't hiding in the least.

Well, perhaps a little. Her change of name had been to secure her place at Miss Emery's. A small bit of dissembling to gain employment and retain her respectability was hardly hiding.

She trailed after the girls as they went up the stairs.

Besides, instead of being in a loveless match, she was free to pursue her own dreams. Now that she'd come of age and gained her inheritance, she could do whatever she wanted.

Really, what did Jack know of her life? Hiding indeed! She was entirely free of the confines that most women had binding their lives.

Yet a small voice inside her teased the issue. *Free to do what?*

She was on her way to Kent to spend the rest of her days as a spinster . . . a recluse. She might as well take her father's fortune and build her own tower, as Albin had.

Oh, yes, if she was free, then Jack was as rich as Midas.

They arrived in their rooms and Miranda set the girls to packing, then escaped to her own small chamber, closing the door between them. Her meager belongings took no time to arrange in her old, plain valise.

Really, she mused, as she sat down on her bed and stared up at the unsmiling woman in the portrait over the mantel, there was nothing wrong with hiding.

Hadn't her attempt to let her "light" shine, per Nanny Rana's advice, been a near disaster? Why, the girls had gaped at her as if she'd gone mad.

And if she was honest, she had gone a little mad. Certainly it was understandable, when one finds out that the world thinks them dead.

Set free by her own demise: it was a laughable notion. What wasn't so worthy of mirth was what her father's lie had cost Jack. He'd been ruined by it, scorned by Society, by his family and finally banished here to Thistleton Park.

Tell him who you are, a strange little voice whispered. *Tell him and set him free.*

She glanced up at the lady inside the frame and said, "Whatever would the truth serve?"

To tell him that she lived? That her father had lied to him, to her?

He'd be furious, and rightly so. And then what? Have him scorn her once again?

Not that he had scorned her the first time around; she had merely thought he had. Yet even that mistaken assumption had hurt her deeply.

No, she couldn't tell Jack the truth. And yet, wasn't

the worse crime not to tell him? To let him go on being censured by his friends and family? Perhaps with his name cleared, with his reputation returned, he could find a life beyond the dreary confines of this house and the dark past that seemed to whisper from the very walls.

She stole a glance up at the dour woman above the mantel. Gads, the first thing she'd do if she were mistress of this house would be to remove all these awful reminders of the past and pack them off to Jack's brother. Let the duke be the caretaker of his mad relations.

If you were mistress of this house . . . that odd little voice taunted. *Now isn't that a fine notion?*

Miranda shook her head. No wonder everyone averred this house to be haunted and cursed. She considered herself a modern lady of reason and science, but truly there was something uncomfortably gothic about this ancient pile of stones.

"I wouldn't accept even if he offered," she told the lady, guessing by her cold, narrow gaze that she must have lived here—and for a good reason. "It isn't as if I expect him to make an offer for me after all these years." Dear God, what was becoming of her? She was talking to portraits! She got up and crossed the room, deliberately putting her back to the fireplace.

But she found she couldn't escape this temporary madness so easily.

I remember her kiss . . .

Jack's confession echoed through her tangled thoughts like a medley of trumpets.

Her kiss! Miranda pressed her lips together, then glanced over her shoulder at the portrait.

Was it her imagination, or was the woman mocking her with that slight tip to her lips?

"Yes, I know," she told her. He'd probably been telling the girls a Banbury tale, for if he had truly been marked by Miss Mabberly's kiss, then why had he been about to kiss her in the foyer?

Because you are one and the same. And while he might not know it, there are some things you can't hide from Fate.

Fate! Miranda scoffed at such a notion.

Then what are you doing here?

Before she could continue this ridiculous argument, the door opened and Felicity burst into her room.

"My *Chronicles!*" she exclaimed. "I've forgotten them. I know you said we are to stay in our room, but Miss Porter, I left them downstairs—"

Miranda glanced heavenward. There was Fate, and then there was Felicity.

"I doubt anyone will bother them," she told her, as she guided the girl back to her room.

"I'm not worried about anyone taking them, Miss Porter. I'm afraid of someone reading them."

Miranda paused. *Reading them?*

The calamity in Felicity's confession now struck terror in Miranda's heart.

Oh, dear God, what if Jack read what was written on those pages?

. . . Miss Porter would be the prefect bride for a former rake of limited means like Lord John.

What if he thought she'd had something to do with their arrival at Thistleton Park? Or worse, if he thought Felicity's nonsense wasn't such a bad notion? As much as Jack could still leave her trembling, marriage to such a man was inconceivable. She might be a bit distracted by the madness of this house, but she wasn't about to lower her standards as to the perfect mate.

A gentleman in all things. An honorable man always. A man of nobility and integrity.

A man whose kiss . . .

Never mind his kiss, she told herself. That was exactly the point of why she needed to get out of this house. Escape this insanity before Felicity or Fate had their way.

Miranda turned to the girl. "Exactly where did you leave it?"

"On the hall table, near the library."

Miranda nodded and threw her shawl over her shoulders. There was nothing to be done but to go fetch it.

Before it was too late.

"Do not leave this room," she admonished the girls before she closed the door behind her and made her way downstairs, quickly and quietly.

"Felicity, do you really think this will work?" Pippin whispered after Miss Porter's steps retreated down the hallway.

Her cousin nodded. "Of course. Did you see them tonight? Jack kept staring at her, and when they ran into each other at the foot of the stairs . . . it was ever so romantic. I would bet my next quarter's allowance that with a bit more time together they end up wed."

Tally sat up in bed. "That might be true, but there was more at work tonight than just your matchmaking, Fe-

licity. I think they could fall in love if it weren't for . . .
for . . ."

"Weren't for what?" Pippin asked.

"I don't know," Tally admitted. "But there was something else going on tonight, something I think we are missing."

"The only thing we are missing is more time," Felicity said, frowning at the door. "Miss Porter is so determined to leave. There has got to be a way to prevent us from leaving tomorrow."

Tally chewed at her bottom lip and thought about it for a few moments. Then suddenly her fair features brightened. "Duchess, do you remember when we had to leave Vienna and Nanny Birgit was in such a state of it?"

"Uh-huh," Felicity said distractedly as she paced about, trying to come up with a new plan of attack.

Tally continued, "And she bribed the stableman to make the horse appear lame so we wouldn't be able to leave for a few more days?"

Felicity stopped midstride, then spun around and looked at her sister, an excited light in her eyes. "I remember. She had that lad do something to the horse's shoe." She turned to her horse-mad cousin. "Pippin, you could do it."

"Do what?" she asked.

"Make one of the horses go lame."

At this, Pippin scrambled out of bed. "I will not harm one of Papa's dear horses."

Felicity shook her head. "You aren't going to hurt the poor beast, just keep it from pulling that carriage Mr. Stillings found." She towed her cousin over to a settee and settled her down on it. "Think. What could you do—" For her cousin's benefit she added, "—that wouldn't harm the horse."

Pippin looked from one sister to another. She wasn't so convinced about all this matchmaking business, but it was so very important to Felicity and Tally. And Miss Porter had seemed different tonight, and Jack . . . She sighed. Jack might be a bit old, but he was rather charming. "I suppose—" she began, the two other girls leaning closer to listen. "If we snuck out to the stables and—"

Just down the stairs and toward the library, Miranda told herself. She'd fetch Felicity's *Chronicles* and be back upstairs before . . .

Before she ran into Jack.

Miranda pulled her shawl tighter.

Tell him . . . tell him the truth, the very walls of the house seemed to whisper.

Oh, perhaps she owed him that much. She'd set him free, and she'd be free as well.

And if he wanted to kiss her, well then . . .

Miranda came to a faltering stop. There would be no kissing. None whatsoever, she told herself sternly. She would tell him the truth and then continue on to her new life in Kent. Where she could spend the rest of her life hiding. Or building a tower . . .

Goodness, she needed to get out of this house, or she'd be as mad as a good portion of the Tremont clan.

From down in the dark recesses of the house came a sound that drew her out of her reverie and sent a chill of fright running down her spine. So much so, that she clutched the railing to keep from tumbling down the stairs like poor Isolda.

For there from the library, came the echo of voices raised in anger.

That would not have been enough to stop her, if it hadn't been for the fact that one of the voices rising in heated argument was female.

A woman?

"What do you mean, you don't have the money?" Jack was saying, his deep voice carrying through the thick door. "How am I to pay Dashwell without the gold you promised?"

"Jack, dear, I did my best," the lady replied.

A woman? He had a woman in there? And he was demanding money from her?

Miranda pressed her lips together. Sir Norris had the right of it. Jack Tremont was no gentleman.

"Your best is not good enough," he was saying. "You promised to have the money in a sennight, and that time, madame, has come and gone."

"I can't very well conjure a fortune out of thin air," the lady shot back. "Besides, I have it on good authority that we are being watched. It isn't as easy to come and go as it was."

"Being watched? Nonsense. There is no one about."

He paused for a moment, and Miranda felt a renewed chill in her veins.

No one but the unexpected arrival of a spinster and three girls, Miranda drew a slow and steadying breath. Surely he didn't think they had anything to do with his problems.

Whatever those may be.

Miranda's curiosity drew her closer, down a few more steps. She told herself she needed to discover the truth of this mystery if only to ensure that the girls didn't become embroiled in some scandal. But honestly, what she wanted to know was the truth about Jack.

"There is your husband," he was suggesting. "Surely, my good Mrs. Pymm, he has the money?"

"Oh, now I'm 'Mrs. Pymm' to you! That's a fine state of things between us."

"Don't think," he shot back, "you can use our familiarity to get out of your obligations."

The lady was married? And owed Jack a fortune?

The small measure of vindication Miranda felt—for she'd suspected all along something wasn't right about this house—also left her feeling more than a little piqued.

What did she expect? Once a rake . . .

Jack's voice rose again. "My gold, Mrs. Pymm. With no more arguments, no more delays."

But what could he need gold for? Blackmail? Debts? She glanced toward the windows and thought about his nightly forays. With the Channel at his back, perhaps he was up to his neck in smuggling.

She slowly slid down the rest of the stairs, keeping to the shadows, her gaze riveted on the library doors as Jack continued his tirade.

"That parsimonious old bastard you married has the money. I know it and you know it. How can you come here saying you don't have the gold I need? I've been more than patient with you on this, but I will not be pushed for much longer. There is too much at stake."

There was another exchange, but Miranda couldn't hear it, so she drew closer.

Felicity's *Chronicles* were forgotten; her fears of him reading the now seemingly innocuous musings of a schoolgirl were far removed from the drama being played out in the room beyond.

"My darling boy, I'll get you the money, but not until I know that you have—"

Miranda stepped even closer still, only to find Mr. Jones looming out of the shadows and into her path.

"Where you going there, miss?" he said, catching hold of her.

"Unhand me," she told him, struggling to get out of his grasp. She pointed at the door. "I heard . . . that is . . ."

The voices inside the library immediately stilled. Miranda's heart lurched as the door opened. What did she care if Jack had another man's wife in his house—other than the general impropriety of the situation?

But for a thousand reasons, none of which she understood, she did care. Suddenly and deeply. He was in there with a married woman. From whom he was extorting a fortune in gold.

What had her father said when he'd sent her away? *Once a rake, always a rake. He'll run through your money and break your heart.*

But for all her wild imaginings of what she was about to witness, to her amazement out came Jack strolling casually as if nothing were amiss. His eyes widened at the sight of his secretary holding her at bay.

"Mr. Jones, what is the meaning of this?" he asked. "Unhand Miss Porter. Immediately."

"But she was about to—"

"Bruno!" he said. "Release her!"

The big man heaved a meaty sigh and reluctantly started to let go.

Miranda shook herself out of his lingering grasp.

"Miss Porter, is there a problem?" Jack asked, as if he were suddenly the most caring and attentive of hosts.

She ignored his question and pushed past him, flying into the library, half afraid of what she was going to find.

Or rather whom.

But to her shock, the room was empty.

The great throne still sat in the corner. The shelves of books lined the walls. His desk, cluttered with account books and correspondence, lay before her.

And there was no one in sight.

She spun around. "Where is she?"

His brow rose in a quizzical arch. "Where is who?"

She paced around the room, looking behind the throne, under his desk.

"Where have you hidden her?"

"Miss Porter, I don't know what you are talking about. I was just working on my accounts when I heard your voice in the hall."

Her hands went to her hips. "Lord John, I know what I heard. And I heard a woman's voice. Inside this room. And you were arguing with her."

He had the temerity to shake his head. "My dear Miss Porter, I make it a rule never to argue with a lady. Perhaps you were just imagining—"

"My lord, I am not prone to fancies."

He swept a glance from the top of her chignon to the tips of her worn slippers. "I don't suppose you are."

Miranda sucked in a deep breath. And she'd been considering setting this wretch free.

She glanced around the library again, and this time her gaze fell on the window. A large one that she suspected led to the gardens.

Crossing the room in a flash, she tugged the curtains aside and began struggling to open it. She pulled and tugged at the sash, but the window held fast.

The rogue came over to her shoulder. "Miss Porter, if you need air, I should advise you to go out the front doors. That window probably hasn't been opened in a century."

Miranda let out a groan of frustration. "What have you done with her?"

Lord John shot a befuddled glance at his secretary, who wore an equally confused look. "Miss Porter, perhaps the day has been a little trying for you. Why don't you sit down and I'll have Mr. Joncs fetch you a restorative."

"I do not need a restorative," she shot back. "Where have you hidden her?"

When neither of them answered her, she went back into the foyer and examined the front door, which was still barred and locked for the night.

From behind her, Jack said, "As you can see, the only woman down here is you." He pushed off the door and walked over to her. "And what is it that brings you out of the sanctuary of your room, Miss Porter?" His eyes raked over her again, and there was a slight smile to his lips.

She looked around and realized that Mr. Jones was suddenly nowhere to be seen. He'd melded back into the shadows from which he'd appeared earlier, which meant she'd been left alone with Jack.

Alone with the rake.

"If you must know," she said, "I came down because Felicity forgot her notebook and was concerned about its welfare."

She dodged past him and retrieved it off the sideboard, holding it up for him to see, so as to prove her point.

"Must be something awful important in there to get you to come sneaking down here to fetch it. Care to share the contents with me?"

"Certainly not!" she told him tartly, at the same time tucking it safely behind her back. "This is Miss Langley's private journal and not meant for public enjoyment."

He shrugged, then grinned and tried to peek around her.

Miranda backed up until she bumped into the wall and found herself trapped.

Jack leaned in close, so close Miranda could see the beginnings of rough stubble on his chin, feel the heat of his breath upon her brow. Her body, unwilling to listen to reason, to remember that he was a rake of the worst kind, seemed to be having a regular celebration at his proximity.

An alarming thread of desire ran through her veins. Her thighs tightened as he drew closer. Her heart beat noisily, like the town crier eager to awaken her every nerve.

"Tell me about him," he was saying. It wasn't really a request but an order.

"About wh-wh-o-o?" she stammered.

"Him. The one missing the button."

She shook her head, her gaze fixed on his jacket, on the plain buttons hanging there by frayed threads. "He is of no consequence."

At least he was now . . . the devious wretch.

"Miss Porter, you are many things, but a good liar is not one of them." He came closer still. "Tell me about this man who haunts you still."

"He does no such thing. Like I said, he was of no—"

"Did he kiss you?"

"Wha-a-t?"

"Kiss you?" he asked, staring at her lips. "Do you still remember his kiss?"

With one hand clutching the *Chronicles*, her other went to her lips. She shook her head.

Jack grinned. "So he kissed you."

"It was only once," she blurted out, trying to find a way around him. He stuck his arm up and planted it on the wall next to her. Beside her, the sideboard kept her locked in place. "Only once, and like I said, it was of no—"

"Must have been some kiss for you to keep his button."

"Lord John—" Miranda protested. The hallway had suddenly grown terribly warm—from the heat of his body pressed so very close . . . and the memory of his kiss, which had always left her feeling flushed . . . and flustered . . .

"Jack," he told her.

"Wha-a-t?" She looked up at him, but it was hard to really look at him and not stare at his lips.

Those dangerous, kissable lips.

"Call me Jack."

"That would hardly be proper."

"I think you left proper upstairs when you decided to come wandering about my house in the middle of the night."

This time his words caressed, they teased, and they offered something that Miranda knew was better left alone.

The last time he'd kissed her, he'd ruined her.

What more could a man do to a woman?

Miranda gulped. She had to imagine that if anyone was capable of answering that question, it was Jack.

And then to her consternation, he showed her.

"Come closer, Miss Porter," he whispered, his eyes dark and full of smoky promise. "I wager I could give you a kiss that would turn your faithless lover into nothing but a distant and poor memory."

Miranda wavered under his mesmerizing spell. He was testing her, teasing her.

He was distracting her.

Distracting her?

Miranda stiffened. The wretched fiend was deliberately distracting her. As he had been all evening.

It certainly explained his sudden transformation from boorish lout to affable host.

Oh, yes, the grand stories, the carefully guided tour through his house, a bit of flirtation, all orchestrated so she wouldn't notice the incongruities.

The secretary who looked like a pugilist, the too-proper London butler. No housekeeper, no regular maids about. And what about the gentleman himself? A man who rode about the countryside at all hours? Lived in ramshackle poverty, when his charm had once made him the darling of Society? The sort who demanded a fortune in gold from a married woman?

And she'd defended him to Sir Norris.

Been about to tell Jack . . . never mind what she'd been about to tell him.

Miranda had never felt such a fool. Jack Tremont was the most despicable rake who'd ever lived.

"Get out of my way," she said, trying to nudge past him.

He closed the gap between them, his mouth dipping down toward hers. "Miss Porter, I thought we were reaching an accord, an understanding—"

She didn't let him finish. Instead, her free hand planted itself on his chest and gave him a good shove. It was enough of a surprise to knock him off balance, but only slightly, and not enough to give her the space she needed to escape. So she pulled out Felicity's *Chronicles* and put them to a better use than matchmaking.

She brought the thick notebook down on his head, where it landed with a solid *thump*.

"I'll breathe my last before I am cozened by the likes of you, Mad Jack Tremont," she said as she shoved past him, crossed the foyer in a flash of muslin, and took the stairs two at a time.

Miranda didn't know what deviltry was about this house, and she didn't care. They'd be gone at first light, and with every mile she gained between herself and

Thistleton Park, she'd utter a prayer of thanksgiving that she hadn't ended up married to this bounder.

But when she reached her door, she paused for a moment and looked back into the darkness behind her, her heart still pounding with the last remnants of the desire he'd teased so expertly from her.

For all her indignation, all her moralistic ranting, deep down inside, she knew that the worst of it was that she had desperately wanted him to kiss her.

And a part of her regretted that she hadn't let him delude her for just a few minutes more.

Birdwell and Bruno emerged from opposite sides of the foyer, their low chuckles revealing that they had seen more than enough of his encounter with Miss Porter.

"I don't see what's so funny," Jack muttered as he rubbed the top of his head. The little minx had given him a good wallop.

"Scared her good, eh, milord?" Bruno chuckled. "Looked like she finished the job for you. Put my money on her, next time you two go a few rounds."

Jack frowned at him. "She's not your usual lady."

"Because she didn't fall prey to your charms, my lord?" Birdwell asked. "Rather, I suspect the lady possesses a rare intelligence."

"Too intelligent," he said, glancing up toward the darkened stairwell and motioning them to follow him into the privacy of the library. "How much do you think she heard?"

Bruno shook his head. "Hard to tell. But she was snooping about for certain. Coming tiptoeing down the stairs. Didn't hear her until she was right next to me."

"You weren't asleep again, were you, Mr. Jones?" Birdwell asked.

"Asleep?" the man bleated. "Why of all the insulting—"

"It wouldn't be the first time" Birdwell pointed out to no one in particular.

"Milord—" Bruno protested.

Jack held up his hand, staving off any more of their bickering, at least for the time being. "All I want to know is how much she heard—she obviously heard enough to know I wasn't alone."

"In Mr. Jones's defense," Birdwell said, "it wasn't like you were using proper discretion. I'm surprised Sir Norris hasn't arrived, hoping to catch you at last."

"That will be the day," Jack said with a short laugh. "However annoying our neighbor may be, he isn't half as worrisome as Miss Porter and her charges. What the devil was she doing down here? A fine excuse, that notebook. No, I don't trust her."

"Hard to trust a woman who can flatten you like that," Bruno offered. "You don't think she was sent to look about, do you?"

Birdwell was shaking his head furiously before Jack could answer. "That's ridiculous, Mr. Jones. What sort of woman would use three innocent girls in such a deception? No, it is impossible that she has been sent here by our enemies."

Jack wasn't so sure. Miss Porter had him at sixes and sevens with her red hair and tart remarks. Could he have been so distracted that he'd mistaken the light in her eyes for desire, rather than the deception it might be?

He'd used his charm on more than one lady to get his way; who was to say a lady couldn't do the same?

"Do you think we're being watched, milord?" Bruno whispered. "Like her ladyship said?"

Jack glanced out the library door and into the darkness beyond. "I don't know. But I mean to find out."

"Miss Porter and the young ladies will be gone at first light," Birdwell said, continuing his defense of their guests. "Even if she heard anything, I am sure she drew the wrong conclusion, given your rather infamous reputation."

Jack shrugged off his butler's assurances. If Miss Porter had heard too much, well, then . . . he didn't want to think about what they would need to do.

Not that Bruno was opposed to such postulating. "Still think we ought to crate the lot of them up and sell 'em to Dash afore they discover what's about. 'Sides, the gold would come in handy since we ain't got what we were promised."

"Dash has taken my word in the past. Let us hope he is in a generous mood when he arrives," Jack said. "In the meantime, I need to go light the lamps and see if we can't lure him across the Channel, despite the fact that another storm is upon us. That cargo is imperative, now more than ever."

"What if I catch her nosing about the place?" Bruno asked.

Jack did his best to ignore the hope in his secretary's voice. "We'll cross that bridge when we come to it."

Bruno rubbed his hands together with glee. "Then I'll get me crates ready." He glanced over at a very indignant Birdwell and added, "Just in case."

Chapter 8

"Ladies, finish your breakfast so we can take our leave," Miranda said to her dawdling charges.

The girls stared down at their food and continued to pick at the tasty feast Mr. Birdwell had provided. Even Pippin, who could be counted on to finish several plates, was being unusually sluggish.

They were, Miranda decided, out of sorts over their failure to make their match.

On the other hand, the prospect of departing was brightening her mood immeasurably.

"This breakfast is marvelous, Mr. Birdwell. Lord John has an excellent cook," Miranda told him. "Please send our compliments."

The man bowed. "Actually, miss, I do the cooking."

Miranda's gaze swung up. Just when she thought

nothing more about this household could surprise her, here was this revelation.

"You, Mr. Birdwell?" Felicity asked. "Where did you learn to cook?"

"My father was the Duke of Haverford's chef. I learned at his able side."

"So why are you Lord John's butler?" Leave it to Tally to ask the question that was on everyone's mind.

Birdwell smiled at her. "My mother was the housekeeper at Haverford House. You could say I have many skills."

"You grew up in the Duke of Haverford's household?" Felicity sounded incredulous. "But they live in the north, and on a magnificent estate, if Mr. Billingsworth's travel account is to be trusted, while Thistleton Park is . . . is . . ."

"Such a steep descent?" Birdwell offered.

"Precisely," Felicity said, never one to dwell on niceties. "I would think you could have employment wherever you would like."

"Life doesn't always turn out as we plan, Miss Langley. No matter how well we think we have matters in hand."

It was the resigned finality to his statement that gave Miranda pause. Suddenly Jack's butler had a secret of his own—something quite substantial if it kept him from the refined and hallowed homes of London or the lofty reaches of Haverford House.

Miranda glanced over at the kindly old man and realized that perhaps Birdwell wasn't so out of place at Thistleton Park as he had seemed before.

"You don't still have any contact with Haverford House, do you?" Felicity asked over her shoulder.

"No, miss," Birdwell told her. "I do not."

That sealed it for Miranda—the once seemingly innocent butler also harbored a dark secret. Was there anything about this house that wasn't embroiled in mystery?

Felicity heaved a sigh. "That's unfortunate. I was hoping you had some information for me on the current duke's heir."

The butler did his best to hide a sly smile as to the girl's tenacity.

"So how is it that you came here, Mr. Birdwell?" Tally asked. Like her sister, Tally thought nothing of prying.

The man came around the table and filled their teacups. "I was previously employed by his lordship's brother, the Duke of Parkerton, at his London residence. When Lord John was"—the man paused and refilled Miss Porter's cup—"given the opportunity to live here, I came with him. It seemed to be where I was needed most."

"Well, I for one am glad you are here," Pippin told him. "I'd hate to see what Mr. Jones would do to the kitchens."

"And I as well," Birdwell told them, offering an uncharacteristic guffaw at such a notion.

Soon the girls were giggling as well, and even Miranda had to suppress a smile at the thought of the large and brooding Mr. Jones amidst the pots and pans.

Their good spirits lasted but for a short time before Tally turned a petulant face to her teacher.

"Miss Porter, do reconsider. I would dearly love to finish my sketch of Albin's Folly," she complained. "A few more hours, and I will be able to catch the very essence of the setting."

"You will have to rely on your memory and imagination, I daresay," Miranda told her, immune to their begging and ploys for a bit more time at Thistleton Park. They'd been making one bid after another to continue their stay since she'd roused them from their beds before dawn.

They had also been quite put out when they'd arrived in the dining room to find breakfast set out with only four place settings.

Apparently their host wasn't joining them.

"Jack will certainly think ill of us if we don't bid him a proper farewell. It will reflect badly on Miss Emery as well," Felicity said. She glanced over her shoulder at the butler standing in the corner. "Mr. Birdwell, doesn't Lord John usually arise early? He was up by now yesterday morning."

"Yesterday was unusual, Miss Langley," the man told her.

Unusual was the word for most everything and everyone around Thistleton Park, Miranda surmised.

Birdwell moved around the sideboard, straightening the trays and collecting the empty ones. "Lord John prefers to keep Town hours, and as such, sleeps until midday."

Leaving them free to flee while the lion was still in his den, or in this case, his bed.

"Lord John will understand if we are gone when he

arises," Miranda told them. "And no, Felicity, I will not listen to any more arguments about propriety, for I have penned a perfectly good note detailing our appreciation that Mr. Birdwell will pass along to our host."

She glanced at the clock on the mantel and sighed. "Really, girls, it isn't like you to dawdle like this over your meals. Mr. Stillings assured me that he would have the carriage ready by now, and if we are to reach Lady Caldecott's by nightfall, we must leave at once."

The girls glanced at each other, and she assumed they were urging one another to come up with some last desperate bid to change her mind.

Too late for that, she mused as the door to the dining room opened and Stillings came in, hat in hand. "Uh, ma'am?"

"Ah, Mr. Stillings, right on time," Miranda said, rising from her seat. "Glad to see someone is following our schedule this morning. If everything is ready, then the ladies and I will be—"

"That's just it, ma'am," he said, interrupting her smooth flow. "There's a bit of a problem."

A chill, not unlike the one from the night before, invaded her bones.

Their driver nodded toward the door. "If I could be having a word with ye, ma'am."

The ominous tone of his words set her teeth on edge, so much so that she forgot utterly to fold her napkin properly and place it where it belonged. Instead, it fell absently to the floor as she hurried after their driver.

"What is it, Mr. Stillings?" she asked once the door

to the dining room was closed behind her and they had moved to the far end of the foyer, well away from prying ears.

" 'Tis one of the horses. The lead beastie. He's gone and lost a shoe."

"Lost a shoe?" Miranda shook her head. Even with her limited knowledge of horses that sounded odd. "How did that happen?"

"I'm at a loss, I am, ma'am. Horses don't just lose shoes like that. Not all tucked up nice in their stalls, they don't."

A draft sped through the hall, bringing with it another chill of foreboding. "Can you put it back on?"

He shook his head. "That's what's so odd about it. I can't even find the damn thing. Pardon me for saying so, ma'am."

She waved at his apology. It wasn't like she wasn't thinking the same thing herself. "How could a horse just lose his shoe, let alone have the thing vanish?"

Stillings leaned in close. "I think this place is as accursed as they say."

"Sir, I doubt very much a curse would affect a horse's shoe."

The man sniffed, as if he thought such ways of the world were obviously beyond her ken, though Miranda had another theory about this unforeseen problem.

Mad Jack Tremont.

She drew a deep breath. "Now how do we go about getting a new shoe?"

As quickly as possible.

"The stable lad says the nearest smithy is in Hastings."

"Hastings! Surely there's someone closer?"

He shook his head. "The old smithy died about four months ago, and his apprentice is as likely to geld the animal as he is to get a good shoe on the poor beast."

"Perhaps he could put on a temporary—" she offered.

But Stillings looked horrified that she'd even consider such a notion. This would have been entirely easier if the earl's driver didn't look after the horses as if they were the actual heirs to the family fortune and title.

"Or perhaps we could just harness two of the horses and make a slower go of it. You did say the carriage you found wasn't as large—"

Given the outraged expression on the man's face, she might as well have suggested they use them to pull the oak out of the way. Really, they were just horses.

But not to their driver, and most likely not to the Earl of Stanbrook. If any harm came to the animals, she had to consider that the blame would land squarely on Stillings's large shoulders. He'd be sacked for certain, the earl reputed to care more for his cattle than for his lands or his family.

She doubted the safety of his daughter would have much weight in the matter.

Meanwhile, Stillings was shifting in place, passing his hat from one hand to the other. "I know you're keen to be going, but I don't see any other way about it than for me to go fetch the smithy."

"Yes, yes," Miranda said. "How long do you think it will take?"

"The morning to get there," he said. "The afternoon to return. See to the shoeing and we could be on our way tomorrow." Seeing the look of shock on her face, he added, "At first light, miss. That I promise you."

Miranda wanted to groan. Another day? She could just imagine what mischief the girls could manufacture in that time.

Not to mention their host.

"Then you had best be going, Mr. Stillings," she told him.

The man bobbed his head and took his leave.

She turned around and found Lord John standing on the staircase looking down at her. He had the same clothes on as the night before, albeit wrinkled and tousled. Why, if she didn't know better, she'd think he'd been up all night.

And if he'd been up all night . . .

"Problems, Miss Porter?"

As if he didn't know. She wouldn't put it past him to have removed the shoe himself. But whatever for?

His angry words from the night before rang out. *I will not be pushed for much longer. There is too much at stake.*

Gold. Money. Miranda did her best to still her pounding heart, her racing thoughts. What if he thought to get the money from them?

"A problem with one of the horses," she said, smoothing her hands over her skirt and not looking at him for fear he'd see the questions . . . and accusations . . . in her eyes. "One of our horses has lost its shoe, and our driver has gone to fetch the smith to remedy the situation. The earl is quite particular about his animals, so I fear we must impose upon on you for another day."

Jack strode down the stairs until he stood before her. "A smith? But that means he'll have to—"

"Yes, ride to Hastings, so it seems." She took a deep

breath. "If our continued presence in your home is an inconvenience, then perhaps other accommodations can be found—"

Now it was his turn to look exasperated. He ran a hand through his unruly mane of hair, then shook his head, leaving it as tousled as before. Really, he was quite the thespian, for he almost had her convinced that he was quite put out at this turn of events.

"Perhaps the inn isn't as bad as Mr. Birdwell believes, and we could remove ourselves—"

"No," he said, cutting her off. He forced a smile to his face. "Miss Porter, there is no need to flee Thistleton Park when it means only another day in each other's company." He ran his hand through his dark hair again. "I know that after last night . . . well, I must excuse myself, I was an utter cad. My behavior indefensible. Please allow me to make it up today, by—"

"Make up what?" came a question from behind them.

Miranda turned to find the girls standing in the doorway of the dining room. Given the way they were grinning, she could only imagine how much they'd heard.

More than enough, she'd reason.

"I must make up for my hasty departure last night," he told them. "It seems you are to stay another day, and I was just about to propose an outing, a picnic if you would like, to the folly."

"We get to stay?" said Tally. "Oh, wonderful."

"You can finish your sketch," Felicity pointed out.

"Lord John is being overly kind," Miranda told them. "But I am sure he doesn't need to need bother himself with our comings and goings. Besides, we need no escort—we found the way quite easily yesterday, and on our own, thank you very much."

Their host, it seemed, had found not only an apology in his bag of tricks but his manners as well. "Miss Porter, I would be bereft if any of you left with the impression that I am a poor host. I suspect my honor is at stake. Not to mention, I have Mr. Billingsworth's description to live up to—"

"Just yesterday you said the man was a pandering fool," she reminded him.

Jack grinned at her. "Even a fool deserves to be proven correct on occasion."

Miranda's hands balled into fists. Wretched man. He could twist the words of a saint.

Standing her ground, she said, "My lord, really it isn't necessary."

He drew closer. "My dear Miss Porter, you must be aware by now that compromise is not in my nature." He had the audacity to wink at her, then turn on one heel and stride toward the dining room. "Birdwell! Birdwell!" he called out. "We need a picnic, my good man." Then he turned back toward Miranda and added for her benefit, "A proper one."

"Harrumph." She wondered if such a thing was possible at Thistleton Park. A picnic at a folly. The irony of such an offer didn't escape her.

She straightened her shoulders and girded her resolve. If he thought a lost shoe would give him enough time to gain whatever boon he was seeking, he was sadly mistaken.

For last night, besides the missing shoe, he'd also lost any claim he might have had on her heart.

* * *

Jack led his guests down the trail to the folly. Better this, he knew, than let them have free run on his property. He didn't think the girls had anything to do with their mysterious and unlikely arrival into his life. Pippin's father, the Earl of Stanbrook, was too horse mad to ever be wrapped up in the sort of havey-cavey business that came naturally to Thistleton Park, while Tally and Felicity's father, Lord Langley, was renown in the right circles for his loyalty to the Crown.

Still, he couldn't shake the warning from last night.

I have it on good authority that we are being watched.

That left only Miss Porter . . . and how convenient was it that their horse had turned up with a missing shoe? Sounded to him like a plan concocted by a desperate woman.

How desperate? he wondered as he looked over at her.

He yawned, then took a deep breath of fresh air. He needed to keep a clear head today, but it was nearly impossible when he was dead tired. He couldn't remember the last time he'd gotten a decent night's sleep.

And every night more that Dash didn't arrive with his shipment, it put everything connected to Thistleton Park at risk.

In truth, the only thing keeping him awake at the moment was the chattering voices behind him. How was it that he'd forgotten how young ladies talked incessantly? His head was fairly spinning from the never-ending volleys the girls put back and forth to each other as he led them down the path toward Albin's Folly.

Miss Porter, he noted, was singularly quiet. And had been most of the morning.

It was as if she was weighing some great body of evidence, as if she thought *him* responsible for their current predicament.

Well, she was either the world's most accomplished actress or mad.

He decided mad would be the best conclusion. He didn't want to consider what would have to be done if she had been sent to ferret out the enigma that was Thistleton Park.

What he needed to do was discover Miss Porter's secrets. He glanced over his shoulder and realized the best place was to start with the allies he knew he had.

"Is it true you can see the coast of France from the top of the tower?" called out Tally, pushing past her teacher and coming up to his elbow.

He glanced down at her and smiled. "Yes, and since the weather is finally clear, perhaps you would like to take a peek at old Boney himself."

"Bother the man," she replied. "I detest him. Father brought us to an audience with him years ago, during the peace in '01. He was a cocky, smug fellow then and even more loathsome now."

"Who's loathsome?" asked Felicity, as she joined them.

"Bonaparte," her sister said.

Felicity's pert lips curled. "Odious, awful man. Whatever are you doing discussing him?"

"Jack suggested we look for him from the top of the tower, since the weather is clear. I think the vista will make a great sketch."

Felicity looked singularly unimpressed. But Jack had to imagine he knew a subject that would get the girl chattering once again.

"Duchess," Jack said, lowering his voice to a conspiratorial whisper. "Tell me about your Miss Porter."

At this, the girl's eyes brightened with a calculated spark. "What would you like to know?"

"Hmm," he said, rubbing his chin and slanting a glance back at the lady. "Where is she from? That is, where did she come from before she was a teacher?"

Felicity pursed her lips. "I don't know. She was there when we arrived three years ago." She turned to her twin. "Tally?"

Her sister shrugged. "Her father was in trade. I think in London, but I remember once she talked about how cold winter is in Northumberland."

That wasn't much to go on, Jack realized. "Has she ever had any visitors? Gone to visit her family? Perhaps had a suitor?"

The girls giggled.

"A suitor? You must be teasing," Tally said.

Felicity explained it further. "Miss Emery strictly prohibits her teachers from indulging in such things. Miss Porter would have been sacked if she'd been discovered keeping company with a man—no matter how eligible he might be."

"And why is it that she's escorting you, not one of the other teachers?"

"She isn't a teacher any longer," Tally told him. "When she gained her inheritance this past winter, she gave her notice."

So Miss Porter was rich? When they'd mentioned it

the night before, he hadn't thought much of it. Now Jack took another look at the lady. There was no evidence of her wealth in her simple gown and decision to travel with three young charges.

Felicity continued. "Must have been a good amount of money, for Miss Browne's maid told us that she heard from the kitchen boy who takes the trays into the teacher's dining room that Miss Porter had taken a house in Kent. And a grand one at that. So it must have been a notable fortune."

"But who left her this money?" he asked.

Felicity shrugged. "I don't rightly know. Though she's paid whoever it is their due respect. She's just come out of mourning this past fortnight, but before that she was in black for a good six months."

Jack remembered the ugly jet bombazine she'd been wearing when he'd been in Bath.

Could it have been her mysterious lover? The man from the button who'd left her this legacy?

Before he could make any further queries, they arrived at Albin's Folly and at Miss Porter's bidding the girls pulled out their sketch books and set to work on their drawings. Then Miss Porter settled on a nearby rock and pulled knitting needles and a ball of yarn out of her bag to work on what appeared to be a sensible stocking.

No French silk for Miss Porter, just good English wool.

"When I am done," Tally said over her sketchbook, "I want to do a drawing of the vista from the top of the tower."

"The top?" protested Miss Porter as she frowned up

at the stony heights. "Why don't you make do with a sketch of the shoreline?"

Sketches of the shoreline? Jack shot a suspicious glance at her.

Really, what Miss Porter suggested was nothing more than innocent sketches. There was no harm in that.

Then again . . .

What would his enemies do with detailed maps of the Park? Or worse, the house? And if they discovered the other secrets the ancient manse held, there would be hell to pay.

Demmit, he wasn't cut from the right cloth for this sort of thing. Smugglers like Dash . . . Dissemblers like Mrs. Pymm . . . His chameleon-like friend, Temple.

But Jack, he was a charlatan in all this. One slipped word, one false step, and lives could be lost.

And then there was Miss Porter's mysterious power over him. The way the lady haunted his thoughts, drove him to distraction.

He groaned and kicked at a stone, which landed at Miss Porter's feet.

She jumped a bit, then glanced up from her knitting.

"My apologies," he said.

"Something amiss, Lord John?"

It could have been an innocent question, but he was filled with misgivings today and was finding enemies in every quarter.

"You really needn't spend your day with us, Lord John," she told him. "We are quite able to find our way back to the house. I would assume you have business to attend to. I noticed that the shipwright and his crew of carpenters arrived this morning. Perhaps you are anxious to oversee the removal of your oak. Undoubtedly, it will be a valuable addition to your coffers . . . if it is properly managed."

"The shipwright has the task well in hand," he told her. "Besides, I would rather spend the day with you lovely ladies." He shot a saucy wink at Pippin, who blushed furiously at his lighthearted flirtation.

Miss Porter sniffed a little and went back to her knitting.

Jack ignored her apparent disapproval and silent admonishment.

A proper gentleman would see to his business ventures himself.

Well, he was hardly the proper country gentleman.

And that was the problem.

"Doesn't your secretary have something to do?" she asked, nodding at Bruno as he loomed over Tally's shoulder, staring moodily down at the girl's work.

"He is very efficient. I am sure he has everything in hand," Jack told her.

"Harrumph. He seems an odd choice for the position."

Jack looked over at the man and shook his head, as if he didn't see at all what she did.

She sighed and set her knitting down, leveling him with a pointed stare. "Mr. Jones looks more like a pugilist than a gentleman's secretary."

Jack glanced over at his bearlike man of letters and shrugged again, if only to vex her. "Believe me, he came highly recommended, and I have yet to see an equal in his skills."

At forgery . . .

But there was no need to add that to the catalogue of incongruities she seemed to be compiling.

"Are you always so outspoken in your observations, Miss Porter?" This time he watched her face, her eyes, and in them he spied a wary light, as if she was considering her next words carefully.

But before she came up with a proper answer, Bruno could be heard saying to Tally, "You've a fine hand, miss."

Both Jack and Miss Porter glanced over at the pair.

"A real talent for drawing," Bruno continued. "But the perspective is a bit off here," he said, pointing at one spot and then another, "and here."

The girl glanced over her shoulder at him and then stared down at her drawing. Looking back up at the tower before her, she nodded. "How right you are. Thank you, Mr. Jones," she said, rubbing out the portions he'd suggested. "Are you an artist, sir?"

He shook his head. "Me dah was. An engraver."

"And you didn't follow him into the trade?" Felicity asked.

"I learnt it alright, but I was—" Bruno started to say.

"Is anyone hungry?" Jack asked, changing the subject, lest too much be said or asked about Bruno's past.

Pippin set aside her notebook and pencil almost immediately, rising up and eagerly offering to help Mr. Birdwell unpack the feast.

While she set to work, Tally made a few finishing changes to her drawing, then rose and gazed up at the tower before them. "I would so love to see the view."

"It is a rather dusty and long climb to the top," Jack told her, hoping to discourage her.

To his dismay, this only seemed to add to her determination, then her sister's as well.

"Lord John, the Duchess and I have climbed far more difficult vantage points than your tower," Tally told him. "As our father would say, the climb will only serve to whet our appetites."

Their appetites were the least of his worries; it was their curiosity that he wanted to blight.

Miranda had no choice but to follow the girls up and into the tower. Her protests about the dangers of such a climb were met with a bored look from Felicity.

What did she expect? The Langley sisters had crossed the Russian steppes in the dead of winter, braved the trip to and from India, and toured the bazaars of Constantinople.

Albin's Folly probably presented no more danger to the intrepid pair than an afternoon tea with one of the more exacting patronesses of Almack's.

Yet she couldn't let them go up there alone with Lord John, so there was no choice in the matter but to trail along behind.

Once inside, she found it wasn't quite as dark and dreary as one might have thought. Daylight stole in from the narrow slits in the stone, crisscrossing the rising stairs like mummers' ribbons.

The stairs curved around the walls, only wide enough for one person to traverse them. The higher they rose, the more dangerous it became, for there was no railing, only the occasional handhold.

Jack strode nimbly up the steps, and only when he was a quarter of the way up did he glance back to see how she was faring.

"Do you need a hand, Miss Porter?" He held his out for her.

"No," she told him, probably a little too sharply, for the idea of having to hold his hand startled her more than the idea of plummeting to her death.

She might be resolved not to trust him, but that didn't mean he still didn't have some influence over her—for even as she watched him climb before her, it was difficult not to give his athletic form a bit of scrutiny. Those broad shoulders, muscular legs encased in tight breeches, and his tight . . .

Miranda closed her eyes and chastised herself for even looking at his . . . his . . . oh, bother, his derrière.

There was no question now, this place was making her as addled as Mrs. Hibbert's second cousin. It was the only explanation as to her fascination with his charms . . . his kiss . . . and dare she admit it? His tight and well-shaped backside.

She shook her head. It was as if every lesson in modesty she'd ever taught had deserted her.

Luckily for her overwhelmed senses, he climbed up into the top of the tower and out of sight. So, she continued onward and upward, silently recounting every lesson she could recall on the evils of unrepentant rakes.

When she arrived, Jack and the girls stood by one of the large open windows.

Miranda came closer, until she looked out and realized just how far down it was to the waves below. Sited as it was at the edge of the cliff, and rising five stories above that, the top floor of the folly made her dizzy.

"Afraid of heights?" Jack asked as she took a hasty step back.

"Not in the least," she told him, steeling herself and returning to the window.

Below, the waves crashed into the shore, while before them, the Channel stretched for as far as the eye could see.

"Can you really see France from here, Jack?" Tally asked, obviously disappointed not to be able to see its foreign shores.

He nodded, and reached up onto a shelf, pulling down a looking glass for her. "See for yourself."

She held it up to her eye and peered through it for a few moments. Then a great smile spread across her face. "Look, Felicity, France!" the girl said excitedly, handing it over to her sister.

Felicity took her turn, then pointed the glass down toward the ground. "There's Pippin waving at us to come down for nuncheon." She handed the glass to Jack. "We'd best hurry or she'll have taken all the cakes for herself." She caught Tally's hand and all but towed her sister down the stairs, leaving Jack and Miranda completely alone.

"That was subtle," he said, smiling at the now empty space beside them.

"What do you mean?" Miranda asked, trying to feign innocence. The last thing she needed was for him to suspect their true reasons for being here.

"Their efforts at matchmaking," he said, circling around her, confirming her worst fears.

She turned slowly, watching him. "I don't think that's at all what they—"

He tipped his head at her as if he expected her to do better than that.

"'Tis a ridiculous notion, sir," she told him, her hands going to her hips. "I have no desire to be 'matched.'"

"Then you had best make sure the Duchess knows of your wishes, or you will continue to find yourself alone with me." He eyed her again, then continued circling her like a tomcat.

Blessed saints, couldn't the man just stand still? What with the heights up here, and his spinning around her like a top, she was about to topple over.

"Their efforts—if you insist on calling them that—will come to naught," she said. "And do stop moving about like that, you are making me dizzy."

"Perhaps it's your corset," he teased.

"My wh-what?" she stammered, feeling as if he'd just tugged her strings tighter.

"Your corset." He pointed at her gown, and she felt her nipples tighten as if he'd touched her there. "I would imagine you have it too tight."

And suddenly it felt too snug, for he was coming closer, closing the gap between them, and she was having trouble breathing.

He's a wretch. He's trying to distract you again, she told herself. But her body wasn't listening. Her breasts felt heavy, her thighs ached, her mouth was dry. In a heartbeat, she was sixteen again, pressed against the wall of the Opera House, and his hands, his lips were upon her . . .

"Leave my corset out of this," she managed to say.

"It would be no trouble, Miss Porter," he said, coming to stand just behind her. "I have a knack for these things."

Oh, yes, well I know . . .

"My lord, if this is more of your infamous charm, I would like to point out that I'm—"

"I could loosen it for you," he offered, moving behind her.

She gasped. *Loosen her corset?*

"So you wouldn't have so much trouble breathing," he said in a low, heated voice.

"I'm . . . not . . . having . . . any trouble . . . breathing," she wheezed.

"Ah, but I think you are," he whispered into her ear, his heated breath fanning across her shoulder, leaving her trembling, unable even to draw a breath.

Then, when she thought she couldn't take any more of this, he caught her in his arms and spun her around so that she faced him. His grasp was sure and commanding, his body hard against hers. That hardness was a shock in itself, for it frightened her and made her long for something she didn't understand.

"My lord—" she managed to whisper.

"Jack," he told her, his hand cupping her backside and tugging her up against him. Up against his masculine length.

"Oooh," she gasped, what sounded more like a moan than a protest. There was no denying that he had her spellbound and full of longing. Willing to give herself over to the inexplicable desires he brought boiling and tossing to the surface with only his touch.

She was lost already, and he hadn't even kissed her.

* * *

Jack had never taken a woman in anything other than mutual seduction, but he knew he was crossing the line with Miss Porter.

Damn the woman and her red hair. She had been a fixture in his dreams for months, and now with her at Thistleton Park, she was driving him mad.

Mad with desire. And that didn't even take into account her meddling ways and her persistent questions.

But she could only act so long, and he was about to test her resolve and see how far she would play this game of cat and mouse.

Staring down at her, he wondered which part in the contest he had. It hadn't taken but a moment of teasing, a second to haul her into his arms, and he'd gone hard with desire. It was instantaneous and downright painful the way this woman tempted him.

Not that he was the only one being affected. Her hips had met his with feline appreciation, rocking against him, tracing his hardness in heady exploration.

His hands roamed over her back, where he could feel the smooth line of her corset, which meant the strings were in the front. From the back of his throat, a growl came out, a male celebration at the idea of opening her corset from the front, of freeing her ripe, full breasts one at a time and taking one of her taut nipples in his mouth.

He nuzzled her neck and whispered into her ear, "Come now, Miss Porter, let me see all your secrets. Let me *taste* them."

She shivered, even as his hand cupped one of her breasts, found the nipple there, and rolled over it.

His hunger for her knew no bounds and so he sought her lips, sought her mouth so he could taste her, while his hand went to work on her knotted corset strings.

What sort of woman knotted her corset strings twice?

But before he could lower his lips to hers, before he could devour her with a kiss, mark her and make her his . . .

"Miss Porter? Miss Porter? Are you coming down?" Pippin called out from the stairs. "Mr. Birdwell says the picnic is ready."

The girl's words were enough to break Miss Porter out of the spell he'd cast.

"Goodness!" she gasped, pushing herself out of his arms. "Leave me be." Her cheeks flamed to a deep blush.

The panic in her words snapped something inside him and he released her instantly, stepping back from her and seeing all too clearly the truth.

What the devil had he been thinking? This was no seductive spy sent to ferret out the secrets of Thistleton Park. One look into her eyes, at the mixture of fear and desire that had driven her into flight, and he knew the truth. She was no more than a spinster.

A passionate one, but from the color of her cheeks, more innocent than not.

And he, a lonely man with obligations that weighed so heavily on his heart and soul that he'd wanted to believe something of her that wasn't true.

And in the process, he'd made a fool of himself.

"I . . . I . . ." he stammered.

"You, sir, are no gentleman," she whispered.

Jack's guilt melted slightly. It wasn't as if he was the only one up here still filled with desire. Her nipples poked out from her bodice, and he had to imagine she was as wet as she was hopping mad. "And you are no lady."

"How dare you!" she sputtered as she snapped up her shawl and wound it back around her shoulders. "And I suppose you are going to claim I encouraged you."

"You didn't protest when your scheming little charges left us up here alone." She sputtered again, but he didn't let her have a chance to get a word in. "Then again I suppose those girls see what neither of us is willing to admit, Miss Porter," he told her.

"And what would that be?"

"We're well matched." With that, he winked at her and left her stammering and sputtering after him as he made his way down the stairs.

Well matched! And he didn't mean in the marital sense, she had to imagine. The odious man. Miranda paced about the top floor of the tower, struggling to compose herself.

How had he overcome her so easily? She paused for a second, feeling foolish. That wasn't so difficult to answer, given the way her heart still pounded furiously in her chest, the ache of longing between her legs—slick and hot and tight from having had his rock-hard manhood thrust up against her.

She was trying with all her might to ignore the fact that her hips had rocked rebelliously against him. Ignore the desire to touch herself there and finish what he'd started.

Oh, if Jack was right about anything, she was no lady. For what kind of woman found herself standing in an empty tower, panting and longing for a man who was the worst sort of rake?

A man capable of almost anything.

Almost anything . . . He had let her go when she had protested. If he hadn't, if he'd continued his determined seduction, managed to gain her mouth, kiss her protests away, she didn't trust that her "no's" wouldn't have turned to sighs of *Please, Jack. Please!*

Cut my corset strings. Strip me of this proper gown. Torment my dreams no longer.

Miranda went to the open window and took a deep breath of the bracing, salty air rising from the crashing waves below. Then another and then as many as it took to clear her thoughts.

She turned from the window and sat down on the only thing in the room, a sturdy sea chest. However was she going to escape him for the next fourteen hours? Until the sun rose again and she could hightail it away from Thistleton Park to her nice, safe house on the far side of Kent?

She rocked back and forth, her knees curled up to her chest, as she considered her choices. Seeking shelter at Sir Norris's was one option, but as improper as Jack may be, Sir Norris was . . . well, Miranda shuddered and dismissed the man from her thoughts.

Her hand dropped absently to the side of the chest and her fingers curved around a thick padlock.

A lock?

This stopped her musings in their tracks and brought forth her natural curiosity. Whatever would one keep up here that required such a sturdy lock? She got up from her perch and stared down at the chest. She couldn't imagine how it had been hauled up here, but in the next instant, she had to wonder what was in the box that had been deemed so important it had been carried up five floors.

She glanced over her shoulder at the opening in the floor where Jack had disappeared. The echo of his tromping footsteps had long since faded away, so he was well and gone.

So she looked back at the chest again.

No, you shouldn't, she tried telling herself. *'Tis improper to snoop.*

Then again, as he'd said to her last night, she'd left proper behind when she'd arrived at his house.

Besides, the lock was fast, so there really wasn't any chance of opening the thing . . . unless the key could be found.

She straightened and looked around the room slowly, her eyes narrowing as she made her sweeping inspection.

If he had taken to a life of crime, say like smuggling, to support himself, then she felt a measure of guilt over the situation.

You are responsible for his fall, she told herself. *If Father hadn't lied about me being dead and Jack had been able to make an honorable offer for me (which I would have refused without question), he might have led a respectable life.*

Then again, probably not, but she couldn't help but feel a little bit of blame.

Taking one last glance around the room, she finally spied it. A bright brass key, hanging on a peg high over the opening to the stairs. She could never reach it, given its dangerously lofty perch, but then she had another idea, and caught up the spyglass, pulled it out to its full length, and used it to flip the key from its hanger.

For a split second she thought it was going to go tumbling through the opening and down the stairs, but she snatched it out of the air just in time.

And before she had any second thoughts, she shoved the key into the hole and turned it until the lock sprang open. Even as her one hand went to the lid, and her other worked to pry the latch open, one startling question sprang to mind.

What are you going to do if you discover something odious in this box?

Like a raft of French brandy?

Or the body of that woman from last night?

She reeled back and eyed the chest with a healthy dose of trepidation. Curiosity was a demanding mistress, and Miranda knew she'd never be able to walk away from this Pandora's box without taking just one small peek.

Really, her hesitation was nothing more than too many hours in the carriage listening to Tally reading aloud from her gothic novels or giving heed to claims of curses.

Then from down below she heard Pippin laughing, a sound full of happy innocence. It sparkled with sunshine and made her dark thoughts seem all that much more ominous.

If those girls were in harm's way, she had a duty to see them safe.

That thought was enough to square up her resolve, and she wrenched open the lid.

As she peered down into it, she discovered that her imagination was as overwrought as Tally's novels.

For inside there was nothing but a pair of lanterns, spare wicks, flints, and a coil of rope.

She sat back and sighed. Hardly condemning evidence this. Nothing unusual, really.

Drawing a deep breath, she let it out. And even as she took her next one, a familiar odor filled her nostrils.

She poked her nose back into the crate and dug around some more, until her fingers curled around the butt of a pistol, her other hand landing on a small powder keg—so that was the acrid scent that had caught her attention. No wonder it was so familiar; her father's warehouse had from time to time held naval commissions of gunpowder.

She searched a bit further when something heavy jangled from beneath the coil of rope. She closed her fingers over it and pulled it free—only to find an evil-looking pair of manacles hanging before her stunned eyes.

A pistol? Manacles?

When added to Lord John's odd collection of servants, the disappearing woman, and Sir Norris's accusations, Miranda didn't know what to think.

This went beyond a little bit of illegal trade in French brandy.

What the devil was going on at Thistleton Park?

Folly of a very dangerous sort, she realized, putting everything back in its place. Glancing out across the sea at the endless waves, she felt more perplexed than ever by this impossible man.

A man who seemed destined to leave her scandalized and, at the same time, adrift with desire.

Chapter 9

Once back at the house, Miranda knew there was no better diversion than a bit of hard work, so she threw the doors to the music room open and directed the girls to set to work cleaning it. While they balked a bit at first, when an exquisite pianoforte was discovered under a Holland cover, Tally was inspired.

"No playing until this room is spotless," Miranda told her. Thus ordered and motivated, Tally bullied her sister and cousin into helping her, all the while gazing longingly at the wonderful and long-unused instrument.

If anything, Miranda reasoned, the labors would leave them too exhausted to hatch any more of their schemes. And to her further delight, Mr. Stillings arrived with the blacksmith. She left the girls to their labors while she went out to listen to their driver's report and pay the craftsman.

Not a minute later, Felicity stopped in the middle of the room. "I don't know why I didn't see this before!" She rushed about the room, yanking off the covers and throwing back the heavy drapes. "This is the perfect place."

"Perfect place for what?" Pippin's nose twitched back and forth. "An airing? This room has a very odd smell to it."

"Romance!" Felicity declared, throwing open the French doors that led outside. Beyond lay a very neglected rose garden that looked like it hadn't seen the touch of a spade or shears in twenty years.

"I don't know," Pippin said, her nose still wrinkled.

"A bit of fresh air and flowers will do the trick," Felicity assured her. "We'll have an evening musical and invite Miss Porter and Lord John. Tally, you can play your Mozart. And then, when the mood is set, Pippin, you will find some excuse for all of us to leave them alone."

Pippin glanced around the dusty room. "I don't see how we can get this room in order in time. Miss Porter is out with Mr. Stillings and the blacksmith right now. It doesn't take that long to fit a shoe back on."

Felicity glanced toward the open door, then lowered her voice. "Then you should have seen fit to take off more than one."

Pippin bristled. "Next time you do it. It was hard enough getting the one off without being caught."

Felicity heaved a sigh. "But they need more time. Perhaps you could remove—"

Her cousin stopped her right there. "I can't very well sneak out and pry off another shoe. It will be too obvious."

"I suppose so," Felicity agreed. "If only there was another way."

Tally, who had been peeking beneath the Holland covers, looked up, her eyes alight. "Do you remember that time in St. Petersburg when we were delayed because the harnesses had been stolen? And Papa thought Nanny Tasha was responsible?"

Felicity grinned at her sister. "Yes, that's it! We'll steal the harnesses tonight."

"Really, don't you think that will be as obvious as the missing shoe?" Pippin pointed out.

Felicity turned to her cousin. "Then what do you suggest?"

The coltish girl paced about the room, as if considering their options. "Perhaps we could loosen some of the stitches, maybe break a couple of the buckles. Father once had a very clumsy stable lad who dropped a bucket of feed on his racing harness and it was completely unusable."

Felicity grinned. "That's perfect! Now all we have to do is lure Miss Porter and Jack in here, lull them with some romantic music, then we'll slip out and see to the harnesses."

Pippin shook her head. "Miss Porter is a stickler for propriety. She'll never remain here with Jack unattended."

"They were up in the tower for quite a while this afternoon," Felicity countered. "And would have remained so if you hadn't gone in there and called her down for lunch."

Pippin shrugged. "It wasn't proper for them to be up there alone." She thought the world of Miss Porter and only wanted her happiness. Sometimes Felicity and Tally were . . . well, a bit overbearing.

Felicity waved her off. "You sound like Miss Emery. Didn't you see Miss Porter's countenance when she came down? She looked particularly flustered. As if she'd been kissed."

Tally's mouth fell open. "You think Jack kissed Miss Porter?"

Her sister nodded sagely. "He is a rake and she is a woman."

Crossing her arms over her chest, Tally shook her head. "Then why didn't she look more pleased? In fact, she looked pale when she came down. And she certainly didn't let us linger over Mr. Birdwell's excellent picnic."

"No, she didn't," Pippin added. "And then nothing but lessons all afternoon up in our room. If she is a lady in love, then I'm not sure I want anything to do with it. It appears to be a miserable state."

"Well, it will all be for naught if we leave in the morrow without them forming an attachment," Felicity declared.

Pippin wasn't done making her case. Besides, she didn't look forward to an afternoon cleaning the music room. "Miss Porter hardly seems amenable to him, and all they've ever done is argue."

Felicity smiled. "But don't you see? They are just fighting nature."

"Ahem," came a discreet cough at the door.

Felicity and Pippin spun around, while Tally scrambled up from her unladylike slouch.

"Mr. Birdwell!" Felicity said, shooting a glance that

cried out caution to her compatriots. "I hope you don't mind, Miss Porter suggested we tidy up this room a bit so we may practice our music."

"Yes, our music," Tally enthused, rising and rushing over to the pianoforte in the corner. "Lord John mentioned he had a fondness for music and we thought—"

"Yes, I know what you thought," the old butler said. Then he winked at them and added, "And I find it an admirable notion."

Gooseflesh ran down Felicity's arms. With Mr. Birdwell's help, there would be nothing to stop them.

Miranda let out a sigh of relief when she arrived at dinner and Jack was nowhere to be found. Felicity, on the other hand, looked ready to go hunt the man up and bring him to the table at the end of a musket.

And apparently she'd have Birdwell's help as well.

"My deepest apologies, Miss Langley," he was telling her, "but his lordship has been delayed by pressing business."

Pressing business, bah! Miranda thought. Perhaps he'd found a new lady from which to extort gold.

Or whom he was seducing . . .

She pressed her lips together and pushed that thought aside.

"Will Lord John be gone all evening?" Felicity pressed.

"Miss Langley," she admonished. "Our host's business and schedule are none of our concern."

Tally poked her food around her plate with her fork. "I'd hoped he'd come listen to me play tonight."

Birdwell smiled at her. "Never fear, Miss Thalia.

When his lordship hears you on the pianoforte, you'll lure him away from his ledger book."

Miranda glanced from Felicity to Tally to Pippin and saw a spark of hope in their eyes. Oh, heavens. Not this again. And before she could nip their plans in the bud, the Duchess was one step ahead of her.

"It seems a shame, Mr. Birdwell," Felicity began, "that Jack never married."

Miranda nearly choked on her wine. "Felicity Langley!"

"Well, it is, Miss Porter," the girl protested. "He is a gentleman, and every gentleman should be induced to wed. Miss Emery says so."

There was no arguing with Miss Emery's prime directive, but there were exceptions to every rule, and there was no better example than Mad Jack Tremont.

"Lord John's life is his own concern," Miranda told them. "And it is not polite to speculate as to what he should or has not done."

The incorrigible Felicity was not to be stopped. "It is a dire shame, isn't it, Mr. Birdwell?"

The butler nodded. "A terrible one, miss."

The girl shot a triumphant glance across the table. Nor did it seem she was satisfied to have just found an ally. Felicity Langley was out to win the war. "I would think a man of Lord John's fine temperament would be lonely here at Thistleton Park. Surely he must miss Town."

And much to Miranda's chagrin, Birdwell fell into line like a career soldier. "A terribly lonely life, miss."

Having suffered under the delusion that she was actually in charge of these girls, Miranda knew she was going to have to make a last stand to halt this runaway matchmaking scheme.

"Felicity Langley, if you do not stop this inappropriate line of conversation, I will confiscate your *Chronicles* and dispatch them to Miss Emery."

Every bit of color drained from the girl's face.

There, that had done it. Now there would be no more of this nonsense, Miranda reasoned.

She'd reasoned wrong.

After a few minutes of quiet and proper dining, Tally dared to speak up. After all, she had no notebook to lose. "Miss Porter, perhaps you could persuade Jack to come listen to me play?"

Miranda's gaze swung up. "Me? Whyever do you think I have any influence on his lordship?"

Tally sat up straighter. "I believe he holds your opinions in high regard."

"Stuff and nonsense," Miranda told her.

"No, it is true," Pippin said, as if on cue. "Jack listens to what you have to say." The girl smiled a sly grin. "And he likes to look at you when you aren't looking."

"That does sound like he has a *tendre* for you, Miss Porter," Felicity pointed out, as if she were the expert on such matters.

And before Miranda could tell them they were all as bird-witted as she'd ever seen, there came a reply from the doorway.

"Who has a *tendre* for Miss Porter?"

She looked up and found Jack lounging in the doorway, a rakish grin pasted on his face. Gone was the scruffy, dangerous-looking man of the past few days, for he'd taken extra pains to dress for the evening.

Shaved and brushed—why, he'd even trimmed his hair, and this time with scissors, she had to imagine. He looked much as he had in his heyday in Town. The dark green coat may be nine years out of fashion, but he still wore it with style and vigor. To his credit, his cravat looked as snowy as if it had been washed and tended by the most lofty and finicky of valets.

She didn't even venture a glance at the tight cut of his buff breeches or the polish on his Hessians encasing his long, muscular legs.

Well, perhaps she did. Dear heavens, when he looked like that, it was easy to forgive him, easy to forget the dangerous man he'd hidden beneath this finery.

"Jack!" Felicity said. "You look so handsome."

"Oh, yes," Tally enthused. "Why, you would put the loftiest of dukes to shame. Your cravat is divine."

"Hardly," he told them. "I had to dig these out of a trunk. But you can compliment Birdwell for the cravat—he took special care to iron it for me. And then cautioned me against creasing it, for he wasn't about to do another one."

Pippin pointed at his jacket. "You are missing a button."

Miranda nearly choked on her wine. *Missing a button?* She looked at the coat again. Gracious heavens! It was the jacket he'd been wearing that night.

For his part, Jack glanced down at the missing trinket and shrugged. "Probably at the bottom of the trunk with the rest of my old Town clothes." He pushed off the doorjamb and came into the room as proud and stately as any Corinthian. "Now, isn't anyone going to answer me?" he asked. "Who has a *tendre* for Miss

Porter? And don't tell me it is Mr. Jones, for I'll sack him for his presumptions."

Tally giggled.

"No one," Miranda managed to tell him, trying to keep her eyes from his jacket. "The girls were just teasing—for really it is a ridiculous notion."

"And why is that?" he asked as he pulled his chair out and settled into the seat.

She only hoped her cheeks weren't as red as they felt. Oh, why couldn't he have just stayed absent?

Stayed away.

Left her in peace.

"My lord, please don't encourage them," Miranda said. "I have no delusions about my place in society. I am well past the age where I waste my time spinning dreams that are foolish at best." This comment she shot toward her erstwhile matchmakers.

None of them appeared to take her hint, for they had turned their heads to see how Jack would respond to this volley.

"I don't think age has anything to do with it," he replied, "when a lady is as pretty as you are, Miss Porter."

Her? Pretty? Spanish coin and false flattery if ever there was.

Tally let out a sigh, full of longing that suggested she couldn't wait for the day that a man said such a thing about her.

"You think Miss Porter is pretty, Lord John?" Felicity prodded, then cast an I-told-you-so glance back at her teacher.

"Miss Porter has a rare quality about her," he said,

and his gaze met Miranda's and held it in a look that could have melted all her resolve to leave Thistleton Park with her corset strings intact.

The way he looked at her, devoured her really, made her spine tingle, her skin grow warm, as if his fingers were on her corset strings and untying them with deft and experienced fingers.

She needed to say something, do something to break his hold on her, to end this ridiculous game, but words failed her. This dangerous rake made her feel dizzy, breathlessly so.

Oh, please say something, she willed herself. *Say something to end this perilous temptation.*

The silence was wearing on everyone, for the girls were now staring openmouthed at the pair of them, and the determined light in Felicity's eyes spoke of triumph.

That was enough to drive Miranda into action.

"Really, all of you are terrible teases," she said. "But I am quite content with my life and have never been regarded as pretty, despite Lord John's assertions." She paused and tapped her lips with her napkin. "Besides, you must remember that Lord John has been away from London for many years, and his memory and standards for beauty are not completely up to snuff."

Felicity's brows creased. Her displeasure over Miranda's continued and obstinate disregard for the prospect of marriage seemed enough to put her in a state of apoplexy. But she wasn't finished yet.

"Jack," she said sweetly, as if tossing out a honey-covered fishing line. "Do you like music?"

* * *

Miranda grit her teeth and entered the music room as if it were filled with French mines. Not only were the girls in open rebellion against her orders not to engage in any further matchmaking but, to make matters worse, Mr. Birdwell appeared their equal in audacity, if not in sheer determination.

Well, she certainly wasn't going to fall for the chicanery of three schoolgirls and a displaced London butler.

Not that Jack was doing her any favors. Why, the beast of a man had taken to Felicity's offer of an evening of music as if it were going to be presented in the finest London salon.

Still, when she entered the elegant room, it had the effect of bringing her back nine years to her own short Season—the candles fluttering in the corners, the flowers in the vases lending the rich scent of roses to the room. No tame hothouse flowers these, but spicy, heady blooms from the tangle of bushes that grew in wild abandon throughout the unkempt grounds of Thistleton Park.

It was a perfume that filled the senses with an air of persuasive temptation.

Like the master of the house himself.

"Upon my word," he exclaimed like a good London rake, "what mischief is all this?" He walked around the room admiring its transformation, seemingly oblivious to the spell it was meant to cast.

"'T'was nothing that a bit of cleaning and some fresh flowers couldn't accomplish," Felicity told him. "'T'was Miss Porter's idea."

Miranda cringed.

"It was?" he asked.

Cleaning, yes. That had been her idea. Not this orchestrated attempt to toss her yet again into Lord John's arms.

"It seemed a small way to repay your hospitality," she said.

Jack slanted a glance at her, the look on his face saying only too well that he'd caught the double entendre to her words.

A small favor for his pittance of hospitality.

He continued into the room, eyeing all the changes, then came to a sudden stop. "I have a pianoforte?" he asked, his brows cocked with a wicked tilt. "Whenever did I acquire this?"

"A tolerable one at that." Tally grinned at his teasing. "It was a wonderful find. Much better than the collection of dust curls we discovered behind the sofa."

He bowed to the three of them. "I should detain you all from ever leaving, for I imagine if I let you loose in the house for, at the very least, another fortnight, you would probably uncover all sorts of treasures—beyond my rare collection of dust."

As the girls laughed at Jack's wit, Miranda wondered just what sort of secrets they would indeed find—for if they were anything like the nefarious items she'd discovered in Albin's Folly, it was certainly better for all of them that they were leaving on the morrow.

Especially for her. For more dangerous than the manacles, the powder, and pistol was the way Jack sent her senses into a wild flight from reason.

Glancing over at the all-too-handsome man, with his dark brushed hair and chiseled jaw, she thought he looked more like a fallen angel than a gentleman.

And angels fell for very good reasons. This one was as mercurial as they came: boorish one moment, charmingly handsome the next, only to turn around and be forcefully seductive.

Which Jack Tremont was the true master of this house, she couldn't say.

The girls stood gathered around their host, chattering about their discoveries of music and rare vases and imported bric-a-brac, but he wasn't paying them any heed. His gaze rose over their heads, sweeping across the room until he found her.

A deep, piercing glance that drew out her desires for him like a summer moth to a candle. She shivered and wrapped her shawl tighter around her shoulders.

Resolve, Miranda, she told herself. *Remember the missing woman. His desperate need for gold.*

She felt a sudden urgency to turn his attention elsewhere.

"Thalia, perhaps you can show Lord John just what a valuable pianoforte he possesses by playing it for us."

Tally bobbed her head and hurried over to the instrument, in all eagerness to begin.

So with everyone diverted as Tally began to play, Miranda walked around the edge of the room, taking in both the music and what the girls had accomplished in the once dusty, unused room.

She stopped before an ancient chessboard, its pieces neatly arranged and waiting in their orderly lines for combat to begin.

Miranda couldn't help herself; she reached down and picked up a pawn. The board summoned forth memories of countless evenings spent sitting across from her father learning the fine art of chess, and listening to the tidbits about business and trade and organization he'd interjected into their games.

Sadly, she had realized only too late that her father had seen her as nothing more than a pawn in his own ambitions—to see her wed to improve his business. Her mother had been of the same bent, even without her knowledge of chess.

Miranda had been but a piece in her parents' ambitions. Yet a stray thought floated into her musings.

Even a lowly pawn could sometimes take the king.

"I am so sorry about today, Miss Porter," came a low voice as contrite and sincere as she'd ever heard. "My actions were most regrettable."

She looked up at Jack, the pawn still clenched in her hand. " 'Tis forgotten."

"Hardly so," he said, glancing across the room, as if gauging whether or not their conversation was being subjected to eavesdropping. "I see it in your eyes."

She glanced away and took a deep breath. "It is forgotten now."

It had to be. It was too dangerous, too uncontrollable. Too unforgettable.

"I'm not usually such a complete and utter ass—"

Turning a calculated glance up at him, she arched one brow in response.

He shrugged, then offered the grin that had served him so well in his madcap days. "Perhaps that is also best forgotten."

Miranda returned the pawn to its place on the board.

"You manage them quite well," he said, nodding toward the girls. "Why, their matchmaking efforts are barely transparent this evening."

"Not as well as I would like," she replied.

They both laughed, and Miranda felt one of the bricks in her wall of resolve crumble. No matter her attempt to contain it, to put the rubble back in place, Jack Tremont was yet again dismantling her determination.

"You strike me as a woman with a military mind, Miss Porter," he said, picking up a pawn and moving it into play. He glanced up at her, his look challenging her to a match.

"Not so," she told him, making a cautious entry into the fray. A battle she wasn't about to lose.

"I think you could manage the French out of Spain much quicker than Wellington ever will."

"Bah!"

"Look what you did to this room in one short afternoon."

"I didn't do anything to this room," she said, concentrating on the board in front of her and not willing to look up at him. "It was all the girls' work."

"Yes," he said, moving a rook. "But I can't believe they fostered this sense of independence on their own. Such a quality in a young lady usually has to be encouraged. Or learned by example."

Miranda felt the implication of his words down to her toes, but she wasn't about to concede to him. Not on this, not on whatever undercurrent he was trying to ply from her. "You don't think that such a thing as independence is a natural occurrence?"

He shrugged and made his next move.

"And you, Lord John? From whom did you learn your . . . your independence?"

"From a lady," he said softly, picking up the queen and carefully moving her into the action.

A lady. But of course. Another brick chinked loose and fell to her feet as a torch of jealousy flared to life inside her. Who was this woman who'd had such an influence on Jack, who'd been able to take that wild thread within him and pull it loose like a spinning top?

Was it the same woman she'd heard last night?

To her ears, the lady from the library had sounded older than Jack, but she doubted he was the type of man who cared about such conventions—especially when the woman ignored propriety and decorum, a lady who boldly marched through life.

The kind of woman who wouldn't run from the secrets and mystery of Thistleton Park but would uncover them brazenly, intently, without a care for the danger they might hold.

A woman whose inner light would illuminate the very night, shine like a beacon into the heavens.

She glanced up at Jack, who was studying the board seriously, and she realized that as much as he stirred her senses, the real danger he posed to her, the real temptation he elicited was the desire he evoked in her to live her life with a daring and audacity that went against her very grain.

To let her spirit shine through the rules and decorum she'd become imprisoned by.

Then once again, her heart staged a perilous rebellion, raising a battle cry that drowned out common sense, trampled the hallowed halls of reason.

What was the use of a life of decorum if she never lived?

Recklessly, she gazed at the board until she saw something she might never have seen if it hadn't been for this discordant tune running through her veins. She pulled her fingers away from the piece she'd been considering and boldly moved her queen into harm's way.

Jack's eyes widened. "Are you sure about that?"

"Very much so," she said confidently.

He moved as she'd guessed he would, taking her queen and striding forward, thinking he had her cornered. "Check."

Miranda feigned surprise. Then coolly reached down and moved the pawn he'd overlooked. "Checkmate."

He did a double take, staring down at the board as if he couldn't believe it, and then up at her as if he was seeing her for the first time. "Miss Porter! You surprise me . . . yet again."

She couldn't speak, afraid as she was of what sort of nonsense would come from her lips, come racing forth from her fast-beating heart.

Pippin rose from her chair and came over to look at the chessboard, studying the pieces. "What a masterful game, Miss Porter. I didn't know you played."

"I did as a young girl," she confessed. "Actually, it has been years."

"You obviously haven't lost the skill," Jack said, still looking at the board, replaying the moves and trying to discover how he had failed to see the entrapment that had been his downfall. When he came to the point where he'd been distracted, he nodded, then grinned at her. "What other secrets do you possess, Miss Porter?"

Miranda felt his probing question down to her toes. As if he were trying to strip her naked. Worse yet, before she could come up with a starchy reply to set him down a bit, Tally answered for her.

"She dances beautifully, my lord," the girl told him.

More like lied.

Miranda's gaze swiveled toward the cheeky little matchmaker. "I do not!" she exclaimed.

Felicity waded in to add to her sister's case. "Miss Porter is infamously modest about her accomplishments. It is why she was the perfect decorum teacher."

Miranda rose from her seat, her mouth opening to deny this charge as well, but apparently the Langley sisters were undaunted even by the threat she'd made before dinner of a month's worth of detention knitting nappies for the Orphan Society for even the slightest infraction.

"Oh, yes, Jack," Tally called out from the bench at the pianoforte, "Monsieur Guise, our dancing master, once declared Miss Porter's skill worthy of the Paris Opera."

An opera dancer! They were comparing her to an opera dancer? Why not just declare her a highly sought after Cyprian and be done with their attempts to push her into his arms?

For his part, Lord John grinned. "Fancy that! I've always had a fondness for opera dancers." He shot Felicity and Tally a saucy wink. "But there is only one problem, Miss Langley," he said, scratching his head and glancing around the room.

"What is that?" Felicity asked, all anxiousness to provide whatever element would promote Jack's attentions.

"A place to dance," he told her. "How could I ask your esteemed teacher to dance without the proper space?"

Felicity's eyes widened in horror as she realized that she'd forgotten one very vital component in her plan. She quickly recruited Pippin to assist her with moving the furniture.

Miranda gazed heavenward, wishing the girls to perdition.

Oh, they were incorrigible, but she knew just how to ensure they never did this again. Oh, yes, by tomorrow evening she would know exactly how many times they were able to write *I will not play matchmaker* between Thistleton Park and Lady Caldecott's. She didn't care if it took every blank page in Felicity's *Chronicles*.

Even worse, Jack appeared to be willing to go along with the girls' plans, for he was helping them rearrange the room. Their sense of mischief obviously appealed to him, devilish rake that he was.

"I have just the music," Tally said, sorting through the sheaves in front of her. "That is, if you are of a mind to try something a little different. The Duchess and I learned this dance just before Father sent us here for school."

Miranda was already shaking her head, even as Jack was saying, "Splendid! How do we start?"

Felicity came forward. "You need a partner, milord," she said, nudging him none-so-delicately toward Miranda.

"Yes, of course. How rude of me," he declared. Clearing his throat with a dramatic air, he then bowed low, as if he were being presented to royalty. When he rose, he said, "Miss Porter, will you do me the honor of partnering me in the next dance—" and glanced over at Tally. "What are we dancing?"

"A waltz," she told him. "Nanny Birgit taught us how when Father was attached to the Viennese court."

"I'm afraid I'm not familiar with it," Jack admitted.

"And neither am I," Miranda added quickly, hoping that would be the end of it. She could well imagine the sort of dance one of the girls' questionable nannies had taught them.

Tally waved off their protests. "It is quite simple, and an enormous favorite all over Bavaria and Austria. Why it isn't danced in England, I am at an utter loss." She glanced at her music and straightened the pages, before nodding to her sister. "Felicity, show Jack how to hold Miss Porter."

"Hold me?" Miranda protested, backing away from this folly until she was greeted by the solid wall behind her.

Jack held out his hands to her. "Come now, Miss Porter, there is nothing to fear in a simple dance from the Continent, is there?"

It wasn't the dance that had Miranda terrified. It was those three simple words that had her quaking in her sensible shoes.

Hold Miss Porter.

Jack found her panic almost amusing. Really, did the woman think he was going to ravish her right here in the music room before her students and Birdwell?

Well, he probably shouldn't answer that considering

his conduct earlier in the day. But really, how scandalous could this waltz be if two young misses not out of the schoolroom knew the steps?

He completely forgot who he was dealing with.

Felicity came forward, all business. "Now you must take Miss Porter's hand, and hold it up," she was saying, catching hold of her teacher's fingers and pressing the lady's palm to Jack's.

It being the country—and Thistleton Park at that— Miss Porter had not stood on ceremony and had forgone her gloves.

So her bare skin pressed against his.

It had been ages since he'd held a woman's hand, let alone a bare one, and the experience caught him unawares.

His fingers curled instinctively around hers, protectively and unhesitantly. He realized he was holding her hand like he had found something precious, something thought long lost.

And when he looked into her eyes, he saw a wary light.

She felt it as well, and it frightened her.

Hell, it was unnerving him. It was the same demmed fire that had nearly driven him mad this afternoon at the folly. It was why he'd gone to great lengths to dress as a gentleman tonight, hoping that his old clothes would infuse him with a determination to behave like a man of honor and integrity.

Truly, he'd been a fool to think her some part of the rumored conspiracy swirling around him. The lady was nothing more than she appeared—a spinster ready to set herself on the shelf.

And that in itself bothered him. Not that it was any of his business, but it seemed a demmed waste of a lady well-trained in keeping a man utterly organized to see her spend the rest of her days in some lonely, tidy house. Look at Thistleton Park since she'd arrived . . . regular meals, clean rooms, a sense of order like he'd never imagined possible in this old pile of stones.

Though he knew that wasn't the only waste to seeing a lady like Miss Porter at her last prayers, for he suspected that as much as she would take the house well under hand, it would also make her the mistress of his nights. . . .

"Now what?" he asked Felicity, hoping to get on with this dance and be done with it.

Felicity frowned at the pair of them. "You need to stand closer together."

Jack took a small step forward.

"Jack," Felicity complained, "you'll never be able to hold her from that distance." Not satisfied at all with the small step he'd taken, she put her hand on his back and shoved him toward her teacher.

Miss Porter's hand flew to his shoulder to steady them both, and they ended up standing as close as one might to a lover. Jack knew without a doubt why this waltz of Tally's had remained on the Continent.

And it seemed the bothersome little Duchess wasn't done with them yet. "Now, Jack, take your other hand and put it on . . . put it on Miss Porter's . . ." The girl cocked her head and stared at her teacher as if at a loss as to how to say it.

"Oh, bother," she finally said, catching up his hand and plopping it down on Miss Porter's hip.

Even as his grasp claimed her, the lady panicked beneath his touch.

"Felicity, I cannot believe this is how this dance is performed," Miss Porter protested. "Why, it is improper, indecent, and morally—"

With each of her protests, she tried unsuccessfully to extract herself from his grasp, but Jack held her fast. It was, he soon discovered, like trying to contain a flame.

Mayhap there was something to this waltz. . . .

"But that is the correct position, Miss Porter," Felicity told her. "It was all the rage at the Viennese court."

"I would imagine so," Jack added, wondering with some bemusement what the patronesses of Almack's would say to such an arrangement of partners.

Then again, those hallowed halls would most likely overflow with every eligible, able-bodied gentleman in London if it meant being able to cavort so openly with your lady-love.

"Well, I hardly think—" Miss Porter continued to protest.

"Sssh," he told her, pulling her closer, until he had her up against him. "As a former teacher, I would think you would be open to learning a new dance."

"I cannot believe this is how this is supposed to be done. At such close proximity," she repeated.

Felicity bit her lip and eyed them. "I believe Miss Porter is correct, my lord. You have her too close."

Not as close as I would like. He bit back the words before they came forth, and shocked his partner. It was enough of a jolt that he was even thinking such a thing.

Felicity eyed them once again, and this time she finally seemed satisfied with her arrangements. "Tally, are you ready?"

Her twin nodded and started to play a piece he thought was Mozart.

"Pippin, come help me," the intent matchmaker asked her cousin.

The two girls paired off, all serious in their determination to make this dance perfect. "Now follow us," Felicity ordered.

Jack squeezed Miss Porter's hand and winked at her, daring her to continue making such an indelicate face. "Come now, Miss Porter, have you never done anything imprudent in your life?"

Not counting this afternoon.

"One, two, three," Felicity was saying, starting to glide through the room with her cousin in tow. "One, two, three."

Before his partner could add another protest, Jack followed suit. Miss Porter stumbled at first, but he held her fast and towed her along.

At first they bumped and stumbled around the music room, colliding with Felicity and Pippin.

Tally stopped playing, and all of them broke into laughter, the girls' giggles delightful, but nothing more startling than Miss Porter's laughter.

It sparkled through the room with the same power as Mozart's tempting notes.

"Jack, that will never do. You must pay more attention," Felicity scolded.

"To what? Miss Porter or the furniture?"

His partner closed her eyes and shook her head, like

any good teacher faced with a recalcitrant but charming student. However, the smile on her lips belied her unspoken protest.

"Just try again," Felicity urged, even as she nodded at her sister to start playing again. "Pippin and I will sit this one out and give you more room."

At the pianoforte, Tally took up the charge, the music flowing once again through the room.

Jack glanced down at Miss Porter—her cheeks flushed and her eyes sparkling with mirth. Worse yet, a stray curl of red hair had come loose from her usually too tight chignon, and it begged to be tucked back into place . . . or toyed with.

He doubted she'd approve of either choice.

"Are you ready?" he asked instead. "I think it is expected."

"One more dance," she said, "if only to put an end to their meddling."

She said it with the certain knowledge that one dance could hardly be a danger.

He even shared her conviction, her resolve, for he had no place in his life for the tangle these girls were trying to wind around him and Miss Porter.

Yet for the rest of his life, Jack would look back at that one simple dance in wonder. What had it been? The seductive music? It had certainly fed his soul, seduced his senses. The blur of spinning around the room until the walls, and sconces, and furniture had seemed to disappear and it was as if they were the only two people in the world.

Suddenly he forgot . . . forgot his duty, his obligations. Dash, the lanterns that needed to be lit. It made him forget all of it. But it wasn't the music or the dance that wielded this magic.

It was the lady herself.

He'd never held a woman and felt so . . . so complete. It took his breath away.

And it seemed she had fallen under the same spell.

While she'd been coltish and stiff at first, ever so slowly she'd thawed until she'd whirled along with him, similarly lost in the magic.

Leave it to the Viennese to get to the heart of the matter—this waltz was nothing more than a seductive prelude.

His thoughts went from dancing, to enticing, to discovering what other charms Miss Porter had so aptly hidden beneath her poor gowns, to discover if her delightful laughter would turn to sensual purrs of rapture as he tempted her beyond her hallowed convent of decorum.

He swept her around and around, his desire for her growing with every note.

"So what do you think of their matchmaking efforts now?" he asked as he whirled her toward the far side of the room, well out of earshot of their eager audience.

She heaved a sigh. "I suppose I owe you an apology. I fear I've underestimated Felicity's determination."

"I would venture that you aren't the first to do so, and you won't be the last." Jack shuddered. "I pity London when she arrives for her Season. She'll have all the men at sixes and sevens, the matrons eating out of her hands, and all the rest of the young hopefuls praying for an invasion by the combined Continental armies to stop her determined conquest."

Miss Porter laughed. "She'll be Miss Emery's best advertisement."

He whirled her past the girls, Felicity and Pippin sitting on the sofa, both with satisfied grins pasted on their faces.

Jack leaned closer. "What do you think they would say if I were to kiss you?"

"Don't you dare, Lord John," she said, pulling back.

"Are you saying that for their benefit or for yours?"

"Both."

He leaned closer still and whispered seductively into her ear. "Are you so certain?"

She stumbled a little, and he had his answer.

And kiss her he would. Kiss her and draw her into his arms, his bed, his life.

Suddenly around him, he saw Thistleton Park shift and change. He saw it as it should have been all these centuries, a home filled with love and laughter.

Even as he found himself being lulled into such a tempting dream, the clock on the mantel chimed the hour. It clanged with a furor he had never heard before.

Hell, the demmed thing probably hadn't been wound in twenty years—for good reason—it was enough to wake the dead.

Yet it served as warning enough. This was Thistleton Park, home to the demented and those inclined to mayhem. With each chime it seemed all his crack-witted and misunderstood relations were howling at the accursed Fates who held them tied to this madhouse.

Including himself.

He stumbled to a halt and let go of Miss Porter like he was shaking himself out of a nightmare.

Marry some miss? He'd finally gone around the bend. It was bad enough to have guests at Thistleton Park, but a wife? She'd expect explanations for his comings and goings that he had no desire to divulge . . . not to anyone.

Glancing up at her red tumbled hair, the pink in her cheeks, and the sparkling light in her eyes, he knew something else.

He couldn't take such a risk with Miss Porter. Put her in harm's way. His life was of no consequence. He'd been resigned to that fact since he'd come here, taken the responsibilities that came with being the master of this house—but by his own choice. But not her, her life . . . that wasn't his to endanger.

Jack glanced at the clock again. "So late?" he said, raking his fingers through his hair, keeping them well out of the way before they reached out and stole Miss Porter's hand.

Before he asked her to waltz again. Beseeched Tally to play until dawn.

To let him while away the hours in Miss Porter's arms and forget the dangers that lurked at the dappled shores of England. That awaited him this very night.

"What do you mean, 'so late'?" Felicity protested. "Say it isn't so, Jack."

"Yes, I fear I have . . . um . . . business matters that I must attend to," he lied. "Yes, that's it. Estate business. Mr. Jones is an exacting task master, and I must catch up on my . . . my correspondence or he will be most displeased with me in the morning if it isn't completed." He bowed low and fled out of the room without another word.

* * *

Miranda watched Jack go. Correspondence, indeed!

One look about Thistleton Park and the grounds said business was the last thing the master of the house attended to.

"But . . . but . . . ," Felicity stammered after him. She heaved a sigh and flounced back down on the sofa, her arms crossed over her chest. "We had it all planned."

"I don't understand," Tally said, rising from her seat at the pianoforte and coming to stand behind her sister. She put a reassuring hand on Felicity's shoulder. "He wasn't supposed to leave yet. Not before he—" Her words halted as she glanced up at her teacher. "I mean—"

Miranda arched a brow at the three of them. "What exactly were you three expecting?"

" 'Tis all for naught now!" Felicity despaired. "We'll leave in the morning and . . . and . . ."

"Lord John will not have declared his intentions for me?"

"Exactly!" Felicity declared. Why, the girl looked relieved to discover that Miss Porter fully understood what was at stake. "He does have a *tendre* for you."

Miranda came over to the sofa and sat down beside Felicity. She offered her a small smile of consolation. "Come sit, Pippin, Tally," she told the others. "Let me tell you where your plans went awry."

The girls settled into their seats with all eagerness.

Miranda drew a deep breath. "You cannot force the affections of a man."

They sat silently for a few moments, as if waiting for more enlightenment on this all too important subject.

"That's it?" Felicity complained. " 'Don't force their

affections'? Miss Porter, you'll have to do better than that. Besides, Nanny Tasha always said any man could be induced with a good meal, the right wine, and proper lighting."

"I don't think she was referring to marriage, Felicity," Miranda told her.

"Oh," she muttered, and then, as it dawned on her exactly what her beloved nanny had been implying, she blushed. "Oh, my."

"Oh, dear," Tally added, having obviously come to the same realization. "We never meant for . . . well, that wouldn't be proper."

"Yes, exactly," Miranda added.

Pippin looked from one to the other. "What? What are you talking about?"

"I'll explain it later," Felicity whispered.

Miranda rose and glanced around the music room. "You really did do a marvelous job of transforming this room."

The girls beamed under her praise.

"Too bad it will all go back under Holland covers and be coated in dust in a fortnight," Tally said. "This house could use a mistress. Have you ever seen such an ill-run place, Miss Porter?"

"No, Tally. I can honestly say I have never been in a house quite like this."

Felicity rose and walked toward the door, as if she was still replaying the events of the evening in her mind and trying to determine what she could have done differently. "Don't you think it is odd that all of a sudden Lord John had to go attend to business? I mean, it is ten o'clock at night." Her hands went to her hips.

"Yes, Felicity, it is odd, but you have to consider the other key element in which you miscalculated."

The girl's head snapped around. "What?"

"You're dealing with a man. And they are neither predictable nor reliable."

"Bother them all," Felicity complained.

"Hold onto that sentiment until you find the right one to bother," Miranda advised. "Now let us retire, for tomorrow we need to arrive at Lady Caldecott's fresh and ready for her capable hospitality."

Well away from Lord John Tremont.

She ignored the protest rising in her heart, the bricks that tumbled freely down on her resolve.

No, this was how it must be.

And even as they gained their rooms and were about to shut the door, Miranda thought she heard the front door open and close.

Harrumph. Business indeed! A tomcat on the midnight prowl, most likely. *No matter his advanced age,* she thought with some mild amusement.

She had to go back to Sir Norris's assessment of the man. Jack Tremont was no gentleman, and it was a lesson they should all have heeded.

Miranda heaved a sigh and shooed the girls toward their respective beds, bidding them to sleep well and retreating to her own adjoining chamber. Unwittingly, she crossed the room and came to stand before the window. The dark of night offered no clues as to where Lord John had gone, not that she sought any.

Despite her silent assertion that she cared not about his foray into the darkness, to her chagrin, she felt an unfamiliar ache. A sense of longing for something she would never know.

What it would be like to be the woman in the night waiting for him . . .

Jack made his way to the tower and lit a single lamp. Placing it in the window, he hoped that this time Dash and his ship would be just out amongst the waves and ready to risk sending a longboat ashore.

But demmit, what was he going to say about the fact that he didn't have the gold the cheeky American had been promised? Dash was so unpredictable, Jack wouldn't put it past him to pull up his oars and never return. He climbed down the stairs and then carefully followed the steep path to the rocky shore.

There was still Bruno's suggestion—offering the girls to the captain in exchange for the cargo.

Jack laughed to himself. Certainly the loss of Felicity Langley would be a favor to all the unwitting and unmarried men of England.

But he liked Dash too much to pull such a fast one on him.

As he made it down to the last few feet to the beach, he looked up and out at the waves.

"Come on, Dash," he whispered. "Don't disappoint me tonight."

Overhead, a few stray stars winked and sparkled in the breaks in the clouds.

Demmit, if the weather continued to clear, the moon would be out and it could make them all too visible. Something neither he nor Dash liked or needed.

Then through the even, never-ending whoosh and swoosh of the waves came a lonely creak. Oars? At least he thought it might be. Then again, it could have been pieces of driftwood butting into each other.

Jack stilled, his eyes straining to see through the darkness. It wasn't until the boat was nearly upon him that he spied it.

If anything, Dash knew his business well. The oars were muffled, the boat painted as black as the waves surrounding it. All of his men were dressed similarly, in dark caps and black wool coats. They blended into the night with the stealth of a band of pirates—which some might claim they were.

Even Dash. Which only gave further evidence to the overwhelming sense of foreboding that had surrounded Jack for a sennight now. Dash in black? The young captain usually wore the most colorful garb he could steal, relishing the awe and fear his wild clothing and danger-ous swagger evoked in those who met him.

Jack waded out to greet them, and as he drew along-side the boat, he realized there was only one extra per-son aboard—and no one else.

His gut clenched—this was all wrong. Where the hell was the rest of the cargo?

"What is this?" he demanded.

"Easy there, Jack, my friend. The rest of your goods are safe aboard the *Circe*," Dash told him, leaping out of the longboat and helping Jack pull it ashore. "We'll fetch them in once I have the gold I was promised."

"You're late," Jack said. "I don't pay for late cargo."

Dash snorted. "You'll pay. Would have been here a week ago if I hadn't had a bit of trouble getting out of

Calais—and then this demmed French frigate chased me out into the Atlantic. Thought I was going to have to go all the way to Boston to shake that frog off my stern." He grinned and winked at Jack. "The devil paid him back with that storm, though. The French haven't the blood for a good wind like that. Last time I saw the bastard he was floundering about like an old woman. So pay up, Tremont, this trip has been more trouble than even I like."

Jack crossed his arms over his chest. "Dash, you know the rules. No gold until my cargo is delivered. All of it."

"But you see, Tremont," the young captain said with that lazy American drawl of his, "I believed that very same promise last month when you offered me a fat reward for making an extra of these little runs to France for you. Then I get back to my ship and count the money, and find some of it missing." Dash leaned against the prow. "Let me rephrase that—most of it missing. I'll not be conned with painted lead again."

So much for Bruno's promise that his cousin's coins would pass muster.

The passenger on the boat got up and started to move to disembark, but two of the crew pulled pistols and pointed them at their "guest."

"Not so fast, Mr. Grey," Dash advised him. "You are worth more to me alive than dead. Worth twice what Jack here promised me, I would imagine."

"Dash, you pigheaded, arrogant bastard—" Jack sputtered. "Don't you know what is at stake here? Give Malcolm over. Give them all over, and I will see you paid thrice what you want."

Dash swaggered closer. "I take that to mean you don't have my gold, despite the fact you look dressed to rob the king himself. Did I bring you out of the ball-room, Tremont? Is that why you are in such a hurry? Got a woman up there waiting for you?" The bastard grinned and laughed.

Jack took a deep breath and reined in the desire to put his fist directly into Dash's smug face. Instead, he cursed his ill luck. The storm, his guests, that skinflint Pymm with the Foreign Office, who never paid his accounts.

For it was Jack's job to see that England's spies and Foreign Office agents made their way from England's shores into the heart of France, and back again. He paid the various and sundry captains—like Thomas Dashwell—who could be trusted (for the most part) to make the perilous crossing with every measure of se-crecy.

The Tremonts of Thistleton Park had used their house, their beach, and now Albin's Folly, as a sort of way station for the king's lesser-known business. Everyone helped: Bruno provided traveling papers, his forger's craft honed so sharply that he could duplicate the ever changing French identity papers in a matter of hours. Birdwell could be counted on to fit a French uni-form or traveling clothes from the closet of extras they maintained.

But to keep it all running smoothly and unobtru-sively, it took gold.

Gold that wasn't always so easily had.

"Have you got the money or not, Tremont?" Dash-well demanded.

Then Jack's luck turned from bad to deadly.

Overhead, a volley of rockets shot into the sky, illuminating the beach and the sea beyond.

The *Circe,* Dash's fleet ketch, stood out suddenly, naked and exposed, as did their position on the beach.

The rockets were quickly followed by musket fire.

"Bloody hell," Jack cursed. "Excise men."

"I see you forgot to bribe them as well," Dash said, even as he pulled his pistol out and returned fire. Once the gun was spent, he laid his shoulder into the prow of his longboat and gave it a hard shove back into the waves.

The gunfire from the top of the cliffs was then matched by cannon fire. And not from the *Circe* but from a warship looming in fast.

"I see we have no friends tonight, lads," Dash cried out. "To the ship, and hard to it."

Oh, this can't be happening, Jack thought, pulling his own pistol and returning fire. He didn't want to kill one of the local militia, but it might deter them a bit. Most of the lads preferred downing pints of illegal brandy at the Henry than getting themselves shot up over it on the beach.

Dash hoisted himself into the longboat, and his men pulled the oars with all their might, heading back to the *Circe.*

With his cargo!

"Demmit, Dash, hand over Grey."

"Not tonight," the captain called back. "Not until I have my gold, Tremont. I'll be back for it. Trust me." His rude laugh suggested something altogether different.

But Malcolm Grey, unlike Dash, wasn't a man disconcerted by a bit of gunfire. He rose up in his seat and was about to jump overboard when another rocket exploded overhead, pinpointing the longboat's position and giving the militia a clear target.

Dash twisted in his seat, and to his credit, tried to pull Grey down, to get the man out of the line of fire, but it was too late.

A bullet hit Malcolm in the chest, the force of it pitching him into the water.

"Tremont, get him," Dash cried out. "They've hit Grey."

Jack waded into the icy waves until he was nearly to his neck. In the flash of another rocket, he spied his friend and caught hold of his coat, pulling him into his arms, then dragging him through the water toward the rocks at the end of the beach.

The *Circe* was returning fire, snipers from the rigging firing at the men on the cliffs, their cannon sending warning shots at the fast-approaching warship.

Dash and his men were already alongside the stern, clambering up the sides like sea rats, and Jack had to imagine the devilish American would once again beat the Fates and slip through this trap.

He couldn't say as much for his own luck as he felt Grey shudder and grow still in his arms.

There was only one chance for them now, and with the tide nearing the high mark, he didn't have much time.

Chapter 10

Miranda discovered that sleep was anything but easily gained that night. Lying in bed, she glanced over at the window, where the shades were parted slightly and the moon was sending in a sliver of light.

The wind was blowing, and a branch from the untrimmed roses that grew up the side of the house banged against the pane, tapping like the staccato questions hammering away at her curiosity.

Where had he gone?

Oh, bother! She had no business caring how Jack spent his nights—doing who-knows-what with who-knows-whom, but it didn't escape her that it must have been him that she'd spied the other evening stealing into the darkness—a phantom for certain, a ghost from her past, a thief capable of stealing hearts.

Was that where he went at night? To some illicit tryst?

She heaved a sigh. That wouldn't surprise her. Even in this empty countryside, she had to imagine that Mad Jack Tremont did not lack for conquests.

She, for one, could vouch for his skill, limited though her experience was.

"Whatever are you thinking, Miranda Mabberly?" she chastened herself. She tossed in the bed and pounded the pillow into a more comfortable position.

The man is the devil himself. Better avoided and forgotten.

Forgotten.

She rolled over again. *Forget about him.*

She hadn't in nine years, so she didn't see why tonight would be any different.

Shutting her eyes tight, she unsuccessfully willed herself to sleep . . . until, that is, a thought of what sleep could offer tempted her to relax: dreams . . . dreams that she could only find in the darkness of night, in the arms of Queen Mab.

And eventually she did fall asleep, drifting off into the embrace of a dark-haired man who bound her in his grasp and whispered of the dangerous passions they would share . . . somewhere, swirling in the mist, she heard the roar of cannons, the sharp retort of guns, echoing like the thunder of the storm that had brought her back to Jack.

"Miss Porter, Miss Porter, wake up!"

The cry in her ear and the violent tugging by three sets of hands roused Miranda out of the restless slumber into which she'd fallen.

"What is it?" she managed. "Whatever is the matter?" She glanced over at Felicity, who was white as a sheet. "Are you having one of your megrims?"

The girl shook her head. "Listen, Miss Porter. There is something very wrong."

The three girls fell uncharacteristically silent, and Miranda shook the last vestiges of sleep from her cloudy thoughts and did the same.

For a few moments the house held all the quiet of a grave, until an unearthly cry rose from somewhere deep in the manor.

It was a cry of agony and pain that tore at the heart.

"The curse!" Thalia gasped. "I knew it the first I heard it. Just as Sir Norris told us."

"'Tis no curse," Miranda told her, rising from the bed and reaching for her wrapper, "but someone in trouble."

The girls didn't look so convinced, especially when another howl rose through the night.

"Whatever should we do?" Pippin asked.

"You three shall go back into your room and bolt the door behind me."

"Behind you?" Felicity asked.

"Yes, behind me." Miranda grabbed up a shawl and threw it over her wrapper. "I will go see if I can be of assistance."

"But the curse—" Tally said, catching Miranda by the sleeve with a grip that could have put a blacksmith to shame.

"Tally, I cannot believe you are paying any heed to what Sir Norris said," Miranda told her, disengaging the girl's frantic grasp. "Ladies of refinement give no credence to such falderal. A lady—a lady of breeding—offers her calm reassurance and able assistance in such situations."

Miranda went to the door and had her hand on the latch when another cry of wretched agony rent the night.

Perhaps it would be better to stay with the girls . . .

But her curiosity and sense of duty outweighed her fears. "Lock the door behind me and don't let anyone in, save me or Mr. Birdwell." Of all of Jack's odd staff, Miranda felt that Mr. Birdwell was probably the most respectable.

If there was such a thing in this madhouse.

The girls nodded, and Miranda paused outside in the hall until she heard the latch click and the bolt slide in place. Clutching her candle, she proceeded down the stairs, wondering with some trepidation if she was about to discover the secrets that Thistleton Park held in its dark shadows.

Jack held a half empty bottle of brandy in one hand, a candle in the other.

"I don't like the look of this," Birdwell said. He caught hold of Jack's arm and drew it closer. "Hold the candle right there. I need all the light I can get."

The three men were bent over Jack's desk, which had been cleared and turned into an impromptu surgery. Atop it lay Malcolm Grey, his shirt torn open to reveal the hideous evidence of a gunshot that had left a gaping wound from which Birdwell was endeavoring to remove the bullet and the missing piece of shirt.

Malcolm was fighting their efforts, but whether it

was the pain or the specter of death that he battled, Jack didn't know.

"Hold him still, Mr. Jones," Birdwell snapped. "I haven't done this in some time."

"He must live, Birdwell," Jack said, adding his own weight to Bruno's to keep his friend still. "He must."

Grey had taught him much in the last four years, saved his life twice when Jack had waded headlong into folly. "Malcolm is one of our best agents. We've got to save him. If he's come back to England, he's most likely discovered who's been selling us out."

"I'm trying, my lord," Birdwell said, "but he's lost a lot of blood." He probed the wound further, then pulled out the bullet, dropping the piece of lead onto the desk.

Jack felt a moment of elation. Malcolm would survive. He had to. But the bullet was followed by a rush of blood.

Birdwell swore, the word itself a shock to hear from the always proper man. "It's like I feared. He's been nicked where it can't be fixed."

"What do you mean—can't be fixed?" Jack put his hand over the wound to stop the flow. He didn't want to hear Birdwell's sigh of resignation. Instead, he put every ounce of strength into holding onto his friend, willing his heartbeat to guide Malcolm out of the icy grasp of death.

But everything that could have gone wrong tonight just seemed to get worse, for Malcolm's tormented cries stilled, until there was nothing left of the man who had always seemed larger than life.

As Jack watched his friend die, the bottle of brandy

slipped from his fingers and shattered on the floor beside him.

Once that would have seemed the greatest disaster of his day, the loss of such a fine French vintage, but tonight he would have tossed a hundred cases of it over the cliffs to save his friend.

Oh, whatever was he to do now?

Even as the human cost of war rose to face him yet again, a knock on the door banged into his grief, into his personal pain.

An insistent, meddling sort of pounding.

"Lord John, is everything well?"

"Blimey," Bruno whispered. "It's *her.*"

Miss Porter? Jack struggled up out of the blinding fog of grief. He glanced at the door and then at the scene that would meet her eye if she dared enter the room uninvited.

"The door is locked," Birdwell said quietly. "I thought it prudent when you brought Mr. Grey in."

Jack nodded. Leave it to Birdwell to get the details right.

The pounding came again. "Lord John, are you in there?"

"Women!" Bruno said under his breath. "Curious as cats and just as troublesome."

"I've got to get rid of her," Jack said. "She can't see this." He turned in a daze and ran into an end table that held their medical kit. It sent the metal instruments and bottles tumbling in a clatter to the floor.

If anything, the sharp sound of the metal hitting the oak floors and the return of Miss Porter's knocking worked to clear his head. He went toward the door, determined to get rid of her.

"My lord," Birdwell hissed.

Jack glanced over at him.

The butler nodded at his jacket.

He looked down to find his coat stained in blood. Malcolm's last evidence of life. Wrenching off his ruined coat, he tossed it aside. "Douse the lights," he ordered.

With the room cast in shadows, he opened the door and forced his way out, pushing the persistent lady aside even as she tried to gain entry.

"Miss Porter?" he said, trying his best to sound surprised. "What are you doing lurking about? Hardly proper, is it? Why, I thought you and your charges had sought your beds hours ago."

She held her candle up high and gave him a searching glance, seeking answers and suspecting everything.

"So it seemed. Until we were awakened by a most grievous noise—" She arched a brow and awaited his explanation.

"Awakened? How unfortunate." He used every ounce of aristocratic nerve he had gained from watching his brother, the Duke of Parkerton, snub any and all who expected him to be forthcoming. "My apologies, Miss Porter. Now if you will excuse me—"

He tried to leave, but she wasn't about to be dismissed so easily.

"Sir, I heard, I mean, we *all* heard, a most dreadful cry. Several of them."

Jack shook his head. "Nothing more than a man complaining when he's on a losing streak. 'Tis just me and a few acquaintances playing a little too deep. Drinking a little too much." He stepped closer until her nose wrinkled at the convincing smell of brandy that surrounded him.

"Sir, that is not what I heard. I heard a man in pain. In agony, and not from losing his last quid," she insisted. Once again, she shot a glance over his shoulder at the door behind him. "If there is someone hurt, perhaps I can be of assistance."

Demmit. They had heard too much. But he couldn't confess the truth. Not to anyone. Not now that another of England's agents had been murdered.

"Cries of agony?" Jack shook his head. "Really, Miss Porter, I didn't take you for the fanciful sort . . . this is twice in as many nights you've come down here with these strange assertions. Have you always been prone to nightmares?"

Her brow arched in defiance, a defiance that he'd certainly never seen in a mere schoolteacher. Why, she had the look of Boadicea, standing there in her nightrail, her candle held like a sword ready for battle.

"Lord John, I am not a woman prone to flights of fancy. Nor am I to be naysaid, especially when I have the welfare of those girls to consider. If there is anything improper going on, I insist—"

Improper. His friend had just died and she was out here nattering on about propriety—as if it mattered.

He'd like to tell her what improper was. Improper was good men like Malcolm Grey lost forever. Improper was enemies who would go to any means to see England fall.

He'd like nothing more than to show her what was

improper and unjust about the world outside of Miss Emery's hallowed walls, outside the protective shell of London Society. The devil take her—didn't she know it wasn't proper for a lady, an unmarried one at that, to go wandering about a man's house in the middle of the night?

Highly improper.

He snatched the candleholder from her hand and stuck it on a nearby table. With barely a pause, he caught her in his arms and hauled her close—right up to his chest, his hands taking every liberty that the freedom of being in one's own home, in the middle of the night, allowed him.

This wasn't right, this was so very wrong. But this night had seemed to be cast by a very different set of rules.

And there was Miss Porter. A woman was a woman, he reasoned, and after so long of being away from the blessed sanctuary they offered a man, he was like one starving as he nuzzled her neck, inhaled her innocent perfume.

His grief pushed him well past proper. Past nobility and honor. Tonight, he was no gentleman.

And she felt like heaven. He went hard, rock hard, as her breasts pressed against him. Soft and round and warm, where his night had been cold and sharp. He knew how they would fit in his hand, how the peaks would rise under his touch, under his tongue. And so he did—touch her—cradling a breast, the weight like gold beneath his burning grasp. His fingers curled around it, seeking and finding that pebbled summit, rising beneath his touch.

"Oooh," she gasped.

He glanced down at her and saw the look of shock in her eyes. A look that burned with outrage . . . and something else.

If it had been only outrage that he'd spied there in the light of her blue eyes, he might have stopped. But there was more to Miss Porter's chagrin.

There was passion. An undeniable passion.

The flame in her eyes drew him like a moth. So that even as her mouth sputtered open to protest, he covered it with his and tasted bliss.

A long-unsated hunger filled him. So he kissed her soundly. Thoroughly. His tongue teased at her lips, swiped aside her requisite objections.

He'd spent the last four years trying to make amends, trying to do the right thing, and the cost was just too much to bear.

His grief and anger and fears poured forth, fueling needs that surprised even him.

His hand found the small of her back and pushed it inward, so she rode right up against him. Could feel every bit of his need, would understand the dangers of the night, wouldn't make this same mistake—of wandering about—again.

Tugging at her nightrail, he pulled it up, baring her legs, her thighs, so his hand could caress her there. Could tease her to open up for him, so he could feel the very heat, the evidence of her passion.

She struggled anew, if in shock at what he was doing or out of propriety, he couldn't tell. But he wasn't about to let go of her, he wasn't going to stop kissing her until . . . until he heard the capitulation that was his triumph, a softly given moan escaping her lips like a traitor.

Holding her fast, his other hand returned to her breast, sweeping aside her impotent layers of propriety and defense—as if a shawl over her wrapper made a difference to a man with intent—and sought out his prize.

Beneath his fingers, her skin enticed him like silk, his thumb rolling over the taut peak, while his touch memorized every detail of her perfect shape.

Gads, how he loved a woman's breasts.

The shape, the taste, the way a man could fill his senses with their silk, their promise, how a lady would writhe and sigh if they were cherished, teased just so. And if one inhaled deeply enough as he devoured her, he could discover her very scent.

As he broke the kiss that had silenced her protests and brought his lips to taste her nipple, to tease and torment her in an altogether new way, this lady and her perfect breasts suddenly brought back memories of another scandalized miss.

Oh, yes, it had been a long time since he'd tasted a woman, enjoyed the pleasures of her silken flesh. And this lady . . . this woman . . . suddenly seemed demmed familiar.

Remember

He paused and then brought his mouth to hers, kissing her again, this time, tasting her, testing her, while memories flooded his senses.

Images of London. The sound of music in the distance. To a young miss with a kiss filled with innocence . . .

A woman who was supposed to be dead.

He wrenched his mouth from hers. "What the hell—"

Miranda's outrage had once again been overwhelmed by the passion she found in Jack Tremont's arms. The wretched bounder had a way of sending her protests scattering away in a flutter, like autumn leaves in a tempest.

And while his hands could tease and torment her, his kiss was an uncontrollable tumult that swept through her every good intention, her very control.

Like the rich odor of brandy surrounding him, he intoxicated her with his kiss.

In his arms, with his lips pressed to hers, with his body covering her, with . . . *that* riding up against her, so insistent in making its presence known, she couldn't keep a single sensible thought from being tangled and tossed aside.

Just as traitorous as her body had been when he'd kissed her at the opéra, or held her in the tower earlier, it once again betrayed her. It began in her toes as they curled up in bliss.

Somehow the rogue knew the effect he had on her, and he pulled her in tighter, indecently so.

Before she could stop herself, she let out a soft moan of longing.

Of desire . . .

Good grief, had she gone mad?

A proper lady wasn't supposed to think about such things, but when he kissed her like this, all she could think about was that dangerous hardness between his legs. Of how she wanted to touch it, to have all the layers between them ripped away so there was nothing left to do but . . .

His hand moved upward, sweeping aside her shawl, her wrapper, moving beneath her nightrail and freeing her breast, his fingers taking possession and moving over her with almost a reverence—surely an expertise, because he had her knees going weaker still, until she thought they would buckle for certain.

Then he broke their kiss and her traitorous lips opened up as if to cry out in torment, to call him back—until his mouth covered her breast and he began to suckle her.

With his tongue lapping at her, his lips drawing her deeper into his mouth, her knees did buckle. He was sending shock waves through her body, tossing aside all the intentions she'd had when she'd come downstairs.

Then just as suddenly as he'd begun this torment, he stopped, kissing her once more, and then pulling his head back and staring at her . . .

And then she saw it—a question in his eyes.

As if he knew who she was!

Impossible. Besides, he knew it couldn't be true. Miranda Mabberly was dead.

But there it was—shock and surprise in his eyes. And disbelief.

Good, she thought. And to distract him further, she shoved him away from her—in truth, what she should have done from the first moment he'd caught hold of her—and sent a stinging slap across his cheek, a warning sally to keep him from ever coming near her again.

To ever discover the truth.

"How dare you!" she sputtered.

His hand went to his now red cheek, and he glanced over at her with narrowed eyes. "I dare, madame, because it is *my* house."

"Well, be that as it may, as a gentleman—"

He stalked toward her, closing the gap quickly, dangerously. His hand snaked out and caught her by the elbow, hauling her once again up against him. "Need I remind you, I am no gentleman. And in the future, if you decide to come seeking my company in the middle of the night, remember well that such an encounter will end in my bed, *Miss Porter.* Is that what you want? To come spend the night in my bed?"

She pressed her lips together, if only because she didn't trust herself not to say an emphatic *Yes, Jack.*

God, how she wanted him.

"Are you staying or leaving, Miss Porter?" he asked in a voice as dark as the night, a temptation that curled around her with dangerous passion.

If she gave in now, she knew she'd never be able to leave him, never escape Thistleton Park. She'd be subject to his whims, his desires for as long as he would keep her.

And then he'd surely cast her back out to face the cold fate that would await her.

Miranda gasped at the thought and shook off his grasp with all her might. Then she fled back upstairs, his mocking laughter chasing her up each flight, only adding to her haste.

When she reached the door, she came to a skidding halt.

Compose yourself, Miranda, she chastened. She tried to still her racing heart. Impossible. Shake off the last vestiges of passion. Equally unachievable. So she made do by patting her hair into place and making sure her nightrail and wrapper were now decently reassembled. Finally, she settled her shawl back over her shoulders and knocked quietly, but firmly, on the door. "Ladies, let me in."

The door flung open, as if they were about to save her from the very hounds of hell. Felicity and Tally stood side by side, while Pippin was huddled beneath the covers of her bed.

Miranda walked in, hoping that she was the picture of composure, that no one noticed the way her knees still wobbled.

"Whatever happened?" Felicity asked. "What did you discover?"

That Jack Tremont can still kiss a lady senseless . . . that we must be away from here before . . .

Brutus circled her hemline, sniffing and growling at whatever he found there.

"There is nothing amiss," she told the twins.

They fell back, looking all too disappointed, while Brutus cast a suspicious glance up at her that suggested the little canine didn't believe a word of what she was saying.

"But the noise," Felicity protested. "We all heard that monstrous noise. *You* heard it." Her hands were on her hips, and Miranda knew the girl wasn't going to be appeased without some sort of plausible explanation.

"Yes, well, it seems one of the servants has had too much to drink." Miranda sent them all a pointed glance. "Unfortunately this house is not very well run, and someone left the wine cellar unlocked," Happily, her words started to sound like another lecture on household management, and her audience was in no mood for lessons.

"I knew this would come to naught," Felicity said to her sister. "You and your curses."

Tally shrugged and made her way back to her bed. "It could have been a curse. You certainly thought so a few minutes ago."

Pippin had never left her bed, and now she pulled a pillow up over her head to drown out the argument that was sure to follow.

"Good night, ladies," Miranda bid them and returned to her own room. She dropped her shawl on a chair and paced about the chamber trying to make sense of what had just happened. Then she caught sight of herself in the mirror.

She stopped in midstep and stared at her reflection in horror. Glancing down at her sleeve where Jack had first held her, where he had caught hold of her and pulled her into his grasp was evidence of something unmistakable.

Blood.

She struggled frantically to get out of her nightrail, pulling it from her body, then staring down at the muslin in her hands.

And yet there it was. A bloody handprint. She looked up at the door that led to the hall.

Drunken revels, indeed! He was up to his neck in something nefarious. Something deadly.

The passion that he'd enflamed with his kiss now seemed quite tame.

She looked again at the door. The door that would lead back to Jack. To an answer to all this mystery.

And yet his threat came back to haunt her.

. . . if you decide to come seeking my company in the middle of the night, remember well that such an encounter will end in my bed, Miss Porter *. . .*

Miranda stared at her ruined nightrail, then wadded it up in a ball and threw it into the fireplace, the coals still hot enough to catch hold of the damning evidence and consign it to the flames.

Perhaps it was better that some questions remain unanswered. For now, she'd take the coward's path and stay in her room, well hidden from Jack Tremont.

A man she couldn't even begin to fathom.

Pippin peeked out from beneath the covers and glanced at the door that led to Miss Porter's. "Is she coming back?" she whispered.

"No, I think she's going to bed," Felicity offered. "Did you manage it?"

"Yes," Pippin said as she quietly climbed out of bed.

"Were you seen?" Tally asked.

"Not that I know."

"What about Mr. Stillings?" Felicity asked. "Miss Porter said he was going to spend the night in the stables."

Pippin sniffed as she shrugged off her cloak and

hung it over the back of a chair near the fireplace. "He was playing cards with the other stable hands."

"And you were able to . . ."

Pippin turned around and grinned at them. "Yes, I cut them. We won't be going anywhere in the morning. Or in the afternoon, for that matter."

Tally sighed. "That is perfect. Now Jack will have no more excuses to keep from declaring his feelings for Miss Porter."

"Yes, but I am worried about her," Felicity said. "She seems quite determined to the contrary."

"Well," Tally mused, rolling over in her bed and reaching down to give Brutus a pat on the head. "We'll have all day to convince her otherwise. I suspect we'll have no problems tomorrow showing her Lord John's finest attributes."

Chapter 11

"**W**hat do you mean the harnesses are cut?" Miranda asked Stillings when he came into breakfast to inform them that their trip would be delayed—yet again.

"Like I said, miss," he replied. "They've been cut. Completely useless."

Miranda turned her gaze on the trio of girls behind her. "Ladies, do you know anything about this?"

"Us, Miss Porter?" Felicity asked, her eyes wide with innocence.

The girl was good, but her sister and cousin were not as successful; Pippin buried her nose in her meal, while Tally turned a bright shade of incriminating pink.

"How long will it take to fix them, Mr. Stillings?" Miranda asked, knowing it was no use questioning the girls together—they probably feared Felicity's wrath far more than hers.

"Actually, not more than an hour," he told her.

"An hour?" Felicity burst out.

"How can that be?" Pippin asked. "You surely can't repair the crupper without—" Pippin's question came to an abrupt halt as Miranda quirked a brow at her.

"Yes, well, Pippin," she said, "it seems we have something to discuss while we wait for Mr. Stillings." She glanced over at the driver. "An hour?"

"Yes, miss, shouldn't take much longer than that." He smiled and winked at Pippin. "You of all people, Lady Philippa, should know I always carry a spare crupper."

Pippin cringed.

"Ladies," Miranda announced, "breakfast is over. Please thank Mr. Birdwell and then join me in the library. It seems we have much to discuss."

The girls rose together and bid their farewells to Mr. Birdwell. Then they followed their teacher to the library like a condemned lot at Newgate, Brutus trotting behind them, his tail waving back and forth.

Miranda didn't even wait to shut the door before she started in on them.

"How dare you!" she said in a voice both deadly and calm. "This is inexcusable. I am going to—"

"Miss Porter, please, if you would but listen—" Felicity began.

"Miss Langley, if I require anything of you, I will ask. Now sit."

Felicity did as she was bid.

Meanwhile, Brutus, who wasn't under any admonition or scrutiny, ignored them all and started sniffing around the library shelves.

"As I was saying," Miss Porter continued. "I shall indeed write your fathers and report that—"

"Grrrrr." Brutus paced before the wall, growling and barking loud enough to drown out Miranda's reprimand.

"Brutus!" she snapped at the dog. "Stop that immediately."

The little dog ignored her and continued to scratch at the shelves, growling and snarling at the volumes.

Tally went to his rescue, plucking up her pet and carrying him over to her seat. "Darling," she cooed at him, "those are just dull old history books, not rats." She looked up at Miranda. "He probably smells a rat."

No doubt explaining his initial reaction to Lord John.

"Now, as I was saying," Miranda began anew. "There is no doubt that Miss Emery will be angry to discover that students of her school engaged in such—"

Meanwhile, Brutus had gotten loose from Tally's grasp and was yet again at the library shelves, scratching and digging at the lower one, even barking at the dusty tomes.

"Brutus!" Tally hissed. "Get over here!" She shot an apologetic glance at Miranda. "I don't know what is wrong with him, he's usually so well behaved."

"Harrumph!" Miranda was of a contrary opinion.

"I'll get him," Pippin said, rushing to keep the peace and ending up stumbling over the hem of her gown. She pitched forward and fell, catching hold of one of the shelves as she went, landing in a heap beside Brutus with a shower of books around her.

"Pippin, what have you done?" Felicity gasped.

"I-I-I was only trying to—" Pippin began.

"Oh dear, look at what you've discovered!" Tally said, pointing over her cousin's shoulder.

Pippin turned around and glanced at the library wall—a wall that had moved, leaving a gaping hole. "A secret panel!" she whispered, rising from the floor and standing before the entrance to what looked to be a dark tunnel down into the depths of the house.

"Stay back," Miranda admonished. "You don't know what is in there."

Brutus, however, bolted into the darkness with the ferocity of a dog twice his size, barking and growling as if he had found an entire nest of rodents.

Tally went after him, probably having already forgotten Miranda's admonishment to stay back, so Pippin followed her, if only to catch her and stop her before she fell into some pit or other problem that would only deepen the mire they were already neck deep in.

But Pippin's progress was halted by Tally, who hadn't gone more than a few steps into the tunnel.

"A-a-a-ah," Tally stammered, pointing down at Brutus, who had something in his mouth. She began shaking from head to toe.

Pippin squinted to see better, and then probably wished she hadn't.

"Miss Porter—" Pippin squeaked.

Miranda was at her side in a moment. "What is it?" She fell silent at the sight before her, then managed an, "Oh, dear heavens!"

Brutus hadn't caught a rat. Rather he had a sheet, which he had pulled back to reveal a man. A very dead man.

Felicity joined them, her eyes growing wide with horror, her lips moving to form a word, but the ability to say it escaped her.

But Miranda knew what it was.

Murder.

It was as she had feared. There'd been a murder last night. How else could one explain the darkened stains of blood across the man's chest, the blood on her nightgown.

The blood on Jack's hand.

"We must be gone from here," she told them, pulling them away from the body and snatching up a reluctant Brutus. "Before anyone sees us." Closing the passageway, she glanced at the library door, her teeth working her lower lip.

While flight seemed the best choice, she couldn't do that. The man inside deserved retribution, but how?

Then Miranda remembered something from the other day.

"Pippin, put those books back on the shelf. Felicity, close your mouth, it is unbecoming. Tally, take a deep breath and regain your composure, then help your cousin with the books."

Tally, not being much of a librarian, began shoving the volumes back in willy-nilly.

"Tally, they have to go in order," Pippin chastened.

"Order? What are you talking about? There is a dead man in there and you are worried about the books being neat?"

"No, we have to make them look like nothing has been disturbed," Pippin said, sorting the books.

"Miss Porter," she asked as she set the last volume, a

thick book on ancient English history, back into place. "What are we to do now?"

"We are going to fetch the magistrate."

Jack had spent the night pacing the floor. Malcolm was dead, and Miss Mabberly . . . well, he wasn't so sure now.

But how could it be that Miss Porter was . . .

The woman he'd long thought dead.

After she'd fled upstairs, he'd stood looking after her for some time, telling himself he was as mad as Lord Albin, as ramshackle as Lord Hal.

Miranda Mabberly couldn't be alive.

Remember . . .

"Remember what?" he demanded of the shadows that seemed to haunt him. "Remember bloody what?"

There was nothing to remember. The chit was dead, and Miss Porter was . . . very much alive.

Hours later, Jack was still toying with the idea of giving Bruno's suggestion about the crates a try.

"I thought they were leaving," he said to Mr. Birdwell, as he watched Miss Porter and her trio of acolytes walking across the lawn at a fast clip. He should catch up with her and demand an explanation, demand she tell him who she was.

But if she did, and she was indeed the woman he suspected her to be, then what?

Not that he wanted anything to do with her. She'd concealed her whereabouts and left him to twist in the wind of ruination even as she'd made a life for herself well away from Society.

While he'd . . . well, he'd been banished here.

"They are leaving," his butler replied, sounding as disappointed as the girls probably were at their inability to secure a match.

"Not you as well," Jack said, turning from the window and glancing at the man.

"I don't see that Miss Porter would be such a bad prospect for matrimony."

Not for him. Not when he looked back at her, spied the curve of her hips, that undeniable hair. Then it hit him again, just as her kiss, her sighs from last night had revived his memories. Gads, she was Miranda Mabberly. How had he not seen it before?

But he had. Back at Miss Emery's, later when she'd arrived in his dining room like a phantom from his past, when he'd held her in his arms. He'd known—and had ignored the truth.

Because to have her back in his life meant that he had a responsibility to her.

No, he didn't. Not now. Not when she'd deceived him.

Birdwell glanced out the window as well. "Odd that Miss Porter would take the girls on a walk now, all things considered."

"Considering what?"

"Well, apparently one of the young ladies disabled the harnesses last night so as to delay their departure—"

Jack shook his head. "You mean they aren't leaving?"

"Oh, yes, they're going. That man of theirs, Stillings, carries a spare set. When I last saw them, Miss Porter had taken them into the library to ring a peel over their head."

Jack's gaze shot up. "The library?"

Even Birdwell paled. "Oh, my lord it never occurred to me that—"

Jack was already out into the hall, charging down the stairs. Despite his rheumy appearance, Birdwell still had some speed in him and was hot on his heels.

There was just too bloody much at stake.

When he gained the library, Jack chastised himself at first for overreacting.

Really, did he think that four women could uncover the secret passageway in the Thistleton Park that had outwitted Cromwell's best agents, not to mention generations of excise men and local magistrates who had all tried to catch the eccentric Tremonts in some nefarious act? None of them had ever discovered the tunnel, the secret passageway that led down through the house and into the sandstone on which it was built, until it reached the beach. There the entrance was hidden by the treacherous waters of high tide and a large rock at low tide. Even then the opening was just enough to slip past at low tide, if one knew it was there to chance.

It was how he'd gotten Grey into the house undetected—though it had been a close go, the tide coming in fast and the tunnel filling higher and higher with seawater with each successive wave.

And it was where he had hidden Malcolm's body until his "guests" departed and he could give his friend a decent burial in the ancient graveyard behind the garden.

"All appears well," Birdwell said, nodding his head approvingly after he'd inspected the room.

Jack agreed, but that didn't explain Miss Porter's odd decision to take the girls on a trip down the cliff path.

A turn about the garden—what there was of it—was not unheard of before one climbed into a carriage before a long day's travel, but a hike?

He couldn't shake the feeling that something was wrong.

Bruno came in just then. "Where are those troublesome gels?" he asked. "Their man out there says he's ready to go." He eyed Jack, who was down on his knees examining the shelf that concealed the latch. "Never knew you to be the bookish sort, milord."

"Do shut up, Jones," Birdwell told him. "We think the ladies might have discovered . . ." He coughed and lowered his voice. "Might have discovered our other guest."

Bruno's eyes widened. "Nah. Go on with ya." The man shook his great shaggy head. "That would be a—"

"A disaster," Jack said, sitting back on his heels and staring in disbelief at the evidence before him. "I can't believe it."

"What is it?" Bruno asked, kneeling beside him and looking at the books before them.

"That," Jack said, pointing at the lower shelf.

"They look just fine to me," Bruno said. "All nice and neat and in order."

"In order?" Birdwell gulped.

Jack nodded, for the butler understood exactly what that meant. The books were all in place, in perfect arrangement, even the one that shouldn't be—an ancient volume on early English history.

"Christ!" Jack cursed, getting up and glancing over his shoulder at the window beyond.

"How could they have discovered the tunnel?" Birdwell asked.

"It doesn't matter how," Jack said, shoving back the curtain and staring unseeing out into the tangle of his gardens. "Which way did you say they went, Birdwell?"

"The cliff path."

Jack groaned. "Oh, demmit. They've gone to Nesbitt Hall. They're off to fetch the magistrate."

Bruno put his two meaty paws together and cracked his knuckles. "Not if I stop them first."

"No," Jack told him before Birdwell jumped in and he'd have to step between the two men he needed to pull off a magnificent deception. "We've got to hide all this before Norris arrives." He turned to Bruno and Birdwell. "And then we'll deal with Miss Porter and her charges."

Bruno rubbed his hands together with glee. "Me crates!"

Miranda had spent the time fetching Sir Norris trying to reconcile the grisly discovery they'd made in the library with the man she'd danced with not twelve hours earlier.

Jack? A murderer?

She couldn't believe it, yet how could she not when faced with so much damning evidence?

The dead man. The manacles and ropes in the tower. The mysterious tunnel.

The blood on her nightrail.

She shuddered. Of all the things she had told Sir Norris—once they'd managed to get the man to leave his breakfast—she hadn't told him about the blood on her nightrail.

How could she? And yet by not offering the evidence that would surely send Lord John to the gallows (which was where, Sir Norris had said more than once in the last hour, that devilish Tremont belonged) wasn't she guilty as well?

"I've got 'em now," Sir Norris chuckled as he led the way along the path, his pack of hounds bounding around them. To the rear of this unlikely parade were several large fellows Sir Norris had summoned from his stables to help take Lord John into custody. " 'Tis a proud day, it is, Miss Porter."

"Yes, well, I just wonder if there is an explanation for all this," she posed, not utterly convinced that Lord John was the vicious criminal Sir Norris claimed him to be.

Certainly the facts, well, were damning, but . . .

No, it was too simple to take Sir Norris's road and dismiss Jack as just another of those "crackbrained Tremonts."

Perhaps Jack was a ne'er-do-well, but she couldn't shake a sense of something else that had been in his kiss last night.

Grief.

He'd taken hold of her like a man drowning. He'd kissed her as if he'd expected to find a balm in her lips, something, anything to take away a pain he couldn't fathom.

They rounded the corner and slipped though the opening in the wall and into the tangled yard of Thistleton Park.

"Disreputable," Sir Norris complained. "But we'll see to Lord John today. Yes, we will."

"What do you mean to do with him?" Felicity asked.

"Why, hang 'em, miss," he replied with glee. "As quickly and straightforward as I can."

Miranda stumbled to a halt. "Hang him?"

Sir Norris spat at the ground. "Now don't be getting

missish about the matter. He's gone and committed murder, and he'll hang for it. No way around it."

"But perhaps there is a reasonable explanation for why this man is dead," Miranda offered, knowing that her words were falling on deaf ears, for Sir Norris was already up the front steps and pounding on the door.

Miranda held her breath and waited for Birdwell to come. Nervously, she glanced around the yard and realized all eyes were fixed on their party. The men working to cut up the oak, the lads from the stable.

Suddenly she felt like a traitor.

But she wasn't the guilty party, she told herself, wishing she could say the same to the men staring at them.

Sir Norris pounded on the door again, and finally it opened, but it wasn't Birdwell who answered but Lord John himself.

He looked as rakish and devil-may-care as ever in his shirtsleeves and black breeches. "Sir Norris, what a surprise! I see you've escorted the ladies home. I was starting to fear they'd gone missing—"

"Enough of your chatter, Tremont," Sir Norris said, shoving the door open and pushing his way in without an invitation. "I got you dead to right this time. You'll hang for sure." The man continued into the house as if it were his and marched straight to the library.

"And good morning to you, as well," Jack said. Glancing back over his shoulder, he smiled at the rest of the party. "Good morning, ladies. How are all of you this fine day?"

The girls filed past him, bobbing their heads politely but eyeing their former hero with disillusionment.

"That bad, eh?" he said. "Miss Porter, what say you? I

doubt you've been struck dumb this morning. You always seem to have an opinion and aren't shy about sharing it."

Miranda shook her head. "I-I-I . . ." she stammered. "I didn't know what else to do."

He eyed her quizzically. "So you invited Sir Norris over? I can think of less drastic steps to take."

"Lord John, you shouldn't jest," she told him.

"Lord John, is it? What happened to 'Jack'?"

She stared down at the tips of her sensible boots.

"Hmm," he mused. "Shall we retire to the library and see what Sir Norris thinks he has against me . . . this time?" He winked at her, then went off toward the library whistling a jaunty tune, as if this were nothing more than a lark.

Miranda shook her head.

"Miss Porter," Pippin whispered, "I don't want Sir Norris to hang Jack."

Neither did she. "I fear this is out of our hands," she told her. Yet she couldn't escape the notion that she was missing something about all this.

"Perhaps there is a reasonable explanation," Felicity offered as they followed their host to the scene of the crime.

Brutus, for his part, trotted eagerly back into the room and went right to the shelf, but instead of growling and making a great fuss, he simply sniffed around once or twice, then with a resigned sigh, left the spot. He hopped up on Lord Harold's throne and made himself at home, curling up and going to sleep as if there were nothing of note to be found.

Miranda eyed Jack. He looked as unimpressed with this intrusion as Brutus.

"Now, Miss Porter, if you would do the honors and show us what you found," Sir Norris said, rubbing his hands together with glee.

She didn't even dare look at Jack but edged past him and went to the library shelves. "This bottom shelf is part of the latch. You just—" She went to move the hidden latch, but the piece held fast. She pushed it again, but nothing happened.

Sir Norris nudged her aside and came down to inspect the shelf himself. "And you say the secret passageway was right behind this wall?"

"Yes."

"Secret passageway?" Jack asked, sounding incredulous. "Finding a pianoforte is one thing, ladies, but you say I also have a secret passageway? Well, that's unbelievable."

"Harrumph!" Sir Norris snorted. "We'll see about this."

The man prodded and pulled and pushed at the shelf, shoving aside the volumes in annoyance to study the wall behind them more carefully.

The determined baronet even had Pippin explain exactly how she stumbled and fell, so as to try to recreate the exact accident that had led to the discovery of the body.

Meanwhile, Jack lounged against the wall, a curious expression pasted on his handsome features, as if all of this intrusion were nothing more than a bemusing entertainment for a dull day.

Finally, Sir Norris rose up and fixed a deadly stare on him. "Don't suppose you would open this wall up for us?"

"Sir Norris, since I have no idea what these ladies have seen, I can't even suppose to know how to open it." He smiled, the epitome of the congenial host, as if he would like nothing better than to help them all. "And what exactly do you think is behind this wall?" he asked, pushing off his post near the door and leaning over to retrieve some of the fallen volumes.

"A dead man, my lord," Felicity offered, speaking up for the first time. "We found him, quite by accident."

"A body?" he declared. "Heavens, you girls are quite determined to remain at Thistleton Park if you are willing to go to such lengths to see me matched to Miss Porter." He threw a companionable arm around Sir Norris's shoulder as if they were old comrades instead of feuding neighbors. "I fear you've been had, my good man. These girls are bent on matchmaking and have gone to great lengths to see that I take a fancy to their teacher—why, they've pulled the shoe off a horse, broken their harnesses, and now, apparently, conjured a dead man to delay their travels. I fear you've been led astray by some misguided schoolgirls."

Sir Norris's bushy brows furrowed. "But Miss Porter, she said—"

"Sir Norris," Jack told him, all conciliation and concern, "even a marriage to me would be better for the old gel . . . well, you know what I mean. Why, just last night she quite threw herself at me—"

"I did no such thing!" Miranda protested.

"No, of course not," he conceded, and then mouthed to Sir Norris, *"She most certainly did."*

"Oh, of all the outrageous lies," Miranda complained, but neither man was paying her much heed, for they'd fallen into that companionable, contrived friendship that men affected when they sensed a female conspiracy of entrapment.

"Goodness, just be thankful," Jack was saying, "the lot of them didn't end up on your doorstep, or you might have been part of their parson's trap."

The toady little baronet blustered and shuddered, muttering about the "inherent dangers of unsupervised females."

Miranda eyed them both incredulously. "Sir Norris, there is a passageway behind that wall and there is a body to be found." She went over to the wall and pounded on it, much as the baronet had, hoping it would resound with the hollow echo that would give credence to her statements. But the wall was as solid as if it had stone behind it, and the shelf that had slipped loose also felt just as solid.

"Now Miss Porter," Sir Norris said, patting her on the arm, "I know your lot is difficult, but really, you could do better than Lord John." His brows waggled in a suggestion that he wasn't opposed to her matrimonial plots.

Miranda ruffled and shook off the odious man's attentions. "Sir Norris, I know what I saw, and I saw a dead man behind that wall."

Sir Norris eyed her once again, and this time, he shook his head, as if there was no hope for her, then stormed out of the room in a great huff.

Jack shot her a triumphant wink.

Oh, the devil take him, she thought. This wasn't over yet.

She strode out of the room, intent on seeing that wall opened if it was the last thing she did.

The girls followed in her wake, as well as a reluctant Brutus, looking quite vexed at having to leave such a comfortable spot. Even still, he trotted along at the hem of Tally's skirt.

"Why wouldn't the wall open?" Felicity whispered.

"I don't know," Miranda replied, as she followed Sir Norris down the front steps. "But I have no intention of letting this rest."

Desperate spinster indeed! Odious, hateful man. She'd see Jack Tremont hang if she had to tie the knot herself. Then she looked up and spied something that might prove her case, even to someone as obtuse as this so-called magistrate. "Sir Norris, I am going to prove that Lord John has concealed a body behind that wall."

Sir Norris snorted. "And how do you intend to prove that, Miss Porter? I haven't got the time for any more of your nonsense."

She walked over to the fallen oak and nodded to the workers, who had all stopped working to watch the spectacle. Taking advantage of their laxity, Miranda picked up one of the axes and, before anyone could protest, spun on one heel and stormed back toward the house looking once again like Boadicea on the warpath.

Even Sir Norris backed out of her stormy path. Then his slow wit finally caught up with her plan—one that was obvious to everyone else. He hurried to catch up with her, then moved to block her path. "Miss Porter, you cannot start breaking down the walls. It isn't done."

"I can and I will," she told him, striding around him.

"I declare, Lord John is correct, you are mad. Now, I demand that you stop this nonsense or I will have *you* arrested."

"Not before I prove my point." Miranda knew Sir Norris was probably right on two accounts—she had gone mad and he was going to have to arrest her to stop her.

She marched on toward the house, ax in hand, until suddenly Mr. Jones came down the steps and caught hold of her by the waist, holding her in front of him, her back to his chest. Jack tried to catch hold of the ax and get it out of her hands, but she swung it at him with impunity, not caring a whit about the sight she presented.

"Put me down," she yelled at Mr. Jones.

"Not so long as you've got that ax, I won't, miss," he said.

"Unhand me!" she protested.

Sir Norris joined the fray, and the four of them continued arguing and hurling accusations at each other, while Tally, Felicity, and Pippin watched in horrified silence.

Then into this fracas came the sound of Brutus barking wildly.

"Whatever is that dog into now?" Felicity said. "Tally, you need to keep him on a tether or something, for he's probably digging in the gardens."

"It's not like anyone will care," Tally protested. "I don't think anything out here has been tended or turned in years."

The barking turned more frantic and now was being joined by a chorus from Sir Norris's ever-present hounds. Their baying quite drowned out the argument on the front steps.

"Oh, bother," Felicity complained. "If you won't see to Brutus, I will." She turned and marched around the corner of the house, to the rose garden near the music room, where she came to an abrupt halt. "Miss Porter!

Sir Norris!" she cried out. When they didn't come immediately, she put two fingers to her lips and laid out an impressive whistle.

Tally grinned. "Nanny Helga taught us how to do that. Quite earsplitting, don't you think?" she said proudly to Pippin.

Their cousin agreed, and obviously so did Miss Porter, Sir Norris, and Lord John. They froze from their antics and all looked over at the corner of the house where Felicity stood.

The girl's hands sat on her hips. "I do believe Brutus has found what we are looking for."

If Miranda felt any confusion it was instantly sated by the pale expression on Jack's face.

"Christ!" he muttered.

Sir Norris stilled for a second, then tipped his head as he listened to his dogs. "Sounds like they've got something."

"I wonder what it could be?" Miranda asked, looking directly at Jack. "Or rather *who* it could be?"

Sir Norris was off on a fast trot around the house, and Miranda followed suit, still clinging to her ax.

Pippin and Tally joined in the parade, and as they turned the corner, they discovered what had become of the mysterious missing body.

Brutus had dug into some newly turned soil in the rose garden and had a hold of what appeared to be a sleeve and a hand.

Chapter 12

J ack was nearly to the library before Sir Norris's
hired hands caught him. No matter that he appeared
the coward for bolting and running at the discovery of
Malcolm's body in the garden: Truly, he could serve
England better alive (and viewed as a coward) than
heroically hanging from the gallows.

He had thought he stood a chance of making it to the
passageway, what with Bruno standing between him and
Norris's henchmen, but with four against one, the odds
for his secretary had not been as good as Jack had hoped.

And they were just as bad for him.

"Caught you, Tremont! Caught you, I have!" Sir
Norris crowed, as if he had captured Napoleon himself.

"To be exact, four women and a mutt caught me, Sir
Norris," Jack replied, still struggling against the two

thugs who had his arms. "You had very little to do with the matter."

The magistrate shrugged. "I'll get the credit of it, that's all that counts. And no one will really care how it came about, once you swing."

Jack felt the chill of the man's words down to the soles of his boots. "Do you really think my brother is going to allow you to hang me?" He shouldn't have asked, for he knew the answer to that. Parkerton might be outraged, if only because he thought he should appear so, but then he would privately raise a glass to Norris for ridding the duke of that "stain to the family line," as he liked to call Jack.

"No matter," Sir Norris declared. "As luck would have it, the assizes will be convened the day after next in Hastings, and I'll see you tried and convicted afore the week is out."

"Sir Norris," Miss Porter protested (at least it sounded like a protest to Jack), "surely you can't just hang a man in such a hasty fashion?"

The old codger just snorted. "Miss Porter, you should leave these matters to those who understand them." He patted her hand, then turned his back to her.

That was a mistake.

"Sir Norris!" she said, bustling around the baronet and planting herself in front of him. "You can't just hang Lord John based on the fact that there is a body in his yard."

As astute and observant and annoying as usual, Jack mused. Whatever was she about? She was the reason he was in this fix, and now she'd had a change of heart and was defending him?

It would have better served him if she'd had this change of heart, say, about an hour ago.

"Why not?" Sir Norris was asking her, looking at the lady as if she were completely daft. "Why can't I hang him?"

"Because you have no proof he committed the crime. Why, anyone could have killed that man. Botheration, you don't even know who that poor soul is."

"He's dead, that's what he is," Sir Norris told her, his temper rising at her interference. "And *that* is enough for me."

"I didn't kill anyone," Jack sputtered. "That man . . . he's . . ."

"He's what?" Sir Norris spat.

Jack pursed his lips together in a hard line. What could he say? That Grey was an agent of the Crown, and that Norris and his militia should be the ones tried—not only for Grey's murder, but for treason for interfering with the Crown's business?

"So who did?" Sir Norris asked. "There was a skirmish with a band of smugglers last night on the beach. Do you know anything about that? Or perhaps you'd like to tell me who that fellow in your garden is?" The baronet's beady gaze bore into him.

Jack could only shake his head.

"I thought not," Sir Norris said. "No matter, murder is a better charge than smuggling. It will assure me that you'll swing."

Jack's chest tightened. And what would happen tonight when Dash returned, looking for his gold and holding the other agents until he was paid? Would they all meet the same fate as Malcolm?

And yet, what could he do? Tell the truth? Reveal the network of spies that used Thistleton Park as their gateway to the Continent and beyond? There were traitors enough trying to bring about the downfall of England, without Jack's revealing the situation to such an indiscriminate old fool as Sir Norris.

Jack's frustration, his anger, his grief over Malcolm's senseless death, the discovery of Miss Porter's identity, all boiled up inside him, and with every bit of strength he possessed, he lunged at Sir Norris.

He managed to get an arm free and immediately shot his balled-up fist directly into the baronet's beak of a nose, sending the man sprawling backwards into the mud of the yard.

"You stupid, dull-witted bastard," Jack seethed, even as the baronet's men caught him anew. "Can you not see that there is a greater good at stake than what your dull wit can comprehend?" If anything, the sight of Sir Norris laying on his arse in the mud was almost worth it all.

Except it turned out to be the last thing he was able to see, for it was then that he was clouted over the head, and he slumped into blackness.

"You've killed him!" Miranda said, rushing forward to Jack's collapsed form, dropping to her knees beside him.

"Better now than costing the Crown the jury fees and the court's time, I say," Sir Norris spat as he regained his feet.

She ignored the repugnant man and pulled off her gloves, her bare fingers seeking out Jack's neck.

"Is he—" Felicity asked, coming forward with her sister and cousin. The girls huddled together in a tight knot.

Miranda shrugged, a sense of helplessness enveloping her as she searched for a sign of life. Then finally, beneath her fingers, she made out the dull thudding of his heart.

"Oh, thank heavens, he's alive," she said, heaving a sigh.

"What's all this?" Sir Norris said, nodding at his men to take Jack away. "You come to my house all ready to see the man arrested and now you want him treated to silks and kid gloves?"

"I just don't think—" Miranda began.

"Miss Porter, I don't care what you think. You can share your misguided notions with the jury."

"What do you mean, the jury?" she stammered, rising to her feet and facing him, all the while her gaze remained on Jack. What had he been saying before they'd struck him? Something about a "greater good"?

Whatever had that meant?

"The jury," Sir Norris repeated. "You will be required to testify. All four of you."

The baronet's words finally sunk in. "Testify?" Surely, she hadn't heard him correctly.

"Of course. You found the body, Miss Porter, you and those girls of yours. You'll have to testify at the inquest."

Testify? Miranda could only manage to shake her head. They couldn't testify, especially in public. Word of it would surely ruin the girls.

And worst of all, their testimony would condemn Jack.

Oh, Jack. Her heart stilled, and for once her reason held sway. There was more to this than met the eye . . .

"I don't think we will be available to testify, Sir Norris," Felicity said, as if declining an improper invitation. "We are expected at Lady Caldecott's by nightfall. And since we would be compelled to tell the truth, it was actually Brutus who found the man." She crossed her arms over her small chest. "We had very little to do with it."

Sir Norris looked at her. "And who is this Brutus?"

Tally came forward, holding up the key witness. "My dog."

Sir Norris choked and coughed. "A dog? You expect the dog to testify?" His face was now bright red, and he turned his displeasure toward Miranda. "You and your charges aren't going anywhere."

She shook her head. "Sir Norris, it is impossible—"

"It is not only possible, miss, but I demand it. Try to leave the shire, and I'll see the four of you locked up beside that villain to ensure your testimony."

"Lock us up?" Now it was Miranda's turn to grow outraged.

The girls looked equally askance.

"Oh, yes, miss. Don't try my patience on this. I've spent years hot on the heels of these wretched Tremonts, as my father did afore me, and now that I've caught one of 'em red-handed, mayhap they'll think twice afore they send another of their lot down here."

"And where exactly do you expect us to stay?" Miranda asked, her temper rising quickly.

The man blew out a disgruntled breath, then he waved his hand toward the manor house. "Stay here. Been good enough for you so far, and now that Lord John is well in hand, at least you won't be sleeping with one eye open to keep these young ones intact." He laughed at his crude joke, then whistled for his dogs.

Jack was tossed none too gently into the back of a wagon that Sir Norris had commandeered from the shipwright. Mr. Jones was already there, shackled and tied down.

Miranda hurried over and peered over the rails at Jack, who lay still and deathly quiet. *What have I done to you?* Unconciously, she reached out to touch his arm, to reassure herself that he was still alive.

"Git yer hands off of 'em," Mr. Jones growled at her.

Even though she knew the giant of a man was shackled, Miranda snatched her hand back at his fierce and protective tones.

"Haven't ye done enough?" he spat. "If only he had listened to me and sold the lot of you off the day you arrived." He shook his head. "Too noble for that. Always doing what's right. Trying to make a good name for himself. Not that I expect the likes of you to understand." He turned his face away.

Miranda took a step back. Those were more words than she'd ever heard the man speak in one sentence, and there was a passion, a faith in them, a faith in Jack, that echoed her own suspicions about this enigmatic man lying between them.

"I didn't mean for this—" she started to tell him but stopped, realizing that nothing she could say would make up for what was about to happen to Jack . . . or to Mr. Jones.

"But Sir Norris, what about that poor man?" she asked, pointing back at the body in the garden.

"I would suggest burying him, miss. A little deeper

this time." He chuckled as if he'd never heard such a fine jest.

"The man deserves a decent committal, sir," Miranda told him, ignoring his mocking tones. "In the churchyard and with the blessing of a man of the cloth."

Sir Norris's gaze rolled heavenward, as if he were searching for his last vestige of patience. "If you want a Christian burial, I'll send the vicar up to give that sot a few words, but don't expect to see him buried in the churchyard. He's probably as immoral as the rest of the lot around here and unfit to lie alongside the good people of this shire. Bury him here, miss. With the rest of the Tremont rabble."

Miranda's hands went to her hips. "Sir Norris, I protest—"

He threw up his hands. "Enough, miss! And don't even think about leaving. Obstructing justice would see you transported at the very least, hanging beside Tremont if I have any say in it."

And then just as suddenly as her world had fallen apart, Sir Norris and his company were gone and Miranda found herself alone with the girls, standing in the yard of Thistleton Park.

"Miss Porter?" Tally asked, coming to stand at her elbow. "What are we to do?"

"We are going to get to the bottom of all this, that is what we are going to do."

Miranda wasn't so sure of her plan several hours later when they still hadn't succeeded in opening the secret panel in the library.

Not that they had spent the entire time trying to open it. They'd had another task to handle first—burying the stranger in Jack's garden. They hadn't been able to find Mr. Stillings, (or Mr. Birdwell, for that matter), so Miranda had pleaded with the workmen to dig a grave. Not one of them could be induced to help until she'd gone and fetched her reticule and offered a ridiculous sum for the task.

It wasn't so much the digging of the hole, one of the lads had confessed. It was digging around the Tremonts already buried there that had made the locals leery.

But finally it had been done and the man had been buried, his grave marked with a bouquet of flowers the girls had gathered. Then Miranda had set forth on the next item of business.

Getting that passageway open. She was convinced it would help to answer their questions. But their attempts had yet to even budge the wall.

Tally and Felicity sat on the couch with Brutus snoring between them. Pippin lay on the floor before the shelves.

"I give up," she declared. "I am bruised from head to toe trying to fall on this again."

Miranda was of a mind to agree with her—there was no way to open it other than her much earlier idea of using an ax.

"Couldn't we offer those men outside an extra bit of gold to break down the wall?" Felicity asked.

"I've already tried," Miranda said. "They won't do it. That Jonas fellow says digging a grave is one thing, but he won't be opening walls and letting out the ghosts that live in this house."

"Ghosts," Tally scoffed, which gained her an arched glance from her sister and cousin. "So I might have believed the stories a little bit last night."

"What are we to do, Miss Porter?" Pippin asked. "They'll move Jack and Mr. Jones in the morning to Hastings and then there will be no saving them."

"I don't know Pippin," she admitted.

"What about Jack's brother?" Felicity suggested. "We could send urgent word to the duke."

Miranda had considered it, but she had to imagine that the Duke of Parkerton's response would be much the same as her father's might have been.

I'll not waste good money after bad.

"I think the better course would be to send word to my solicitor." She had money . . . and there was no one to naysay how she spent it. And she would spend it, she thought, looking around for a pen and paper. Every last shilling if it meant helping Jack.

At least to see him fairly tried, she reasoned as she attempted to reconcile the blood on her nightrail with the man who, as Mr. Jones said, was "trying to make a good name for himself."

Pippin rose from the floor and stared at the wall, her hands on her hips. "I wish Mr. Birdwell hadn't disappeared as well," she sighed. "For it is well past supper and we missed nuncheon and tea." With this complaint she shot Miranda an aggrieved look. When that didn't result in any sympathy, she turned her attention back to the library wall that was the root of all her problems. "I am fair to famished with all this work." She kicked the bottom shelf with her slippered foot, and then leaped back as it creaked and then moved, leaving an opening wide enough for someone to slip through.

Miranda rushed forward. "What did you do, Pippin?"

"I don't know," she admitted. "I just gave it a good kick."

"And that is the answer to many things," came a rattled, cronish voice. "Men and dogs, sometimes all they understand is a good kick."

Tally and Felicity bounded to their feet, and Miranda stepped in front of them, pulling Pippin behind her as well to face this newest surprise.

"Who goes there?" Miranda asked.

From out of the opening in the wall came a spry old woman. She must have been seventy if she was a day, but she moved with the agility of a young lady in her first Season.

"Oh, stop gaping like a bunch of mackerels at the market. It's not like you didn't know the passageway was there, or so Dingby tells me."

"Who are you?" Miranda demanded.

The lady's regal brow rose in a noble arch of displeasure. "I am the lady of this house, if you must know, you impertinent piece of baggage."

Tally's brow furrowed. "You mean you are Jack's wife?"

The old woman laughed—well, cackled, as if she had never heard anything so funny. "Married to that bounder? I think not. That lot belongs to another." At this, she sent Miranda a pointed glance.

Shaking off the chills that ran down her limbs, Miranda looked a little closer at the woman, a wild notion taking hold. "Lady Josephine?"

The old woman eyed her slowly, taking Miranda's measure, then nodded. "Just as that no-account nephew said, you are too smart for your own good. Yes, I am Lady Josephine."

"But you're dead," Pippin said, taking a step back.

"Never believe everything you hear, young lady."

"But Sir Norris told us—" Felicity said.

"Sir Norris? That horse's ass? He hasn't the wit to clean out a stall, let alone to know what end the mess came from."

Miranda looked at the woman again, let her words resonate through her memory. She had heard this lady's voice before. "You were in the library with Lord John the other night. You're Mrs. Pymm."

Lady Josephine nodded. "Yes. And you were snooping about."

"I was not snooping."

The old lady laughed again. "I would suggest going with the first theory, for if you weren't nosing about, then what were you doing seeking out my nephew's company at that hour of the night?"

Miranda blushed at the lady's accusation.

"They share a *tendre* for each other," Tally confided.

"A *'tendre'*? Is that what they call it these days?" Lady Josephine snorted. "We called it something else. A grand passion. Now that's a phrase that means something. One you don't waste your time dillydallying over either."

"Lady Josephine, what is the meaning of all this?" Miranda asked, determined to steer everyone back to the matters at hand. "Why are you hiding in your own house? And where is Mr. Birdwell?"

"Birdwell? Who the devil is—" She smiled, then nodded her head. "You mean Dingby? He's somewhere back there." She poked her head back into the crevice and called out, "Dingby, Dingby Michaels? Where the devil are you?" She rubbed her chin. "He was right behind me. For a highwayman, it's hard to believe he can't find his way in the dark." She nodded to Pippin and pointed a bony finger over at the sideboard. "Fetch that brace of candles for me, like a good girl."

Pippin did as she was bid.

"A highwayman?" Miranda sputtered, still trying to reconcile the fact that Jack's infamous great-aunt was alive. "There is a highwayman in there?" she said, pointing at the cavern and pulling Pippin away from the entrance by the back of her skirt.

Lady Josephine heaved a sigh. "It isn't as if the place suddenly got rats. And I can honestly say there have been far worse criminals come through that hole than Dingby." The lady blew out an aggrieved breath and took the brace of candles from Pippin. Then she poked them into the entrance and called out, "Dingby, do be a love and come out. That idiot neighbor of ours is long gone and there isn't a noose in sight." She shot an apologetic glance at her audience. "Even after all these years, he still gets a mite skittish when the magistrate comes calling." She glanced back into the passageway. "There you are. Thought I'd lost you. Come now, the young ladies have been looking for you."

And out of the passageway stepped a rumpled and

dirty Mr. Birdwell, looking much older and a bit tattered from his experience.

"Mr. Birdwell!" Felicity said, coming forward to help her ally in matchmaking. Then she paused. "Or rather, Mr. Michaels. 'Tis good to see you well and safe."

Miranda was glad to see the old butler as well, but she had to wonder if anything at Thistleton Park was what it seemed. Its dead mistress was alive. The dignified and proper butler was a highwayman.

"A former highwayman," Birdwell said, as if having heard her thoughts. "I gave over that profession years ago."

"Not that it doesn't come in handy on days like today," Lady Josephine chuckled, then she looked over Felicity, her eyes narrowing. "You're Langley's girl, one of the—" Her words trailed off as she looked over at Tally. "Ah, yes, the twins. That explains much. Took after your mother in looks and inherited your father's nerve and wit. You'll be a formidable pair one day."

Miranda watched the two puff up with pride. Goodness, all they needed was encouragement from the likes of Lady Josephine.

"My lady, Mr. Birdwell," Miranda said, "we can go on all night getting acquainted and worrying about tea, but meanwhile Jack . . . I mean to say Lord John and Mr. Jones are going to be transported tomorrow to Hastings and then—" She didn't want to finish her statement, because even saying the words "will be hung" seemed tantamount to giving up. "We must do something. Tonight."

The woman shot a glance at Birdwell, who nodded at her, as if giving his agreement that they could be trusted.

She then cast her intense gaze over each of them. "What I have to say is to be kept in the utmost confidence. There are more lives at stake than just that of my no-account nephew. I will have your word on it, each of you."

The girls each promised, as did Miranda.

And then they listened as Lady Josephine explained everything to them.

And at the end of her unbelievable story, Miranda glanced out the window and into the darkness.

Jack, oh, Jack, why didn't I see it?

The man she'd loathed, the man she'd thought a wastrel, was everything she had ever dreamed a man could be.

And now once more, she was about to lose him.

But this time, she wasn't going to let propriety or decorum or the ideas of others stand in the way. Now that she could see that Jack wasn't the dissolute rake she'd thought, it was time for her to be the woman she had hidden all these years.

The woman she was meant to be, Nanny Rana might say.

"Then there is only one thing we can do," Miranda announced as she rose from her chair and threw her shawl around her shoulders. "When Sir Norris arrives in the morning to take them to Hastings, I think it only fair he find an empty jail."

Clearing his throat, Birdwell said, "That is a fine plan, Miss Porter. However, there is only one problem with it."

"What could it be?" Miranda asked.

"They're locked in," Lady Josephine pointed out.

"But your spirit does you credit." She got up and paced about the room. "Too bad Malcolm is gone. He was a dear boy with explosives. Quite handy in such circumstances." She glanced over at the girls. "Any of you have a talent with gunpowder?"

Felicity looked horrified, Tally disappointed, and Pippin almost willing to give it a try just to please the old gal.

"Really, my lady, it is a rather small jail," Birdwell interjected. " 'T'would do more harm than good."

"Pity," Lady Josephine said. "Might give Sir Norris a fateful case of apoplexy to have his jail blown up."

"If only Mr. Stillings was here to help us," Pippin said.

Birdwell cast a glance over at Lady Josephine, who, if it was to be believed, looked like she was blushing. "I believe, Lady Philippa, I can solve that mystery," he said.

Taking up the candlestick, he went down into the cavern, then returned leading a bound and gagged Stillings.

"My sincerest apologies," the butler offered. "But I am afraid he saw us moving Mr. Grey's body out of the house, and Bruno knocked him out before Lord John could stop him. With Sir Norris about to arrive, we all thought it best that Mr. Stillings recuperate in the tunnel."

Mr. Stillings was untied, and after he got over the indignity of the entire situation, Pippin and Miranda were able to convince him to help them.

However, as it turned out, the driver knew nothing of explosives and even less about breaking into jails. His only thought was seeing to the horses, and so he excused himself.

With his departure, Lady Josephine sighed and

rubbed her chin. "Then we will just have to do it with less flair. Find someone to pick the locks."

"I think I can be of help with that task," came a reply that surprised everyone.

All eyes turned toward Tally. The girl grinned. "I can pick a lock."

Lady Josephine reached over and with one finger pushed Miranda's lower jaw closed. "Miss Porter, close your mouth. 'Tis unladylike to gape."

Jack awoke in near darkness. His head hurt like hell and the rest of him didn't feel much better. He tried to rise up from the cold, wet stone floor, but his head spun, and he collapsed back down.

Even as he fell, he heard a laugh that sent a chill through his bones that had nothing to do with the cold stone floor beneath him.

"So the mighty Tremont is finally waking up. Keeping London hours, eh, Dandy?"

"Sir Norris," Jack muttered, more as a curse than a greeting.

Then it all came back to him. Malcolm's death, Miss Porter's betrayal—make that Miss Mabberly's betrayal.

He didn't know which stung more, the fact that she was alive or the fact that she hadn't come to him first. Asked him about the passageway, about Grey.

Oh, yes, and he would have told her the entire truth, he thought, rubbing his aching skull. No, trust had always been in short supply around Thistleton Park.

And then there was Dash. Unreliable, unpredictable Dash.

If Jack wasn't back on that beach tonight, there with Dash's gold, who knows what the arrogant, crack-brained Yankee would do with a cargo more precious than all the jewels in London. Probably sail back to France and sell the other agents he now held hostage to Bonaparte.

The ironic fact in all of it was that Bonaparte would most likely pay him more money than Pymm would.

He struggled to his feet. "Let me out of here." Jack clung to the bars, if only to hold himself up. "You don't realize what you are doing. I have to be—" Then he stopped, not knowing how far he could trust Sir Norris. Though the man was a magistrate, he wasn't the smartest or most discerning of fellows.

And he certainly wasn't the first person Jack would want to trust with the fate of England.

"Be where, you bastard? Back on that beach? Stealing my livelihood right out from beneath my very nose? Well, I'm done looking the other way on your little midnight forays. You've skimmed from my profits for long enough." He slammed his walking stick across the bars of the cell, nearly taking Jack's fingers off—if Jack hadn't pulled them back just in time.

"Sir Norris, you have it all wrong. If you would just hear me out—"

"Hear you? Hear the word of a Tremont? Lies and deceptions. Your aunt was always one to talk at me until she had me in circles. A regular vixen, she was, what with her wiles and charms." The man stepped back and shook his head. "I'll not listen to a word you have to say. Unless you want to tell me what is coming ashore tonight and who your supplier is. I'm always in the market for a new source for brandy."

Jack sat back on the floor and shook his head.

"Not brandy, eh?" Sir Norris said. "Tea, perhaps? Fetching a good price in London right now." He snapped his fingers. "That's it, isn't it? Tea. I thought as much. I'll be rich by morning. Negotiate a good percentage with your fellow and have all the business from Hastings to Dungeness to myself. Or at least my fair cut of it."

"You'll be dead if you go down there," Jack told him.

"And good riddance," Bruno muttered from his corner.

"Kill me?" Sir Norris let out a mighty snort. "Think you can frighten me with your lies? Why the devil would he kill me? It is really quite simple; either he gives me his cargo or I light off a few rockets. Then my regular contacts—let us call them our friends from Calais, who have been after this fellow for months— will solve the problem for me. They'll have his ship before he can get through the surf. I've seen to that."

Jack sprang from the floor and shook the bars. "You can't do that. Everyone on board that ship would die."

"Then I suppose I won't have to negotiate a percentage with the fellow, will I?" Sir Norris sneered. He reached down and snapped open his pocket watch. "Time to go. Got some tea to unload." He turned to leave, his henchmen at his heels.

"No, you can't do this!" Jack protested. "The man coming ashore isn't one for games or negotiations."

"Everyone negotiates," Sir Norris told him. "Or else they find themselves in the same position as your friend in the garden." He opened the door and started to leave.

Jack had nothing left to lose. For everything was lost if Sir Norris went down to that beach.

"The very fate of England is at stake, man! Do not do this!"

Norris stopped and turned. "The fate of England?" He laughed. "Your aunt could have come up with a better tale than that. And been a might bit more convincing." And then he left the jail.

Left Jack to his fate.

Chapter 13

"Picking locks, Miss Thalia?" Miranda said over her shoulder as they quietly approached the village jail.

Tally had the cheek to grin from ear to ear. "Would you believe it if I told you I hadn't the skill until I came to Miss Emery's?"

Miranda groaned. "You aren't going to cozen me into believing you learned larceny at Miss Emery's. In truth, did you learn this from one of your countless nannies?"

"No, it's true. Kit Escott taught me," she said quite proudly.

This caught Miranda's attention, and she turned around and stared at Tally. Miss Kathleen Escott was one of Miss Emery's finest triumphs, having married very well, even though it was rumored that the circumstances had been rather questionable.

Not that such a thing ever mattered to Miss Emery: A good marriage was all she asked of her former students. It was better advertisement than an ad in the *Morning Post*.

Still, Miranda was having some trouble believing Tally. "Are you telling me the Countess of Radcotte taught you how to pick locks?"

Tally nodded and grinned. "I'm certainly not as accomplished as she is, but she claimed I was the most adept student she'd ever trained."

"We shall see exactly how adept you are, Miss Thalia," Birdwell said, dousing the lamp he held and pointing toward the low, squat building that sat in the middle of the village square.

Miranda glanced around the little huddle of houses and shops that sat at the crossroads. It looked like so many other English towns that had grown up bordered by great estates, or sitting as this one was, at the intersection of two roads.

And luckily for them, the jail was not much more than a small stone cottage.

"Do you think anyone else is in there?" Miranda asked Birdwell.

"No. Sir Norris is too tightfisted to pay someone to stay the night."

Miranda nodded, then glanced back at the jail, which was situated out in the open, as bright and obvious as a plum atop a cake. And to make matters worse, the full moon overhead seemed to have settled its bright beams directly on the front door.

"Not the best of nights for this," Birdwell muttered. "Would be better if it were a few nights from now and pitch black."

"Spoken like a true highwayman," Miranda whispered back at him. "But you are right, the moonlight could reveal our intentions if someone happens along. I want you to stay back here and act as a lookout—"

Birdwell sputtered a protest. "Miss Porter! I will not be left behind—"

"It is better if you stay here," she told him. "If we are caught, we will have the protection of our names and families to rely upon. But you, Mr. Birdwell, if your true identity were revealed, would hang."

He still shook his head.

"It is better this way," she told him, placing her hand on the sleeve of his coat. "One of us must go with Tally to help. If you were to go and the two of you were caught, that would leave only me left to save Lord John. I haven't the aptitude for picking locks or your experiences with evading the law. If we fail, Lord John will be better served with you to act as our backup."

The butler heaved a sigh and nodded. "If anyone happens along, I will make this whistle." He made an odd little chirping. "Drop down and throw your cloaks over your heads, you will blend into the shadows and most likely not be seen."

Miranda nodded, then started quietly and quickly across the village square with Tally beside her.

"Are you sure you can do this?" Miranda asked her, still dubious about taking one of Miss Emery's students on a midnight raid of one of the King's jails.

"I hope so," Tally whispered back.

The village around them was unsettling in its quiet. Not even a bit of rough laughter arose from the nearby inn, the common room dark and empty.

Tally knelt before the door and fumbled in her bag for her tools. "Odd that Lady Josephine had a pick set, don't you think?"

Given what they had learned of Thistleton Park this evening, Miranda couldn't imagine anything about Lady Josephine that would surprise her.

Or about Jack . . .

The lock rattled stubbornly as Tally first tried it, and Miranda's heart sank. Dear God, what if they couldn't set Jack free?

That would leave Felicity, Pippin, and Lady Josephine to wait for Dash's arrival alone.

Tally continued to try her hand at opening the locked door, muttering what Miranda suspected was not only Russian but also not in the least ladylike.

More of Nanny Tasha's lessons, no doubt.

Then, after one last oath, the lock made a loud click and the door gave way.

"I did it!" Tally whispered. "I did it!"

"You did!"

"The only other thing I've ever opened," she said excitedly, "is Miss Emery's wine cabinet."

Miranda paused and looked at her.

"I mean . . . I didn't really . . . Oh—" Tally finished her rebuttal with another bit of Russian.

"Let's just pretend I didn't hear that," Miranda told her.

"The curse or the wine part?" the girl asked.

"Both." Leading the way, Miranda moved slowly inside the jail. "Jack?" she whispered. "Jack, are you in here?"

"Miss Porter?"

Miranda blinked her eyes in the darkness. Only the barest sliver of moonlight fell inside through one of the narrow windows high in the wall. And when finally her sight adjusted to the meager light, she saw him.

He was on the floor beside a figure, which she presumed was Mr. Jones. Crossing the room in a flash, she knelt beside the bars. "Is he hurt?"

"Aye," Jack said, without looking up. "But not too bad. His hand is broken, but it should heal just fine if we can get it set properly."

"Jack, I—" she started to say, but she stopped when he finally looked at her, his blue eyes narrow and dark.

"What the devil are you doing here?" he said. "I would have thought you and your charges would be to Hastings by now, comfortably and properly encamped at Lady Caldecott's."

"Our plans changed," was all she could mutter past the lump in her throat. There was so much more she wanted to say.

Tally, in the meantime, had gone to work on the lock on the cell door.

Jack glanced over at the girl, then back at Miranda. "Is she doing what I think she's doing?"

"How do you think we got in here?"

He let out a short laugh. "No wonder Parkerton pulled his daughter out of that school. Just what exactly do they teach at Miss Emery's . . . besides decorum and larceny?"

"How to apologize," she said ever so softly.

"Apologize for what?" he asked.

"For this," Miranda said, daring to look up into his eyes. "For everything." *For having ruined you all those years ago. For driving you from Society. For believing in lies for so long. For being unable to forget.*

And in a tremulous moment, Miranda felt a sense that he had not only heard her unspoken plea but also knew. Knew what was in her heart. And once Tally freed him, she would have nowhere else to hide.

Instead of scaring her half to death, it made her want to tear the bars free.

Tally finally got the pick to work, and the lock turned. She grinned at both of them as she pulled the door open. "What a difference a good pick set makes. Why, the ones Kit gave me aren't anywhere as good as the set your Aunt Josephine has."

"My who?" Jack said, slowly turning around and looking at first Tally, then Miranda.

"Lady Josephine," Tally replied as if the sudden arrival of Jack's deceased aunt into their midst were barely worth repeating, least of all mentioning.

Miranda nodded when he looked at her again. "Your aunt arrived a few hours ago."

"And so you know—"

Miranda nodded again. "Yes, we know." Then she smiled. "Probably more than you would like."

"That means if Aunt Josephine is back, then—"

He didn't finish, and Miranda had to imagine that he still wasn't ready to give away any more secrets than he had to.

So she helped him along. "Yes, she returned with the gold."

He went over to the door and glanced up at the moon. "It's just after midnight, isn't it?"

"Yes."

"So I might still have time—" He strode back and helped Bruno to his feet.

"To get the gold to the beach?" Miranda suggested. "You needn't worry. That's been taken care of."

He swung around and stared at her. "What the devil have you done?"

Miranda bristled at his tone. "Helped you, if you must know. While we are getting you out of jail, your aunt is poised to deliver the gold to Captain Dashwell."

Jack shook his head as if he couldn't believe it.

Mr. Jones was more eloquent. "Bloody hell."

"Whatever is wrong?" Miranda asked. "I believe your aunt is quite capable of—"

"Being murdered."

"Murdered?" Miranda whispered, a chill of premonition running down her spine.

Jack stormed out of the jail, and Miranda followed hot on his heels.

"Who is going to murder them, Jack?"

He spun around on her. "My aunt is walking into a trap. Sir Norris has the militia and excise men poised to intercept Dashwell's ship. He thinks the thing is full of tea and lace, and he means to help himself to it. And if he doesn't get what he wants . . ."

Miranda felt her blood run cold.

Behind her, Tally took a deep breath. "Felicity! Pippin!" she finally managed to say.

Jack looked from one to the other. "Don't tell me those two girls are down there with her?"

Miranda nodded. "Oh, Jack, what have I done? How will I ever forgive myself if something happens to—" She wavered again, and this time he caught her. Hauled her into his arms and held her close.

"Nothing will happen if we get there in time," he promised.

Down on the beach, Felicity and Pippin flanked Lady Josephine. Behind them, Mr. Stillings stood, having finally been recruited, albeit reluctantly, to aid his country.

The moon overhead cast an eerie light over the beach, giving them a good view of the waves beyond. Pippin held the spyglass to her eye yet again, but she didn't see any sign of the ship they were awaiting.

"Is this Captain Dashwell trustworthy?" Felicity asked.

Lady Josephine snorted.

Apparently not.

"What if he doesn't come?" Pippin asked.

"He'll be here," Lady Josephine said with conviction. "There's gold to be had."

And even as she said the words, Pippin rose up on her tiptoes to see over the waves and was rewarded with the sight of a ship coming around the point. "There!" she said, gesturing at the arriving ketch.

Lady Josephine snatched up the glass and searched the vessel from stem to stern. Then she snapped the spyglass shut. "'Tis him." She handed the glass back to Pippin, then hoisted up the hem of her gown.

Much to Pippin's amazement, the lady had a pair of pistols holstered to each ankle.

She pulled the first two free and handed one to Felicity and one to Pippin. "Know how to use them?"

Both girls nodded.

"Good. Nice to know not every miss in England is as useless as that gaggle of geese they trot about London." She pulled the other pair free, tucking one pistol into the sash at her waist and holding the other at her side. "Never hurts to be ready"—she glanced at one, then the other—"for anything."

Pippin drew a deep breath and held the pistol a little tighter.

The ship had dropped a longboat into the water, and a handful of people were scrambling down the lines to get into it.

Pippin's heart was hammering as she watched it come ashore. She glanced over at Felicity, who, to all intents and purposes, looked as calm as if she were waiting for the next course of dinner to be served. But Pippin knew better. She could see the way her usually composed cousin's hand trembled, the pistol in her grasp wavering ever so slightly. It was the most she had ever seen her cousin unnerved.

That Felicity, with all her Continental manners and experiences, was frightened actually calmed Pippin's nerves. For once, they were on equal footing.

The longboat cast off and started to row ashore.

Lady Josephine stood regal and erect, and Pippin did her best to effect the same pose.

As the boat came through the surf, surging toward the beach, a tall man leaped from the bow and caught hold of the rope. Another joined him, and they pulled the boat in, stopping in front of Lady Josephine. If this was Captain Dashwell, he was much younger than Pippin had thought he would be.

"Well, if it isn't the old girl herself," he said, doffing his plumed hat and bowing low. "I see reports of your demise were premature. That or the devil tossed you out of hell'?"

Instead of being insulted, Lady Josephine grinned and took the man into a hug. "Dash, you are the most incorrigible, impertinent young man."

"And you wouldn't have me any other way," he said, extracting himself from the lady's grasp. Then he stepped back and eyed Felicity and then Pippin. "And who do we have here?" He sent Pippin the most audacious, saucy wink, the kind that suggested he didn't have an inkling of propriety or proper introductions.

And worst of all, it made her knees go weak with a sense of danger and something she'd never felt before.

"You leave them alone, Dash," Lady Josephine told him. "They aren't your type. And they both know how to shoot a rat when they see one."

"My lady, you wound me," he said, his hand covering his heart.

"Enough of this nonsense. Unload your passengers right this minute," she ordered. "Can't believe you didn't put them ashore last night. It isn't like you wouldn't be paid."

He snorted, much as Lady Josephine had earlier. Apparently he trusted his English counterparts as much as they trusted him.

"You'll get your cargo when I get my gold," he told her.

Lady Josephine nodded toward a pile of driftwood behind them, where the mule had been tied.

He grinned and strode up the beach, flipping open the first pack and pulling out a handful of gold coins. Nodding in satisfaction, he whistled, low and soft, like a seabird to the men in the longboat.

They pulled up one man, then another, and cut the bindings that had their arms tied around their backs. The pair were then shoved roughly over the side and into the surf.

From the water rose a tall, darkly clad man, who came ashore with all the elegant stride of a Corinthian. The other, not quite as tall but dressed in similar clothes, followed at his heels.

The first man wasn't but a few feet from them when Felicity gasped. "Uncle Temple!"

The man stopped dead in his tracks and stared open-mouthed at her. "Duchess? Is that you?"

"Uncle Temple," she said again, running to the man's arms. "What are you doing here?"

"You've found me out, I daresay," he said, giving her a good hug, then tucking her hand into the crook of his arm and escorting her up to Lady Josephine.

"Lady Josephine?" Temple said, a sense of delight and wonder to his words. "How is this?" He shook his head. "More of Pymm's machinations, I daresay."

"You know my husband," Lady Josephine declared. "Always one step ahead of our enemies."

"And his friends," the man muttered. "But it is very good to see you again."

He took her hand and kissed it.

"You know Lady Josephine?" Felicity asked.

Temple nodded.

"And so you are—" She stopped short of saying the

obvious. "So all those times you visited us and Papa, you were actually—"

"Helping, where I could," he demurred.

Felicity nodded. "And my father? He knows?"

"Lord Langley," Lady Josephine announced, "is the finest agent the Foreign Office has ever had."

In the meantime, Dash had brought the mule down to the edge of the water, where he was trying to unload the beast into the longboat, but the animal was balking at being so close to the surf.

Pippin went over and caught hold of the reins, her other hand stroking the poor thing and talking softly to it until it settled down.

"You have a way about you," the cheeky young captain said as he walked back and forth, working alongside his men.

Pippin tried to remember what Miss Porter and Miss Emery had said about such situations, but she couldn't remember a single lesson on meeting wayward Americans in the middle of the night. So she thought it was better to say nothing than to encourage the rogue.

"Do you have a name?" he asked when he returned for the last of the gold. This close she could see that he wasn't much older than she.

And he was the most handsome man she had ever seen. None of the pallid features of the dandies her brother brought home, but tanned from the sea, with his hair tied back in a queue like a pirate.

"What? No name?" he pressed, coming closer still, until she could smell how the very sea seemed to envelop him—odors of salt, pitch, tar, and gunpowder drifting forth.

And an air of masculine power to him that she had never experienced and had to imagine she never would.

She pursed her lips shut, but he stood before her, his brow arched, his eyes dancing with a teasing light.

"Pippin," she whispered. Certainly telling him her nickname wouldn't be a breach in etiquette. It wasn't like they would ever meet again.

"Pippin, eh?" he said. "I would call you something else. Something befitting such a pretty lady. I would call you Circe. For truly you are a siren to lure me ashore."

She felt her cheeks color. "I don't think that is proper," she said, mustering a bit of courage.

"Not proper?" the man laughed. "Not proper is the fact that these bags feel a bit light." He turned toward the party on the beach. "My lady, don't tell me you've cheated me yet again?"

Lady Josephine winced, but she had the nerve to deny her transgression. "Dash, I'll not pay another pence into your dishonest hands."

"Then I shall take my payment otherwise," he said, and before anyone could imagine what he was about, he caught hold of Pippin and pulled her into his arms.

She gasped, first at how quickly he moved, then at the strength with which he held her.

"I've always wanted to kiss a lady," he said, just before his lips met hers.

She thought at first he meant to plunder her, like one would think a pirate might, but his kiss was nothing like that.

Sure and tempting, he kissed her, sweeping aside her protests, and letting his lips ply hers. His tongue swept inside her mouth, sweeping over hers and leaving her breathless with the intimacy of it.

She tried to breathe, she tried to think, but it was impossible.

This was her first kiss, and she had never imagined that it would be . . . be . . . so incredible.

And then, as his hands started to roam over her body, taking liberties that were certainly not proper, he lit a fire beneath her skin that stole what was left of her breath.

His kiss had her hearing the screech of rockets overhead, until she opened her eyes and realized that the night had erupted into day. Suddenly, it seemed, Captain Dashwell had come to the same realization.

He wrenched away from her and looked up.

Overhead, to her amazement, there *were* rockets, streaking across the sky.

"Christ!" he swore. And as gently as he had held her, he shoved her down face first into the sand and threw himself over her as the first of the militia's bullets started to pepper the beach.

Miranda struggled to keep up with Jack. She'd never seen a man so determined, as if he had the devil at his heels.

Even when Lady Josephine had told her that Jack was an agent with the Foreign Office, running operations from Thistleton Park, and, at times, going on missions into France, she hadn't quite believed it.

In her mind, Mad Jack Tremont was a devil-may-care rake, certainly not a man of action and danger.

Now here he was, charging into the fray like . . . like . . . well, like a hero.

Miranda didn't know whether to be terrified or to fall in love.

Terrified. Most decidedly. The latter had already happened.

For here was Jack, charming and heroic, elegant when he wanted to be, and even, on rare occasions, a gentleman, not to mention the power he could wield with his kiss—everything she had ever wanted.

And she'd been too blind and prejudiced to see it. Hadn't she known all along that something wasn't right at Thistleton Park? She'd jumped to an ill conclusion as to his character rather than give the man the benefit of the doubt.

If only he would be able to forgive her for what a mess she'd made of his life.

So lost in her thoughts, she didn't see that Jack had skidded to a halt at the foot of the tower. Miranda blundered to a stop behind him just in time to hear him curse, "Demmit! That bloody fool!"

She tried to catch her breath, to ask him what was happening, when a volley of rockets went screeching into the night sky and exploded overhead, illuminating the scene before them.

Halfway down the cliff path, a line of men—the militia—had the party on the beach cut off.

The rockets had done their work well, for Miranda could see quite clearly Lady Josephine and Felicity diving down behind a large pile of driftwood, along with two other men.

But there was no sign of Pippin.

Even then, Sir Norris gave the order to fire.

To Miranda it sounded like Wellington's entire army

was upon them. Muskets and pistol shots pierced the night.

Her heart stilled, until another rocket exploded and she could search the beach anew—this time seeing Pippin lying in the sand at the water's edge, a man covering her.

"Jack!" she said, pointing toward the waves. "There. Dear heavens, has she been hit?" *No, not Pippin,* she prayed, her knees faltering beneath her.

Bruno, Birdwell and Tally arrived just then, and it was evident they'd seen Pippin as well, from the shock on Tally's face.

"We're too late," Miranda whispered.

"No, we're not," Jack said, turning to Birdwell. "How many pistols do you have?"

"My usual," the man said.

Jack nodded. "Good. Give me two of them."

The once staid and proper butler threw open his coat and revealed a stash of weapons that would put a regiment to shame. Pulling two large, wicked-looking pistols free, he handed them over to Jack, who tucked them in his waistband. "Careful with that one on the left," Birdwell warned. "The trigger is a bit touchy."

"Excellent," Jack said as he hefted another pair. "I'll point it at Sir Norris's head." He turned to his secretary. "Can you shoot, Bruno?"

"Not with me good hand," the man said. "I fear my aim might be off."

Jack nodded and took the next pistol that Birdwell offered and handed it to the man. "No matter, I don't want you to hit anyone."

"Whatever do you think you are going to do?" Miranda asked as she found the next pistol from Bird-well's stash thrust into her hands.

"We are going to give Sir Norris a lesson in military planning."

"Whatever do you mean?" she asked.

Jack handed the next pistol to Tally. "Do you know how to fire one of these?"

She nodded, a look of determination in her eyes.

"Foolish of me to ask," he said. "You just broke me out of jail."

"Jack, what do you think you are going to do?" Miranda said, catching hold of his arm. "March down there and order Sir Norris to cease fire?"

Then to her shock, he grinned at her. The dark flash of his eyes and deep crease to his brows made him look as wicked as Lord Douglas's portrait in the gallery.

"That's exactly what I plan on doing." He reached over and cocked the pistol in her hand. "And you are going to help me."

Miranda knew this man would never change.

He would always be Mad Jack Tremont. And that gave her more courage than if they'd had the King's army behind them.

Sir Norris stood in the middle of his men, ordering them to continue firing, to cut off the longboat from leaving the shore.

"He's got a king's ransom in gold in that boat, I wager, and I'll give twenty guineas to the man who—" His words were cut off as he suddenly found an arm wound around his throat and a gun pointed at his temple.

"What the——" He twisted his head around until he could see his assailant. "Tremont, you devil! Let me go!"

"Good to see you, Sir Norris," Jack said. "Now stand down your men, or I'll blow your head off."

"You wouldn't——"

Jack pulled the trigger back and grinned. "I wouldn't wiggle about too much, for I was told this pistol is a bit touchy. Has a terrible habit of just firing."

Sir Norris gulped, then called out his order. "Stop! Stop, I say," he squeaked.

"Louder," Jack told him, shaking his hand and the temperamental pistol.

"Hold your fire," the man screeched. "Do it."

Jack dragged the squire back a few feet, so all of his men could see him. "Tell them to put down their guns."

"Tremont, do you think you can take my entire militia single-handedly?" Norris said, his initial fears wearing off enough that he could finally find some courage. "Once you kill me, they'll cut you down like a dog."

"But I'm not alone," Jack told him coolly. He tipped the baronet's hat off his head with the muzzle of his pistol.

A second later, shots rang out, and bullets pinged and spit up sand all around the militia. That was enough for the local lads—they tossed aside their issued weapons and ran into the darkness, most likely not stopping until they reached the cozy confines of their cottages.

Apparently not even Sir Norris's offer of twenty guineas was worth losing their lives to an unseen force.

Not to mention the fierce sight of one of the Mad Tremonts brandishing a pistol.

"Brave lot," Jack commented as the last of the men were encouraged to leave by a few well-placed shots. "Loyal as well."

"You'll hang for this, Tremont. Mark my words. Years of smuggling. Now you can add to it interfering with the King's business. Not to mention threatening the King's appointed agent," Norris blustered.

"I could add killing the King's appointed agent if you don't shut up and listen to me for a demmed minute."

Norris, never the brightest of His Majesty's appointed lot, wasn't about to stop. "Oh, I should have seen you swing for your aunt's murder, but this . . . this . . . is the final straw."

Jack shook his head and began to tow his prisoner down to the beach. "Sir Norris, I didn't murder my aunt." They stopped when they reached the rocky shoreline. "Temple? Aunt Josephine? Are you well?" he called out.

"Jack, my boy," his aunt called back. "Is that you?"

"Aye, Aunt Josephine. 'Tis me. It's safe to come out."

"Lady Josephine?" Sir Norris whispered.

As the lady rose up from behind a log, the man sagged against Jack in shock. "But it cannot be!" he protested. "You're dead."

"Sir Norris, still as slow-witted as ever. Do I look dead?"

The man shook his head. "How can this be? What trickery is this?"

"No trickery," Jack told him. "But may I introduce you to the other King's agent in the shire—my aunt, Lady Josephine."

"A woman? An agent of the King? Preposterous,"

Norris protested, more vehemently than he had to the news that Lady Josephine was alive.

"Norris, you are a nitwit. I've been working for the Crown for nigh on forty years."

"Lady Josephine, that is the most unseemly thing I have ever heard," he told her. "I fear I will have to withdraw my attentions from you."

"I thought I had already done that by dying," Lady Josephine shot back.

Jack wasn't about to listen to another word of it. "Is everyone safe?"

"Seems to be," his aunt said, nodding toward Felicity and, to his relief, the Marquis of Templeton, along with the other agent they were awaiting, the Earl of Clifton.

Jack's heart constricted when he saw Clifton. He and Grey had been partners. *Had been.*

That still left one more person to find. Pippin.

He twisted around toward the water's edge, where he'd last seen her, and he heaved a sigh of relief as he saw Dash help her to her feet. But his relief turned to something else as he watched the cheeky American captain take the girl into his arms and look like he was about to . . .

Jack suddenly knew what Mrs. Mabberly must have felt when she'd spied her daughter in his arms that night at the opera. Four words came to mind as he realized that Dash was about to do the same to Pippin.

Over my dead body.

He shoved Sir Norris into Temple's grasp and marched down the beach, cocking his pistol and aiming it at Dashwell. "Get your hands off her, Dash, or it will be the last thing you do."

The American heaved a sigh but brazened another quick peck before he shoved Pippin toward Jack, then dove into the waves, swimming for his longboat, which awaited him about twenty yards out to sea.

"Later, my sweet Circe," he called out. "I'll find you again, very soon."

"Come along, you little siren," Jack told the blushing girl as he towed her up the beach.

Pippin's gaze never left the waves, not until her pirate was well and away.

Bruno, Birdwell, and Tally were just arriving, leading a ragtag prisoner.

"Who've you got there?" Jack asked.

"A Frenchie," Bruno said. "Miss Porter heard 'em talking fancy like near the tower, so me and Dingby decided to delay this one a bit." Even one-handed, Bruno Jones was a force to be reckoned with. "Miss Porter is fetching the manacles out of the tower."

"Well, well, well," Jack said, turning to the baronet. "Consorting with the enemy, Sir Norris?"

"I don't know who that fellow is," the man blustered. "Never seen the bastard before in my life."

"Who the hell are you?" Jack demanded.

"My English, it is not so good," the man said, struggling to escape Bruno.

His lack of English was about to become the least of his problems.

Jack caught the small man by the scruff of his neck and raised him up until he stood on his tippy-toes. "Hear me well, monsieur," he said in perfect French. "This pistol is not all that well made. French, I believe.

And sadly, I am not very good at using it. A dangerous combination, don't you think?" He lifted the fellow up a little higher until the man's feet pedaled in the air. "Who are you? What are you doing here?"

"Go to hell," the man spat.

Jack pulled back the hammer and laid the muzzle to his temple. "You first."

"Jack, don't kill him," Lady Josephine protested, also in French. "We'll never get what we need from him if you kill him. Besides, it's a good six hours before the tide gets up and carries his rotten carcass out to sea. If you must shoot him, take him down to the water's edge."

The man looked ready to soil himself as both aunt and nephew argued the best options for getting information out of him but also killing him in the most efficient fashion.

That is, until a shot rang out, taking with it Temple's hat, and nearly his head.

"That was a perfectly good hat," the marquis lamented as they all dove down. Another shot ripped into the sand around them.

"Sir Norris, call this fool off," Jack said. "Call off your militia."

The Frenchman laughed. "That is no Englishman, but my partner. Prepare *your* soul for a journey to hell, monsieur."

Chapter 14

Miranda made her way up into the folly and got the sea chest open once again. It wasn't as easy in the dark, so she paid extra heed as she carefully removed the small powder keg and coil of fusing wire, tucking the flint into her pocket, before she rummaged around for the manacles.

The last thing she wanted to do was accidentally blow up the place.

Down below she heard the door creak open. *Jack.* She turned to call out to him, but something inside her made her stop.

What if it wasn't Jack?

Then Lady Josephine's warning from the other night rang in her ears.

I have it on good authority we are being watched.

Bruno had been able to sneak up and catch that

French fellow who'd been loitering nearby, but what if that man had a partner?

Footsteps echoed on the stairs, rising closer and closer.

Oh, demmit, she cursed, where had she set her pistol down?

Unable to find it, she caught up the powder keg and fusing coil.

And what are you going to do with these, Miranda? she asked herself. *Blow up Albin's Folly? And you along with it?*

She looked around in panic for a place to hide and cautiously and quickly tucked herself behind the sea chest, next to the opening in the floor. Hopefully whoever it was would not see her and she could slip past them.

And still the footsteps came closer.

She tried to breathe but couldn't. It was like a chess game. One move, then the next.

And the best move was to be prepared, her father had always said. *Think, think, think.* Why is someone coming up here?

To signal a ship offshore? Not with everyone on the beach, she reasoned. A signal lantern would draw them up to investigate.

So why come up here, when they would be in plain sight?

She drew a shaky breath as one reason became clearer than any other. Whoever it was would have a fine view of the beach below when they reached the top of the tower. And a clear shot at the people below.

Miranda's heart chilled. Jack. The girls. Birdwell.

Lady Josephine. She even gave Mr. Jones and Sir Norris a moment of consideration. They were all in danger.

Pulling the plug on the keg, she stuffed an end of the fusing into it, her hands shaking, her heart hammering.

Oh, what was she thinking? She couldn't blow up Albin's Folly. It was hardly sensible and in no way proper.

Well, she had no need for propriety now. For she had to imagine that if she survived this night, the first thing she'd do was anything but proper. She'd find Jack and make him finish what he'd started all those years ago.

With his kiss.

The thought of Jack, his kiss, his arms around her, buoyed her courage.

And when the large, looming man came up through the hole in the floor, went to the window and aimed a pistol at the beach below, she knew exactly what she needed to do.

Jack and Temple worked their way up the path, keeping to the shadows but still drawing the fire of their unknown, unseen assailant.

Finally Jack spied where the shots were coming from.

"He's up in the tower," he whispered over to Temple.

The man nodded and drew his pistol, for the marquis was a crack shot and if anyone could hit a target or an enemy, it was Temple.

Jack glanced back down at the beach to see if everyone was safe. He counted one by one, until he came up short.

Where the devil was Miranda?

Then he remembered what Bruno had said.

Miss Porter is fetching the manacles out of the tower.

He reached over and snatched Temple's arm down just as he fired, the bullet pinging off the stone wall, far from its target.

"What the devil did you do that for?"

"Miranda is up there," Jack told him.

"Miranda who?" Temple asked.

"Miranda Mabberly."

Temple looked at him closely. "You haven't been hit, have you?"

Jack shook his head.

"Because then I must be, for I thought you said Miranda Mabberly is in that tower."

"She is."

Another shot pierced the night, this time ripping into the side of Temple's coat. "First my hat, and now my new coat. This fellow is immensely vexing and positively knows nothing about good fashion."

They scrambled up a little higher, gaining better cover. "Save your droll remarks for Town," Jack told him. "We need to get to Miranda."

Shooting another glance up at the tower and then one over at Jack, Temple said, "Are you telling me that you believe Miss Mabberly, the woman you ruined all those years ago, the woman, I would like to point out, who is *dead,* is the one shooting at us?"

"No!"

Temple heaved a sigh of relief. "That's good, because I thought you'd gone around the bend for certain. I've told Pymm I don't know how many times that he needs to let you come up to London periodically. That house of yours is enough to make anyone dicked in the nob, but living without—"

"Shut up, Templeton," Jack told his friend as they eased their way up the final few feet to the top of the cliff. "Miranda Mabberly is in that tower."

Temple rubbed his forehead, as if trying to make sense of the insensible. "This life has turned you mad. Diana is right—I'll be as odd as Pymm in a few more years, and now I am starting to believe her. Look at you."

Jack was done explaining, or trying to explain. He needed to figure out how to get into the tower and stop this fellow without harming Miranda.

So they could find a way to reconcile all their differences. He still couldn't quite believe it.

Proper Miss Porter, breaking a man out of prison.

While it didn't explain the lies that lay between them, the lost years, it gave Jack a glimpse of a woman he'd always suspected lurked behind that tight chignon, beneath that overlaced corset.

And when he held her in his arms again, he swore he'd find a way to undo everything.

Including her corset.

"Let me get this straight," Temple was saying. "You think a deceased debutante is up in your cousin's folly?"

Another shot ripped past them, this one hitting the heel of Temple's boot, damaging his glossy Hessians. "That is an insult no man can endure," he said, and this time he aimed his pistol before Jack could stop him and would have fired if it hadn't been for one small problem.

Albin's Folly, the poor man's enduring monument to his lost love, the lighthouse that had guided spies and friends across the Channel, exploded above them.

*   *   *

Torches and lanterns, ropes and tools were fetched as quickly as possible, but that didn't deter Jack from digging in the rubble with his bare hands in search of the one thing he feared the most.

Finding Miranda.

The top of the tower had been demolished in the explosion, with the stones and rubble falling inward and around it. It truly looked now like an ancient relic, charred and damaged by time.

As they waded into the debris, Jack nearly stumbled over the body of a man. Once they'd pulled him free and rolled him over, Temple stepped back and shook his head.

"It cannot be," he whispered, catching up the torch that Birdwell held and bringing it closer. "Jean-Marc Marden? How is this possible?"

The other Frenchman was brought forward, and with some convincing, he explained how this man, of all men, was here . . .

And what the wily spy wouldn't tell, Temple filled in.

The marquis had captured and stopped Jean-Marc Marden, one of Napoleon's most dangerous agents, nearly a year before (and saved his beloved Diana in the process). However, Marden had managed to escape the English authorities and had come searching for his adversary and all those connected with him.

"He sought revenge for all he'd lost," their captive told them.

"And may have gained it," Jack said softly, his heart torn with grief.

Undaunted by Marden's fate, Temple and Jack dug through the rubble, pulling aside the heavy stones, digging through the wreckage of the explosion. It wasn't until dawn that Jack spied a hint of red hair peeking out from beneath the buried stairwell.

Quickly, he and Temple tore away the stones that lay around her. At first, Jack's worst fears seemed to be true—she was truly lost. Then Temple pressed forward, placed his fingers to the lady's neck, and said the words that gave Jack hope.

"I think she's alive."

When she was freed, Jack carried Miranda all the way back to the house and laid her in the music room.

Everyone gathered around and waited for the surgeon who had been summoned.

"This is your fault," Jack said, pointing a finger at Aunt Josephine.

"My fault?" she said. "I don't see how—"

"Only you would come up with such a harebrained scheme. Going down to the beach with two schoolgirls, no less. Breaking into a jail."

"Saving your life," Felicity muttered.

"I'll get to you, Miss Langley, in a moment," Jack told her, before he turned back to his aunt and started giving her a wigging that would have put Miss Emery to shame.

Temple pulled the girl aside. "Let him scold, Duchess. He's in a foul mood and of no mind to listen."

"None of this would have happened if he had just admitted he has a *tendre* for Miss Porter," she protested.

"Miss Porter?" Temple asked.

Felicity nodded over at the sofa. "Our decorum teacher. At least she was until the end of this term. She inherited a large fortune last winter and is off to live in Kent, and they will never realize that they are meant to be together." She sighed. "Lord John thinks he is cursed to remain true for the rest of his life to his long-lost Miss Mabberly. Uncle Temple, can't you convince him otherwise? Miss Porter is the perfect lady for him, if only he'd believe."

Temple took another look at the woman on the sofa. The red hair, the face. Then he looked a little bit harder.

No, it couldn't be.

For dear God, Jack wasn't mad. This Miss Porter *was* Miranda Mabberly. Alive all these years.

It had been nine years since he'd last seen her, a girl barely older than Felicity, and betrothed to the Earl of Oxley. The mere thought of that arrangement still made him nauseous. But he had never forgotten her, and had thought her death a terrible shame. Now he realized that old Mathias Mabberly's grief hadn't been so much at the loss of his daughter but at his inability to marry the scandal-ridden heiress to some other worthless, easily manipulated sot like Oxley.

"Duchess, my dear girl, I wouldn't worry about Jack," he told her.

Besides, the man was still ringing a peel over his aunt's head. "And furthermore, now my folly has been blown up—"

"There is a jest in that statement somewhere," Temple mused to no one in particular, "but I daresay now isn't the time."

"It wasn't her fault," came a weak voice.

Jack turned. "Pippin, I don't see how you—" His face paled as he realized that the confession hadn't come from her.

"Do stop scolding everyone, Jack," Miranda told

him, her eyes open at half mast. "You are giving me a frightful megrim with all your yammering."

He rushed to her side, dropping to his knees and taking her hand in his. "You're all right."

"Of course I am," she said, struggling to rise, but he held her down.

"Stay still until the doctor has a chance to look you over."

She opened her eyes and looked around. "How did I get here?" Then, as if the events of the night came back in a rush, she struggled up, despite Jack's hold. "The tower. I was in Albin's Folly."

"Yes, and it blew up," Jack told her. "The Frenchman who was there, shooting at us, his name was Marden. He must have used the powder keg in the chest as a last resort. Perhaps in hopes of destroying the tower."

She shook her head. "No, that's not it at all. He didn't blow it up."

Jack sat back and stared at her. "If Marden didn't, then who did?"

" 'T'was me."

"Mademoiselle, get up and stand where I can see you," the man by the window said in a low and deadly voice.

Miranda reluctantly rose, leaving behind the powder keg but carefully unwinding the fuse coil behind her.

"Très bon." he said. "If you dare move or say a word, my next bullet will be for you."

Silence filled the tower, and Miranda didn't know what to do.

"Do you understand?" he snapped at her.

"Of course," she bit back, suddenly finding a bit of irony in the situation. "But you told me not to speak."

He snorted, as if he had to admire her spunk. "You have a sharp tongue for a woman who is going to die."

"Then I might as well put it to good use," Miranda said brazenly, realizing the more she spoke, the less time he had to shoot. "Who are you?"

"That is unimportant," he told her, firing down at her friends.

She flinched at the sharp retort. And did so again as he pulled another pistol from his jacket and took aim. "It is important to me," she insisted. "I'd like to know the name of the man I am going to consign to perdition."

He laughed a little. "You think so? Then if you must know, it is Marden. Jean-Marc Marden." He bowed his head slightly to her.

"Monsieur Marden, why don't you just put that gun down. Perhaps we could settle all this—"

The man whirled around and aimed the pistol at her. "'This,' as you so blithely put it, will be settled when I have killed my enemies, the men who have ruined my career." His voice held a tightness to it that hinted to Miranda what his "career" might be.

Goodness, what was it about this spy business that made all the people involved ever so unhinged?

But that might make it to her advantage, since her only claim to insanity was when she was near Jack.

Jack . . .

The urge to stop this man, to end all this madness filled her heart with courage and a rage that burned like a torch. She'd bring an end to this Marden before he harmed Jack or anyone else.

The Frenchman fired again, then reloaded, which he did with alarming speed.

But in those precious seconds, Miranda hoped she just might have time to . . .

Glancing back behind her at the black and eerie stairwell, she paused, then fingered the fuse coil in her hands, mentally measuring the length and trying to calculate the seconds it would take to ignite the keg . . .

Her father had dealt in these goods and she knew them well, though that didn't mean she'd ever done something like this.

Mostly because she also knew what would happen if she failed.

Miranda took a slow, deep breath. No, she couldn't consider the notion that she wouldn't make it down in time. She just had to.

Marden was taking aim again, and while he did, she got the flint out of her pocket. She'd have to get it lit on the first strike, for there would be no other chances.

The beast fired, and Miranda sent up a small, urgent prayer that his bullet was like his intent—unbalanced.

Marden cursed, and not in a triumphant way, so Miranda had to believe her plea had been answered. He'd missed.

Just let his next shot go awry as well . . .

Even as he fired, the retort echoing piercingly through the tower, she took her chance and struck the flint.

It sparked, and for a second nothing happened. She thought for certain that she'd failed, but then the fuse ignited, in a hissing, burning fury.

Miranda dropped it to the ground and fled down the stairs, in an equally furious flight.

Ten . . . nine . . . eight, she counted as she whirled down the staircase. Above her she heard Marden curse again, and this time it wasn't because he'd missed.

Five . . . four . . . three . . .

Oh, dear heavens, she'd never make it to the bottom in time.

And so she leaped into the darkness, falling the last story. She hit the ground even as the powder keg exploded.

Rolling beneath the stairs, she looked up to find the tower blasting into a shower of flames. She ducked and covered herself, with only one last thought, one tiny prayer rising from the bottom of her heart, the depth of her soul, and hopefully above the din around her.

Please, let me have just one more kiss from that rake of mine. . . .

Miranda finished her story, and Jack stared at her in disbelief.

Miss Porter, Miss Proper By-the-Book, Decorum-Loving Porter had blown up Albin's Folly.

And risked her very life in the process. Risked everything to stop Marden.

"What the devil were you thinking?" he exploded, not unlike the powder keg she'd ignited.

Miranda rose up in the face of his fury, sputtering back, "What else was I to do? Stand there and let him shoot all of you? I asked him to stop, but he wasn't of a mind to see reason." She sniffed a little and shot Jack a disapproving glance as if he *(yes, him)* had just made some social faux pas. Like forgetting to remove his hat, or leave a proper calling card in the salver.

"I, for one, applaud your ingenuity, Miss Porter," Lady Josephine said.

She would, Jack thought, his anger rising with every second. Demmit, didn't she see the danger she'd been in? And igniting a powder keg? This was her solution? Oh, there would be no more of that sort of nonsense!

Meanwhile, his great-aunt was showering Miranda with unsolicited and unwanted praise. "You showed a splendid amount of courage, Miss Porter, and, might I say, imagination. Why, I think the next time we need someone—"

"Enough, Aunt Josephine," Jack said, cutting her off, ignoring the stubborn light in her eyes. Oh, she was a Tremont all right, and one of the "mad" Tremonts at that, but she was no longer in charge of this house.

He was. And it was about time he took the reins of this manor and ran it as he saw fit.

"There will be no next time," he told her.

"But Jack, my dear boy—"

He rose from Miranda's side. "There will be no next time. For any of you. I have had enough of seeing my friends, my family, let alone the woman I love risk life and limb, and for what?" He paced the room. "There will never be an end to this if something isn't done, so I am ending it. Here and now."

"But Jack—" Miranda protested.

He swung around on her. "And not a word from you. Do you think I want my wife risking her life in such an improper fashion?"

"You love me?" she whispered.

"Yes," he barked at her.

She grinned up at him. "You want to marry me?"

"Should have years ago." He paced back and forth. "I lost you once, Miranda, I shall not lose you again." He crossed his arms over his chest and glared at everyone in the room, daring them to defy him.

Felicity managed to speak first. She whispered over to Temple, "Oh, heavens, he's gone mad from the curse. He thinks Miss Porter is Miss Mabberly. This will never do!"

"I think you will find that love can be a blessed curse," Temple said, clearing his throat. "But perhaps we should leave them alone for a little bit, to sort matters out." He started shooing everyone from the room.

Birdwell, Pippin, and Tally rose happily, glowing in the triumph of their matchmaking scheme. And besides, Tally was still seething with jealousy over Pippin's adventure on the beach.

"Is it true that pirate kissed you, Pippin?" Tally asked.

Pippin nodded, a dreamy expression on her face.

"Oh, bother," Tally complained. "How is it that you have all the luck?"

The glow on Pippin's face said the girl couldn't have been happier to have for once done something before her sophisticated and experienced cousins.

She didn't even mind when Jack sent a warning sally in their direction.

"I shall deal with the rest of you later," he said.

Sir Norris huffed at this. "And I you, sir. Breaking out of the King's jail. Accosting his appointed agent. We shall see about this." But still, he left quite willingly as well.

Not so Lady Josephine and Felicity. They remained seated, as if they wouldn't give up their places for any boon, intent on staying until the final act.

Temple caught Josephine and then Felicity by the arms and towed them out of the room.

"Uncle Temple, you must make him understand that is not Miss Mabberly. If he doesn't propose to Miss Porter, it won't be a proper betrothal—"

"Come along, Duchess," Temple said, pushing her the last few feet out of the room. "There is no stopping a man in love. Believe me, this I know from experience."

Closing the door behind them, they left Jack and Miranda to sort out the future that, up until now, had seemed unimaginable.

Jack knelt before her and carefully and ever so gently brushed her tangled hair back from her face. "Oh, Miranda. How I thought I lost you . . . yet again."

Miranda? She must have hit her head harder than she thought, for she could swear he'd been calling her Miranda. "What did you say?"

"Miranda," he repeated, a wicked light sparkling in his eyes. "Miss Miranda Mabberly. 'Tis your name, isn't it?"

He knew. He knew who she was.

"Temple told you," she said, shooting a glance at the closed door. Leave it to the astute and observant marquis to uncover the truth.

Jack shook his head. "I knew before."

"Before? How? When?"

Jack grinned. "Not as long as I should have. Only since we kissed."

Her fingers went to her lips. The lips that had betrayed her secret.

He hugged her close. "As I said the other night, Miss Mabberly, your kiss was impossible to forget."

"My kiss?" She still had a hard time believing such a notion. But the idea thrilled her down to her toes, even as she recalled the one thing she considered unforgettable.

His kiss . . .

"Yes, yours." To make his point, he kissed her again, his lips covering hers, insistent and demanding. His tongue swept over hers, teasing her, sending desire racing through her veins. The desire she'd spent so many years denying.

Never again, she promised. *Never again.*

But she needed to tell him the truth. Miranda pulled away and looked up at him. "I wasn't dead."

"I gathered as much."

She shook her head. "No, you don't understand. My parents sent me away. I never knew they'd told people that I was dead. I lived with my mother's cousins until they died a few years ago, and then I went to work at Miss Emery's."

"And I suppose your father never told you that I offered for you?"

"No." *He'd offered for her . . .* This time she believed him. With all her heart.

"What would your answer have been?"

"No," she whispered.

"No?" Jack sat back. "What do you mean, no?"

Oh, dear. Perhaps she shouldn't be *that* free with the truth.

"Well, you were a terrible rake back then. You told

everyone you mistook me for an opera dancer! An opera dancer, indeed!"

Jack flinched.

"And you were a terrible wastrel. Why, you'd have run through my dowry before we'd been wed a year." She glanced around the halls. "And this house isn't exactly the most sterling example of your capacity for management."

"Ah, but my darling Miranda, that is where you excel," he said, gathering her up in his arms again. "I have to imagine you'll have this house worthy of even Billingsworth's purple prose."

"Don't try to cozen me, Jack Tremont," she said, the warmth of pride spreading through her veins. "My refusal then had nothing to do with your ne'er-do-well reputation; it had everything to do with your kiss."

"My kiss?" His hand covered his heart, as if she couldn't have wounded him deeper. "Miss Mabberly, I will have you know that my kiss—"

She placed a single finger on his lips. "Is unforgettable. Dangerously so. Your rakish, devilish kiss has left me trembling and breathless for nine years. Left me quite unfit for any other man." She paused and smiled at him. "It ruined me." At this he grinned back at her. "So do be quiet, stop trying to win me over with flattery, and finish what you started all those years ago."

His gaze met hers with an intense, dark inquiry. "Is this really what you want?"

"Please, Jack, make love to me." Could she say it any clearer?

He glanced up at the open door, looking out into the

fading night beyond. "Miranda, I don't know . . . perhaps we should wait until the doctor has a look at you."

"Bother the man, I feel well enough." She put her hands on her hips and stared at him. "Don't tell me you've gone proper on me?"

Jack laughed. "Well, I do try to think of myself as a gentleman these days."

A gentleman? Heavens, that would never do!

To make her point, she pressed her lips to his, kissing him boldly, her hands splaying over his chest, tracing the muscles beneath his shirt, while her hips, oh, her hips were being rakish quite on their own—they rocked against him so she could feel his manhood come to life, straining against his breeches. *"Please, Jack?"*

He looked down at her and grinned. "Nine years is an awful long time to wait, I suppose," he said, catching hold of her hand. "But not here."

Catching her up in his arms, he carried her to the wall. Then he reached up and pressed something in the wainscoting. Moments later the panel opened to reveal a door.

"Is there a room in this house that doesn't have some secret?" she asked, as he handed her a candlestick.

"No," he told her. "But this is one of my favorites."

"Why?" she asked.

"You'll see," he said as he carried her into the shadows and up a staircase. When it came to a dead end, he pulled down on a latch, and the wall opened and they were in a bedchamber.

"Whose room is this?" she asked.

"Mine," he told her.

How like a rake to have his own private entrance to his bedchamber.

Jack lay her on the bed and followed after her eagerly.

None of this was proper, she knew. Why, it went against every lesson in decorum she'd ever taught, but none of that mattered as Jack began to kiss her again, this time without any restraint.

With his mouth covering hers, his hands went to work divesting her of her clothes. Her modesty had gone the way of her good sense, for when his fingers ran over her bare skin, it sent waves of desire through her, had her moaning softly with need.

Before she knew it, her gown was up and over her head, her shoes, stockings, and garters were flung away, and all that remained was her corset.

Her too-tight, binding corset. The one he loosened now, ever so slowly.

She writhed beneath him. "Be done with it."

"As you wish," he said, grinning, and the corset followed her other clothes. And then in hasty fashion, his clothes went the same course.

And then suddenly they were both naked, tangled in the sheets of his bed, and Miranda relished the feeling of it—the crisp hair on his chest, the muscles of his back, the way his legs twined with hers. She stretched like a cat, trying to find every bit of pleasure she could.

Not that Jack wasn't doing his rakish best. His lips, his kiss; there was a good reason she'd never forgotten him.

His hands ran up the length of her body, cupping her bottom and bringing her right up against him, his manhood sliding between her legs. The place that ached for him.

"Oh," she whispered. "I never imagined."

"My dear Miranda," he said, "I haven't even started."

Then he did. His mouth dipped down to her breast, his lips catching hold of a nipple and sucking on it until it became hard and pebbled. Then he took the other one and did the same. Back and forth, he tormented her. She arched up toward him, delirious as her body became enveloped in a haze of passion and desire.

She tried to breathe, tried to imagine there could be more to his talents, when his fingers plied her in a place she'd never been touched by a man. Her hips swayed almost obediently as his hand charmed her thighs to part. He delved between her legs, slowly parting her there, until his fingers came to touch her and stroke her anew.

This time she moaned loud and clear, so loud that Jack covered her mouth with his and kissed her as thoroughly and deeply as his fingers were now exploring her.

She quaked as he slid a finger ever so slightly inside her, and then it returned to the nub. Back and forth, he teased her body until it trembled and rocked with need.

Her hands, which had been clinging to the sheets to keep herself steady, now clung to Jack, running down his back. His body was tense and starting to glisten with sweat.

He kissed her again, this time so deep and hard, so full of a hot, fierce need that she knew he was asking her for more—that he wanted more than just her tentative explorations.

She reached out and caught hold of him, that hard length, and began to stroke him, following his example, drawing her hand from the root to the wet tip and back down again, over and over until he was groaning with pleasure.

But it wasn't enough. Not for either of them.

She knew what came next, wanted it with a woman's desire. What she had said before, about his kiss frightening her, that had been true. But she was a woman grown now . . . a woman who had waited far too long.

Catching his hips, she pulled him close, so the tip of his length pressed into her. Her hips rocked to invite him forth. She stretched and clung to him, aching to feel every bit of him inside her.

Jack murmured into her ear. "Are you sure about this?"

"Please," she told him, her hips arching up to close the gap between them.

"I have never wanted a woman as I do you," he told her as he filled her. Slowly, he pressed himself into her, moving back and forth.

And when he came to her barrier, that tiny hint that spoke of her innocence, he broke it quickly and kissed her back into passion's embrace, even as he drove himself all the way into her.

He pulled himself back out, nearly all the way, and her eyes flung open. That couldn't be the end of it, could it?

But he was grinning at her, and he filled her again, and she felt a delicious sense of hunger rising within her. Then he did it again, stroking her over and over against the restless tide that threatened to overwhelm her.

Miranda clung to him, her body rocking with his. She found herself rising, felt him pushing her higher and higher.

She was headed toward madness, there was no other explanation. This house, this man, this love, it was utter insanity, and now she was about to succumb to it entirely.

And then she did, in an explosion of passion.

What was this heaven? she wondered, even as it enveloped her.

Her eyes flew open and her gaze met his. There was an expression of wonder on his face as well, as he moaned deeply and drove into her one more time, filling her. He gasped and kissed her, his mouth hungry anew, even as the tension in his body seemed to drift away.

"Miranda, you are magnificent," he told her.

She tried to speak but found herself unable to say a thing. Instead, she grinned and nuzzled in close to him. She sighed, letting the sound carry away all her fears from the past nine years.

Never once in her life had she felt as complete or as at home as she did in the arms of this man.

This rake of mine, she mused.

His fingers ran through the tendrils of her hair, pushing them away from her face.

She smiled at him and said, "Now I know why you were such a successful rake. And I must say, you've been wasting your talents playing the gentleman, Jack Tremont."

Chapter 15

J ack awoke an hour or so later and looked over at the sleeping form beside him. Miranda. His passionate, obstinate Miranda. He had meant what he'd said about ending the secrecy and danger that permeated life at Thistleton Park. She'd nearly lost her life meddling in his work, and he knew she would continue to do so as long as he continued his work.

So there was only one solution.

Pulling on his clothes quietly and quickly, he went in search of Temple. He could make his report about Malcolm and then resign. He found the marquis eating a late breakfast, entertaining the girls with a rendition of his infamously stodgy and lofty grandfather.

Jack caught his eye from the door and nodded toward the hall. "I need to speak with you. In private."

The marquis excused himself and followed Jack into

the music room. When the door was closed, he said, "So I suppose you want me to apologize for thinking you crack-witted back on the beach?"

Jack, who was making a beeline for the sideboard, came to an abrupt halt. "What did you say?"

"I thought you'd finally gone round the bend when you kept insisting Miss Mabberly was in the folly," Temple said, pointing his lorgnette in the direction of the ceiling and Jack's bedroom. "However did you discover the truth?"

It wasn't the subject Jack wanted to broach, but he knew Temple well enough to realize the man wouldn't rest until he had the entire tale. "She found me, or rather those girls out there found me and brought her along— crazy as it sounds, they had a notion we'd suit."

"Ah, I thought this had a touch of the Duchess's hand in it," Temple said. "Still, it must have been a shock to see Miss Mabberly again when she arrived."

Jack flinched and said nothing.

"You didn't recognize her at first, did you?" Temple said, with what sounded like a chuckle.

There was no use denying it to the man. "No, I didn't," he said. "But then again, I was so far gone that night at the opera, I wouldn't have recognized her half a minute later."

Temple shook his head. "So how was it that you finally came to recognize her? Or dare I ask?"

Jack knocked back his entire drink. "I think it better that you don't ask."

"Oh, what an *on dit* it would make," Temple said with an air of regret, pacing about the room in his overly exaggerated Corinthian style. "That's the demmed shame of this business, the delicious pieces of gossip that come my way, and yet, how can I share them without revealing too much. Why not two months ago, I overheard something utterly remarkable about—"

"Malcolm is dead," Jack blurted out. He hadn't wanted to tell Templeton like that, but the man had a way of going on and on, and he needed to get this interview over with.

When the marquis turned around and stared at him, he was no longer the affable buck of a few moments ago. "What did you say?" The frivolous air had been replaced with a deadly intent.

"Malcolm. He's dead." Now Jack could barely get the words out, the sting of guilt filling his heart anew.

Temple sank into the nearest chair. "How can that be?"

Jack knew exactly what he meant. Malcolm Grey had slipped past the French more times than anyone could count. "On the beach. The militia was firing at us and he . . ." Clenching his fists and shutting his eyes, he tried to blot out the memories . . . the retort of the pistols, the splash as Malcolm hit the water, the bright stain of blood on his hands.

"Have you told Clifton?" Temple asked.

Jack shook his head. He had wanted to tell Temple first, if only to gauge how best to do it. After all, it was his fault the man was dead.

"Oh, bloody hell," Temple murmured. "I don't envy you the task of telling him."

Telling Clifton had been his first and only thought, since they were brothers. Half brothers, that is. Still, for heir and bastard they had had a deep and abiding friendship that had spanned the gulf of legitimacy separating them.

Clifton, their father's heir. And Grey, a by-blow from a tavern girl in the village.

And now Malcolm was dead.

"Tell me exactly what happened," Temple said.

Jack explained how Dash had come ashore and refused to let Malcolm get out of the longboat until he'd had his money. Then the militia had sent up the rockets and all hell had broken loose.

"And he didn't say anything to you when he got back to the *Circe?*" Jack asked.

"No, the greedy bastard," Temple cursed. "He just said the militia was out looking for smugglers and you and Malcolm had made for the cave."

"That part was true."

Temple's brow furrowed. "Dash probably knew Clifton well enough to realize that if he told the man his brother had taken a bullet, he'd go overboard and dare the surf and rocks if only to see what had come of Malcolm. With the two of us still aboard, at least Dash had a chance of being paid in full." Temple cursed roundly. "We ought to let that bastard rot in France for the remainder of the war."

While Jack was still furious with Dash, blamed him to some extent for Malcolm's death, he had to give credit where it was due. "Don't think too ill of him—he tried to save Malcolm. Risked his own life to pull him down, but it was too late."

Temple nodded. "Where is he?"

Jack knew what he meant. "Birdwell told me that Miranda and the girls got the workmen to dig a plot for him in the graveyard behind the house." Jack felt the hot sting of tears that he hadn't been the one to see to the task. To put his friend to rest. "She buried him alongside Lord Albin. I don't know how Miranda knew, but I have to imagine it is where Malcolm would have wanted to be. Ironic, don't you think?"

"Yes, very ironic," Temple said, wiping back tears with no shame. "I can only hope that Malcolm's soul finds the peace that he fought so hard to gain."

Jack went to the sideboard and caught up the bottle of brandy. *French brandy.* He put it back and opened the cabinet, digging around until he found something a little more appropriate.

Whisky. Good Scottish whisky. The one Malcolm loved.

As Jack poured out the amber liquid, its heady fumes brought back a raft of memories. Clifton and Grey arriving in the middle of the night, arguing good-naturedly about who had discovered what on their latest mission.

And now that was lost.

Jack and Temple raised their glasses in a silent toast to their fallen friend.

And then Jack went in search of Clifton, to finish the assignment he'd failed so utterly.

Miranda made her way downstairs well after midday. She'd awakened, naked and alone, in Jack's bed. At first, she'd stretched like a cat, relishing the memories of their lovemaking, but when she'd looked up at the sunshine streaming in through the windows and realized the time of day, another thought had come to mind.

Everyone would know what they had done!

At first, her long-held sense of propriety sent a trumpeting roar of panic through her. Why hadn't she thought of that before?

Before Jack had carried her upstairs and . . . ruined her, truly and utterly.

She groaned and buried her head beneath the covers. How would she ever go down and face everyone?

No, it was decided. She would remain in Jack's bedroom until a special license was secured, the vicar fetched, and they were lawfully and respectably wed.

Heaving a sigh, she sat up and made herself comfortable. Yet something niggled in the back of her mind. She shifted again and looked around the room.

In all the heated passion, in letting herself get lost in the desire his kiss brought forth with such rakish delight, Miranda couldn't help but think that she'd forgotten something.

Something awfully important.

Like, perhaps, a marriage proposal.

Miranda tried to breathe and found she couldn't.

Jack had proposed, hadn't he? She quickly sifted through everything he'd said and done.

Well, he hadn't actually gotten down on bended knee as she'd always imagined her true love and hero would. Nor had he ever actually asked her. More like just declared it.

What had he said?

Do you think I want my wife risking her life . . .

And hadn't he also said that she was the woman he

loved? She crossed her arms over her chest and smiled as she thought of just how much he'd shown her that during the last few hours. Yes, he loved her.

Certainly he had to have been speaking of her when he'd said "my wife."

At least she hoped he'd been referring to her.

Miranda's panic burrowed a little deeper. This was Mad Jack Tremont, and he had seemed a bit over-wrought at the time. What if he had changed his mind by now? Proclaimed his declaration of love as nothing more than a momentary fit of madness?

She took a deep breath. She was simply being ridiculous. What she needed to do was get dressed, go downstairs, find Jack, and make sure he had meant her when he'd said "wife" and "love." Then she'd gently suggest that he see to it that procuring a special li-cense, as well as the vicar's services, was on his agenda for the day.

Then she could face everyone in the now overflowing house.

She buried herself under the covers and considered perhaps it would be better just to wait for Jack to return. But after a few moments of hiding, her practical side took over.

Dear heavens, if she stayed up here, that left Lady Josephine and Felicity downstairs and in charge of the household.

Her soon-to-be household.

They might even be planning her wedding. Ordering hothouse flowers, special cakes from London, and a dress from Paris—war or no war.

Propriety was one thing, but the idea of those two together for any length of time was enough to send Miranda rooting around the floor and under the bed in search of her discarded clothing. She dressed quickly and went to the door, wondering how she was going to find her way downstairs; she'd never been in this part of the house and for the life of her couldn't remember exactly which panel they'd come through when they'd snuck up into Jack's bedroom.

She counted her blessings that she didn't run into anyone until she was nearly to the foyer, when Birdwell came around the corner. At the sight of her, the butler broke into a wide smile. "Miss Porter, how good it is to see you up and about."

Miranda felt as if she were blushing all the way down to her toes. "Thank you, Mr. Birdwell." The man continued to stand there, grinning at her, and she knew she'd die of embarrassment if she didn't get matters settled, so she asked, "Do you know where I can find Lord John?"

The butler glanced over his shoulder, his brow furrowed. "His lordship is out in the garden with Lord Clifton."

"Thank you," she said, starting down the stairs.

"Miss Porter," Birdwell said, "you may want to wait a few more moments before you go out there."

"I don't think they'll mind," she said, though she didn't know how many more people she could face before she knew the answer to her question.

Did Jack mean to marry her?

She started forward, but this time the butler caught her by the arm. "Miss, you had best wait."

"Whatever for? This isn't more Thistleton Park intrigue, is it?" She smiled at him and tried to shake his grasp free. But he held her fast.

"No, miss. His lordship is telling the earl about Mr. Grey. About what happened."

"Oh," she said. "Were Lord Clifton and Mr. Grey good friends?"

"No." Birdwell shook his head, then looked her steadily in the eye. "They were brothers."

Miranda's knees wavered. "Oh, heavens," she whispered. "I didn't know." She swallowed and glanced toward the front door. "How terrible for Lord Clifton." *And for Jack,* she thought, remembering the blood on his hands—from trying to save his friend's life. "It won't be easy for Jack to tell him."

Birdwell nodded in agreement.

Just then the front door opened and a white-faced Clifton walked in, his back ramrod straight, his expression tight and emotionless. He walked past Miranda and Birdwell as if he didn't see them and continued up the stairs without a word.

"Oh, dear, I daresay that didn't go well," Miranda whispered, once Lord Clifton disappeared from sight. If the look of grief on the earl's face was any indication of how the news had gone over, she had to imagine Jack was feeling a similar devastating sense of loss.

"Lord John will bear the responsibility of this," Birdwell said sadly.

"But how is it Jack's fault?" Miranda set her jaw. "The militia shot Mr. Grey. If anyone is at fault, it is Sir Norris."

"It is not how Lord John will see it. It was his job to see Grey and the others ashore safely, and . . ." Birdwell sighed. "I think he hoped to redeem himself when he came here, prove to one and all that he wasn't such a wastrel, make his life complete and meaningful, but now . . . I daresay after his speech this morning, he'll never complete his work here."

She knew he didn't mean just Jack's obligations to the Foreign Office. He meant achieving a sense of worth and nobility that had been missing all Jack's life.

Miranda blew out a deep breath. Lady Josephine had made a point of telling her all the good and brave things Jack had done. The loss of Grey was chilling, but what about all the lives he had saved?

And now he meant to quit? For her? Never!

Instead of going straight outside to find him, she turned and ran upstairs to her room. She dug around in her valise until she found exactly what she was looking for.

The button from his jacket.

And suddenly she knew exactly why she had held onto it for all these years.

Jack stood in front of Malcolm's grave, his head bowed. He should never have taken on the responsibilities of Thistleton Park. How could he have ever thought he could rise to the challenges that Malcolm, and Clifton, and Temple made look so effortless.

Even Aunt Josephine, with her dizzy ways and madcap schemes, was a better hand at these trials than he would ever be.

But no more. For continuing would lose him not only his slight grasp on his sanity but Miranda as well.

And how and why and when she'd slipped into his

heart, he didn't know. Perhaps he was cursed, had been since the first time he'd kissed her. He glanced over at Albin's grave and wondered if his great-great-uncle would have understood the feeling of helplessness and longing that filled his heart every time he looked at Miranda.

Someone, probably Tally or Pippin, had left a nosegay tied in a blue ribbon on the stone. He smiled at it. They had probably been out here writing their Tremont play.

He wondered what they would say about him . . . hardly a hero, and no doubt as mad as the rest of the Tremonts resting around his feet.

"Jack," came a whisper, as soft as silk, tying its way around his heart.

Miranda. He turned around and found her standing just behind him. He'd been so lost in his thoughts that he hadn't even heard her approach.

"How are you?" she asked, coming closer and taking his hand. The strength and warmth of her fingers as they twined with his was like balm, a lifeline. "Lord Clifton looked bereft, so I had to assume you weren't doing much better."

He closed his eyes, for he didn't trust himself to speak. The irony of it all didn't escape him: Here was Malcolm, buried beneath his feet; the grief of losing his friend was almost too much to bear. Yet in Miranda's arms, making love to her had been like finding a haven. In those glorious hours, he'd forgotten the pain, forgotten his obligations, the sacrifices that came with living at Thistleton Park at the edges of a war that threatened to consume everything he loved.

No, he'd bar the gates, close up the tunnels, never

hang a lamp outside again. He'd keep her safe from harm if it was the last thing he did.

"I was a fool to think I was cut out for this life," he told her. "I killed him as surely as if I had pulled the trigger."

Miranda shook her head. "No, Jack, that isn't true and you know it." She squeezed his hand.

Shaking off her reassurances, he said, "I ruin everything I touch. Perhaps I am cursed, as my brother likes to say. Look what I've done with my life—I ruined you. If it hadn't been for my mistake in judgment, you would be the Countess of Oxley right now." He dared to look up at her, to see her scorn.

He was right. Her brows rose, her lips drew into a tight line.

And then she exploded.

"The Countess of Oxley?! You think you ruined my life by ending my betrothal to that man?" She shook her head. "Jack Tremont, you are mad." Then to his amazement, she laughed, laughed until there were tears streaming down her cheeks. "Don't you dare look back at that night with regrets." She reached out and took his hand, placing it on her breast. "Have you ever met the Earl of Oxley?"

Jack shrugged, then nodded.

"And what did you think of the man?" She waited, and when he didn't answer, she continued. "What would you think of me in his bed?"

At this Jack's gaze swung up, and he was filled with anger, a swell of jealousy like the stormy waves that had rocked the Channel the other night. Oxley? Touching Miranda?

"My feelings exactly," she told him. "You saved my life that night."

"But I thought you said you thought me a worthless sot?"

"You were that as well," she told him, taking his hand and leading him away from the graves, the dead, the past. "But I also knew you were something else."

"What was that?" he dared to ask.

"A hero," she said, opening his palm and putting his button into his hand.

"Your mysterious button," he said, wondering why she would want him to have this.

"Your button," she told him.

Jack didn't understand.

"This button fell from your coat that night. I saw it on the floor and picked it up as my mother dragged me away. I've held onto it all these years. I held onto it because I knew the moment my toes curled up in my slippers I had found the man my heart longed for." She smiled at him. "And you know I am too practical to fall for anyone less than a hero."

Jack held the button that had vexed him and intrigued him and realized he'd been right to begin with—it had belonged to a fool.

"I am no hero. And I have no intention of continuing to pretend that I am."

"I beg to differ," Miranda said. "Lady Josephine told me about last winter when you stole Sir Norris's yacht and sailed alone across the Channel to bring Temple and Clifton home, when no one could be found to dare the trip."

"And nearly got swamped in the swells," he told her.

"But you dared. And you succeeded." She held him at arm's length. "Birdwell tells me you spend most nights out in the folly, watching for ships, charting their movement and sending along your reports to the Admiralty. That you've saved countless lives and helped Temple's cousin, Captain Danvers, capture numerous French warships."

He shrugged.

"That three months ago, when Malcolm was trying to get back to Clifton in Spain, you bribed his way onto a ship out of Hastings—and then you and Birdwell and Bruno ate very little for the next month and a half."

"Well, we did have a full cellar, so it is much easier to wash down gruel with a decent vintage."

She beamed at him, her smile warming his heart. "You cannot quit. Not for me. There are too many lives at stake."

He shook his head. "No. I did those things you said, but I was scared stiff the entire time. Always filled with the dread of failure. This life is making me mad."

"Then perhaps you need a little help," she offered.

He knew what she was saying. "No, never. If you think you are going to—"

"I am and I will. With or without your blessing. I have to imagine Lady Josephine can introduce me to this deplorable Mr. Pymm of hers, and then I plan on offering my services in your stead."

"You will not," he told her, his temper getting the better of him. "I forbid it."

"Piffle!" she told her, in perfect imitation of Aunt Josephine. "I will, with or without your help."

"Why, Miranda? Why, when you have seen the cost, seen the consequences, would you want to do this?"

"For us," she told him with a passion that left a spark in his heart.

A tiny fire of hope that started to kindle.

"What kind of future are we to leave our children if we do nothing? If we don't fight the very tyranny that threatens at our doorstep?" She waved her hand back at the Tremonts buried behind them. "Do you think their sacrifices are for naught? Lord Douglas over there helped supply ships during the Hundred Years' war. Letitia Tremont hid royalists and sabotaged Sir Norris's ancestors' attempts to aid Cromwell. You are a brave and noble link in this lineage, and you have a destiny to carry out."

He looked at her and saw the passion in her eyes. Demmit, if she wasn't crazy enough to believe in him.

And her faith, her trust caught fire in his heart.

And something else she'd said. *"Our children."*

He looked around Thistleton Park and suddenly saw it as Miranda envisioned. A home. A haven. With green lawns and the laughter of children echoing across the open spaces.

He reached over and caught hold of her and pulled her into his arms. "I cannot do this alone."

"Of course you can't," she told him. "No one expects you to. Temple has his Diana, Malcolm had his brother. And you need me, as I need you."

She laid her head on his chest and Jack believed. Believed in his destiny, in their future, in the shining light of their children.

Children? He looked at her again, remembered how they'd spent the morning.

"Demmit," he muttered. "We need to get married."

Instead of being insulted by his less than romantic proposal, his dear, sweet practical bride heaved a big sigh.

"Oh, thank goodness," she said. "I had hoped you hadn't forgotten or changed your mind."

He laughed and leaned down to kiss her. Kiss her deeply and thoroughly. Letting his heart soar with the hope of happiness, the joy of love.

That is, until they were interrupted.

"There you are, Tremont!"

Jack glanced up, his brow furrowed with annoyance. "Sir Norris," he said, letting his annoyance drip from each word. "To what do we owe this pleasure."

"The pleasure is all mine," the baronet said, waving for his hired hands, four large brutes capable of putting a shiver of fear through even Bruno's stout heart.

"What is this, sir?" Jack demanded, tucking Miranda behind him. He looked over at the house and spied Temple and Clifton crossing the lawn at a fast clip.

"I've come to arrest you," Sir Norris announced.

"Not this nonsense again," Jack said. "If anyone should be in that jail it should be you for murdering Malcolm Grey."

Sir Norris colored a bit at this, but the stubborn fool refused to give ground. "Not here about that, what I am here for is the fact you broke out of the jail and accosted me last night, during my duties as a sworn officer of His Majesty. Could have you hung, but in light of . . . well, shall we say, your other obligations, I have a writ here for your arrest." He held out the summons, and Jack took it.

"Thirty days!" he said. "You can't lock me up for thirty days." He handed the paper to Temple, who scanned the contents and then gave it over to Clifton.

"You are a demmed fool," Jack told him. "You can't arrest me for last night."

Sir Norris bristled, his paunchy chest puffing out. "I certainly can, and I will." Then he leaned closer. "Don't you see that I must, Tremont? What are people to think if I, their magistrate, let you get away with this? I'll have a mutiny on my hands, never have any order in the ranks, if you know what I mean."

Jack looked up to find Temple nodding in agreement.

"I see what you mean, Sir Norris," Temple was saying. "A devilish quandary. But this would seem a good solution."

Jack coughed and sputtered. Had his friend gone mad as well? "Templeton, you can't mean to agree with this"—he restrained himself from saying "nitwit" and instead said—"this fellow." He dug into his pocket and pulled out the bullet Birdwell had extracted from Malcolm. "Here is my proof that you ought to be in that cell, Sir Norris. This is the bullet that felled a good and noble man, and it is you who should be paying for it, not me."

Sir Norris looked down at the piece of lead in Jack's hand and shook his head. "That isn't English."

"What do you mean, it's not English?"

"'T'isn't from a musket, not the kind my men use," Sir Norris told him.

"But this is the bullet that killed Malcolm," Jack insisted.

Then to his chagrin, Miranda leaned over his shoulder. "That isn't English, Jack. 'Tis a French ball, for a pistol."

Jack looked up at Temple and Clifton, and they all came to the same realization.

"Marden," Temple said.

Jack shook his head. That bastard had been in the tower that night waiting as well. And had used the cover of the militia fire to take his revenge. "I'm going to find every last soul who helped this man and make them pay," he vowed, then he turned to Sir Norris. "I suppose I owe you an apology, sir." He would smooth this rift with his neighbor, then help Clifton and Temple map out their plans.

"Make it from your jail cell," the man said.

"You still want to arrest me?"

"Of course," Sir Norris said. "I have appearances to keep, and if I let you run afoul of the law, then every other rapscallion fellow will think he can as well. Now come along." He waved his hand for Jack to follow.

He turned to his friends. "Do something!"

Temple shrugged, as did Clifton. "It will work to conceal your activities if Sir Norris locks you up," the marquis agreed. "And secure your rather disreputable place in Society."

Clifton nodded. "I remember one time Malcolm spent two months in a cell for larceny rather than lose credibility. 'Tis all in the line of work."

Jack shook his head at them. "But I am planning on marrying Miranda."

She nodded and took his arm, adding her support to his argument. "We can't be wed if Jack is in jail."

Temple looked more bemused than convinced. "Well,

I'd say thirty days ought to give the vicar time to read the banns, and Miss Mabberly time to plan a proper wedding." Temple nodded to Sir Norris, "Take him away."

Miranda tried to block their path, but Temple pulled her back while Jack was towed away by Sir Norris's henchmen.

"How can you do this?" she demanded of him.

Temple laughed. "One day you'll thank me for this. He needs the time to plan for his future—a future with you, Miss Mabberly, and it will keep him from doing anything rash and foolhardy to redeem himself."

Miranda crossed her arms over her chest and watched as the odious Sir Norris hauled her betrothed off to jail. "If he changes his mind and decides not to marry me at the end of the month, I'll hold you both responsible."

Temple laughed until she turned her determined gaze on him.

And Templeton, one of the Foreign Office's most daring agents, knew the true meaning of fear. As he turned and retreated toward the house, Miranda heard him say in an aside to Clifton, "Thank God she's on our side."

Epilogue

J ack paced back and forth in his jail cell. A month in this tiny prison had nearly driven him mad.

Mad from not being able to spend every night with Miranda. She'd come to see him each day, as she'd promised, telling him of the changes she was making to Thistleton Park, the treasures she and the girls had found in the attics and cellars, and, in a whispered voice, the agents who'd come and gone.

And every day, he'd pull her as close as he could, what with the thick metal bars between them, and kiss her. Kiss her until her knees went weak and she wobbled out of the jail with a devilish smile on her wickedly tempting lips.

But today was the end of his sentence, and Sir Norris should be here any minute to release him.

And then there would be no bars between them.

Jack had fantasized about this day for one long, hard month, and nothing and no one was going to stand in their way tonight.

Demmit . . . this afternoon, if he had any say in the matter. And he doubted Miranda would protest, given the requests she'd whispered in his ear yesterday.

Outside, the crunch of carriage wheels could be heard, and Jack stopped his pacing to listen.

The carriage stopped outside the jail. Sir Norris! About demmed time. And arriving in his carriage. Trying to make this mockery of justice look as official as possible.

Now that the baronet knew the truth about Thistleton Park, he'd become a regular bosom-bow. Offering his suggestions for landing places, names of his various contacts in Calais. All but hinting that he would love to do his part for King and country. Jack was of half a mind to send him along with Temple the next time the marquis went across the Channel.

Serve Templeton right for siding with Sir Norris over his imprisonment.

But when the door opened, it wasn't the toady little baronet but a tall, dignified man who looked around the tidy but small jail and sniffed.

Jack took a step back. "Parkerton!"

"Nice to see you recognize me," he said, entering the room as if it were a London salon, setting his walking stick at a jaunty angle and tipping his nose up just so.

No one was more ducal than Parkerton.

"What the devil are you doing here?" Jack asked. While the rest of the family kowtowed and toadied up to the duke, Jack could never quite bring himself to be awed by his brother's position.

"I think the better question is what are you doing here?" Parkerton looked around and sniffed again. "Not that this sight isn't a surprise. Mother always said you'd embarrass us utterly one day."

Jack tamped down his irritation. Once Sir Norris got here, he'd no longer have to listen to his brother's sermons and he'd find Miranda. "Is that all?" he said. "Come to crow and lecture? Well, be done with it. I have plans for the day."

"Yes, well, as impatient as ever," the duke said. "Imagine my surprise when a wagon arrived at Parkerton Hall and I received this impertinent letter."

He held out the piece of paper, and Jack came over to the bars and took it. He didn't recognize the handwriting, so he began to read.

To His Grace, the Duke of Parkerton
Parkerton Hall, Somerset

Your Grace,

As the future mistress of Thistleton Park, I have compiled an inventory of the house and determined that there are numerous paintings and belongings that have, through no misfortune of their own, found their way here.

Thus, I hereby return these paintings of your ancestors and consign them to your care. It is my suggestion . . .

Suggestion? Jack snorted. Miranda's suggestions were rather like Parkerton's. Orders offered with the subtlety of a lit powder keg.

He continued to read.

It is my suggestion that you offer them the hospitality of your home as is due any Tremont. Perhaps by welcoming them home, you may well lay to rest the rifts that have divided your esteemed and noble family over the centuries.

Yours respectfully,
Miss Jane Porter

Jack coughed, trying not to laugh completely out loud. The cheeky chit, she'd gone and antagonized Parkerton. Oh, he didn't know what he could ever do to repay his gratitude for seeing his brother look so vexed.

"Well?" Parkerton demanded.

"Well, what?" Jack asked.

"How the devil did you find such a magnificent woman?"

Jack's gaze flew up and met his brother's.

Parkerton was smiling. No, not smiling, grinning. "I came down here immediately to give this impertinent miss a lesson in manners and nearly fell over when I found Aunt Josephine in the music room playing the pianoforte." His brother arched a brow, as if expecting an explanation or some sort of apology for not being part and parcel of this deception, but Jack wasn't going to offer any.

So Parkerton continued, "I was further accosted by a

Miss Langley, who grilled me for over an hour as to the merits of every unmarried duke in the realm." He shuddered. "I fear for my peers when she comes of age. Then I was cornered by two more misses, one of whom bears a startling resemblance to the other little chit running about your house. Apparently they are composing a play based on our family's trials and tribulations and wanted to know how I was afflicted by the Tremont madness so they could add my curse to the final act, which they have for some reason entitled 'A Pirate's Revengeful Kiss.'" Parkerton rubbed his forehead and shuddered. "However, I was rescued by Mr. Birdwell, who thankfully has never changed—"

Not that you know of, Jack mused.

"And was finally shown to Miss Porter, who was busy with your secretary updating your ledgers." The duke heaved a sigh. "I never knew that Thistleton Park could manage a state of profitability, but Miss Porter has made it so. Though I am not sure all of her enterprises are entirely proper or lawful." He arched a brow and shot a glance at Jack that suggested he wasn't amused at these less than legal ventures.

Jack shrugged. What was he to say? In a month, Miranda had improved their percentages on the little bit of smuggling he did engage in to cover Thistleton Park's other comings and goings, and now the estate was turning a tidy profit.

His brother had more to say. "If you weren't about to marry her, I would consider hiring her to manage my estates. A more formidable, sharp-witted woman I have never met."

Jack chuckled.

Parkerton smiled as well. "I asked her if she was sure of her intentions, that she wanted to marry my ne'er-do-well brother, and she nearly threw me out of the house, declaring me an impertinent devil." He heaved a sigh. "As I said, she is quite a lady."

Jack cursed his luck. He would have loved to see Miranda giving his brother a wigging. A sight to behold indeed, especially if it had left his brother like this, nearly a humble wreck of his usual ostentatious and overbearing self.

"So I have come to offer my blessings on this union and bring you a decent suit of clothes to wear to your wedding."

Parkerton turned and rapped on the door, and a parade of liveried servants brought in wash basins, hot water (most likely obtained from the public house), and a suit of clothes, along with Parkerton's esteemed valet, Richards.

They stood, crowded hoof to jowls, in the tiny jail, with Jack still locked in his cell.

From behind the bevy of servants came a familiar voice. "Get out of my way, the lot of you," Sir Norris called out. He barged and prodded his way through them and nearly bowled over Parkerton in the process. He got to the cell and, with as much pomp and ceremony as he could muster, made a great speech, declaring Jack's sentence over and declaiming the importance of justice in a civilized society, until Parkerton rapped him with his walking stick and made a very ducal suggestion . . . er, order. "Unlock the door, sir."

"Oh, um, certainly, Yer Grace," Sir Norris said, fumbling with the keys and finally setting Jack free.

"What is all this?" Jack demanded.

"My wedding present to you. Rather a promise to a friend that I would see you married today."

Templeton, Jack had to imagine. The marquis had told him of Miranda's threat—so leave it to the marquis to ensure the deed was done. He'd enlisted Jack's brother as honorary best man—or, rather, enforcer.

Not that he had any objections to marrying Miranda, but he had something else in mind for the present time.

An afternoon in bed with Miranda.

The vicar could wait. But apparently not his brother.

Before Jack knew it, he was scrubbed and dressed and properly presentable. Parkerton escorted him outside to the ducal carriage and drove him straight to Thistleton Park.

"Quite something," Parkerton said as they drove through the gates.

"Remarkable," Jack said, as he climbed out of the carriage and walked up the steps. Why, he barely recognized his own house. The yard was tidy and neat, the ivy and roses trimmed, the lawns cut just so. And inside the changes were just as evident. No longer dreary and dark, his house was as scrubbed and presentable as its master.

And then he saw her. Miranda. Beckoning to him from the music room. She had on a gown of green, and she looked like Spring personified. Delicious and bright and full of promise.

He glanced over his shoulder and saw that his brother was preoccupied in a discussion with the vicar, so Jack had his chance.

And when the duke turned around, his brother was gone from sight.

"Where is Lord John?" he said, his voice commanding the immediate attention of all those around him.

One of the twins—Felicity, he thought—said, "I saw him go in the music room with Miss Porter."

Parkerton went over to the doors and threw them open, ready to stop the pair before there was any more scandal, but the room was empty. "Where the devil have they gone to?"

Aunt Josephine and Birdwell looked at each other, then up at the ceiling at the bedroom above them, and knew exactly what the passionate bride-to-be and her groom were about. They both burst out laughing.

"'Tis highly improper," Parkerton declared, having also shot a glance at the ceiling. "And here I thought marriage to Miss Porter would reform my brother's rakish character."

And with all the pearls of wisdom that Felicity and Tally carried from their nannies', as well as their own experience, it was Pippin who set the record straight for the duke. She nudged him and waggled a finger at him to come closer.

"Once a lady has been kissed by a rake," she said, "she is never quite the same. I daresay Miss Porter prefers Jack just the way he is."

"This is entirely improper," Miranda said as Jack teased her out of her gown. "We aren't even married yet."

"We will be before this day is out," he said, as if that made it perfectly right.

Miranda opened her mouth to protest again, but he bested her by covering her lips with his and kissing her objections away until she was trembling in his arms. His tongue swept over hers, teased her, while his fingers continued to loosen the bindings of her corset.

There was something I was going to say, she thought, even as his fingers dipped inside her bodice and freed her breasts.

It could wait, she had to imagine as he hoisted her in his arms and tossed her onto the bed. He fell upon her like a man starved and had her quickly writhing with a need that matched his own.

"I thought I'd go mad every time I saw you," he whispered in her ear, "and couldn't do this." His lips curled around one of her nipples and lapped and teased it to a burning point.

Madness, this is utter madness, she thought.

Her back arched and her hips rocked back and forth, anticipating the blissful torment to come.

"I thought of you as well," she confessed.

"How, Miranda?" he whispered, urging her to let go of any last vestiges of propriety. "How did you want me?"

The passion in his eyes emboldened her.

"Naked," she said brazenly. "Naked and atop me."

"And what else," he said, catching hold of her and pulling her beneath him, more than willing to give her whatever she desired, fantasized.

His hardness pressed against her. The feel of it made her breathless. She wanted to touch it, caress it, put it in her mouth and taste him. But there would be time for that later. Her body ached for him, she ached for something only he could give her.

"Inside me," she said, opening her thighs, her hips

rising to meet him. He wasn't the only one who had ached for this for thirty long nights. "I wanted you inside me."

She caught his hips and pulled him closer, and he answered her by filling her quickly and deeply.

Miranda cried out, with delirium, with pure joy at the desire that sparked through her veins.

His desires, his needs, pent up like hers, raged through them both, and in a heated, fast, hard fury, they rode together to completion. Miranda's eyes fluttered open even as her body shuddered with joy, even as he was gasping for air, filling her until he could press himself no further.

"Oh, Jack," she said. "Oh, yes."

From the rakish light in his eyes, the groan of passion that wrenched from his lips, she knew that he too had gained what had been denied them for these past few weeks.

Completion.

And after some quiet moments in each other's arms, touching each other and sharing the warmth of the afterglow, Jack stretched and looked over at her.

"Now let's go downstairs and make this proper," he suggested.

Miranda sighed and stretched as well, her legs twining with his, her hands running down the length of his torso until her fingers found him. Still hard.

"Hmmm," she murmured. It seemed such a waste . . .

As practical as ever, Miranda pulled her rake back into her arms. "Not just yet," she said before she kissed him hungrily, whispering words in his ear that left him in no doubt as to what she wanted.

To be ruined yet again.

And as he did so, eagerly and enthusiastically, bringing her to those dizzying, blissful heights of passion once more, Miranda realized something very important.

Proper had its time and place.

And now wasn't one of those times.